#1 *NEW YORK TIMES* BESTSELLING AUTHOR

MIKE EVANS

BORN AGAIN

A NOVEL *of* ISRAEL'S REBIRTH IN 1948

TimeWorthy
BOOKS

P.O. BOX 30000, PHOENIX, AZ 85046

Born Again: A Novel of Israel's Rebirth in 1948

Copyright 2013 by Time Worthy Books
P. O. Box 30000
Phoenix, AZ 85046

Design: Lookout Design, Inc.

Hardcover: 978-1-62961-007-8
Paperback: 978-1-62961-006-1
   Canada: 978-1-62961-008-5

This book is dedicated to my friend and mentor,

the late Menachem Begin,
Prime Minister of Israel.

He was, without question, one of Israel's greatest leaders.
My own life has been enriched by the rare privilege of
friendship with this brilliant man and statesman.

— CHARACTERS AND TERMS —

Jacob Schwarz: Holocaust survivor from Poland who immigrated to Palestine with his wife, Sarah

Sarah Ginsburg Schwarz: Wife of Jacob Schwarz

Avi Livney: Sarah's cousin

Yaakov Auerbach: Young American from Chicago who came to Palestine to work in a communal farming settlement (kibbutz) at Degania near the Sea of Galilee

Suheir Hadawi: an Arab girl who lives with her family on a farm near the kibbutz at Degania and with whom Yaakov Auerbach has a relationship

Natan Shahak: Born in Palestine to an Austrian couple, left home to work on the kibbutz at Degania

David Ben-Gurion: Chairman of the Jewish Agency for Palestine; became Israel's first prime minister

Eyal Revach: Assistant to David Ben-Gurion

Golda Meir: Head of the political department at the Jewish Agency for Palestine; later became Israel's fourth prime minister

Gedaliah Cohen: Head of Haganah, a Jewish paramilitary organization that later became the Israel Defense Force (IDF)

Noga Shapiro: Head of Irgun, a Jewish paramilitary organization later disbanded and incorporated into the Israel Defense Force (IDF)

Tuvia Megged: Assistant to Noga Shapiro

Yitzhak Jeziernicky: Head of Lehi, a Jewish paramilitary organization later disbanded and incorporated into the Israel Defense Forces (IDF)

Mickey Marcus: Colonel in the United States Army who volunteered to help organize the Israel Defense Forces (IDF)

Abba Eban: Israeli diplomat

Folke Bernadotte: Swiss mediator appointed by the United Nations to broker a peace agreement in Palestine

Ralph Bunche: American diplomat who worked for the United Nations and assisted both the United Nations Committee on Palestine (UNSCOP) and Folke Bernadotte Israeli

Israel Defense Forces (IDF): Army of the State of Israel

Jewish Agency for Palestine: Authorized representative organization for Jewish settlers in Palestine under the League of Nations' mandate for the administration of Palestine, later continued by the United Nations

Kibbutz: Communal Jewish farming settlement

PROLOGUE

SWEAT TRICKLED DOWN JACOB SCHWARZ'S BACK as he sat on the pew at the synagogue. Wedged between his mother and older sister, the air was stiflingly hot and he squirmed for room to get comfortable.

Located on Twarda Street, not far from the Vistula River in Warsaw's Jewish Quarter, the synagogue usually was a refuge for Jacob, a haven from the harsh world he encountered every day. Basking in the soft glow of candlelight, his mind was often transported to another place and time, —where no one hated him for being a Jew, where he was no longer required to wear the gold Star of David with word Jude on it—but not that morning. Filled to capacity, the room was too hot, his sister too close, and the service too long. The collar of his shirt chafed against his neck and he longed to unbutton his sleeves at his wrists to let in some air and feel—

The sharp jab of his mother's elbow caught Jacob's attention. He looked up to see his father, Nissim, rise from his seat, step onto the Bema, and make his way toward the lectern. It was his father's turn to serve as cantor, and Jacob loved the sound of his voice as he read the scriptures.

On the lectern before Nissim was a parchment scroll which was wound from either end onto two ornate dowels. He gently pushed the rolls apart, exposing the correct text, then drew a breath to speak. Jacob's eyes were riveted to him, his ears attentive to every sound.

"Today's reading comes from the Book of Isaiah," Nissim began. "Hear these words from the prophet." He paused to clear his throat, then said in a strong, clear voice,

"Who has ever heard of such a thing?
Who has ever seen such things?
Can a country be born in a day
or a nation be brought forth in a moment?
Yet no sooner is Zion in labor
than she gives birth to her children…"

When he finished reading, Nissim returned to his seat and Rabbi Eliashiv came to the lectern to deliver the day's lesson. His voice, unlike Nissim's, was thin and he spoke in a monotone, each word carrying the same weight and emphasis as all the others. Jacob tried to listen, but with the air hot and stuffy his mind soon wandered. Before long he imagined a landscape with lush green hillsides and pleasant meadows. And while the images filled his mind, words from the day's scripture played over and over. *"Can a country be born in a day…a nation in a moment?"* Hashem—the Lord, so high and holy that even His name could not be spoken—He could do it. He formed the earth in a single day. Surely creating a nation would not be too much trouble. A country as lush and green as the one in his mind, born in a…

Another nudge to the ribs brought Jacob back to the moment and he glanced around to see the service had ended. "Come," his mother said. "It is time to go."

"Were you asleep?" his sister chided.

"No." Jacob felt his cheeks blush with embarrassment. "I…I was—"

"You were asleep," his sister needled. "Mama, Jacob was…"

"Hush," Mama commanded, cutting her off. "We must be going. The others will be waiting." Then she shooed them toward the aisle and they made their way toward the door.

On the sidewalk outside they joined Yehonatan Gur, Jacob's grandfather, and Emile, his uncle. While Mama visited with them, Jacob walked slowly in a circle; his arms spread wide, letting cool air flow through his shirt. After a moment, Nissim joined them and they started up the street together for the return trip home.

"Papa," Jacob asked quietly, "what did it mean?"

Nissim glanced at him with a puzzled look. "What did *what* mean?"

"The scripture you read today."

"Did you not hear what Rabbi said about it?"

"I heard, but he didn't talk about a country being born."

"Ah," Grandpa said playfully, "do we have a young Zionist among us?"

"The boy is only curious," Mama answered. "He wants to know about the scripture. That's all. He's not asking about the Zionists."

"Zionism has nothing to do with scripture anyway," Emile scoffed. "It's about preserving our identity, finding freedom from persecution, and creating a state in which we are a majority. It's not a religious movement."

"What are you saying?" Grandpa wondered. "That the faithful cannot return to Palestine to worship?"

"This is what I was hoping to avoid," Mama sighed as the conversation turned toward an all -too -familiar topic. "Always it's about Palestine and the Zionists."

"The return to Palestine is not about finding a place to worship," Emile continued, responding to Grandpa and ignoring Mama's comment.

"Then what's it about?"

"It's about survival," Emile argued. "Building a nation together. Ruling ourselves."

"Politics," Nissim goaded his brother-in-law. "Politics. You Zionists are all about politics."

"Yes," Emile nodded. "Some are attracted by the political reasons. Many of us, in fact."

"So," Grandpa argued, "if they can go for politics, why can't they go for religious reasons, too?"

"I suppose someone could," Emile conceded.

Nissim's voice grew louder as he spoke, "We have Labor Zionists, and Liberal Zionists, and National Zionists. Why not Torah Zionists?"

"Nissim," Mama scowled. "Lower your voice. This is the Sabbath."

"Is there no place for Judaism in Eretz Israel?" Nissim asked, his voice still much too loud to please Mama.

"You don't understand," Emile sighed.

"We don't understand," Grandpa chortled. "You are the one making these claims about Zionism. Is not the establishment of a new Israel a Zionist aspiration?"

"Yes," Emile nodded. "But we are not attempting to fulfill a prophecy."

"Does that matter?"

"What do you mean?"

"Does it matter that you are not attempting it? Cannot Hashem use you for His purpose in spite of your intentions?"

"If that was what He wanted to do," Emile shrugged, "I suppose He could."

"You are right," Grandpa nodded. "Hashem can fulfill His promises by any means He chooses. But that is not the crux of the matter for you, is it?"

"I'm not sure what you mean."

"The problem for you is that you do not believe Hashem wants to establish Israel again. That is the key point. You think the return to Palestine is only a human endeavor."

"I suppose."

"And the root of that notion lies in the first point...you do not believe."

Emile looked embarrassed. "I admit I find it difficult."

No one said a word in response and they walked in silence to the next block, then Grandpa put his arm around Emile's shoulders and said softly, "I pray for you every day."

"I know, Papa. I know."

At home, Mama and Jacob's sister disappeared into the kitchen. Grandpa and Emile settled into comfortable chairs in the front room. Nissim took Jacob aside in the hallway. "You asked a question when we were walking home," he began. "And then Emile and I got into a discussion. What did you want to know?"

"I wanted to know about the scripture you read."

"What about it?"

"It sounded as if Hashem wanted to rebuild Israel."

"Yes," Nissim nodded. "That is correct."

"But there is no Israel."

Nissim had an indulgent smile. "You are right."

"So does He still want to rebuild it?"

Nissim knelt on one knee to look Jacob in the eye. "When Isaiah said those words, he was speaking about the return of our people from captivity thousands of years ago. They did return and Jerusalem was rebuilt."

"So, He won't do it again?"

Nissim smiled, "Some like your Uncle Emile might say so, but the verse we read today is not the only place where the prophets have spoken about the rebirth of Israel."

Jacob's eyes opened wide. "There are more?"

"'In that day the Lord will reach out his hand a second time to reclaim the remnant from Lower Egypt, from Upper Egypt, from Cush, from Elam, from Babylonia, from Hamath and from the islands of the sea.'"

"That is in scripture?"

"It's in Isaiah."

"So Hashem will do it a second time? He will restore Israel again?"

"Yes," Nissim nodded. "A second time. Hashem will do it a second time. And as many times after that as it takes."

"So when will it happen again?"

"I think Hashem is doing that right now." Nissim lowered his voice and leaned close as if he had a secret. "But don't tell your Uncle Emile that. He thinks the idea of returning to Palestine is something he and his friends came up with solely on their own."

"Is Uncle Emile going to Palestine?"

"I do not know. He talks about it, but talking and doing are two different things and I do not know if he will get there."

"Will we go to Palestine?"

Nissim glanced away, his face clouded with a look of disappointment. "I think that is not possible for your mother and me. And Grandpa is too old. Besides, he would never leave the neighborhood anyway." Nissim smiled at Jacob again. "But when you get older, you could go."

"And would that make me a prophet?" Jacob beamed.

"Only Hashem can make a prophet, but you can choose to believe."

"I do believe," Jacob nodded.

"I know," Nissim whispered.

"Would you be sad if I went there?"

Nissim's eyes were full. "Palestine is far away and I would be sad not to see you when I come home at night, or hear your voice when I awaken in the morning, but," he grinned, "I would be proud. Very proud." He rested a hand on Jacob's shoulder. "And I would say to everyone I know, 'My Jacob went to Palestine to see Israel born again.'"

CHAPTER 1

JACOB SCHWARZ STOOD at the ship's rail, face to the wind, and let the humid salt air blow through his hair. Beside him, was Sarah Ginsburg, his wife, and Avi Livney, Sarah's cousin.

The ship on which they sailed was appropriately named the *Exodus*. An aged American freighter, it was seaworthy only in the sense that it floated and took on no more water than the bilge pumps could handle. Its engines ran, most of the time, and it had a rudder that seemed to keep them on course. But it had few amenities and not much more food than the Nazi concentration camps from which its passengers had only recently been freed. Some said the ship was owned by Haganah, the security force created to protect Jewish settlers who'd already arrived in Palestine. Others said it was owned by the Allies who hoped it would sink. Jacob, Sarah, and Livney didn't care who owned it, just as long as it took them away from Europe and closer to the Middle East.

"We aren't far from Palestine," Livney observed.

"Soon we shall be home," Jacob said wistfully.

"Ah, yes. Palestine," Sarah added with mock enthusiasm. "The home of our ancestors." She glanced in Livney's direction and he smiled back.

"I heard you," Jacob droned. "And I know what you're trying to do."

"Not difficult to get you started," Sarah laughed.

Jacob shot a look in her direction. "You wish to return to Europe?"

"No." She shook her head. "But our families lived many generations in Poland. *That* was the land of our ancestors. It will take just as many before

Palestine feels the same."

"Perhaps not that long," Jacob replied. "Unlike Warsaw, there are no Nazis in Tel Aviv."

"Don't be so sure," Livney responded. "We know there will be Arabs, and that's almost as bad."

"We have as much historic claim to the region as the Arabs," Jacob groused.

"A long time has passed since this was Israel," Sarah noted.

"Time does not matter to the heart." Jacob gave her a smile. "You should know that."

She squeezed his arm and rested her head on his shoulder. "That much is true."

"Well, I don't care who has the whole place," Livney said. "Just a little spot. That's all I want. Just a place to live and be left alone."

"If we are patient," Sarah added in a playful tone, "perhaps we can have it all." She knew the comment would be too much for Jacob to resist.

"And that's the point!" he said in a burst of emotion. "We don't know if 'perhaps' will ever happen. We can have a state now if we act boldly and courageously. The world has seen what the Nazis did to us and they are ready to give it to us. We've bought it with the blood of our own families and this is the moment God has given us!"

"You would give up the whole," Sarah goaded, "for only a part?"

"No," Jacob retorted. "I would give up a *dream* for the whole in some distant future—I would give up the illusion of holding it all—for the *reality* of having a part here and now."

"*You* are the dreamer," Sarah chided. "States require work. First, we must do the hard work. Then we will see the result."

"And on that we agree," Jacob nodded. "Work. Build it by hand, on our own soil, bought with our own money, and improved by our own labor. But I am not a dreamer." He looked back over the railing toward the sea. "This is our moment."

"But," Livney joined in, "do you expect the Arabs to greet us with open arms?"

"Of course not," Jacob replied. "They will never accept us, but that doesn't change things."

"So you are resigned to a life of constant conflict?" A frown wrinkled Livney's brow. "I thought we left Europe to get away from that."

"We left to avoid persecution," Jacob corrected. "But we will never escape a life of struggle."

"But what about peace?" Sarah asked, stoking the argument to the next level.

"Peace is the province of established governments. The luxury of people living far away." Jacob was on a roll now and both Sarah and Livney seemed to enjoy encouraging him to continue. Livney smiled at her as Jacob ranted, "Established governments have a vested interest in peace. We do not. We have only—" A jolt from below caught his attention and he stopped in midsentence.

Sarah's eyes opened wide. "What was that?" She glanced around nervously. "Did we hit something?"

"The ship's stopped," Livney replied.

"Why?"

Sarah pointed to the water. "What's that doing out here?"

A British warship appeared at the stern of the *Exodus*, plying its way through the choppy waves. In a few minutes, it came alongside, only a hundred meters away.

"They're going to ram us," Livney blurted out.

"I think they mean to board us," Jacob pointed. "They're armed." Onboard the warship, sailors stood at the ready along the rail, rifles in hand.

Someone standing to Jacob's left had an amused grinned. "Relax," he chuckled. "Probably just a routine customs inspection. They can see we're loaded to the top with passengers."

Jacob had a puzzled expression on his face. "A customs check? From the British?"

"The British control Palestine."

"We're close enough for that?"

"By my reckoning," the man opined, "we're less than fifteen miles out."

Jacob's mouth gaped open in surprise. "Palestine?" he said softly.

"Palestine," the man nodded.

"That's what I was telling you," Livney reminded. "Before you went off on that speech about Jewish statehood. We're almost there."

Jacob slipped his arm around Sarah's waist and they stood with Livney watching as the *Exodus* slowed to a drift and the warship bobbed a short distance away. In a few minutes, the British lowered a gangway to the waterline, and a winch eased a power launch into the blue-green water of the Mediterranean. A seaman held it steady at the foot of the gangway while men came down from the deck and boarded it, then they pushed off. When the launch reached the *Exodus*, a voice on a bullhorn shouted up at the passengers, "We are from Her Majesty's Royal Navy! Stand back from the rail and prepare to be boarded!"

In the launch, a sailor stood and lifted a shoulder-fired device, much like an oversized rifle, into which a grappling hook was loaded. The hook was attached to a rope that trailed from the device to a coil that lay in the bottom of the boat. With the help of a mate, the sailor aimed toward the ship and squeezed the trigger. A bright flash burst from the muzzle followed by a puff of gray smoke. The hook shot from the device and sailed through the air toward the *Exodus*.

The crowd along the railing gasped and backed away just as the hook clanked into place on the second rail. Moments later, a sailor in the launch started up the rope, followed by another, then another, moving hand over hand, lifting themselves toward the deck.

Farther down the ship, other launches appeared with more grappling hooks striking the rail. Jacob leaned over the railing and was about to ask where they came from when he saw a second warship just off their stern. Then a cloud of black smoke wafted overhead and they turned to see a third British vessel on the opposite side.

Suddenly, thick black soot belched from the *Exodus'* stack and the ship lurched forward. At the same time passengers appeared along the railing. Angry and determined, they elbowed their way through the gawking crowd. One of them stood near Jacob and shouted down at the sailors below, "We are a private ship! Properly registered and bearing the flag of Honduras. Sailing in international waters. You have no right to board us!"

Then he drew a knife from his belt and cut the rope from the nearest grappling hook. The sailors climbing up from the launch fell with a splash to the water below.

Others along the ship's rail did the same and a shout of approval went up from the crowd, followed by cheering and clapping. Seconds later, a burst of white smoke appeared on the deck and the crowd shrank back. "Tear gas!" someone shouted. The crowd turned into a stampede as everyone surged toward bow and stern. Jacob backed away from the rail and pulled Sarah with him into a narrow passageway behind an air vent. Livney joined them as panicked passengers pushed and shoved their way past.

A second canister hit the deck followed by a muffled rumble as it burst open, then came the clank of additional grappling hooks and minutes later the sound of an Englishman. "Stand back and no one will get hurt!"

Ten minutes later, the deck swarmed with British sailors, each of them armed with a rifle, ready for use at a moment's notice. Then an officer appeared with a bullhorn and shouted, "As passengers without authorized entrance documents, you are forbidden to enter Palestine."

Someone shouted, "How do you know we have no documents?"

"Any of you possessing valid documents, please identify yourselves. Those of you with valid papers will be allowed to disembark. Anyone presenting forged documents will be prosecuted as a criminal."

"We are here to start a new life!" someone shouted.

"You'll have to find it somewhere else," the man with the bullhorn replied.

Then a woman along the rail pointed and shouted, "Look! I can see the coast."

The crowd fell silent as everyone turned in that direction. Far in the distance, barely visible above the horizon, the hazy gray shoreline formed a thin ribbon against a backdrop of blue sky. Then a voice to the left said, "Let's swim for it."

The crowd surged forward. Sailors along the rail stiffened and pushed back. "Stand back," one of them shouted, "or we'll be forced to respond!"

A murmur went up from the crowd, followed by a chorus of protests. Someone threw a bottle that bounced off a sailor's shoulder and hit the floor. A bucket sailed through the air, and the crowd grabbed for everything not secured, sending chairs, plates, cups, and an assortment of objects raining down on the sailors.

Jacob turned to Livney and shouted above the fracas, "This is why we must break free now! This is why we must have our own state." He jabbed the air with his index finger for emphasis at every phrase.

"How dare you oppose the Crown!" a sailor shouted, and struck Jacob in the forehead with the butt of his rifle. The force of the blow sent him reeling as he staggered backward into the person behind him. Someone grabbed him about the waist and held him up.

Livney, enraged by the sailor's conduct, stepped forward and shouted angrily, "I'll send you to the grave for this!"

Another sailor, caught off-guard by the intensity of the response, raised his rifle and fired. A bullet struck Livney between the eyes and he collapsed to the deck. Jacob could only watch as Sarah fell on her cousin's body, weeping and moaning.

CHAPTER 2

IN TEL AVIV, DAVID BEN-GURION sat at his desk, studying the latest reports from an incident at an outlying settlement. Two nights earlier, Arab gunmen stormed the settlement compound and killed three people. Four of the assailants were killed in the process, but Ben-Gurion was curious about how the intruders made their way past the sentries who were supposed to be on duty around the clock. A knock at the door interrupted him and he glanced up to see Eyal Revach, a young assistant, standing in the doorway.

"They did it," Revach declared with a somber tone.

"Who did what?"

"The British. They boarded the *Exodus*."

"No," Ben-Gurion snapped. "How stupid can they be?"

Revach moved closer. "It gets worse."

Ben-Gurion arched an eyebrow. "What happened?"

"Three of the passengers are dead."

"Dead?" Ben-Gurion roared, standing to his feet. "The British shot them?"

"Yes," Revach nodded. "They survived Hitler only to take a bullet from a British sailor."

"We have to find housing for all of them. The whole shipload. And jobs, too. I want the world to—"

Revach held up his hand. "It's not that simple."

Ben-Gurion seemed put off. "What do you mean?"

"According to the immigration office, the passengers are to be loaded onto British prison ships and sent back to Europe."

Ben-Gurion walked around his desk and strode toward the door. "Get my car!" he shouted, and a secretary who sat outside his door snatched up the telephone receiver to relay the demand. Ben-Gurion glanced over his shoulder in Revach's direction. "Come on."

"Where are we going?"

"To pay a call on the British."

Ten minutes later, Ben-Gurion and Revach arrived at the British army's local command center. They bounded from the car, pushed their way past the guards, and rushed inside. An assistant rose to greet them but they ignored him and moved down the hall toward Gerald Simpson's office. Simpson, a lieutenant general, was standing near the window as they entered. He turned to them with a curious expression that quickly dissolved into a stony glare when he saw them. "How dare you come in here like this without an appointment," he said coldly.

"And how dare *you* fire on innocent civilians?" Ben-Gurion shouted.

Simpson thrust forward his chin in disdain. "What are you complaining about now?"

"Passengers onboard the *Exodus*," Ben-Gurion snarled. "Your sailors shot three of them."

"They aren't my sailors." Simpson sauntered toward his desk. "I have absolutely no control over them."

"You have control over everything that happens in Palestine. Those passengers are Holocaust survivors. Your sailors treated them worse than Hitler."

"Mr. Ben-Gurion," Simpson sighed as he dropped into his chair behind the desk, "we've made it clear to you on more than one occasion that we simply will not tolerate illegal immigration. Not a single passenger onboard that ship had valid authorization to immigrate to Palestine. You and your cohorts knew that but you sent them anyway."

"Fifteen hundred people per month is not enough. That quota is already filled for the rest of the year."

"That is not my concern," Simpson replied. "And it is, by the way, precisely why we have restraints. Otherwise there would be even more chaos here than there already is. The cabinet has made its position clear on that, as well, and they will not raise the immigration quota."

"They would if you had insisted."

"Fifteen hundred Jews per month is the limit."

Ben-Gurion leaned over the desk and lowered his voice. "Why do you always side with the Arabs?"

"We aren't siding with the Arabs. The quota is a Jewish one. It has nothing to do with the Arabs."

"Yes, it does," Ben-Gurion retorted. "They are the ones who demand you set such a ridiculously low limit. And you give in to them solely to appease members of the Arab League, who supply most of England's oil."

"They demanded we halt immigration altogether." Simpson sat upright. "And I resent the implication we were influenced by any consideration other than the cold, hard facts evident to all of us here in the region."

Ben-Gurion struggled to control his anger. "Mr. Simpson, you can resent the implication all you want. We resent being discounted, disregarded, and disparaged. You've all but ended Jewish immigration, restricted the areas in which we can make land purchases, and sided with the Arabs on every major violent incident in recent memory."

"I'm not getting into all of that," Simpson sniffed. "We've argued about it many times. These attempts you sponsor to bring in more immigrants than we allow will do you no good. We won't permit you to circumvent the quota. You put those people on that ship. Their condition is your fault."

"Regardless of how they came to be onboard that ship," Ben-Gurion fumed, "the situation must be resolved."

"Oh, you are quite right about that," Simpson nodded. "Resolving it, however, is a British affair that I assure you we shall address in a most expeditious manner." He turned sideways in his chair and gave a dismissive gesture with the back of his hand. "Good day to you, sir. Come back when you've made an appointment."

As they left the building Revach asked Ben-Gurion, "Do you think you got anywhere with him?"

Ben-Gurion shook his head. "I have never seen a more arrogant man in all of my life."

"I didn't think that would go well." Revach opened the car door and held it while Ben-Gurion crawled inside, then he got in and pulled it closed.

"The committee is still in town," Ben-Gurion decided. "Let's see what they think of this situation."

Revach appeared quizzical. "Do you think they can help?"

"I think we can turn this in our favor," Ben-Gurion smiled confidently. "And then perhaps those three passengers will not have died in vain."

"Can you go over Simpson's head?"

"No, but I think we can at least get something out of this that will help us."

The committee to which Ben-Gurion referred was the United Nations Special Committee on Palestine, known to most by the acronym formed by its initials—UNSCOP. It had been created to investigate British administration of the region, which had been assigned to them following World War I by the League of Nations and continued by the UN General Assembly. The committee's task was to evaluate Arab and Jewish claims to the region and the desire of displaced European Jews to immigrate there. All three problems—Arab occupation of the region, Jewish historic claims of priority, and a plan for the future of the hundreds of thousands of Jews left stranded at the end of World War II—clamored for the United Nations' attention. The general assembly hoped the committee could find a solution.

Chaired by Emil Sandström, a judge from Sweden, the committee had been in Palestine only a few days when news of the trouble aboard the *Exodus* first broke. The committee traveled throughout the region to hold hearings and conduct interviews in an attempt to gain insight into how best to address the issues it faced, but it was keenly aware of the ship and the crisis developing around it.

Leaving the British command center, Ben-Gurion and Revach rode to the Tel-Aviv Museum, where the committee was conducting hearings. They found Abba Eban, the Jewish Agency's liaison, seated at a table to one side of the proceedings. Ben-Gurion caught his attention and motioned for him with a wave. Eban rose from his chair and the three men stepped outside to talk. Reporters who accompanied the committee on its trip were seated in the back of the room. Several of them noticed Eban as he moved from the table but no one followed.

"The British seized the ship," Ben-Gurion began when they were alone.

Eban was puzzled. "The *Exodus*?"

"Yes."

"Why?" Eban asked.

"They hate us."

"The British don't know what they are doing," Eban agreed, "but I doubt they hate us."

"No," Ben-Gurion answered, wagging his finger in protest. "They hate us."

"They certainly seem to be on the Arab side," Revach added.

Eban turned the conversation back to the topic at hand. "What will they do with the ship?"

"They're bringing it to Haifa."

"Then what?"

"Our best intelligence tells us they're going to send the passengers back."

"Send them back?" Eban asked. "To where?"

"France."

"Why France?"

"The ship sailed from Marseille."

"Will the French take them?"

"Not if I can help it," Ben-Gurion quipped.

"So, they're going back to France but the British are bringing them here first?"

"Yes," Ben-Gurion said with a twinkle in his eye. "And they are transferring them to prison ships."

"This could get ugly."

"Already is," Revach observed. "The British killed three passengers when they boarded the ship."

Eban thought for a moment before saying, "What can we do?"

"We need to get the committee up to Haifa for the arrival. They need to see the British in action for themselves." Ben-Gurion rested his hand on Eban's shoulder. "Can you do that? Can you get them up there?"

"Yes," Eban nodded. "That will not be a problem. You realize the reporters who are traveling with us will be there also."

"Yes," Ben-Gurion grinned. "I am counting on it."

"And whatever happens, they'll report it or not at their own choice. There's nothing we can do to control them."

"Good," Ben-Gurion smiled. "We'll have a crowd waiting." He gave Eban a pat on the shoulder. "Everything will turn out fine." Then he turned and walked toward the door.

On the ride back to the office, Revach looked over at Ben-Gurion. "You are sure we want the press to cover this?"

"Absolutely. The British will show their true colors tomorrow, and when the reporters see it they will tell the world about it."

"But how can we be certain they will? You heard what Abba said. They can always choose not to report it."

"Yes," Ben-Gurion nodded. "But if I am correct, this will take most of the day and there will be little time for anything else noteworthy to happen. Reporters have to file their stories daily, especially those who cover a trip like the committee is on. And with nothing else to report, they will write about the British forcing helpless civilians from a ship in Palestine."

"Are we sure there will be a crowd?"

"Oh yes," he nodded. "I am certain of it."

"How so?"

"Golda will take care of it."

— • —

At the Jewish Agency building, Revach and Ben-Gurion found Golda Meir in the workroom, surrounded by assistants and volunteers. A large table sat in the middle of the room and they were bent over a map that was spread upon it. She glanced up as they entered. "You heard about the ship?"

"Yes," Ben-Gurion nodded. "We need to talk."

"We're in the middle of something. Can it wait?"

"Not really."

They stepped across the hall to an empty room. When the door was closed Ben-Gurion turned to Golda. "You know that three passengers were killed?"

"Yes, we knew there could be casualties when we set this up. That's why we took so long in selecting the passengers." She gestured over her shoulder. "We were in there just now reviewing locations where we can house them when they arrive."

Ben-Gurion gave her a solemn expression. "I'm afraid that has changed."

Golda folded her arms across her chest. "What do you mean?"

"The British are sending them back to Europe."

Golda's face turned white with anger. "You can't mean it."

"I'm afraid it's true."

"Have they lost their minds?" She threw her hands in the air. "You have to go see them. You have to meet with Simpson and protest. This is unthinkable."

"We've just come from Simpson's office."

"And he won't budge?"

"Not at all."

"Well, we will have to do something." Golda began to pace. "We can't let this pass."

"They are bringing the ship to Haifa to transfer the passengers to prison ships."

Golda stopped her pacing and turned to face them, her mouth open wide in amazement. "Prison ships?"

"Yes," Ben-Gurion nodded.

"Those poor people. This is not what they signed up for. What are we going to do?"

"I've talked to Abba," Ben-Gurion explained. "He will have the UNSCOP committee at the dock when the ship arrives. I need you to make sure the people of Haifa know what time we expect the ship to arrive."

Golda frowned. "The people?"

"We need as many people as possible waiting at the dock."

A wry smile spread over her face. "We'll have to do this just right."

"That's why we came to you," Revach added.

"It has to appear spontaneous." Golda began to pace once more. "It can't look like we're trying to create an event."

"Why not?" Revach offered. "They killed three of our people. Innocent civilians just trying to make a life for themselves. Why shouldn't we make our indignation obvious?"

"Good point," Ben-Gurion nodded, then turned back to Golda. "Don't worry about whether it's obvious. If anyone asks, tell them we simply told the people what happened."

"Right," Golda nodded. "We'll need to get the word out to people there. And we'll need buses."

Revach shook his head. "I'm not sure how many buses we can arrange in Haifa."

"Not there," Golda answered. "Here. We need buses here, to haul people from Tel Aviv up there, to make certain we have a large crowd." She grinned. "And to give them a chance to show their anger at the British."

Ben-Gurion stepped to leave. "You can take care of it?"

"Yes."

"Good." He opened the door. "We want as large a crowd as possible. The British will do the rest on their own."

CHAPTER 3

LATE THAT AFTERNOON, Ben-Gurion sent a message to Yechiel Diskin, a rabbi from a Karaite Jewish congregation that met in Joppa, asking to meet with him that evening. Diskin arrived at Ben-Gurion's official residence a few hours later. They met upstairs in the study. Ben-Gurion was seated at the desk. "I trust you had no difficulty getting here."

"None at all." Diskin took a seat opposite the desk and gathered his robe around him. "But I was curious why you contacted me. There are many rabbis right here in Tel Aviv."

"But none of them are Karaite."

"I see."

"They all follow the teaching of the Talmud and the Mishnah as if it were as authoritative as the Torah."

"And you have a problem with their tradition," Diskin nodded.

"I have a problem with many things." Ben-Gurion leaned back in his chair. He was in no mood to discuss theology. "Right now, my most pressing problem is with the British."

Diskin wagged his finger in protest. "I cannot be a party to this conflict."

"Party. No party. That is not my issue this evening," Ben-Gurion said with a wave of his hand. "A few days ago," he continued, "a ship called the *Exodus* sailed from Marseille. It was bound for Palestine with four thousand passengers."

"No doubt a continuation of your illegal immigration policy."

Ben-Gurion's lips tightened as he struggled to retain his composure.

"One pressed upon us by the British policy of restricting Jewish immigration to a mere fifteen hundred per month, while we have thousands—even hundreds of thousands—of displaced persons in Europe wishing to settle here."

Diskin seemed to sense Ben-Gurion was on the verge of losing control. "And what of this ship?"

"Earlier today the British boarded it and seized control." As he spoke, Ben-Gurion relaxed and his voice took a more hospitable tone. "They plan to bring the ship to Haifa where they will transfer the passengers to prison ships and send them back."

"To Marseille?"

"Yes."

"And the French will take them?"

Ben-Gurion's eyes darted away. "We are not sure of that yet."

"How does this relate to me?"

"In taking control of the ship, British sailors killed three of the passengers. So far as we can tell, all of them were Jewish. The bodies remain onboard the ship."

Diskin frowned. "They did not bury them at sea?"

"No."

"They must be buried before sundown tomorrow."

"And that is where you come in," Ben-Gurion explained. "I would like for you to meet the ship in Haifa and see if you can obtain the bodies from the British. Those three could not live here, as they wished. The least we can do is bury them here."

"I will require the assistance of a rabbi from Haifa."

"You know someone?"

"Yes."

"A Karaite?"

"Certainly."

"Good," Ben-Gurion smiled. "I trust your judgment."

Diskin scooted forward in the chair to stand. "Is that all you need?"

"No. There is something else." Ben-Gurion gestured for him to remain and paused a moment to take a breath. "There will be a crowd at the dock when the ship arrives."

"I will see the British first thing in the morning. I'm sure they will give me the bodies without protest. I've had a good relationship with them. They're usually reasonable if approached on their own terms."

Ben-Gurion demurred. "I need you to make your request on the dock. After the ship arrives."

"They know I will be there? They are expecting me?"

"Not exactly."

"Oh," Diskin sighed. He slid back in the chair and placed his hands in his lap.

Ben-Gurion continued. "I need you to approach them at the ship as if you presume they'll give you the bodies. Not really asking, just announcing that you are there to collect them." He gestured with his hand as if offering an explanation. "You know. It's our tradition. Bury the dead within a day's time. That sort of thing."

Diskin nodded. "I see."

"It *is* our tradition."

"Of course."

Ben-Gurion propped his elbows on the desk and laced his fingers together, resting them on the desktop. "You understand my situation?"

"Yes." Diskin nodded once more. "I understand."

"Will that be a problem?"

"No." Diskin shook his head. "It is no problem at all." He took a deep breath and let it slowly escape. "You should come to temple sometime, you know."

Ben-Gurion leaned away once more. "I think you know how I feel about that sort of thing."

"Yes."

"A feeling I think you share," Ben-Gurion added, "as a Karaite."

"But I notice you don't hesitate to call on the rabbis when it suits your purposes, Karaite or not."

Ben-Gurion shook his head. "This isn't the time for that discussion."

"That's the problem between us," Diskin replied. "It's never the time to discuss that topic with you."

Ben-Gurion turned his chair toward the window and looked in that direction. "Have you ever wondered if we aren't on the precipice of a truly historic event?"

"I wonder that many times."

"And perhaps we all have a role to play in something much bigger than ourselves."

"You mean we rabbis have religious work to do, but your role is to ignore us?"

"I mean, for things to happen the way they're supposed to, some have to take on a role they might not otherwise seek."

"Many of us see it in prophetic terms."

"I didn't know you were one of them."

"If by *them* you mean those who await the fulfillment of the promises of the prophets—the rebuilding of Jerusalem, the restoration of Judah—then yes, I am one of them."

"Maybe you can help me. I've had this quote in my head the past few days." Ben-Gurion laced his fingers together and rested his hands on his chest. "'He will raise a banner for the nations and gather the exiles of Israel; he will assemble the scattered people of Judah from the four quarters of the earth.'"

Diskin raised an eyebrow. "That's from Isaiah."

"Yes. It is." Ben-Gurion glanced at Diskin. "And I sometimes wonder if that isn't what is happening here."

"Many of the people around you would not be happy to hear you say that."

"Many of the people around me aren't happy with the things I say now," Ben-Gurion chuckled, then turned serious. "But this thing we are doing seems much bigger than those of us who are doing it."

"I am sure it is," Diskin replied.

They sat in silence a moment, then Ben-Gurion straightened in the chair and cleared his throat. "You'll meet the ship in Haifa?"

"Yes," Diskin nodded. "I will take care of the bodies."

"Good. We have arranged to bury them in the Haifa cemetery." Ben-Gurion rose from his desk to escort Diskin to the door. "We shall place them in Martyr's Row."

— • —

That night onboard the *Exodus*, twenty kilometers off the Palestinian coast, Arnon Ullman sat with a group of passengers on the first level below the main deck. Jacob Schwarz was there with Sarah. Ullman's eyes seemed to focus on them as he scanned the gathering. "You are familiar with Haganah?"

"Yes," Jacob replied.

Several nodded in response. "They own this ship," someone offered.

"That's correct," Ullman noted. "And I am a member of Haganah. Yitzhak Rabin sent me here to help you."

"How do we know that is true?" someone asked.

"You don't," Ullman answered with a smile. "You'll just have to trust me."

"Why should we?" another voice asked.

"Because your life may very well depend on it." Ullman paused a moment before continuing. "Tomorrow we will reach the dock at Haifa. British soldiers will be there to meet us. They and the sailors onboard now will tell you to disembark—to get off the ship. You must not cooperate with them. No matter how much they shout and yell. Not matter how angrily they demand. You must resist their efforts to remove you."

"Most of us are civilians," Jacob spoke up. "We have no training in combat. How are we to resist?"

"You must fight back by any means possible."

"They have weapons," Jacob answered. "We do not."

"You have your fists and your feet," Ullman explained. "You can hit and kick. And if you can't do that, you can sit passively on the floor and refuse to move."

"What good will *that* do?" Sarah asked in a derisive tone.

"They will be compelled to remove you by force and that is what we want."

"She is a woman," Jacob argued. "She cannot be expected to engage soldiers in a show of force."

Sarah elbowed him in the ribs. "Speak for yourself." The group laughed in response.

A broad grin broke over Ullman's face. "You should listen to her," he suggested.

"But we would be deliberately provoking them," Jacob insisted, unwilling to yield to a sense of embarrassment at being the butt of Sarah's humor.

"Yes," Ullman said sharply. "Provoking them to show their true side, as a means of showing the world what they are really like." He focused on Jacob. "You remember the beatings they gave you this afternoon?" Jacob nodded, as did heads all around him. "And you remember your friend they shot in anger?" Jacob glanced at Sarah and saw a tear trickle down her face. He slipped his arm around her as Ullman continued. "In Palestine, they do that much and more. Just last month, they looked the other way while an Arab gang killed an entire busload of people in Jerusalem. Men, women, and children slaughtered under the watchful eye of British soldiers. They regularly stand by and watch while Arabs rape, loot, and destroy all that we have built. All of you have seen what they are really like. The world thinks they are saints, but we know they are as bad as the worst among us. Sometimes even as cruel to us as the Nazis. We must give them an opportunity to show that side to the world. We will have a chance to do that tomorrow."

Ullman continued to talk to them for another twenty minutes. As the meeting broke up, Jacob turned away and climbed the steps toward the main deck. A sailor met him there. "You are not supposed to be up here."

"It's hot down there. I do not wish to cause a problem."

"Well," the sailor sighed. "Just for a few minutes."

"Thanks," Jacob replied. He stepped out on the deck and leaned against the rail. A moment later, Sarah appeared at his side. "It's a nice night," she glanced around. Jacob did not reply but stared into the distance. She slipped her arm in his and rested her head on his shoulder. "Are you angry with me?"

"You made me look like an idiot in front of the whole group."

"I'm sorry."

"No, you're not."

"I am sorry I hurt your feelings. I am not sorry for the point I made."

"He is talking about resisting British troops. It could get very rough."

"You don't think I can take it?"

"I could not take seeing *you* hit in the forehead with the butt of a rifle."

She ran her head lightly over his brow. "Does it still hurt?"

"Yes." Jacob winced at her touch.

She squeezed his arm tightly. "Palestine is so close."

Jacob turned to her. "You are feeling better now?"

"About Avi?"

"Yes."

"I miss him, but I did not know him quite as well as you might think."

"You were distraught this afternoon."

"They killed him right in front of me," she lamented. "Of course I was distraught. But I have resolved to express my sorrow by doing something."

"What?"

"By coming with you to Palestine, no matter what. No matter how. No matter when." She kissed him gently.

"You are certain of this?"

"Yes."

"When we left, you still had reservations."

"Those reservations died with Avi this afternoon." Tears formed in her eyes. "They will not stop us," she vowed softly as tears flowed down her cheeks. "They will not stop us."

"No," he replied. "This will be our home. But I am not sure how that will happen."

CHAPTER 4

THE NEXT DAY, BEN-GURION traveled with Revach to Haifa. They arrived at the dock as the *Exodus* approached and found the area filled with people from the street to the water's edge. "Golda did a good job getting out the crowd," Revach commented.

"Too good," Ben-Gurion groused. "I don't think we can get to the water. We're supposed to meet Gedaliah Cohen at the end of the pier."

"Come on," Revach offered. "I think we can make a way."

With Revach in the lead, they picked their way through the crowd and twenty minutes later caught up with Cohen near the water. As commander of Haganah, Cohen had assigned a squad of men to stake out a position for them at the foot of the dock the night before, ahead of the crowd. Anyone entering or leaving the ship would come right past their location.

When they were settled in place, Ben-Gurion scanned the crowd and saw Noga Shapiro across the way standing with his assistant, Tuvia Megged. Shapiro, a German-born immigrant, came to Palestine with the hope of farming on his own, but repeated attacks by Arabs forced him to join a kibbutz where he was placed in charge of defense. His experience there served him well when he later joined Irgun, a paramilitary group that split from Haganah over disputes about how to respond to Arab militancy and British arrogance. Megged ran Irgun's day-to-day operations.

Ben-Gurion scowled in Shapiro's direction. "What are they doing here?"

"Who?" Cohen asked, glancing around.

"Shapiro and Megged."

"Watching, I suppose," Cohen replied. "Like the rest of us."

"Maybe Shapiro's just watching, but Megged's probably waiting for a chance to claim credit for whatever good happens today." Ben-Gurion glanced in Cohen's direction. "They won't try anything now, will they?"

"Irgun isn't the one you have to worry about," Cohen chuckled. "It's Lehi that bothers me. If Shapiro is here, no one in Irgun will act without his order and he won't give it. That's not his style. But Lehi might blow up the dock even with Yitzhak Jeziernicky standing on it."

"Yeah, but I like Lehi," Ben-Gurion smiled. "Jeziernicky doesn't mince words. And he isn't bound by conventional wisdom. He doesn't talk. He acts. And he has inspired deep loyalty among his men." He clasped his hands behind his back. "Don't get me wrong. I'm not condoning what they do. Robbing a bank to fund a mission against the Arabs isn't my way of solving our problems. But you have to admire their pluck. And Jeziernicky wants nothing but to lead his men. Shapiro…I'm not so sure about."

"Shapiro won't be a problem," Cohen replied. "He's not that kind of guy."

Off to the right, wedged between a squad of British soldiers and a group of schoolchildren, Ben-Gurion caught sight of Rabbi Diskin standing with six men who, from the way they were dressed, appeared to be rabbis also. All around them people jostled and shoved one another in an attempt to see, but the rabbis stood motionless, eyes forward, hands resting together at the waist, as if unaffected by all that was happening. Ben-Gurion watched from a distance and wondered how Diskin had found so many Karaite rabbis.

In a few minutes, Golda Meir appeared and came to Ben-Gurion's side. "Well," she beamed triumphantly, "we have the crowd."

"Yes," Revach replied. "Good job."

"I knew you could do it," Ben-Gurion added. "That's why I gave you the job."

"Bringing extra people from Tel Aviv helped."

"Where's Abba and UNSCOP?" Ben-Gurion asked.

"I don't know," she shrugged. "I've been up here all morning getting the local crowd mobilized. You didn't see them before you left?"

"I haven't seen Abba since yesterday."

Cohen nudged him. "The ship's almost here."

Ben-Gurion looked up to see the *Exodus* less than a hundred meters from the dock. He watched in silence with the others as it slowly eased into the berth and seamen secured it with mooring lines.

As the gangway was being slipped into place, a commotion in the crowd caught everyone's attention. Golda pointed in that direction. "That looks like Abba there."

The others turned in time to see British soldiers manhandling the crowd, beating them back with batons and shoving them aside with their rifles. Behind the soldiers came Abba Eban and the members of UNSCOP, most of them wide-eyed at the size of the crowd and the soldiers' brutality. Eban guided the committee to the foot of the dock and placed Emil Sandström, the committee chairman, at Ben-Gurion's side. Ralph Bunche, an American working with the committee, was with them and members of the traveling press corps gathered around.

"Glad you made it," Ben-Gurion said.

"We had a terrible time getting up here," Sandström complained. "Then once we arrived the place was packed. Abba had to get the soldiers to lead us through."

Ben-Gurion leaned to the opposite side, where Eban stood, and whispered with a grin, "Nice touch."

"Yes," Eban nodded. "It was, even if I didn't plan it that way."

Sandström was aghast. "I have never seen such brute force exercised on a civilian crowd in all my life."

"Yes," Bunche added in disgust. "This is unheard of from a trained military like theirs."

Twenty minutes later, the gangway appeared ready, but nothing happened. Then an officer appeared on the deck and waved down to the soldiers who had escorted the committee. The troop dutifully filed up to the ship's deck and disappeared inside.

Half an hour later, an officer came from the ship and approached Ben-Gurion. "The passengers won't disembark," he explained.

Ben-Gurion looked puzzled. "They won't disembark?"

"No. They won't get off the ship. Will you tell them to leave the ship and assemble on the dock?"

"No," Ben-Gurion shook his head resolutely. "I cannot do that. I know what you intend to do with them and if I tell them to cooperate I would be telling them to return to where they came from."

"They won't budge for us, but they would for you."

"I will tell them to rush the gate," Ben-Gurion reiterated. "But I will not tell them to return to Europe. You cannot expect me to turn them away."

The officer's face turned red with anger. "Very well," he hissed. "We shall remove them ourselves."

As the officer returned to the ship, the already unruly crowd grew even more restless. Someone began to chant, "Free them! Free them!" Then others picked it up and before long the sound of their voices was a deafening roar. Reporters spread out, snapping pictures and scribbling notes. Ben-Gurion had a satisfied grin.

Minutes later, two soldiers appeared at the top of the gangway. Each held the foot of a man who was lying flat on the deck. Then the soldiers started down the gangway, dragging the man behind them. His head bumped against the rough boards with each step. The soldiers seemed oblivious to the image it created and laughed all the way down to the dock where they unceremoniously dropped him. As he lay there, still and unflinching, one of the soldiers shouted down at him, "Get up!" When the man they'd dragged did not respond, the soldier kicked him in the side. "Get up, stupid Jew! Do I have to kick you to death right here? Get up!"

Still laughing, the other soldier waved off his companion and picked up the man's foot. "Get that one," he said. "We'll drag him the rest of the way." Reluctantly, the first soldier picked up the other foot and together they dragged him from the dock and past the crowd where soldiers had cordoned off a pathway.

Ben-Gurion was livid at what he'd just witnessed and rushed forward, blocking their way. "What are you doing?" he shouted. "You can't treat him like this! He's not just a slab of meat or a piece of freight."

The first soldier thrust out his forearm to push Ben-Gurion back. "Stand aside, old man. We're coming through."

When Ben-Gurion stiffened and refused to move, the soldier looked him in the eye and said, "We asked you to help and you refused. Now get out of the way or you can join him."

Eban stepped forward and took Ben-Gurion by the arm. "Come on, David. This does us no good."

But the crowd began to chant, "Ben-Gurion! Ben-Gurion!"

He waved to them and turned to Eban. "It does us a lot of good to make our point."

— • —

Onboard the ship, British soldiers worked their way methodically through its levels, dragging and carrying passengers to the main deck and down to the dock. After three hours, they reached Jacob and Sarah. An officer pointed to Jacob and barked to two enlisted men, "This one. Get him off."

"What about her?" one of them asked, pointing to Sarah.

"We'll bring the woman later."

They reached for Jacob but he stood on his own and shrugged them away. "I can walk," he snapped.

"Then do it," a soldier ordered.

Jacob turned to offer Sarah his hand. "Come," he said. "Let us be going."

"I'm not leaving on my own."

"I'm not asking you to leave on your own. I'm asking you to accompany me at my request."

She sighed and stood. "Well, if you put it like that," she smiled, "who could refuse?"

The soldier barked, "They said for her to come later."

"You would rather drag a woman out by the hair like you did those others than to have her leave on the arm of her husband?"

With Sarah holding his arm, Jacob led the way up to the main deck. From below, they had heard the crowd but seeing them now by the tens of thousands was overwhelming. They paused at the top of the gangway to take it all in.

"This is Palestine," Jacob grinned.

"Yes," Sarah acknowledged. "This is Palestine. And already it feels like home."

Jacob pointed to a building in the distance. "If we had an apartment over there, we could see the water from our—"

"Get moving!" a soldier shouted, interrupting their conversation. He prodded them with a shove that caught Jacob off-guard. He stumbled forward and caught himself against the rail. Sarah turned to say something to the soldier but Jacob drew her back. "Come on," he said softly. "Let's not give them the satisfaction of determining our fate."

With Sarah once more holding his arm, Jacob led the way down to the dock, waving to the applauding crowd as he came. When Jacob and Sarah reached the end of the dock, they walked as far toward the crowd as the soldiers allowed. Then Jacob bent down and picked up a stone, which he placed in his pocket and shouted at the top of his voice, "Palestine is my home! I will be back!"

The crowd roared in approval as soldiers led them toward a large warehouse a short distance away.

— · —

For the remainder of the day, British soldiers continued to bring passengers from the *Exodus*, dragging, carrying, shoving, and beating them in the process. Many were already bloodied and battered from the treatment they had received at the hands of the sailors onboard the ship. Once on the ground, they were herded like animals to a warehouse and guarded by armed soldiers. Members of UNSCOP continued to watch in horror.

In the afternoon, Field Marshal Alan Cunningham, British High Commissioner for Palestine, arrived at the dock to review operations. He was accompanied by Gerald Simpson, the lieutenant general from the British command in Tel Aviv, and by a large entourage of assistants and armed guards. Emil Sandström and several members of the committee met with them at a warehouse near the dock where the passengers were being kept.

Sandström asked, "What will you do with these passengers?"

"Detain them until we can make ships ready to take them back," Simpson replied.

"Back to where?"

"To France."

"They can't stay here," Cunningham added.

"Why not?"

"The quota is full."

"And they have no valid entry documents," Simpson offered.

"But they are here," a committee member argued.

"And they're going back," Simpson insisted.

Sandström was obviously disturbed by the situation. "And in the meantime?" he asked.

"In the meantime they will be housed and cared for like any other detainee in British custody," Cunningham sniped.

"Where?" Sandström asked.

"There," Simpson pointed over his shoulder. "In those warehouses. Right where they are now."

Ralph Bunche spoke up. "Do you have sanitation facilities in that warehouse?"

"That is not my problem," Simpson answered.

"What do you mean it's not your problem? You detained them. You have a responsibility to treat them in a humane manner."

"I assure you, Mr. Bunche, we are processing them as quickly as possible."

"Processing them?"

"These things take time, you know."

"Need I remind you that you hold your mandate for control of this region under the authority of the United Nations?"

"Well," Cunningham said in a superior tone, "that remains to be seen."

"Do you propose to keep them in this warehouse overnight?" Bunche continued.

"Yes," Simpson replied. "I suppose so."

"Then how do you plan to care for their sanitary needs?"

"As I said earlier, they are being treated in accord with—"

"They are being treated like animals!" Sandström shouted.

"Now, see here," Cunningham retorted. He stepped forward and jabbed

Sandström in the chest. "We treat them as we see fit. If they wanted to be treated differently they should have obeyed the law."

Sandström was taken aback by Cunningham's conduct but refused to back down. "Do you plan to feed them?" he asked, jabbing Cunningham in the chest for emphasis.

"Unhand me," Cunningham shouted angrily, "or I shall have you arrested at once."

Sandström lowered his voice. "Do not threaten me, Cunningham! Or I'll have the committee file a report with the general assembly that will leave your United Kingdom stuck with this place for another twenty years."

Cunningham straightened his jacket. "You wouldn't dare."

"Try me. If England wants out of Palestine, I'm expecting to see some cooperation with the committee's work and the condition of these passengers you've detained."

— · —

When all the passengers were removed from the *Exodus*, the British soldiers who'd come aboard to assist filed off. They were followed by the sailors who'd brought the ship to port. Behind them came James Staveley, the commanding officer of the boarding party. When he was halfway down to the dock, Rabbi Diskin and the six men who'd accompanied him moved to the foot of the gangway and blocked his path. Staveley addressed them with disdain. "What do you want?" he asked.

"I understand some of our people are dead," Diskin replied.

"What of it?"

"It is our tradition to bury the dead within twenty-four hours. I have come for their bodies."

Ben-Gurion, Eyal Revach, and Gedaliah Cohen stood nearby, watching. Sandström and members of the UN committee watched, too, as did Cunningham and Simpson.

Staveley was obviously uncomfortable and tried to maneuver past them. "They are in British custody."

Diskin refused to step aside to allow him pass. "And we've come so that you may turn them over to us," he continued calmly.

Bunche, who was standing with the committee members, spoke up. "What else are you going to do with them? Take them back to England?"

Soldiers who'd been holding back the crowd stood a few meters away. One of them chuckled aloud, "Feed them to the fish."

Staveley glanced nervously at Cunningham, who simply shrugged, then turned to a soldier and ordered, "Tell them to bring out the bodies."

"We will go get them," Diskin insisted.

Staveley nodded his approval and Diskin started up the gangway with the six men he brought with him. The crowd, which still numbered in the thousands, murmured in response.

A few minutes later, Diskin appeared at the top of the gangway with the others who were carrying three bodies wrapped in white linen shrouds. The crowd fell eerily silent as they moved to the dock and then out toward the street.

Eban turned to Ben-Gurion. "You have someplace to bury them?"

"Yes," Ben-Gurion nodded. "It is all prepared."

"Good," Eban nodded. "I think the British have done all they can do for us today."

"They made our point very well," Ben-Gurion smiled.

CHAPTER 5

THAT EVENING, BEN-GURION convened a meeting of the Jewish Agency's principal leadership at his official residence. They gathered in the study upstairs. Golda Meir was present along with Gedaliah Cohen from Haganah, Aharon Hartman from the Haganah general staff, and Walter Eytan from the Jewish Agency's political department. Abba Eban joined them along with several others. Ben-Gurion began by asking what UNSCOP members thought of the day's events at the dock in Haifa.

"UNSCOP was appalled by the conduct of the British soldiers and sailors," Eban reported with glee. "Sandström was particularly incensed."

"What about the others?"

"I think to a man they were appropriately offended by the entire incident," Eban said with satisfaction. "When they began their work, the committee was deeply divided. A few had originally favored a unified government for all of Palestine. Others supported Arab demands without question. Fewer still were unquestioningly in our favor. Most of them, however, wanted to extend the British mandate for another five years to give time for a different solution to arise, but after what they saw today no one favors extending the British presence. And they have begun to discuss among themselves the need for a Jewish state. I think the British showed today exactly why Jews need a place where they can determine their own fate." He looked over at Golda. "That crowd was a brilliant idea. Nicely played."

"Thank you," she smiled. "I was merely following orders."

"You did it well."

Walter Eytan spoke up. "I think we unified the committee to our cause and the issues we face. But we are still divided among ourselves over whether to opt for a partitioning of Palestine that gives us only a portion of the area, or hold out for control of the entire region. Weizmann has not been in favor of partition and he has worked against us diplomatically at every turn."

"He has certainly done his best to undermine me," Ben-Gurion added.

Indeed, as all of them knew, the rivalry between Ben-Gurion and Chaim Weizmann had marked the history of the modern Zionist movement. Since becoming chairman of the Jewish Agency, Ben-Gurion had favored an immediate push toward an independent Jewish nation, even if it meant controlling only a portion of Palestine. Weizmann, dean of the movement, favored a slower, long-term approach that hopefully would give them control of the entire region. The two had butted heads repeatedly.

"I know he has been difficult at times," Eban nodded, "but I think he has begun to change his mind. I talked to him recently in New York and he seemed to think this might be our last and only hope for a homeland."

Ben-Gurion was encouraged. "That would be good news if he has. What does Sharett say?"

"He thinks the UN will never agree to give us full control of the entire region, and, with that in mind, something now is better than the promise of something later. He favors partition."

"I agree," Golda added.

Ben-Gurion's eyes opened wide. "You've changed your position?"

"I have changed my position," Golda affirmed. "The promise of something in the future is the promise of nothing in the present. We need a place now. Hundreds of thousands of Jews in displaced-persons camps in Europe need a place to go. We need a national identity and the only way we'll get that is through an international coalition of support. The British will never help us obtain it. The American government will do so only reluctantly. But the broader international community is gathering behind our cause. This is our time."

"You're right about the British," Eytan acknowledged. "They will always favor the Arabs because they have oil and England does not."

"The British are stuck in a colonial mind-set," Ben-Gurion grumbled. "To them, the value of a people is solely in the goods and services they can produce, or the natural resources they control. They will favor the Arabs, even if it means our complete demise."

Hartman spoke up. "That's a little harsh, don't you think?"

Ben-Gurion's eyes flashed with anger. "Have you not seen how they treat us?"

"Yes," Hartman conceded. "But they are in a difficult position, playing peace-keeper between two groups with equal historic claims to the same region."

Golda gave a heavy sigh. Walter Eytan shifted uneasily in his chair. And Ben-Gurion was furious. "Equal!" he fumed. "How can you say their claim is equal to ours? Our forebears settled this land thousands of years before Mohammad was born! We were a nation, a people, thousands of years before the Arabs had any collective identity." He shot an angry glare in Cohen's direction. "Would you command men in battle to defend such a measly, ill-defined position as mere competing claims?"

"I'm just saying," Hartman retreated, "the British are in a difficult spot."

"They put themselves there." Ben-Gurion paused to collect himself and shot another glare in Cohen's direction. Cohen seemed to understand and excused himself to step outside with Hartman. When they were gone, Ben-Gurion leaned back in his chair and ran his fingers through his hair. "We are such an unassimilated group."

"Yes," Golda said in a lighthearted tone, "and it is our diversity that makes us strong."

"But frustrating," Ben-Gurion quipped. He took a deep breath and then turned back to Eban. "What about President Truman?" He tried his best to get the conversation back on track. "Any progress in arranging an appointment to speak with him?"

Eban shook his head. "Truman is refusing to speak with representatives from either side."

"Eliahu Epstein doesn't know how to reach him?"

"Eliahu is a good man, but these kinds of things require relationships."

"The longer the better," Eytan chimed in.

"Weizmann is the only one who can do this," Eban continued. "We need him on this."

Ben-Gurion bristled at the suggestion. "I can go to the White House and speak to Truman."

"You could go to the White House," Eban conceded, "but you wouldn't get past the guard at the door. Truman won't speak to you. He won't speak to anyone from either side."

"Well," Ben-Gurion countered, "he might not know me personally, as he does Weizmann, but he knows I am the head of the Jewish Agency for Palestine."

"Yes," Eban nodded, "and that is the very reason he won't see you."

"So what do we do?" Ben-Gurion sighed.

"The Russians seem to favor us," Golda suggested. "Perhaps we should look to them for the support we'd hoped to find in America. Gromyko's recent speech about the need for a Jewish homeland was astounding."

"That's true," Ben-Gurion noted. "And others have expressed their support as well."

"Yes," Eban nodded, "but America's approval is still key to acceptance in the global community. They are essential to our existence, if for no other reason than to act as a counterweight to the British."

"So," Ben-Gurion pondered, "what should we do?"

"To get the Americans," Eban explained, "we'll need Weizmann. I understand you and he have a history between you, but he has some connections that may prove very advantageous."

"Connections?"

"He not only knows Truman, he knows others who know him, too. Americans. People who were close friends with Truman before he came to office. That is the kind of influence we need to move him from his current position."

"Perhaps," Ben-Gurion scowled. "If Weizmann doesn't give away the entire region in the process."

Eban shrugged. "I think we have no choice but to let him work whatever advantage he might have."

Golda spoke up. "Let Weizmann handle the White House. He's good at that sort of thing. It can be his contribution to the effort. The rest of us will push forward at the things we do well, too, and lean on our own strengths."

"Yes," Ben-Gurion agreed. His countenance brightened and he smiled at Eban. "You and Moshe Sharett should continue to pursue the best solution with UNSCOP, which seems to be partition."

"I agree."

"And we will continue to move forward here with issues on the ground that we face every day. The main thing," Ben-Gurion emphasized, "is that in the end, we obtain a Jewish state. That's the main thing. That's what we've been working for and dying for all these years. With a state we have a place, and with a place we can build a future."

"Good," Eban nodded.

"And make sure you keep Eliahu Epstein apprised of the situation as it develops," Ben-Gurion added. "We want him to carry his own weight with his colleagues in Washington, and with Weizmann. We can't have the White House thinking Weizmann is our authorized representative on all matters. And we need to prepare his successor, someone who has cultivated those strategic relationships and can carry on for us in the future."

The door opened and Cohen returned alone to the meeting. Ben-Gurion gestured toward an empty seat, and Eban took the conversation back to UNSCOP and the matter at hand. "As to the committee, we need to work the delegation from Guatemala and Uruguay very closely. Dr. Granados is a reasonable man and Professor Fabregat should be sympathetic to our cause. I think we could lock up their support with a little effort and that would narrow the vote on the final report to just a few delegates."

"Sandström is with us?" Golda asked.

"Very much so."

"Good," Ben-Gurion added. "Any others we should know about?"

"Australia is part of the British commonwealth. I suspect their representative will go with the British position for political reasons. But they don't control the process and in these kinds of committees, process is everything."

"Who controls the process?" Golda wondered.

"Edmundo Sisto is the committee's secretary. He's from Uruguay also. He and Ralph Bunche, the American, keep things running."

"Is Bunche with us?"

"As an American of African descent, he's very familiar with our situation. He told me after we left the docks that he'd seen better treatment of Blacks in the American South than he saw today from the British."

"So, he's with us?"

"He's with us. As is Edmundo Sisto. But that only gives us the process, not the final vote."

"What do we need for that?" Ben-Gurion asked.

"Intelligence," Eban answered. "We can work the committee and control the process, but we need intelligence to stay ahead of the delegates and the British. They and the Arabs are hovering around us all the time."

Gedaliah Cohen nodded. "We can provide intelligence."

"Good." Eban turned to face him. "Just let me know what you need from our side and I'll do my best to set you up."

"Where will they convene to deliberate their report?" Ben-Gurion asked.

"Geneva."

"We will be there," Cohen assured.

Golda spoke up once more. "Our operatives can do this without being seen?"

"Absolutely," Cohen replied. "Shai has grown from a tiny network into a force of well-trained intelligence operatives. Reuven Shiloah and Nahum Admoni have them in top form."

Walter Eytan spoke up. "Just make sure they don't get out of hand. We need intelligence but we don't need to overreach."

"What do you mean?" Cohen frowned.

"Right now we are the victim," Eytan explained. "Great Britain is the bully and the Arabs are seen as totally unreasonable. We need to keep it that way as long as possible and play it to our advantage."

Ben-Gurion turned to Eban. "Tell me a little more about Ralph Bunche."

"Ralph is a brilliant man," Eban said with a grin. "Seasoned diplomat. Polished. Smooth. But a little frustrated with the committee's lack of experience and focus. He and Edmundo Sisto are handling all the committee details right now from travel, to questions for the hearings, to interview lists. He'll probably be the one who writes the final report. None of the rest seems capable of the task. You should meet with him and do your best to make a favorable impression."

"We'll have him for lunch," Ben-Gurion suggested.

"Dinner might work better," Eban offered.

"Good," Ben-Gurion smiled. "Can you keep the committee here a few more days?"

"Maybe. Why?"

"The British will transfer the *Exodus* passengers to prison ships in a day or two for the journey back to Europe. It would be good if the committee was on hand for that."

"They want to go up there tomorrow and check on conditions at the warehouses. I'm not sure we can extend their stay long enough to see them off on the ships."

"Maybe that is how you could present it to them. Take them to the warehouses, show them how the passengers are living, then suggest they need to remain a few days to monitor their conditions."

"I'll give it a shot," Eban agreed. "But I can't guarantee it. They're on a rather tight schedule that has already been blown by yesterday's events."

Gradually, the conversation wound to an end and Ben-Gurion stood. "This has been a productive session. I think we're making progress. But it's late and we have another full day tomorrow."

Walter Eytan started for the stairs with Golda and Abba Eban close behind. As they made their way to the first floor, Ben-Gurion called after them and asked Golda to remain. She returned to the second floor and stood near the desk. Ben-Gurion waited until he heard the door close downstairs, then said quietly, "If Abba is correct, and the UN committee is leaning toward partition, war is coming and we should get ready for it."

"Okay," Golda said slowly. "What should we do?"

"The first thing we must do is play this *Exodus* incident to our advantage as far as it goes."

"We've done a good job of that, I think."

"I want you to go to Paris," Ben-Gurion continued. "Talk to the French. See what their position would be on handling the passengers from the *Exodus*. If the British are returning them to Marseille, we need to be ready for what will happen next."

"What do you want them to do with the passengers?"

"I prefer that they send them back to us, of course. But I know they won't. We just don't want them to condemn us for arranging the voyage or condemn the passengers for trying."

"The British have the public in their corner on this matter," Golda noted. "Most people think they are experts on the Middle East, and yet they have made a complete mess of this region."

"Yes," Ben-Gurion agreed, "but the Americans know what they are really like, even if they won't say it, and the French don't care what either of them thinks, which works in our favor. If we can work cooperatively with the French on this we might be able to cultivate a friendship that will be of greater advantage to us in the days that lie ahead."

"When I was there a few months ago," Golda offered, "I spoke to members of their foreign office and they were sympathetic to our cause."

"That might be helpful," Ben-Gurion nodded. "They have a large supply of German weapons in their country that they seized after the Allied invasion. I understand they would like to get rid of it. I'm hoping this trip and the contacts you make will give us an opening with them on that topic. Perhaps they would be willing to sell to us quietly. Maybe even at bargain terms. If we gain statehood, whether by UN resolution or our own declaration, the Arabs will attack us. They are all far better armed than we."

"As if they aren't attacking us already."

"Right. But this would be much worse. The local Palestinian Arabs would be joined by regular armies from all the countries in the region."

"If we purchased our own armaments, how would we pay for them?"

"I don't know," Ben-Gurion shrugged. "But see what they have to say about it if you get the chance. And do your best to make the chance."

"Imagine that," Golda said, shaking her head at the irony of it. "German arms helping Jews throw off the Arabs, who were German allies in the war."

"At this point, I really don't care where they were manufactured, just so long as we get to use them. Do you know Vincent Auriol?"

"I've met him, but don't know him. I have a good relationship with Leon Blum. Maybe he can get me in to see President Auriol."

"Okay. He would be helpful. See if you can meet with him first."

As they finished their discussion, Ben-Gurion led Golda downstairs to the door. They found Gedaliah Cohen waiting there, and when Golda was gone the two men talked.

"I do not mind our soldiers having a difference of opinion," Ben-Gurion began, "but when the army speaks it must speak with one voice."

"Your voice," Cohen nodded. "I told Hartman that."

"I will not accept anything less than a top-down structure. I as the civilian head; you as the commanding general."

"I made that clear to him."

"And all lines flow down from us."

"That won't be a problem in the future."

"You're sure of it?"

"We had a long talk."

"How many others share his convictions?"

"I'm not certain. We haven't conducted doctrinal surveys."

"Do you think it's necessary?"

"Not so long as they follow orders."

"It's easier to condone free thinking and the expression of thought among the enlisted men, but with officers and leaders we must be as one, at least in our purpose. I doubt any of us agree on exactly how to accomplish our goal. But we can all agree on the goal."

"We must," Cohen added.

"Yes," Ben-Gurion said with resolute finality. "We must."

CHAPTER 6

AROUND MIDMORNING THE FOLLOWING DAY, Abba Eban and the UNSCOP members returned to the docks in Haifa to check on the condition of the passengers from the *Exodus*. As was his practice, Ralph Bunche accompanied them, along with members of the traveling press corps. They found the detainees housed in three warehouses with no windows, no forced circulation, and only one bathroom, each equipped with a single toilet, none of which functioned properly. To make matters worse, the temperature inside was sweltering. There were no cots or chairs. Coupled with the stench of urine and feces from overflowing toilets, conditions were all but unbearable.

Some of the passengers were ill. A few were in such bad shape they required medical attention that could only be rendered in the hospital. Many at the warehouses were hoping they would be sick, too, and left behind when the British ships sailed for France. One or two had escaped in the night, but a rumor was circulating among the passengers that the missing had been killed by the British.

Seated on the bare concrete floor, they clustered together in random groups around the building. Committee delegates wandered among them, talking to those who felt like responding. Enrique Fabregat, the UNSCOP delegate from Uruguay, and Vladimir Simic from Yugoslavia, found Sarah and Jacob Schwarz sitting alone on the far side of the building. After an introduction, Jacob and Sarah agreed to talk. Reporters gathered around, once more taking notes and snapping pictures as the interviews proceeded.

"You came from Europe?" Fabregat asked.

"Yes."

"Just the two of you?"

"No," Jacob replied. "Sarah's cousin, Avi Livney, was traveling with us."

"But he's not now?"

"He was killed on the ship."

"Oh. I did not know the names of the victims," Fabregat said with a hint of sympathy. "I am terribly sorry." He glanced at Sarah. "If you would rather not talk, I don't mind."

"No," she shook her head. "It's okay. They wouldn't let us attend the funeral, so we've been talking about it since it happened. We might as well talk to you, too."

"You were not allowed to attend his funeral?"

"No," Jacob answered.

Fabregat's eyes were wide with concern. "That is unheard of."

"We thought so, too," Sarah said as she wiped her eyes.

"So, what happened?" Simic asked, picking up the conversation. "Onboard the ship. What happened to your…cousin, is it?"

"Yes."

"What happened?"

"We were standing at the rail when they came aboard," Jacob explained. "They were shouting and yelling."

"They?"

"British sailors."

"They looked very young," Sarah added. "And very nervous."

"One of them confronted us," Jacob continued. "Told us to move back or something like that. It made me angry and I said something back to him. That's when he hit me with the butt of his rifle." Jacob pushed back hair from his brow and pointed. "Right there. You can still see the bruise on my head." Simic and Fabregat winced. "Avi was really angry and yelled at the guy."

"What did he say?"

"Avi?"

"Yes. What did he say to the sailor?"

"Something like 'I'll see you in hell—'"

"The grave," Sarah corrected.

"Yeah," Jacob nodded. "That was it. 'I'll send you to the grave for this.' Then the sailor next to him flew into a rage and shot Avi squarely in the middle of his forehead."

Tears trickled down Sarah's face. "And just like that he was gone," she whispered. Jacob slipped his arm around her and pulled her closer. She rested her head on his shoulder.

Simic paused a moment as if reflecting on what they'd said, then continued. "They say you were recruited for this voyage."

"I suppose so," Jacob answered. "We were approached by someone who said they could get us to Palestine at no cost to us."

"You didn't have to pay?"

"No."

"Who approached you?"

"Someone from Mossad LeAliyah Bet. They organize groups of people to emigrate from Europe to Palestine."

"Where were you when they approached you?"

"A displaced-persons camp outside Berlin."

Fabregat had a quizzical expression. "How did they know to ask you?"

"We told them," Sarah offered.

Both Simic and Fabregat appeared puzzled. Jacob explained. "We indicated that was what we wanted to do when the staff at the camp interviewed us. When we were processed into the camp—the displaced-persons camp—they wanted to know if we had a place to go. We had no place but knew we wanted to go to Palestine."

"This was after the war?" Simic asked.

"Yes. When the war ended I was at Auschwitz. Sarah was in hiding. We had no place to go, so the Allies sent us to a camp in Germany with many others who were in a similar situation. Our homes in Poland had been destroyed or appropriated by others. We had no place."

"And they couldn't just give you back your property?"

"I suppose not. It has been years since we were last there."

"So," Fabregat turned the conversation back to the voyage, "you wanted to come to Palestine."

"He did for certain," Sarah noted. "I wasn't that enthusiastic about it at first, but I came because he wanted to."

"And now?"

"We will stay if they let us," she said. "And if not, we'll keep trying until they don't turn us away."

After an hour or so in the warehouses, Emil Sandström, the committee's chairman, had seen enough. He stepped outside and located the officer in charge, William Baker, a lieutenant, standing with a group of soldiers smoking cigarettes in the shade. Sandström approached him directly. "I wish to lodge a complaint."

"About what?" Baker asked.

"About the deplorable conditions under which these people are being held."

"I appreciate the situation they face," Baker paused to take a draw on the cigarette before continuing. "But there is nothing I can do about it."

"Nothing you can do about it?" Sandström's forehead wrinkled in frustration. "Pray tell, why not? Are you not the person in command here?"

"Yes," Baker nodded as he exhaled smoke. "I am in command of the soldiers. But our job is to guard the detainees and keep them confined to the buildings. We are not responsible for providing services to them."

"Then who is?"

"That would be Lieutenant General Simpson, sir."

"And where might he be located?"

"His office is in—" Just then a car turned from the street and came toward them. "I believe that's him now," Baker pointed. "You can speak to him if you like." He tossed his cigarette on the ground and rubbed it out with the toe of his shoe.

"Thank you," Sandström replied. "I shall indeed."

When the car came to a stop, the driver stepped out and opened the rear door. Simpson climbed out and placed his hat upon his head. Sandström did not wait to be invited but approached him at once. In quick fashion, he gave similar notice indicating his objection to the passengers' condition. By then Ralph Bunche and Abba Eban had joined them.

"There are over four thousand prisoners in custody," Simpson groused.

"What do you expect me to do?"

"Passengers," Sandström corrected.

Simpson was perplexed. "Excuse me?"

"You referred to them as prisoners. They are passengers. Civilians."

"Innocent civilians," Bunche added.

"Right," Simpson acknowledged. "And there are more than four thousand of them. We have no other place to put them. It's not that we have a better place and refuse to move them. We simply have no other place to put them."

Eban spoke up, "We have plenty of room in the Negev. We could put them all there."

"Can you not smell the stench these people are forced to endure?" Sandström implored. "Surely you can smell it."

"Yes," Simpson agreed. "Of course. It is most regrettable."

"Can you not at least repair the toilets?"

"I was not aware they were malfunctioning."

"From where did you think the odor arose?"

"I only just arrived," Simpson said defensively.

"This is your first visit since yesterday?"

"Yes. I gave orders for the men to see to their needs. I can't do everything myself."

By then, reporters had spotted them talking and gathered around to listen. "Lieutenant Baker there," Sandström said, gesturing to the soldiers who stood nearby, "seems to think caring for the passengers is not his responsibility. That he is here only to keep them confined."

"I'll take care of that," Simpson said tersely.

"Have they eaten?" Bunche asked.

"The soldiers?"

"No," Eban retorted. "The passengers."

"They receive two meals per day, which is standard for prisoners."

"There you go again," Bunche said. "They are civilians. Even if they attempted to do as you claim, entering the country without authorization is not a crime."

"And," Eban continued, taking this opportunity to educate the reporters, "in fact, they never even attempted to immigrate. You seized them before they arrived, while they were still in international waters."

"Look," Simpson said in a sharp tone, "we have rules. And we must follow them even when it inflicts misery on people like these. I didn't create this problem."

"You aren't doing much to solve it, either."

"That will take place on the morrow," Simpson sighed.

"Tomorrow?" Eban asked.

"Yes."

"And what shall you do for them tomorrow?"

"We shall send them back to Europe, where they belong. They will sail in the morning."

— · —

That night, David Ben-Gurion, Abba Eban, and Golda Meir entertained Ralph Bunche with dinner at Ben-Gurion's residence. They talked about the passengers from the *Exodus*, the critical Arab-Jewish issues facing the people of Palestine, the possibility of partition, and the manner in which the Arab and Jewish populations were concentrated in the region. Later in the evening, Ben-Gurion turned the discussion to a more personal topic. He wanted to know more about Bunche in hopes of better understanding what he might be thinking of their situation—the deeper thoughts Bunche might entertain but never articulate publicly.

"Ralph," he said, approaching the topic with caution, "you seem to be deeply interested in these issues. Personally interested. Not just as a job."

"Yes," Bunche nodded. "I am."

"I assume you aren't Jewish."

Bunche shook his head. "I am not."

"So, as an American who is not a Jew, what makes our situation important for you?"

"Well," Bunche began slowly, "I am not merely an American. I am a black American. Our people have been subjected to some of the harshest racially-based discrimination in the modern world." He glanced around the table at the others. "And I say this with all due respect for the misery that Jews have endured. Ours was perhaps not the worst treatment any group ever received, but it was certainly among the harshest. And as a young boy I began to wonder why. Not merely from the traditional explanation of slavery and Jim Crow laws and so forth, but the more fundamental question of how the treatment we received fit into the world social order. Once I began to explore that idea I realized that racial prejudice is not just an American phenomenon, but international. So then I began to ask myself what there was about the nature of mankind that made us that way and whether there was something about individual groups that made them susceptible to that sort of treatment."

"Did you find any answers?" Golda asked.

"No definitive ones yet," Bunche smiled. "But the search for answers on an international scope brought me to the Jewish situation and I saw that Jews face the same sort of problems with Europeans as Blacks do."

"Which is?" Eban asked.

"People of the traditionally European tribes do not like us," Bunche replied.

"If that's so," Golda said, challenging his premise, "then why do the British seem to fawn over the Arabs?"

"Oil," Bunche replied, "to give you a short answer."

"Is it more than that?"

"The British see an advantage to courting the Arabs," Bunche explained. "They have oil. England needs oil. Beyond that, the British have a long history in the region and the sands of the desert have come to hold a romantic allure for them. They spent many years trying to decipher the artifacts their expeditions uncovered in Egypt and seem to view at least some Arabs as their intellectual peers. I think they also feel that the Arabs are a group they can control. At least, certain ones of them. For Jews, they have no leverage and no prospect of control."

"They seem to think we're after their money," Eban offered.

"That, too," Bunche noted.

"For a piece of literary trash," Golda sighed, *"Protocols of the Learned Elders of Zion* has planted a most insidious seed of conspiracy in their minds."

"Yes, it has," Bunche readily acknowledged. "And in the minds of the Arabs as well."

"So, they fear us?" Ben-Gurion asked.

"They envy you," Bunche countered. "And yes, they fear you. But it's not just you. They see the world changing around them and know they have little control over it. England is in decline. America has arisen with no limit in sight. The British know they are not the nation they once were, but they can't figure out exactly what they are becoming."

"They are floundering," Eban added.

"Exactly," Bunche nodded.

The conversation continued as Bunche talked of America, home, and his children he hadn't seen nearly enough because of the demands of his work. As midnight approached, Golda turned their talk back to the passengers from the *Exodus*. "I understand the British are moving the passengers onto ships tomorrow."

"That is what they told us this morning."

"We haven't been able to get a word out of them directly about it," Ben-Gurion grumbled.

"Simpson told us when we visited the warehouse." Bunche shook his head. "Otherwise, I doubt we would have known."

"Will the committee be on hand to see them off?" Golda asked.

"Sandström wants to. Some of the others are anxious to get on with the remainder of the trip. We have a September 1 deadline to issue our report. They haven't been concerned about it until now, so I'm hesitant to curb that enthusiasm. They need to begin thinking in terms of recommendations."

"So you don't know if they'll be there or not," Ben-Gurion observed.

"No," Bunche responded. "I don't know yet. I'll probably have a message about it when I return to the hotel."

"It would be good if they could be there," Golda continued. "They bring international reporters with them and that would give the passengers a sense that the world knows their plight."

"Yes," Bunche acknowledged. "I'll see what I can do."

— • —

At the warehouse in Haifa, Jacob and Sarah lay beside each other on the hard concrete floor. The room was stuffy and the air stale, but the floor was cool against their backs. Neither could sleep. "What will they do with us?" Sarah asked.

"Return us to France, I suppose. That is what everyone was saying today. You think they mean to do something else?"

"Will they just herd us from the ship and leave us on the street?"

Jacob could hear the worry in her voice. "I don't know," he rolled on his side and placed his arm across Sarah's abdomen. "But whatever happens, we will be together."

"I am not so sure."

"Why?" he asked softly.

"We're here, in this warehouse, without even a pillow for our heads. It makes me think of the camps and the war and not knowing where you were." Her voice broke. Jacob gave her a hug. with one arm. "That won't happen," he whispered. "It won't happen again."

After a while, the conversation between them lagged and Sarah's breathing slowed to the easy rhythm of sleep. Jacob, however, was wide-awake. Rather than lying there staring up at the darkened roof above them, he rose from the floor and walked to the door on the far side of the building.

The night air was heavy with moisture from the ocean, and the gentle sound of the sea was a stark contrast to the tension they'd been under the past few weeks. A guard was supposed to be at the door but Jacob saw him standing fifty meters away, smoking a cigarette.

As he stood there, staring out at the docks and the sea beyond, he thought again of the long conversations he'd had with his father. Every night after supper, and often well into the early hours of the morning, they sat at the dining room table poring over the prophets, his young mind thirsty for the things they had to say about the restoration of Israel.

"I will bring you from the nations and gather you from the countries where you have been scattered"—a voice to the left caught his attention and he turned to see a man dressed in black standing an arm's length away. "Who are you?" Jacob gasped, startled by the man's sudden appearance

"...with a mighty hand and an outstretched arm and with outpoured wrath," the man said, finishing the quote. "I see you are familiar with Ezekiel."

A frown wrinkled Jacob's forehead.

"Sorry to scare you. I am Rabbi Diskin." When Jacob gave him a puzzled frown, he added, "The one who took your cousin from the ship."

"Oh," Jacob said. "My wife's cousin. Yes."

"You were not at the service."

"No," Jacob shook his head. "They wouldn't let us."

"I was afraid that was the case," Diskin replied. "Many people were there."

"I heard," Jacob nodded. "Avi would be impressed."

"You knew him well?"

"Yes," Jacob replied.

"As well as you know the prophets?"

"I don't know about that," Jacob smiled. "I'm not sure how well one could know either of them."

"I can't speak for your cousin, but the prophets are a bit of a mystery. You came to Palestine to make it your home?"

"Yes."

"And I'm guessing those scriptures had something to do with it."

"A little."

"Well, do not worry," Diskin smiled. "You are a young man. You have much of your life ahead of you. I think you will return and see things more wonderful than you can imagine."

"I want to."

The sound of footsteps caught Jacob's attention and he glanced around to see the guard coming toward him. "They don't want you out here," the guard said in a gruff voice.

"We were just talking."

"Who?"

"Rabbi Diskin and I," Jacob said with a gesture to his left. "We were just—" He stopped in midsentence when he realized Diskin was gone.

"You okay?" the guard asked with a concerned expression.

"I'm fine," Jacob sighed. "It's just not easy to sleep on that floor."

"Yeah. I can imagine. Want a cigarette?"

"No, thanks," Jacob replied. "I don't smoke."

CHAPTER 7

AT SUNUP THE NEXT MORNING, Jacob Schwarz was awakened by the sound of trucks outside the warehouse. He walked to the doorway and saw British soldiers arriving by truckloads. Sarah appeared at his side, groggy from a restless night on the hard floor. "What are they doing here?" she asked.

"They are coming to move us, I think." Jacob pointed to the dock. "The ships are here." Across the way, three vessels were moored at the pier.

Sarah leaned on his shoulder. "I would like a hot bath and breakfast in bed."

"I'm sure they'll give you that," he chuckled, "right after they give you your papers to stay."

They watched a moment longer as soldiers took positions around the warehouses, then an officer appeared at the doorway and asked them to move back inside. "We will tell you when it is time to go," he ordered tersely.

Jacob opened his mouth to respond but Sarah pulled him away. "Come on. Let's not make a scene now."

Reluctantly, he turned away and walked with her back to their spot on the opposite side of the building. "We're supposed to resist," Jacob whispered when they were safely beyond the soldier's hearing.

"And what did we learn from that before?" she asked.

"That it makes our point but it hurts," he said with a dour expression.

"Exactly. And I'm not interested in hurting today or in seeing you get injured again. We're going back to France, or wherever else they decide to take us, and we should get used to the idea. We can try again to reach Palestine later."

"But isn't the point of how they treat us a point worth making?"

Sarah halted abruptly and turned to face him. "Listen to me, Jacob. Avi is dead. Your head is badly bruised and you're lucky your brains didn't spill all over that ship. Reporters from America, England…the Soviet Union…the world saw what happened when we arrived and heard us talk about it yesterday. I think we've made our point." She took him by the arm. "Now let's walk over there, sit in our place, and await our turn."

"Wait our turn?"

"When they come for us to take us out of here, we will stand and walk out with our heads held high, just like we did when we left the ship."

"But not before they get to us."

"No," she agreed. "Not before they get to us."

An hour later, soldiers entered the building. A man dressed in civilian clothing appeared with a bullhorn and shouted, "It is time for you to board the ships! Gather your belongings and exit through the door over here." He pointed to the left. "Follow the path to the dock and walk all the way to the gangway for the third ship. The last one on the pier. That's your ship." In spite of the terrible conditions inside the building, no one moved. "I must warn you," the man with the bullhorn continued, "we are authorized to use force to remove you from this warehouse and place you onboard the ship." Still no one moved. "Very well. We will proceed as we see fit."

For the next several hours, Jacob and Sarah watched and listened as soldiers methodically worked their way through the warehouse, moving passengers from the building to the ship. Some they carried, some they dragged by the feet. Others fought back, using their hands and feet to ward off the advancing guards. Those who did were beaten and kicked into submission, then dragged from the building. Several were injured so badly they were taken away by ambulance. Sarah wondered aloud if it wasn't a ploy on their part to be left behind.

Finally, near the middle of the afternoon, two soldiers stepped before them. "Get on the ship," the first one demanded and reached for the baton that hung from his belt.

Jacob stood. "We are able to walk," he held out his hand for Sarah. She took it and stood. The soldiers stepped aside and watched them walk toward the door.

They emerged from the building and found a crowd had gathered, filling the area between the warehouse and the docks. It wasn't as large as the one that had greeted them when they arrived, but it was supportive and energetic just the same. A cheer went up as they walked out together and made their way toward the pier, following the pathway lined with soldiers.

Ben-Gurion was there, standing at the edge of the crowd behind the row of soldiers. Jacob recognized him at once and started in that direction. When he was a few meters away a soldier stepped out to confront him and struck Jacob across the shoulder with a baton. Jacob crumpled, his weight resting on one knee. The soldier raised the baton to strike him again but as he did, Sarah reached up with her hand and caught it as it began its downward arc. The soldier's eyes were wide with amazement at the sudden interruption.

"He was only coming to say hello to Mr. Ben-Gurion," Sarah explained calmly.

The soldier lowered his baton and straightened his shirt. He glanced around nervously, checking behind him. When no one seemed to notice he placed the baton on his belt and growled, "Get onboard the ship."

Jacob stood and once more offered Sarah his arm. With their heads held high, they made their way onto the dock and up the gangway to the deck of the ship. When they reached it, Jacob paused and turned back to the railing.

"Come on," Sarah said, tugging at him. "The guards will only rough you up again."

"Not yet," he gazed out at the shoreline. "I want an image of Palestine in my mind. So that when I lie down at night I will see it and never forget."

"We'll see it again, when we return. Now come on," and she nudged him once more. "We need to get below."

Footsteps approached and Jacob turned to see a soldier coming toward them. "You there!" he shouted. "What is the meaning of this?"

"Just one last look," Jacob replied as he led Sarah toward the door and down the steps into the belly of the ship.

CHAPTER 8

THAT EVENING, AHARON HARTMAN came to the Dan Hotel in Tel Aviv, where most of the UNSCOP members were staying. He inquired at the lobby desk for Ralph Bunche, and a clerk sent a runner up to the room. While he waited, Hartman took a seat on the opposite side of the room, away from the large windows that faced the street.

When Gedaliah Cohen had escorted Hartman from the meeting at Ben-Gurion's house the night before, he knew he would never fit in with the organization Ben-Gurion had created. He had ideas of his own for solutions to Palestine's problems. He also had his own opinion about who should lead the way in bringing those solutions to pass. None of that aligned with the plans put forth by Ben-Gurion and those who surrounded him. If Hartman was going to see his ideas put into effect he would have to reach outside the structure created by the Jewish Agency. Ben-Gurion held that firmly in his grasp. No one there would oppose him. No one *could* oppose him. Cohen had made that clear when he refused to allow Hartman to return to the meeting, and for Hartman that had been the defining moment.

In a few minutes, Bunche appeared in the lobby. Hartman rose from his chair and crossed the lobby to meet him. After a brief introduction Bunche gestured toward the rear exit of the hotel. "Let's walk out back for a view of the beach. We can talk in private there."

They came to a patio situated between the building and the Mediterranean shoreline. A table with four chairs stood to the right. Hartman led the way over to it. When they were seated Bunche checked his watch. "I don't have much time. We're really working on a tight deadline."

"This won't take long. I just wanted to make sure you heard all sides of the Jewish argument before you left."

"I've heard a lot. And seen even more."

"I know," Hartman nodded. "But I'm not sure you're getting the full picture from Ben-Gurion and his assistants."

Bunche had a puzzled frown. "What's this about?"

"I'll get right to the point. I've been here in Palestine a long time and I know from experience that partition of the region into separate ethnic states won't work. I realize Ben-Gurion wants to have a Jewish state. Golda is for it. So is Abba Eban and the others. But it won't work and I think many of them know, they just won't admit it."

"Why do you think it would fail?"

"If we divide Palestine and create a separate, independent Jewish state, we will be fighting each other for centuries."

"I'm not certain you won't be fighting each other regardless of what we do," Bunche stated flatly.

"That could be true." Hartman leaned back in his chair. "But at least with my approach we have the chance of peace. With theirs, we get only continual conflict. We will create for ourselves a culture of constant warfare."

"So, you have a better idea?"

"Yes. An idea that takes into account the political reality already present in the region. The politics of this region all comes down to competing claims for the same land. Ben-Gurion and others try to make the case that the Jewish claim has historic priority—that our ancestors occupied this land from a time that predates the Arabs. But our descendants also abandoned this place."

"They had a little help from the Romans," Bunche pointed out with a wry smile.

"Nevertheless, they left. And while they were gone, other people moved in and took their place, just as we witnessed in Europe the last fifteen or twenty years with Jews removed from Germany, Austria, the Netherlands, and transported to Poland. One group was moved out, another moved in. No one is suggesting Jews should be allowed to return to their former residences and reclaim their family estates."

"Maybe," Bunche conceded. "But still there are tens of thousands of Jews in camps around Europe—maybe hundreds of thousands—and they all want a place to live. Wouldn't it be good if a solution to Palestine's problems included a solution for that problem, too?"

"I don't have a total solution." Hartman glanced away. "Of course, they could always come here, I suppose."

"Not if the Arabs control the region," Bunche argued. "If they are in control—or as it is now with the British in control—you'll see practically no Jewish immigration in the near future. And meanwhile all those people are left sitting in European camps, wondering about their future and enduring various degrees of hardship that could be alleviated if they were in a productive society somewhere else. The only way you're ever going to solve the problems facing the Jews is to view it as a whole, in its totality as a related set of circumstances, and the only solution for that is with a Jewish state. I see no other way."

"But," Hartman countered, "partition of Palestine will displace Arabs."

"Perhaps," Bunche nodded. "That depends on how it's done."

"And," Hartman continued, "displacing the Arabs now would be at least as disruptive as what the Jews have endured, in terms of displacement, and just as upsetting to Arabs as the Nazi uprooting of Jews was to the Jews."

Bunche checked his watch again. "So what's your solution? Do you have any specifics?"

Hartman leaned forward and rested his forearms on the tabletop. "The only way this will work—with Jews and Arabs living in the same place—is through a unified Palestine. We could divide the country into provinces and some would have a majority of Arabs and others a majority of Jews. That way, each ethnic group could control its own local destiny, even though the national government would be dominated by whichever group held a nationwide majority."

"That's a nice idea," Bunche had a skeptical tone. "But you have one problem."

"What's that?"

"Palestine is a small place with limited resources. It would be very difficult to have more than two or three flourishing provinces. You just don't have the resources or the space for more than that."

"Maybe," Hartman shrugged. "And maybe they wouldn't have to be traditional provinces. They could be some other kind of political subdivision—tailored specifically for this situation—with a broader layer of government between them and the national government. The regions are pretty well racially divided already. All we'd have to do is preserve the status quo and give the people a chance to determine their own local destiny. Put them in control of the politics. That would put an end to the violence."

"I think you're past that now," Bunche sighed.

"Past the violence?"

"No." Bunche shook his head. "Past the time when Jews and Arabs could live together without fighting."

"That's rather shortsighted, isn't it?"

"It's a realistic picture of the political situation you face." Bunche scooted forward. "Palestinian Arabs outnumber the Jews by more than two to one. You are surrounded by Arab countries with armies that are far better armed and trained than yours. If I know this, they know it, too. Don't you worry just a little that they will slaughter you the moment the British leave?"

Hartman shook his head. "The greatest military threat to us is from Transjordan and Egypt—that much is true. They both have modern armies with new equipment. But their leaders are only interested in Palestine because they want to expand their own territory. They feign interest in Palestinian Arabs but what they really want is an excuse to grab pieces of the region for themselves. They don't want another independent Arab state."

Bunche leaned back in his chair. "But you're proposing one."

"No." Hartman shook his head again. "I'm proposing an independent state, made up both of predominantly Arab and predominantly Jewish political regions. With Jerusalem as the capital of the national government. I suppose the Arabs could claim it was an Arab country, so long as they hold the national majority, but Jews could claim they have a homeland, too."

"Not if the Arab-dominated national government prohibits Jewish immigration."

Hartman shrugged. "There are still details to be worked out."

"Tell me something," Bunche stared Hartman in the eye. "Have your superior officers approved this plan of yours?"

"Not officially." Hartman glanced down at his lap. "They don't know I'm here. And anyway, I'm not here as an officer or a member of Haganah. I'm here as me. A private citizen."

"I'm not certain they would separate the two."

— · —

At Ramat Gan, a community on the east side of Tel Aviv, Noga Shapiro convened a meeting of Irgun leadership. Formed in 1931, the group had developed around the belief that all Jews everywhere had a right to return to Palestine and that armed resistance of both Arab and British aggression was the only way to preserve that right. As a result, they had been involved in military actions throughout the region.

When they were assembled, Shapiro faced them and said in a matter-of-fact tone, "The British have left us no option. We must respond to what we witnessed on the docks at Haifa these past few days."

"Yes," someone replied. "And the sooner the better."

"Ben-Gurion can meet with members of the UN committee and talk to the British until they are out of breath. The only thing our enemies know is force and power. That is the only thing they respect. Words mean nothing to them. Action is everything."

Tuvia Megged spoke up. "If we don't make it painful for them, they will never leave."

"This latest business with the *Exodus*," another added, "has shown just how brutal the British can be, and how inept Ben-Gurion is when it comes to dealing with things of this nature."

"Not inept," Shapiro countered. "David Ben-Gurion is a capable man. But he's wrong in how to approach the British. Negotiation will get us nowhere because they don't see us as equal parties. And while he is talking to the British and the UN delegates, the Arabs are stealing the promise of our future."

"To the British, we are nothing but subjects. And to the Arabs, we are their next victim."

"So, we have to craft a response. What can we do to make a statement?"

"There are two bridges across the Jordan River," Yoel Harnoy suggested. "Both are of strategic importance. The Arabs use them to reinforce and resupply troops from the east, through Jerusalem. We could blow them up."

Gil Benari spoke up. "But what does that say? They kill our people, we blow up their bridges?"

"The bridges are of strategic importance," Harnoy argued.

"I like that idea," Shapiro nodded. "A response but with minimum possibility of casualties on either side. Is there something else?" Shapiro asked as he shifted restlessly in his chair. "Surely that is not the only idea for a response."

"We could blow up their headquarters," Benari offered.

"In Haifa?"

"No," Benari answered. "In Jerusalem."

Everyone sat in silence a moment, then Shapiro responded somberly, "That would mean blowing up the King David Hotel. You want to blow up the hotel?"

"Yeah," Benari nodded.

"Many people would die. Some of them our own people."

"Not the entire hotel," Benari countered. "Just the wing where they have their offices."

"I don't know," Harnoy said solemnly. "Ben-Gurion and Haganah would come after us in full force."

"Yoel is right," Shapiro agreed. "It is too much." He ran a fingertip over his chin as if thinking. "An action like that would call everything into question."

"How do you mean?" Benari asked.

"Right now," Shapiro explained, "the world sees the British as we do—brutal and callous. If we blow up the hotel and kill large numbers of people, especially civilians, they will see us the same way."

They talked awhile longer discussing a range of options, then Shapiro folded his hands in his lap and said, "We've talked enough. Prepare a plan to detonate the two bridges and move forward with that operation. Report to Tuvia on your progress and let him know when you are ready to proceed."

"What about the hotel?" Benari asked.

"No," Shapiro said, shaking his head. "It is too big and it will produce too many casualties."

"We need the casualties."

"Not while I'm in command," Shapiro said tersely. "And certainly not among our own people. These are human lives we're talking about. Not merely pawns in a chess match."

Megged stepped in. "Okay, it's late. We'll conduct a planning session in the morning." He looked over at Harnoy. "Yoel, you're in charge of the bridges. Think about who you want on your team." And with that, the meeting ended.

— • —

Back at the Dan Hotel, Ralph Bunche sat at his desk reading through a draft of his ideas about the recommendations UNSCOP might make. He was weeks ahead of the committee, perhaps even months; they were far behind and the days available for work on their review of Palestine were rapidly diminishing. Members of the committee came to their task with few diplomatic skills and little knowledge of Arab or Jewish history and tradition. And they'd done little to address either of those since their appointment. Most of their time had been devoted to petty squabbles about seating on the airplane and the view from their rooms at the various hotels where they'd stayed. Until the incident with passengers from the *Exodus*, they'd done very little serious work on the task assigned them by the General Assembly.

In spite of those limitations, Bunche found his work with the committee exhilarating. Not only did it afford him the opportunity to develop firsthand knowledge of a key region, it allowed him to meet the next generation of leadership—both Arab and Jewish—which offered the prospect of a continuing relationship for years to come. Regardless of the committee's final recommendation or the General Assembly's final decision, he could participate in the development of Palestine throughout the remainder of the current century.

As he continued to work into the night, he thought also of his conversation that evening with Hartman. Some of his points had made sense. Creation of an independent Jewish state would destine its citizens for a life of conflict with the Arabs. Bunche had already reached that conclusion on his own. But that was also the history of the Jews—a history of struggle with its neighbors that began with Abraham and the arrival of the Hebrews in Palestine, then continued with the birth of his sons, Isaac and Ishmael. Neither the committee nor the UN could change that, certainly not in the short term. But the conversation had been troubling, too.

Hartman was an officer in Haganah. By reputation, he was one of their ablest and best-trained leaders. Few could match his combat and command experience. Yet he had come to Bunche under cover of darkness for a private meeting about issues that went to the core of Ben-Gurion's approach. He wasn't certain, and Hartman had seemed deliberate in avoiding the topic, but the unstated message of the meeting was that Ben-Gurion was not capable of a vision for Palestine that encompassed more than merely imposing the Jewish will on all who opposed it. Bunche was certain that Hartman saw himself as the better alternative. Army officers weren't supposed to voice those kinds of opinions.

"If I'm correct," he whispered to himself, "David Ben-Gurion is not only fighting a war against the Arabs, he's also fighting a war against his rivals. And judging by Hartman's boldness in approaching me, the final outcome of that battle is still very much in doubt."

— · —

Meanwhile, when the Irgun leadership meeting broke up in Ramat Gan, Tuvia Megged followed the others outside and caught up with Gil Benari. "How would you do it?"

"Do what?"

"Blow up the hotel."

"He's already said no."

"I know what he said. I'm asking what it would take operationally to do it."

"Not much," Benari shrugged. "A couple of well-placed charges would collapse the building into the basement."

"You know this for a fact?"

"I've been there many times," Benari explained. "They have a café in the basement of the wing where the British have their offices. Support columns that hold it up run right through the café. We put the charges there, we can rock the foundation. The entire structure will collapse." He gestured over his shoulder. "But what about Shapiro?"

"Let me worry about him," Megged replied. "If we are careful, no one should ever know who did it."

"You're really thinking about doing it?"

"Yeah. But he's right. The casualties would be high."

"Unless we warned them ahead of time," Benari offered.

"That's an option," Megged nodded.

"But if they don't respond to the warning, they'll be in trouble," Benari cautioned. "I mean once the charges are in place, we won't be able to stop it. We'd use a timing device to activate the detonator. Stopping it would require going back inside the hotel, which I don't think will be possible. Not without being caught."

"But warning them would give them a chance to get out of the building before it blows up. If they do, then the loss of life is greatly reduced but the statement is the same—the building will fall to the ground. And if they ignore the warning, the loss of life will be on their shoulders."

"It will soften the impact," Benari noted. "Fewer bodies will mean less political emphasis."

"It's the King David Hotel," Megged replied. "Collapsing a wing of it will be enough." He gave Benari a pat on the back. "Recruit your men and develop your plan of operations, but don't move forward until I say so."

"You can handle this with Shapiro? If?"

"Yeah."

"Because if we do this, I don't want to get left holding the bag on it."

"I'll take care of it. Just see me before you do it."

CHAPTER 9

ON THE OPPOSITE SIDE OF THE ATLANTIC, Peter Howard, the British ambassador to the United States, sat in the back of his car and watched out the window as it made its way through the streets of Washington, D.C., toward the State Department building. He'd made this trip many times in the past ten years, as he and a succession of US secretaries of state worked to keep the Allies together in opposition to Germany and the Axis powers. Now that the war was over, he and George Marshall, the current secretary of state, met regularly to keep each other abreast of the latest developments and to ensure that their respective countries—the United States and the United Kingdom—promoted, at least in public, policies on which they mutually agreed. After all, as Howard often pointed out, they had recently defeated the Axis war machine together. Perhaps they might now owe it to future generations to lead the world away from war.

As secretary of state, Marshall controlled the US professional diplomatic corps. The diplomatic machinery of the State Department was firmly in his grasp. Truman, however, was prone to making important decisions on his own and, though Marshall had direct access to the president, some aspects of US foreign policy were beyond his control. As a result, he and Truman often played a cat-and-mouse game with each trying to box the other into a position that produced their desired result. Both were frustrated by the process. Howard was well aware of their relationship and hoped to use it to his advantage.

When he arrived at the State Department building, an aide escorted

Howard to Marshall's office. Marshall guided him toward a table near the window where they sat and enjoyed a cup of coffee. The chatter of old friends quickly gave way to the topic of Palestine.

"I understand UNSCOP is leaning toward partition now," Marshall noted.

"I knew they shouldn't have gone over there," Howard said with a condescending tone. "They can hardly find the restroom at the Waldorf, much less discern sane policy for a region as troubled as Palestine."

"The Arabs didn't help themselves by refusing to cooperate."

"No," Howard sighed. "I suppose not. They appear to be rather inept at diplomacy."

"And out of touch with world opinion."

"I don't think they care about world opinion."

"This poses a serious challenge for us."

"Yes, it does. Especially since the Jews show no hint of accepting the fact that they are still a minority in the region."

"I understand your troops were a little rough on the passengers of the *Exodus*."

"On the contrary," Howard said sharply. "They performed admirably in light of such blatant provocation."

"The passengers didn't appear provocative to me," Marshall countered. "Did you see the newsreels?"

"One or two. I never pay much attention to that stuff. I prefer the wireless broadcasts from reporters who were actually present and who aren't afraid to be heard. Newsreels give me the sense that someone is hiding behind the camera. Afraid to come out and be known for the opinions they offer. Just an unknown voice with pictures."

"That was quite a crowd at the docks."

"Totally staged," Howard shook his head. "I understand all of it was arranged in advance by Golda Meir."

"She's quite good at her job then."

"Yes. I suppose so."

"You know, Peter," Marshall said in a professorial tone, "we can't disregard that what the world saw from Palestine these past few days has reshaped and galvanized public opinion. Public sentiment now overwhelmingly favors the Jews."

"The masses will always go where we lead them."

"I'm not so sure that is the case now. Things are changing."

"Time marches on, as they say."

"Things changed while we were fighting the war. Women taking jobs previously filled by men. Tending family and home on their own. That brought about fundamental changes to lifestyles in both our countries. People have seen what they can do and it has opened new vistas. I don't think we can move them like we could before. They have minds of their own."

"It most certainly is evident over here. But look," Howard said, shifting his weight in the chair. "What were we to do with them? There were over four thousand passengers on that ship. Were we to leave them there? They had to go through with it. I mean, the passengers onboard the ship were attempting to immigrate illegally. Cunningham couldn't let them in. Otherwise, the ocean would be filled with shiploads of Jews trying to get to Palestine. The place would descend into utter and complete chaos."

"Peter, it's pretty nearly there now."

"Yes, it is. And I must admit things have gone rather badly for us there these past ten years. The Jews no longer trust us, and our people have little respect for the Jews." He looked over at Marshall. "Are you able to exert any influence on them through Weizmann?"

"He and I have a good relationship and he seems to understand that a Jewish state will never work."

"Certainly not now," Howard paused to take a sip of coffee. "Perhaps twenty years from now, but not now."

"A lot can happen in that time," Marshall mused. "One can hope it would be for the good."

"And in twenty years we'll have Arab oil locked up with contracts and leases and then the Jews can do whatever they want. If the Jews are still around," Howard chuckled.

Marshall's face wrinkled in a scowl at the comment. He had been in Europe during the war and had seen the Nazi death camps with his own eyes. The Jews stirred many feelings in him, but those camps had brought home the reality of their plight during the war and left an indelible imprint on his psyche. There were limits to how far he would entertain anti-Semitism. Howard was touching those limits. "No one in this administration wants that to happen," he said, staring Howard in the eye. "No one."

"I understand," Howard said with a dismissive wave of his hand. "I was only trying to smooth it over. Just making a joke."

"Did you see the death camps?"

Howard glanced down at the table. "No. I'm afraid I missed them."

"You should have seen them," Marshall replied. "Then you would know why they distrust us all." Marshall picked up his coffee cup. "And you would know why this is no laughing matter to them."

— · —

The following day, Shapiro met with Yoel Harnoy to review plans for destroying the two bridges that lay on the east side of Jerusalem. Shapiro was surprised that they were ready so soon. "That was fast. Have you covered every contingency?"

"I think so," Harnoy answered. "We worked on it all night. If we're responding to the *Exodus* incident, we thought we should do so immediately. So that the event and our response are contemporaneous. Otherwise, if we're too late, an attack would seem like one more random act."

"Okay," Shapiro nodded. "What do you have?"

Harnoy handed him a sheet of paper. "This is what we came up with."

On the paper was a list of eleven bridge sites. Shapiro quickly scanned them. "You want me to choose one?"

"No," Harnoy replied. "We want to destroy them all."

Shapiro looked concerned. "You want to destroy all of them?"

"Yes."

"On the same night?"

Harnoy grinned. "Our men dubbed it 'The Night of the Bridges.'"

Shapiro leaned back in his chair. "How do you propose to do such a thing?"

"Teams of six will move under cover of darkness. Place the charges and detonate. Then scurry away. With only six men, no one will ever see them."

Shapiro was skeptical. "Teams of six?"

"Yes. They'll need to move quickly."

Shapiro handed him the list. "With that few men, it will only work if you aren't spotted."

"Yes. We know."

Shapiro waited in silence a moment, "Okay. But I want an extra team of fourteen for each location, in case there is trouble."

Harnoy sighed. "Now we're talking twenty men per bridge. That's over two hundred total."

"You can do it?" Shapiro asked.

"Yes. But it will take some time to get them ready and in position."

"How much time?"

"A week."

"That won't be a problem," Shapiro assured. "What about casualties?"

"If we don't get in a firefight, there should be none."

"But the bridges are guarded."

Harnoy nodded. "Most of them are."

"The guards are all soldiers?"

"Yes. Some of them British, some of them Arab."

"But no civilians?"

"No," Harnoy shook his head. "Most of these sites are in remote locations. Several of them are unguarded, but the ones that are usually have guards on either end. No one in the middle. Loss of life should be minimal."

"Very good," Shapiro said. "We will inflict economic damage not loss of human life, and if the British don't understand this as a response to the *Exodus*, we'll find a way to make it clear to them."

CHAPTER 10

ONE WEEK LATER, in response to Abba Eban's report cabled from Tel Aviv, Chaim Weizmann requested a meeting with George Marshall. It was his tenth such request that year and part of a long-running attempt to arrange a meeting with President Truman to explain the Jewish perspective on Palestine. So far, he'd come no closer to entering the White House than Marshall's office.

Weizmann had begun his career as a chemist, studying in Germany and Switzerland before moving to Manchester, England, where he was a professor at Manchester University. While there he became acquainted with Arthur Balfour, a relationship that proved vital in procuring Great Britain's initial endorsement of an independent Jewish state in Palestine, later known as the Balfour Declaration. Weizmann's involvement in Zionist causes and organizations led to his election as president of the World Zionist Organization, which put him at the forefront of efforts to rescue Jews from Nazi Germany. He was well-known among heads of state around the world and had an entrée into many of the finest palaces and capitols. But try as he might, he could not convince Truman to see him. The meeting he requested with George Marshall was his final attempt at arranging an appointment through traditional channels. If this failed, he would be forced to call on one of those strategic relationships for which he was so well-known.

As he had on many prior occasions, Marshall granted Weizmann an appointment immediately. Weizmann flew from his home in New

York the following day. Marshall met Weizmann at the elevator near the front entrance of the building and guided him to a parlor across from his office. A tray of breads and sweets awaited them with an urn of hot coffee. Weizmann took a seat opposite Marshall and waited while a porter filled his cup. He hoped to speak first and bring the conversation straight to his point, but when they were alone, Marshall spoke up. "It's always good to see you, Chaim, but I know why you're here and we both know the answer to your question already."

"I was hoping for a different result this time," Weizmann replied.

"The president isn't seeing anyone from either side on the issue of Palestine. He won't even talk to me about it."

"And Peter Howard?" Weizmann glanced at Marshall with a raised eyebrow. "Does he get to see the president?"

"Not on this issue. The president wants to take his counsel from his own sources."

"If he's not talking to you about it, to whom is he turning for advice?"

"To be frank, I don't know exactly."

"I know you do not favor an independent Jewish state, as you have mentioned many times before."

"No," Marshall shook his head. "I do not. Not in Palestine. And not now."

"I'm afraid no other location would do and I'm not certain we will ever have another opportunity."

"It's too disruptive now," Marshall argued. "Both in terms of Palestine and the international community."

"The Jews have been displaced and no one seemed to mind."

"Now, Chaim," Marshall challenged, "that's not true."

"I noticed it took ten years for this State Department to acknowledge that Hitler had despicable plans for us."

"That was a different administration and the United States had plenty of things clamoring for our attention. We couldn't address every issue at once. We had to fight some battles first."

"And the battle for six million Jews was not at the top of your list."

"We've talked about this at length. We were working to help the British withstand the German onslaught. If England had fallen, you and I would not be having this conversation today."

"As I am well aware."

"The world has been through war since 1938. Most of the nations who support your cause are tired. They want to put aside conflict and get on with their lives."

"The Middle East has been in turmoil since the British took over," Weizmann spoke quietly, his eyes focused on a piece of bread as he buttered it. "And not just in Palestine. We need peace, too, but we have no place where we are not subjected to the will of someone else." He looked over at Marshall. "Tell me, George, where could we go? To America? You would accept the hundreds of thousands of Jewish refugees from Europe? Tell me yes and I will load the ships with them tonight."

"You know the answer to that."

"Exactly. America has been as supportive of the Jewish cause as is politically feasible, but even America will not make a place within its own borders for displaced Jews. So if America, with all its power and resources, will not open its doors to us, then where are we to go? And if we are to go anywhere, why should we not be in Palestine, our home? Our ancestors occupied that land before the Arabs were conscious of their collective identity and long before Mohammad existed."

"The British have tried to help. I know it doesn't seem that way now, but they tried. You would do well to remember that when you meet with them."

"They tried because they need Arab oil," Weizmann replied. "You want them to have it because you don't want to sell them yours."

Marshall sipped his coffee in silence for a moment, then looked across the table at Weizmann. "Chaim, I need to tell you, we here at the State Department favor an extension of the mandate, if not with the British then with an international force if necessary. If I have an opportunity to discuss Palestine with the president, this will be my recommendation."

"You have made up your mind?"

"Yes. An extension would give both sides time to work out their differences in an amicable manner."

"That is disappointing. I had hoped you would reconsider."

"I don't know what the president will do. Or the UN."

"UNSCOP was appalled at what they saw in Palestine."

"I think their reaction was understandable given the circumstances. They will have a better perspective when they arrive in Geneva for the real work of creating a comprehensive report. If you agree now to an extension, you will have the full support of both the United States and the United Kingdom. Can you get Ben-Gurion under control?"

"No one can control him. Do you have any indication at all where Truman stands on partition?"

"None."

"So, he doesn't want to choose sides?"

"You can view it that way if you like. I wouldn't think of him that way, though. Not too long ago, you were not in favor of partition either."

Weizmann ignored Marshall's comment. "Truman doesn't want a fight with the Arabs any more than the British do. I can understand that. What I'm worried about is not extending the mandate per se, but how to prevent our annihilation in the process."

"I don't think the world would stand by and watch that happen."

"They did in Germany."

"Yes. I suppose they did. But we—"

Weizmann interrupted. "Are you prepared to deploy the US military to enforce the mandate?"

Marshall's eyes darted away. "I don't get to make that decision."

"If the United States deployed its forces to patrol Palestine, and if they ensured the peace and safety of the Jewish people, I could convince the others to hold off on demanding an independent Jewish state."

"You know I can't make that offer."

"Then neither can I accept anything less."

CHAPTER 11

WORKING FROM THE INSTRUCTIONS provided by Tuvia Megged after the Irgun meeting, Gil Benari gathered a team of six men to discuss how best to obtain the necessary material for the bomb he intended to place in the King David Hotel. In the past, operations of this size had been broken into compartmented segments and spread among independent teams, each performing a portion of the whole but none knowing the work or identity of the others. This time, however, the team would do it all—planning, procurement, execution, escape. Benari was convinced this was the only way to maintain the required level of secrecy.

"This may be the most important operation any of us undertakes," he began. "It will certainly be the most memorable. If we do this correctly, an entire wing of the King David Hotel should be reduced to rubble. I think that will be remembered for a long time but more importantly, I think it will send a clear message to the British." He paused a moment and took a breath. "So, it's important. It's crucial. It will create and draw a big response. But it is not a complicated operation. The first thing we need is explosives. Anyone have any ideas?"

"What kind are we using?" Yoni Shalit asked.

"Dynamite," Shlomo Avital offered. "It's the obvious choice. Biggest bang. Takes up the smallest space. Safe to transport and handle. Low risk of accidental detonation."

"You prefer it over nitrogen and diesel fuel?" Dover Kastner asked.

"Too bulky," Avital replied. He glanced over at Benari. "Didn't you say before that this has to fit in a small container?"

"Yes."

"How small?" Shalit asked.

"milk can," Benari answered.

"You mean those metal things that they use to carry it in bulk?"

"Yes."

"Why milk cans?"

"Because that's something the café receives all the time," Benari explained. "I've been there. I've seen them. If we put the charges in milk cans we can appear as deliverymen. No one will question our presence. We'll get in and out of the building without a problem."

"Good idea," Shalit nodded.

"Well, if that's the case, then I suggest TNT," Avital said. "It's safe. Powerful. We can fill the cans to the top. And it's readily available."

"Only one problem," Shalit needled.

Avital was perturbed. "What's that?"

Shalit had a cocky smirk. "Where are you going to find TNT?"

Oded Laslo spoke up. "The British have tons of it."

"You know where they keep it?" Shalit asked in a challenging tone.

"They have a storeroom full of it at Haifa."

"Full of TNT?" Shalit made no attempt to hide his disbelief. "A storeroom filled with boxes and barrels of it?"

"No," Laslo said confidently. "The storeroom's filled with armor-piercing shells."

"And the shells are filled with TNT," Shalit groused with a nod and a roll of his eyes.

"Exactly," Laslo grinned. "All we have to do is steal the shells and extract the TNT from them."

"Without blowing ourselves up in the process," someone added.

"Maybe it would be better if we found some dynamite," Kastner commented dryly.

"Packing enough dynamite into a milk can would be tedious," Avital replied. "And I'm not sure we could get enough in one of those cans to do the job."

"Okay," Benari said, keeping the conversation on track, "we need to think about how to get inside that British storeroom."

"That part's easy," Laslo chuckled. "We dress as British soldiers. Walk in through the front gate. No one will ask any questions."

"We'll need uniforms," someone suggested.

"And a truck," another added. "We can't carry the stuff out by hand."

Kastner spoke up. "I know where we can get the uniforms. A lady on the east side of town does laundry for them. Washes it in a tub, hangs it out to dry. Clothesline behind her house is always full of army uniforms. We can get all the shirts and pants we need right there."

Avital looked over at Shalit. "Think you can hot-wire a truck from the British compound?"

"Yeah," Shalit nodded reluctantly. "I can do it."

"Okay, then," Benari smiled. "Let's get ready. We go to the storeroom tomorrow night."

— • —

Early the following evening, Benari and the team dressed as British soldiers and rode in two cars to Haifa. The British compound was located along the lower end of Herzl Street, not far from the docks where the *Exodus* had been moored. The main entrance faced west, toward the water. Avital was driving and parked the car on a side street two blocks away. They left it there and walked down to the gate, pretending to be army buddies returning from a night out. As Laslo suggested, the guards paid them no attention and they entered the compound without incident.

According to the plan, the second group, led by Shalit, was supposed to enter through a gate on the east side of the facility. Benari and the others hadn't seen them since they'd turned onto the side street to park the car.

Using information developed by Laslo from a friend, the first team made its way to a small warehouse near the northern edge of the compound. The wooden rectangular structure stood apart from the other buildings, separated by a broad thoroughfare on all four sides. It was windowless and doors were located on either end with a single guard posted at each.

Benari gathered his men behind an armored car that was parked about thirty meters away. He glanced at Laslo. "Are you sure this is the place?"

"This is it," Laslo replied.

"Okay," Benari glanced around at the group. "We do this as planned. I'll take Kastner with me and eliminate the guard on the opposite side. Give us five minutes to get into place, then the rest of you take out the guard on this side. Got it?" They all nodded in agreement, then Benari and Kastner slipped away.

When they were gone, Avital turned to Laslo. "Oded, you know what to do?"

"Yes," Laslo nodded, checking his watch. "I've got it. Move into position. Time is getting away fast."

"Right," Avital replied and then he slipped from behind the armored car and disappeared from sight.

Laslo checked his watch once more and waited as the seconds ticked past. Five minutes later, he nodded to the others and they stepped from behind the armored car into the open. Walking in a group, they made their way casually toward the guard on the near side of the building. "Nice night for a walk," Laslo said as they approached.

The guard jumped at the sound of Laslo's voice and lowered his rifle to his waist, pointing it in Laslo's direction, his finger on the trigger, ready to shoot. "Halt!" he shouted. "Identify yourself."

"Come on," Laslo laughed, waving his hands innocently and giving his best impression of a British accent. "It's me. Charles. Don't you recognize me?"

"Charles?" the guard frowned. "Charles who? State your full name and rank," he demanded. "Give it at once."

"I'm Charles," Laslo evaded. "From London." He took a pack of cigarettes from his shirt pocket and poked one in his mouth. "Just thought I'd come out for a walk and a smoke." He returned the cigarette pack to his pocket and took out a matchbox. With a flick of his finger he opened it as if to light one.

The guard stepped forward, suddenly more alert than ever. "No smoking!" he shouted in an excited voice. "No smoking! Smoking is prohibited in this area."

"That's just an army regulation," Laslo said with a smirk. He struck the match against his belt buckle and it burst into flame.

The guard started toward him in earnest. "Are you crazy? You're gonna blow us all up!" Before he could reach Laslo, a noise from the opposite end of the building caught his attention. "What was that?" he asked, wide-eyed with fear, and he wheeled around in that direction.

As he did, Avital slipped from the corner of the building and grabbed him with an arm around the neck in a choke hold, then thrust a knife between the guard's ribs, burying it in his chest up to the handle. The guard gasped, then collapsed in Avital's arms. Avital pulled his limp body around the corner and out of sight.

With the guard out of the way, the others stepped to the door. Laslo reached for the handle to open it but before he could grab it, the door slid back and Benari appeared. "Come on," he whispered with a grin. "This place is full of stuff."

— · —

The following morning, Tuvia Megged asked Benari to meet him at a safe house in Tel Aviv. Benari assumed he was invited there to report on his team's progress toward bombing the King David Hotel. He arrived to find a bodyguard posted just inside the door. The guard patted him down, then gestured toward the hallway. "He's in the back room."

Benari made his way in that direction and found Megged seated in an armchair with his back to an interior wall. "Sorry for the security," Megged apologized as Benari entered the room. "Things are getting a little tense around here these days. Had to bring in some extra people."

"Did something happen?"

"Not yet, but we think it will."

"Anything I need to be concerned about?"

"Not at all." A chair sat across from Megged and he gestured toward it. "Have a seat."

Benari settled into place on the chair and propped his elbows against the armrests. "If you're worried about our part of the program, we made good progress last night and now have all the—"

"Wait," Megged gestured with a hand to stop him. "I don't want to know the details."

"Okay," Benari said slowly. "I assumed you asked me here to receive a report on our efforts so far."

"I'm sure you're doing a good job." Megged crossed his legs and shifted his weight to the opposite side of the chair. He hesitated, "I think you should do this. It's a good idea and I'm confident you have a good plan in mind to make it happen. But I want you to wait."

Benari's forehead wrinkled in a puzzled frown. "How long?"

"Other operations are in process and I think this one, together with those others, would be much too big."

"I thought that was the point," Benari countered. "To express our indignation over the *Exodus* in an unmistakable way."

"Yes," Megged smiled. "But blowing up a wing of the hotel at the same time we do these other things might be seen as a declaration of war. The British would see it that way. I'm concerned they might launch a major military offensive against us."

"We wouldn't want that?" Benari shrugged.

"We couldn't survive that," Megged said emphatically. "And it would derail all of the Jewish Agency's political maneuvers."

"Don't we want to derail them?"

"Maybe," Megged nodded. "But only after we are ready to implement our own plan for Palestine's future. Until then, we don't want to ruin all the possibilities merely by our own stubborn intransigence."

"You mean we might fail in the end and not achieve the result most of us in Irgun want. And if that happens, the country needs a viable alternative."

"Exactly," Megged nodded. "And if we do it now, I'll catch a lot of heat from Shapiro. And that's trouble I can't handle right now. So let's put this on hold for now."

"I think you're wrong about the impact," Benari replied. "But I don't know what other operations are planned and if this is how you want it, then okay. I'm a soldier. I follow orders."

"Good," Megged smiled. He stood and offered Benari his hand. "Continue to plan your operation. Get ready for it. Continue to make your preparations. But let's hold this operation in abeyance for now."

CHAPTER 12

AS UNSCOP NEARED THE CONCLUSION of its work in Palestine, Abba Eban left them in Walter Eytan's care and flew to New York to review the latest developments with Moshe Sharett. As the Jewish Agency's primary diplomatic officer, he was the official liaison between the fledgling Jewish community in Palestine and the United Nations. The two men met in a back room at Ratner's, a kosher dairy restaurant on Delancey Street.

"I understand the *Exodus* passengers have not yet reached France."

"Apparently the British are sending them the slowest way possible."

"But they made a complete show of themselves in the process."

"Yes. They played right into our hands."

"Who coordinated the crowds?"

"Golda."

Sharett smiled. "She's good at everything she does."

"Yes," Eban nodded. "She is."

"Did you attend the funerals for the passengers who were killed?"

"Yes."

"I was surprised Ben-Gurion arranged for the rabbis to do that."

"He's not opposed to Judaism. In fact, he's very much a believer. He just doesn't care for the rabbinate."

"More of the Karaite persuasion," Sharett nodded. "I knew that. But I was surprised he did anything about it. The rabbis hold a lot of power but Ben-Gurion can't be seen as yielding to them or the socialists will get upset."

"I haven't heard any negative response about it. I think most people saw it as a national expression of sympathy and never thought about it in political terms."

"My parents believed in the old ways, too," Sharett added. He paused to take a drink of water. "Walter was comfortable taking care of the committee so you could come over here?"

"Very much so," Eban nodded. "He's fully capable of doing either of our jobs."

"Speak for yourself," Sharett quipped.

"He's doing well." Eban paused to take a bite of dinner. "How are things in Washington?"

"Weizmann met with Marshall a few days ago," Sharett noted. "It seems Marshall favors extension of the mandate."

Eban arched an eyebrow. "He wants the British to remain?"

"I think he would prefer it that way but would settle for an international force if it meant getting an extension."

"What did Weizmann say in response?"

"He told Marshall that if the Americans agreed to take over the mandate and deploy their army to assure our safety, he could convince the rest of us to go along with it."

"Arrogant old man," Eban scowled. "I love him but sometimes he says too much."

"He'd have a good chance of doing it," Sharett countered. "We aren't nearly as unified in our goals as Ben-Gurion makes people think."

"Maybe so," Eban shrugged. "I assume Weizmann was meeting with Marshall to request a meeting with the president."

"Yes."

"And I assume the reason I haven't heard about a meeting at the White House being scheduled is because Marshall turned him down."

"Marshall said the same thing he's been saying since Weizmann started asking. The president isn't talking to either side about Palestine."

"Not even the British?"

"Marshall says not."

"I would be surprised if that's true."

"I think Weizmann would agree with you," Sharett nodded. "He thinks the British are getting their information in front of Truman, one way or the other."

"I thought Weizmann had some special connection he was going to use."

"He does. Said he wanted to try this one more time. After the trouble with the *Exodus* he thought maybe things had changed."

"But not that much."

"World opinion has shifted decidedly in our favor," Sharett said with a hint of optimism, "but Truman still doesn't want to be seen as choosing sides."

"Can't really blame him," Eban acknowledged. "Even if he favored us, if he talked to representatives from the Arab League many would see it as an endorsement of their view, and that would shift policy against us. If he talks to us, the same thing happens in the opposite direction." He took a serious tone. "You know, Ben-Gurion will never agree to an extension of the mandate."

"I know," Sharett nodded. "What about the others?"

"Golda now says she favors partition."

"That's a change."

"Yes. Ben-Gurion seemed surprised by it."

"Should have seen it coming. Underneath all that enthusiasm and energy she has a practical mind. What about the rest of them?"

"I didn't talk with any of the others. We met at Ben-Gurion's residence, not the office."

"Which residence?"

Eban was surprised. "He has more than one?"

"He has several."

"I didn't know that. This one is located on Keren Kayemet Boulevard."

"That's the official residence. You didn't meet with the entire administrative executive committee?"

"No. Just the group at his home. They took a consensus of those in the room—Golda, Gedaliah Cohen, Walter Eytan, several others. And a general named Hartman."

"Aharon Hartman."

"You know him?"

"Yes."

"I'd never met him before."

"He's a good man. I'm not certain he supports Ben-Gurion's plans, though."

"Oh?" Once more Eban was surprised. "What makes you say that?"

"Just rumors I hear about conversations others have had with him. I think he favors a unified Palestine. Majority rule on a national level. Ethnic rule on a local level."

"That would work except that the Arabs would be in the majority and they would end all Jewish immigration."

"And then they would slaughter us." Sharett paused to take another drink. "So they favor partition?"

"Yes. I suppose they would prefer control of the entire region, but their perception of political realities has pushed them to see partition as the only option."

"I think it's the only option that has a chance of gaining international approval. As I've said many times before, the UN isn't going to hand us total and complete control of Palestine."

"I told them as much."

"So, during the entire time you were there, you didn't meet with the full thirteen members of the council?"

"No. We had discussed it before I went over there and I thought I would get to meet with them, but it didn't happen."

"Well," Sharett said thoughtfully, "perhaps all of them are not of one mind."

"Or," Eban added, "Ben-Gurion is suspicious of me. This is more likely."

"Maybe." Sharett reached over and patted Eban on the shoulder. "Don't take it personally. He's suspicious of everyone."

CHAPTER 13

AT BEN-GURION'S URGING, Golda departed Tel Aviv for Paris on the first available flight. She traveled without an appointment, hoping Leon Blum or one of the other contacts Ben-Gurion mentioned could assist in getting her an appointment with President Auriol. However, when she arrived she learned that Blum was out of town and not expected to return for at least another week. She did the best she could to gain an audience with as many government officials as possible but had little success doing so.

With nothing left to do but wait, she phoned Lou Kaddar, a friend she'd met years before when she passed through Paris on her first trip to Palestine. Lou had been born in Paris but curiosity and an inherent need for adventure sent her around the world at an early age. The result was a cosmopolitan personality that Golda found infectious.

Together, they hit all the traditional tourist stops—rode the elevator to the top of the Eiffel Tower, ate lunch on the Boulevard du Montparnasse, and visited the newly reopened museums. When Golda grew tired of that, they took the train to Normandy and toured the battleground where the D-Day invasion took place. Even though four years had passed since that epic military operation, many areas were still off-limits as crews continued to remove land mines and unexploded ordnance. After a three-day trip, they returned to Paris and Golda phoned Blum's residence. Finally, she learned, after what had been an exhilarating and yet frustrating two weeks, Blum had returned and would see her that afternoon. She put aside all other activities and began immediately to prepare for the meeting.

Blum was a rare combination in France; indeed, in all of Europe. He was both very much Jewish, very much French, and a consummate politician. That combination of talent, intellect, and experience opened many doors for him. Rather than enrich himself by it, he used every opportunity to serve the French people. On two different occasions before the war he held the office of prime minister and was president of the French Provisional Government after the country was liberated by the Allies. In between, he held any number of ministerial posts and was loved by all. Golda knew all of that before her arrival at his residence but nevertheless was surprised by the warmth of his greeting and his genuine delight in seeing her.

"I have heard so much about you," he beamed. "And all of it splendid."

"Give me a list of everyone who told you that," she laughed, "and I'll personally thank them one and all."

"And such humor," he chuckled as he offered her his arm. "You and I shall get along just fine."

They walked a short distance up the hall and took seats in the front parlor, then spent the next hour regaling each another with stories from their experiences in the world of international politics. Blum knew everyone and had a story to tell about them all. Golda enjoyed listening and when he began to lag contributed her own anecdotes to keep him talking.

At last, as the afternoon began to wane, the conversation turned to the purpose of her trip and Blum took a curious expression. "When they told me you had phoned and wanted to meet, I was glad to accede to your request. I've heard so much about you and I thought at last I have a chance to visit with her, but you must have had some specific purpose in traveling all this way to call on me."

"Yes," Golda nodded, her voice now serious and her approach professional. "As you are no doubt aware, a ship recently docked in Haifa bearing over four thousand people who wished to immigrate to Palestine."

"Yes," Blum replied. "The *Exodus*. I've read about it and listened to reports on the radio. Dreadful what they did. Should have let them stay."

"Thank you for saying that."

"I'm only stating the obvious." Blum took a questioning tone. "But how does that affect me?"

"I was wondering if you could help me get an appointment with President Auriol."

"Oh," he said with a start, "I should be delighted. Sit right there one moment." He stood and walked to the doorway, then disappeared down the hall. Golda waited, wondering what would happen next.

In a few minutes Blum returned with a smile. "President Auriol will see you tomorrow afternoon," he announced.

Golda was surprised. "You phoned him?"

"Yes," he nodded excitedly. "I talked to him personally."

"Just like that?"

"Just like that." Blum was still standing. "You should come back here in the morning. Around eight," he suggested. "So we can meet with Pierre Schuman before you see Auriol."

Golda was puzzled. "Pierre Schuman from the foreign office?"

"Yes. You know him?"

"Only by reputation."

"He will be very helpful. Has a lot of influence with Auriol." Blum stepped closer and offered Golda his hand. "And now, if you would be so kind as to join me, we shall have dinner."

Golda smiled as she stood. "I didn't know we were dining together."

"Certainly," he said in a matter-of-fact manner. "It is the dinner hour. You are a lovely young lady. Why should we not enjoy our meal together? Besides," he tucked her hand beneath his arm, "I would like to hear more about my friend David Ben-Gurion."

— • —

Promptly at eight the next morning, Golda returned to see Blum. They were joined by Jules Stavisky from the Paris office of the Jewish Agency. "Jules and I have been friends a long time," Blum explained. "And he knows Schuman well, too."

"Schuman and I play tennis together," Jules said proudly.

"I never learned that game," Golda replied. "Never lived anywhere that had a court."

"It's very relaxing."

"Always seemed too much like work to me."

They talked a while longer, then Blum led the way through the house to the front entrance and out to a car that was parked nearby. From there, they traveled across town to the foreign office. They arrived early and waited while Schuman finished a previous meeting. When it was concluded, he came from his office to get them and after an exchange of greetings they sat together over tea in Schuman's office.

"You had some trouble in Palestine over the *Exodus*," Schuman said when the conversation turned serious.

"Yes," Golda nodded. "Quite a bit. That's why I've come to see you."

"Our representative in Palestine told us the British are returning the passengers to Marseille."

"That's what they told us," Golda commented, "but so far the ships have not arrived."

"Our best information indicates they went to Cyprus."

"I heard that earlier," Golda acknowledged, "but we have no confirmation about their final destination."

Stavisky spoke up. "I believe there was some disagreement at the cabinet level about what to do with them."

"Yes," Schuman confirmed. "We receive cables regularly from our embassy in England and have a continuing presence in Syria. Contacts in both places indicate there was major disagreement about how to handle the passengers, but I think they have ultimately settled on the original idea of returning them to us."

"They have certainly taken their time about bringing them here, but assuming they do return the passengers to you, what will you do with them when they arrive?"

Schuman gave her a knowing smile. "What would you like for us to do with them?"

"Take custody of the passengers," Golda said without hesitation. "Send them back to us immediately."

"Yes," Schuman grinned. "I'm sure you would." He paused to take a sip of tea. "Am I correct that this incident involves more than the four thousand passengers?"

"Yes," Golda nodded. "Approximately four thousand two hundred, I believe."

Schuman set aside his cup. "We French find the British are as arrogant as everyone else does, but we're in a difficult position with them. We need their help with the Americans. Our economy is in a fragile condition right now. I'm not sure how much we can do to assist in this manner, though we are not unsympathetic to your cause. The British, it seems, have become as much a problem for you as the Arabs."

"Yes," Golda agreed. "They have."

"We experienced little difficulty with the Arabs in Syria, but we took a very different approach from the British."

"They should have learned from you."

"The British, as I'm sure you know by now, rarely learn from anyone."

— · —

In the afternoon, Golda traveled to Élysée Palace where she met with President Auriol. They sat opposite each other in overstuffed chairs arranged around a low table in the corner of his office. Auriol was familiar with much of Golda's work in Palestine as well as the trips she'd made abroad and he asked about several of her speeches. As she responded, the conversation took much the same tone as her discussion with Blum the day before—a friendly exchange of stories about the places they'd been and the people they'd met. After a while, however, the conversation moved on to recent events in Palestine and the Jewish experience with the British. But just as Golda was about to bring up the topic of the *Exodus* and the status of its passengers, Auriol turned the conversation away from the present toward the future.

"Tell me, if you would," he spoke rather abruptly. "We've heard rumors that the Americans are now favoring an extension of the British mandate. Have you heard those same rumors?"

"From what I know," Golda replied, "that is the current position of the State Department. George Marshall is of the opinion that the mandate should be extended, either with the British carrying out supervision and security tasks or with an international force. But President Truman has refused to discuss the matter with Marshall or any of the other traditional US foreign policy experts."

"Really?" Auriol leaned back in his chair. "He's not even talking to the British about it?"

"Some wonder if he might be," Golda said. "But officially, he is refusing to receive any visitors, Jewish or Arab, and really any visitors at all, about matters related to Palestine."

"I should think he'd have a difficult time putting off the British on the topic."

"Perhaps," she nodded. "But Weizmann put that question to Marshall recently and Marshall insisted that Truman was refusing to see them in that regard."

"And not even Marshall?"

"No."

"Then with whom is he talking?"

"No one seems to know."

Auriol sat up straight in his chair, "I'll see what more I can learn of that and let you know."

"We would appreciate any help you can give," Golda assured him. "And on that subject, you are aware of the recent incident in Tel Aviv with the *Exodus*?"

"Yes." Auriol seemed troubled. "I understand the British have said they intend to return those passengers to us."

"That's what they said before the ships sailed. What they might actually do and when the passengers might actually arrive, I do not know."

"Apparently they put in at Cyprus while the cabinet in London debated the matter further," Auriol offered, "but I believe they are under way again and on their way here now. If not, they will be shortly."

"What will you do with them when they arrive?"

"That has been debated. Some favor accepting them. Others think we should refuse."

"And what do you think?" Golda prodded. "Which position to do you favor?"

Auriol thought for a moment, then said, "I believe the prudent course of action is to allow those who wish to disembark to do so and accept them freely. But I am not inclined to accept passengers forced off by the British."

"I'm sure the passengers would appreciate that. Some, no doubt, would wish to make a statement by resisting the British to the bitter end. Others, though, might think of it in more practical terms."

"I think you are correct," Auriol agreed. "When I first heard they were sending the passengers back it seemed as though the British were attempting to dump their problems on us. My initial reaction was not to help them out at all and refuse the ship access to our ports. The British created this problem; they should be forced solve it and do so as humanely as possible. But as I have considered the matter further I have come to the conclusion that the passengers are going to be delivered to a location other than Palestine—the British will not allow them to return now—and if any of them want to come here, we would be glad to receive them and assist them to the fullest extent of our abilities. So long as they do so of their own volition. We will not accept any whom the British attempt to forcibly remove."

Golda felt it was all they could ask him to do, but she wanted to make certain he was being forthright. "Have you communicated this position to the British?" she asked.

Auriol glanced away, "No, but I have instructed our ambassador in London to communicate this to his peers." He had a nervous smile. "Right now we are, as you know, rather dependent on our allies for assistance as we continue to recover from the war. It is in our best interests not to provoke them unnecessarily. When the time comes, we will make our position clear. But until then, I think it best to handle the matter by unofficial means."

Auriol shifted his position in the chair as if to stand, but before he could get to his feet Golda spoke up. "There was one more issue I wanted to explore."

"Oh?" Auriol settled back in the chair. "What might that be?"

"It is our understanding that you are currently holding German armaments seized at the end of the war."

"Yes," Auriol nodded. "We have a rather large supply of their equipment. Why do you ask?"

"UNSCOP is working on a proposal for solutions to the issues in Palestine. As you know, their report is due to be submitted to the General Assembly in September. They've been in Palestine recently talking with us and with the Arabs, though the Arabs have not been forthcoming in their responses." She was talking in circles while slowly creeping up on the topic. "From discussions with committee members and from their reaction to the *Exodus* affair it seems there is some possibility the committee might recommend partition."

"You would accept partition?" Auriol looked at her with interest. "A state that does not comprise the whole of Palestine? Ben-Gurion would accept such a thing?"

"Yes. We would."

"Is that your personal opinion, or has there been some official decision?"

"We've not acted on the matter formally but we have reached a consensus among ourselves. If offered partition, we would accept."

"If that recommendation made it out of the committee," Auriol mused. "If the committee proposed it, I suspect you could gain enough support in the assembly to see it enacted."

"That would be a wonderful day," Golda said with a smile. "But when it occurs, there is the very real probability that we would experience increased violence." She was hesitant to reveal the certainty of invasion by neighboring Arab countries for fear Auriol might see it as a reason to withdraw his support entirely. "With the British gone from the region, we would be responsible for our own defense and for maintaining order. To do that, we need equipment."

"What kind of equipment did you have in mind?"

"What do you have?" she chuckled. "We need it all—rifles, tanks, armored vehicles, aircraft, ammunition, uniforms, helmets—I could go on at length, but you understand. Thus far, we have defended our settlements with paramilitary units. If partition occurs, we would need to equip a formal army. Perhaps rather quickly."

Auriol paused a moment, then said confidently, "You met with Pierre Schuman this morning?"

"Yes."

"He is the person to see about this. I will instruct him to cooperate with you fully. We are interested in disposing of the equipment. However, some of it is under the control of the Americans. As to the disposition of those items, I cannot say. You would probably need to take that up with them, and we will assist you in every way with that if you like." He paused again before saying, "Perhaps you might not want to contact them just yet. But as for the equipment we control, Pierre Schuman would be pleased to work out an amicable arrangement for the transfer of any of it you can use." Auriol stood. "This has been a delightful visit," he said with a broad and genuine smile.

"Yes," Golda replied as she rose and extended her hand. "It has been wonderful. And I look forward to many more similar visits in the future."

He guided her toward the doorway. "No doubt," he said as he held the door open for her, "we shall see each other often."

CHAPTER 14

THAT SAME NIGHT, Irgun's teams went into action across Palestine as they unleashed the Night of the Bridges attack on key elements of Palestine's transportation system.

At the Yarmuk River, Shaul Metzger led five Irgun members beneath a railroad bridge. Situated along the border between Palestine and Syria, the bridge provided a crucial link between Damascus and the northern half of the Galilee. Normally, it was guarded by British soldiers, but with the region sparsely settled, and facing increased violence near Jerusalem and along the coast, the British army was occupied elsewhere. As a result, the bridge was unguarded.

For three hours, Metzger and his men worked diligently to place charges in exactly the right location to ensure the bridge was destroyed on the first try. Even though few people lived in the area, a blast like the one they planned would draw a response. To escape cleanly, they had to get it right on the first attempt.

When the charges were set in place, the men climbed from beneath the bridge and stretched wires up the hill a safe distance away. Metzger attached the wires to a detonator and checked again to make certain his men were accounted for. Then with all eyes fixed on the bridge, he pressed a button on the detonator. Instantly, the ground shook from the force of the explosion as the charges erupted simultaneously. A thick black cloud enveloped the structure and rolled into the night sky. Timbers flew in every direction, followed by a loud crash from the bottom of the gorge as the bridge collapsed into the river.

— • —

Far to the south, Yoel Harnoy and a six-man Irgun team worked their way beneath a highway bridge over Nahal HaBesor, a wadi that bisected the coastal highway a few kilometers south of Gaza. Behind them, along the crest of a hill to the north, a dozen men from the backup unit lay out of sight, watching for trouble, ready to spring into action at a moment's notice. To the south, on the opposite side of the wadi, a second unit was poised to respond should anything happen from that direction.

There were twenty-four men in the support units and seven in the bridge team—thirty-one in total and far too many for Harnoy's comfort. With that many it was impossible to travel lightly and move quickly. He preferred to get in and out before anyone knew they were there, and leave little evidence behind, but with so many men that was impossible. "This group is about as nimble as a herd of elephants," he grumbled to himself.

The highway bridge was old and worn, having been constructed decades before as an open wooden railroad trestle and only later converted to a roadway, but it was a crucial part of the coastal thoroughfare that stretched the length of the coast from Egypt to Haifa. All commercial traffic moving north from the border traveled that road and crossed that bridge. For that reason, it was guarded by two dozen heavily armed and well-trained British troops.

Harnoy and his men began at the southern end of the bridge and worked their way north, setting charges in place as they went. The plan called for them to finish on the north side of the wadi, detonate the bridge, and escape with little or no British pursuit. The team proceeded as scheduled until they reached the midpoint of the bridge. Then, they perched on a timber near the top of the structure. The sound of footsteps pounded overhead, followed by an excited voice that shouted, "I see them!" Harnoy and his men froze in place.

Footsteps continued across the bridge as the sound moved down the bridge to the south. Minutes later, gunfire broke out from that direction and Harnoy knew the southern support team had been spotted. "Work fast," he whispered. "We must get out of here before they check the bridge."

Just then, a sound from above caught their attention, and seconds later a torso appeared at the edge of the roadway as a soldier leaned over the edge from the roadway to see the structure beneath. His eyes grew big and round as he caught sight of the explosive charges. A look of terror swept over his face and he shouted, "They're blowing the bridge! They're blowing the bridge!"

Harnoy drew his pistol from his belt. "Everyone out!" he shouted. Then with expert aim he fired a single shot in the soldier's direction. A red dot appeared on the man's forehead, followed by a thick red trickle of blood that ran down the bridge of his nose and dribbled from the end in large drops. For a moment he hung there, eyes fixed, body suspended in air. Then his hands let go their grip and he tumbled headfirst into the wadi.

Suddenly gunfire erupted from the northern end of the bridge as the second support team moved down to attack. Caught in the middle, the British soldiers had no choice but to stand their ground and fight. While they were occupied, Harnoy and his team scrambled through the bridge structure, stringing detonator wire behind them. A panicked voice in front cried out, "We're cut off to the north! They're coming from the south! How will we get out?" To which Harnoy replied calmly, "Just keep moving."

"Just keep moving," Harnoy repeated in a calm tone.

Minutes later they reached the north side and huddled against the bridge abutment. Harnoy counted heads. All six of his men were present. He glanced at them and smiled. "Think we can blow it from here without getting killed?"

"Wait," one of the men said, and before anyone could react he started up the nearest support column. They watched as he climbed to the top, detached the detonator wires from two charges, then hurried back down. When he reached the ground he announced in a huff, "We can survive the blast now."

"But will it blow the bridge?" someone asked.

"It'll drop," another replied.

"I don't think we have a choice," Harnoy said as he attached the lead wires to the detonator.

"I think we have as good a chance here as we do out there," someone offered.

"Then take cover," Harnoy nodded. He waited a moment while every-one crouched against the abutment, then he picked up the detonator, pressed a button on the side, and covered his head with his arms.

A thunderous explosion ripped through the bridge as all the charges detonated at once. The ground shook beneath their feet. Fire rushed upward and a huge ball of smoke engulfed them. Timbers flew through the air. Shards of timber and roadway pelted Harnoy and his men, but as the smoke and dust cleared, the section above their heads was still in place. The remainder of the bridge lay in ruins on the floor of the wadi.

— • —

Long before sunrise the next morning, news of the night's events reached the Jewish Agency in Tel Aviv. Staff at the office contacted Eyal Revach. After a briefing from Shai, he drove to Ben-Gurion's home and awakened him from a deep sleep. "We have a problem," Revach said.

"What is it?" Ben-Gurion asked, still only half awake.

"A dozen bridges have been destroyed."

"The stupid Arabs," Ben-Gurion growled as he bolted upright in bed. "Who would do such a thing?"

Revach shook his head. "It wasn't the Arabs. We're all but certain it was Irgun."

Ben-Gurion was angry. "Irgun," he muttered. "They will ruin us all." Ben-Gurion rolled to a sitting position with his feet dangling over the side of the bed. "We must put an end to these random operations." He rubbed his hands over his face, trying to get fully awake. "An army with a central command," he continued as he stood and pulled on a robe. "Every country has an army with a central command. None of this business with everyone making it up as they go."

"Yes," Revach agreed. "But right now we must decide how to respond to the British."

Ben-Gurion turned to face him with a puzzled frown. "The British?"

"Many of the bridges that were destroyed were guarded by British soldiers."

Ben-Gurion struck the wall with his fist. "How many are dead?"

"We don't know for certain but it looks like dozens, at least."

"Violence does us no good now! We had public opinion in our favor. It was bought with the bodies of those three men from the *Exodus*."

"The people are frustrated."

"I understand the frustration with the British. They arrest our people yet watch as the Arabs commit atrocities twice as bad." Ben-Gurion moved toward the closet. "But now we have to respond to this." He glanced in Revach's direction. "And what do we say?"

"Say what you just said," Revach argued. "That violence is deplorable in all its forms, but that you can understand the frustration our people have with both the Arabs and the British. Recount for them the horrors of what we saw and experienced with the *Exodus*. Remind them that this is how our people are treated every day. Then say you do not condone the attacks on the bridges and will work to see that no one is deprived of food and water because of transportation disruptions caused by the attacks."

Ben-Gurion smiled. "I knew there was a reason I kept you around." He reached into the closet and took out a suit. "That's exactly what I'm going to say."

— • —

Later that morning, Ben-Gurion held a press conference before a dozen journalists, most of whom had been covering the *Exodus* incident and remained behind after the passengers departed to write follow-up stories. He strayed from the text of his prepared remarks a few times but said almost verbatim the words given to him by Revach early that morning—he denounced violence in all its forms but understood the frustration people felt with the way the British conducted themselves. When the conference ended, he returned to his office.

Moments later, the office door flew open and Field Marshal Cunningham, the British High Commissioner for Palestine, appeared with Ben-Gurion's secretary trailing behind. She started to explain but Ben-Gurion waved her off.

"How dare you attack soldiers of Her Majesty's Army!" Cunningham roared.

"We didn't attack anyone," Ben-Gurion replied calmly, still seated at his desk. "Haganah had nothing to do with this."

"Eleven bridges were destroyed. Numerous casualties, including fifteen British soldiers, were incurred."

"We had nothing to do with it," Ben-Gurion repeated.

"But you know who did." Cunningham pointed an accusing finger in Ben-Gurion's face. "And you'll bring them to me within twenty-four hours."

"Or what?"

"Or I'll round them up myself."

"You treat us like second-class citizens, as if we're less than the Arabs, and you expect me to cooperate with you?"

"I expect you to—"

Ben-Gurion leapt to his feet. "The *Exodus* incident," he shouted angrily. "Your soldiers dragged our people off by their feet, some by the hair of their heads. Then you stored them in warehouses without even the minimum sanitary services or adequate ventilation. Now you're hauling them back to Europe in prison ships."

"You set that up with your—"

"All the while your soldiers chided us and ridiculed us with their racist anti-Semitic slurs. Every day your men stand and watch while Arab terrorists rape and murder our people. Yet when a Jew tries to defend himself, you arrest the Jew and let the Arab goes free."

Cunningham scoffed. "We don't—"

"I don't think violence is a good way to deal with you," Ben-Gurion continued, "but I understand the frustration of our people. They are forced to live with barbarians who masquerade as soldiers, racist anti-Semites who hold themselves out as friends, and Arab collaborators waiting for a chance to betray us." Ben-Gurion straightened his jacket and lowered his voice. "I've already condemned the bombings, but even if I knew who did it I wouldn't give their names to you. The last time we did that, you turned the men over to an Arab mob that beat them to death."

Cunningham's face was red and he pounded the desk. "How dare you! How dare you!" Then he turned and charged from the room without further response.

— • —

That afternoon in Washington, D.C., George Marshall traveled across town to the British Embassy. Peter Howard greeted him as he stepped from the car and they walked together to Howard's office.

"I met with Weizmann," Marshall said when they were alone.

"What did he have to say this time?"

"He's leaning toward partition."

"I thought he was opposed to that idea."

"Somehow," Marshall said dryly, "Lord Cunningham and his army have changed his mind."

Howard did not respond and they walked in silence the rest of the way to the office. He gestured to a seat as they neared the desk. "Sit here," he said in a less-than-friendly tone. He took a seat behind the desk and propped his elbows on the armrest of the chair. "I should think the Jews would be grateful to us."

"I suppose they prefer you to the Arabs."

"Our presence," Howard said in an imperious tone, "has kept the Arabs at bay for most of this century."

"On the whole, your presence has been viewed as generally beneficent."

"On the whole?"

"You removed passengers from the *Exodus* and forced them back to Europe—on prison ships at that."

"They were illegal aliens," Howard sniped.

"You've already indicated your desire to leave Palestine," Marshall reminded him.

Howard took a professorial tone. "But until we do, we are bound by the rule of law."

"Peter," Marshall said in a parental voice, "your soldiers dragged them down the gangway by the hair of the head."

"I thought you were on our side."

"I am, but I'm not in favor of treating Jews as second-class citizens. I saw what happened to them in Europe during the war."

"Yes," Howard sighed with a hint of arrogance. "You've reminded me of that several times." He stared past Marshall. "I suppose some of our men got a little carried away."

"Weizmann did say he could convince the others to hold off on partition demands if we deployed our army to Palestine."

Howard leaned back in his chair. "I don't suppose there's any chance of that happening, is there?"

"Not even the slightest. I think Weizmann and Ben-Gurion see this as their last best chance for establishing a state. I know that's Ben-Gurion's view and it appears Weizmann is moving in that direction."

"The Jews and their state," Howard said with derision.

"Well, after what happened in Europe—"

"They didn't help themselves there much," Howard interrupted.

"Oh?" Marshall was surprised. "You blame them for what the Germans did to them?"

"No. Of course not. But they didn't do much to fit in to society either."

"Well," Marshall said, "I think we could all do a better job of tolerating each other." They sat in silence a moment before Marshall continued. "You still think that if you let this go on long enough the Jews in Palestine will collapse?"

Howard smiled at him. "The consensus in London is that when we withdraw, the Arabs will step in, and that will be that."

"And I suppose you're counting on our support."

"We all need their oil." Howard gave Marshall a cold stare. "Unlike you, Europe has no Texas."

"Well," Marshall replied, "momentum for an independent Jewish state seems to be building. I don't think you can stop it, regardless of the ultimate outcome."

"I wouldn't be too sure of that." Howard opened a desk drawer and took out a folder, which he tossed over to Marshall. "Take a look at that."

The report gave details of the attacks in Palestine that occurred the night before. Marshall was taken aback. "They hit a dozen places on the same night?"

"And killed at least as many British soldiers," Howard added. "Some in the cabinet are calling for all-out war."

"Against whom?"

"Our intelligence says this was the work of the Jews."

"Do you really want the world to see the British army crushing defenseless Jewish villages?"

"That's not my decision," Howard said, glancing away. "But they won't let this pass without a response. Cunningham will have to do something and he'll do it against the Jews."

CHAPTER 15

AS WITH UNDOCUMENTED IMMIGRANTS detained in Palestine in the past, British ships bearing passengers from the *Exodus* sailed to Cyprus where others attempting to illegally enter Palestine were being held. Instead of docking there, however, as rumor had suggested, the ships loitered off the coast while officials in London argued over what to do next. Finally, after weeks of discussion, the ships sailed for Marseille, the port on the southern coast of France from which the *Exodus* had departed several months earlier.

Throughout their journey, first from France to Palestine and then from Palestine back, passengers from the *Exodus* had been loosely organized by deck and section under the direction of men associated with Haganah. Jacob and Sarah Schwarz were housed in the forward section of the second lower deck under the direction of Yossi Olmert. As the ship neared the French coast, Olmert gathered with the passengers. "The British have decided to take us to Marseille," he began. "We will arrive there in a few days."

"Where are we now?" someone asked.

"Loitering off the coast of Cyprus," Olmert answered.

"It takes days to get to France?"

"Only if you move at the British pace," Olmert chuckled. He paused as laughter tittered through the group. "When we arrive, we expect the British will attempt to force us from the ship as they did in Haifa. I know that was rough for some, but you must resist every effort to remove you from the ship."

"Will the French help us?"

"We don't know."

"But you're certain they will take us off here?"

"We aren't sure," Olmert replied. "But if they try, we must resist."

Jacob and Sarah sat in the corner, away from the group, listening. As Olmert spoke, Sarah rested her head on Jacob's shoulder. "I just want to be home," she groaned.

"We have no home but Palestine," Jacob replied.

"You know what I mean," she argued. "Off this ship. In a room with a real bed. And no one fighting or arguing." She looked up at him. "I don't want to hear arguing and shouting anymore."

"Do you think Jews will ever find a place to live in peace?"

"And the ransomed of the Lord will return. They will enter Zion with singing; everlasting joy will crown their heads. Gladness and joy will overtake them, and sorrow and sighing will flee away."

"Isaiah."

"How many times have you quoted it to me?"

"That was one of my father's favorite passages from one of his favorite chapters."

"It didn't seem so hard to believe when I was a girl," she lamented.

"I'm not sure it was so easy back then. I don't think it was quite like we remember."

"Will you fight back when they come for us?"

"To take us from the ship?"

"Yes," she nodded. "Will you fight back?"

Jacob looked away. "I think I shall walk off with dignity, if you will walk with me."

"If I wasn't with you," she persisted, "would you fight back?"

"That is an impossible question to answer."

"Why?"

He leaned over and kissed her. "If I was not with you, I would not be me."

— · —

Two days later, the ship on which Jacob and Sarah were traveling arrived at the port in Marseille. As before, British sailors ordered the passengers off the ship and as before, no one moved. But unlike in Palestine, this time the sailors did not attempt to remove them by force. Instead, they waited.

After three hours Yossi Olmert appeared on the deck where Jacob and Sarah were seated. "Apparently, the British think they can wait us out."

"What does that mean?"

"They aren't going any farther," Olmert explained. "They plan to wait until we decide to get off."

"How long can we remain here?" someone asked.

"They have food and water for three more days," Olmert informed them.

"And after that?"

"No one knows. But we don't want to wait until then. We're calling for a hunger strike now."

"I'm already hungry," a voice offered.

"I've been hungry since we left France the first time," a second added.

"I've been hungry since 1939," still another called out.

"No food," Olmert said with a wave of his hand for emphasis. "And only water when you must."

"Will this make any difference?" someone asked.

"Won't this only make things more manageable for the British?" another suggested.

"Yeah," another chimed in. "If we don't eat, they don't have to provision the ship."

"It's the only weapon we have right now," Olmert explained. "We'll use it to draw attention to our situation."

"Attention from whom?"

"From the newspapers."

"We have journalists onboard?"

"They are coming tomorrow with representatives from the Red Cross."

As instructed, for the next three days Jacob and Sarah avoided all food and consumed only enough water each day to keep from fainting. Representatives from the Red Cross appeared on deck but no one talked to them and they didn't come forward to be heard.

On the fourth day, a British officer appeared near the stairway. "May I have your attention, please," he shouted. "This is your last opportunity to leave the ship. The French government will accept any of those who wish to disembark on their own. We will not remove you from the ship, nor will we force you out by any other means, but if you wish to leave the ship now under your own power, you may do so."

A voice to the left called out, "Where are we going?"

"Germany," the officer said tersely.

"Germany?" someone shouted. "You are sending us back to Germany?"

"We only narrowly survived there before."

"You are going to displaced-persons camps in the section of Germany controlled by Her Majesty's army," the officer elaborated. "I assure you, there will be no Germans there. At least, not as you remember them."

Four days later, the ship arrived in Hamburg and was moored at the dock. In an hour, the British began forcing passengers from the ship. Many onboard the ship were physically sick, all were tired of being at sea, but the sight of British soldiers driving them from the ship by force set the passengers to action. Using whatever means at hand, they turned years of frustration on the soldiers and sailors, but the more they resisted, the harder the British pressed, wielding batons and clubs in a hail of violence that was shocking even to the officers in charge.

As before, Jacob and Sarah, trying to ignore the shrieks, screams and angry voices that filled the ship, sat quietly until a British officer approached. Flanked by a sailor on each side, he appeared grim and determined. Jacob kept his eyes on them as they drew nearer and when it was evident they'd come for him and Sarah, he stood and said confidently, "I can walk. She can, too," he added with a nod in Sarah's direction. The sailors watched while Jacob extended his hand to her and helped her to her feet.

"At last," the officer sighed, "a Jew with common sense."

To which Jacob replied, "I make my own choices. You cannot make me go. Nor can you make me come. The Nazis tried to rule me. I survived them. You will not do what they could not." Then with Sarah's hand tucked beneath his arm, they started toward the stairs.

From the docks in Hamburg, Jacob and Sarah were transferred by bus to a holding facility near Bergedorf where they were screened to determine whether they had a criminal background. With only an identification card from the displaced-persons camp where they'd been shortly after the war and an old card from Poland, convincing the British that they were not wanted by authorities took three days.

The next morning, they ate breakfast in a former barracks building that had been converted to a dining hall. None of the food was kosher but they ate it anyway. When they were finished, an officer appeared and ordered everyone to form a line outside. Jacob and Sarah did as they were told and huddled together on the street.

Thirty minutes later, under armed escort, they were marched through the camp and past the fence that ringed the facility to a large building. Inside, they formed lines once more and waited. Two hours later, they were taken together to an interview room where they appeared before an Allied representative.

Once more, they produced the ID cards issued at the displaced-persons camp and the cards they'd held in Poland. And once again they were subjected to interrogation about past criminal activity and association with known incorrigibles. When the officer was satisfied with their answers, they were sent to the medical department for examinations.

For Sarah's sake, Jacob did his best to comply with every direction. He didn't want to cause trouble for her or give the British a reason to separate them, but the facility and the fence and the soldiers brought back memories of his time in the Nazi concentration camp. Memories of those days flashed through his mind—guards shouting at him, soldiers beating him about the head and screaming in his ears, doctors probing every orifice of his body.

The medical examination that day was nothing like the kind he'd received from the Nazis during the war, just a routine check of basic functions. No one demanded that he remove his clothing. When he was finished, he stepped outside the examination room and waited for Sarah.

A few minutes later she joined him and he took her by the hand. "Are you okay?" he asked quietly.

"I am fine," she nodded. "It was nothing."

"Did he make you take off your clothes?"

"No. And it was a female doctor."

"Oh," he said with surprise. "I didn't know they had those here."

"Yes. An American. Very nice."

A guard directed them to a door on the left but as they chatted together, Jacob simply walked straight ahead, paying little attention except to Sarah. No one stopped them and when they reached the door, Jacob pushed it open. He held it while Sarah stepped through and then followed her out. He squinted against a brilliant glare and saw that they were outside the building—and outside the fenced area of the camp.

Still talking about the experience inside, Sarah stepped forward as if to continue. Jacob stopped and pulled her up short. "We are outside the building," he said, his eyes wide with excitement.

"Yes," she nodded, glancing around. "We're outside."

He pointed to the left, not sure she realized exactly where they were. "The fence is over there."

"I know," she nodded, still unaware of what it meant.

"But we are beyond it."

She fell silent as she glanced around, turning in every direction and gazing with wonder at the rolling German countryside that stretched before them. "We're beyond the fence," she gasped.

"Yes," Jacob grinned. "Beyond the fence and free."

"What do we do?"

"I don't know," Jacob shrugged. "Do you think they will they let us back inside?"

"I don't know. Perhaps they would think we were outsiders trying to get in."

"Why would anyone on the outside want to get into a place like that?" he shook his head. "Maybe we should just keep walking."

"But we have no money," she worried.

"We will find some help somewhere."

"Are you sure?"

He gestured with his thumb over his shoulder. "Do you really want to go back in there?"

"No," she said, shaking her head slowly. "But I'm scared of what might happen if we don't."

"Yes," Jacob nodded. "And I'm scared of what might happen if we do." He put his arm around her shoulder and drew her near. "So let's throw our fears away and see what we can find over that next hill." Then he took a step forward and she joined him.

CHAPTER 16

WHEN UNSCOP CONCLUDED its review of conditions in Palestine, it traveled to Geneva, Switzerland, where members were expected to continue their deliberations and begin work toward a final report. Official sessions were scheduled for the Palace of Nations, a sprawling complex once home to the League of Nations. Committee members and most associated delegations, both Jewish and Arab, were booked into rooms at the Hotel Beau-Rivage, an historic hotel overlooking Lake Geneva.

Nahum Admoni and a team of operatives from Shai, Haganah's intelligence arm, arrived in Geneva weeks in advance. Posing as hotel employees, they gained access to utility panels and telephone switchboards, which allowed them to tap any telephone line in the building. As the committee's arrival date drew nearer, they determined actual room assignments for members and other attendees and planted listening devices in every room, then routed lines from those devices to a room on the fifth floor that they converted into a command center.

At the same time, additional Shai members obtained legitimate jobs as waiters, housemaids, attendants, and custodians. Scattered throughout the facility, they provided unquestioned access to sections of the hotel too risky to surreptitiously penetrate with nonemployees. They also provided access to rumors and stories circulating among hotel staff, even the most outlandish and unbelievable of which were carefully analyzed for new information.

All of that took weeks of work and almost a hundred agents, but by the time the committee arrived, Admoni's network of agents and eavesdropping devices were in place. They didn't have to wait long to see the value of their efforts.

Emil Sandström, chairman of the committee, was placed in a suite on the seventh floor. Located near the top of the hotel, it had a large seating area, private dining room, three bedrooms, and four bathrooms. As one of the most lavish accommodations in Switzerland, it was a much sought-after retreat for the hotel's wealthiest clients and almost always occupied, which made it difficult to access. Shai operatives had succeeded in planting only a single small microphone in each room, most of them hidden inside the light fixtures in the ceiling. It was less than perfect—ideally they wanted multiple devices in every location—but the microphones were sensitive and picked up most conversations.

After dinner on the evening before the committee's first session, Sandström met in his room with his assistant, Paul Mohn. Working from the room on the fifth floor, Elia Strauss, a Shai agent, switched on a tape recorder, adjusted the headphones over his ears, and listened.

"In the morning," Sandström began, "as our first item, I would like to take up this question of visiting the displaced-persons camps."

"You want this to be first on the agenda?" Mohn asked. His voice belied a sense of doubt.

"Yes. The General Assembly directed us to do so. It's right there in the commission."

"They implied it," Mohn countered.

"But strongly," Sandström reiterated.

"Some will object."

"They are certainly free to raise any objection they like."

"There'll be an argument. You want to do that on the first day?"

"Who would object?"

"Well," Mohn sighed, "delegates from countries with large Arab populations for certain. India, Iran, and Yugoslavia."

"Why would they care about whether we go to the camps or not?"

"Because the people in those camps are predominantly Jewish."

"But we need to know if they want to return to Palestine," Sandström insisted. "That is one of the driving issues behind this controversy. The

Jewish Agency says they want to return. Others question whether that is correct. That's why the General Assembly included it in the commission they gave us. If they want to return, we have an issue that supports the Jewish view, of course. But if they don't, it strengthens the Arab position. The Arab countries shouldn't be upset, unless they know already that the Jewish Agency is correct."

"I don't think they'll see it that way."

"Well, I don't really care how anyone sees it," Sandström retorted. "This is our job. To find the truth. And we need to see the camps to know the truth. Besides," he continued, softening his tone, "those three Arab countries are only three votes. They can't stop us from going."

"What if Canada and Australia join them?" Mohn suggested.

"Why would Canada and Australia oppose such a visit?"

"The British generally favor the Arab position," Mohn explained. "Canada and Australia are part of the British Commonwealth."

"Well, that still isn't a majority," Sandström said in a dismissive tone. "And it's my job as chairman to keep the committee focused on the direction given us by the General Assembly. They can argue all they like. We talked about this in New York at the beginning, and we talked about it in Jerusalem, and both times we tabled a final decision. We're putting it to a vote tomorrow and we're doing it as the first item of business."

As the conversation moved on to other topics, Strauss scribbled a note, stuck it in an envelope, and handed it to a runner. "Take this to Nahum Admoni. Immediately."

Five minutes later Admoni entered the room on the fifth floor. "What do you have?" he asked. Strauss rewound the tape and played it for him. "Very good," Admoni said as the recording came to an end. "We need the locations of those camps."

"They haven't said where."

"Are you certain?"

"Yes sir, I listened carefully. They haven't said."

"Okay." Admoni started toward the door. "I'll see what I can find out. Keep listening."

— • —

Admoni left the room on the fifth floor and took the elevator to the hotel lobby. He found Abba Eban seated at a table in the bar, sipping a drink. "Come on," Admoni said. "We need to talk."

"Talk right here," Eban groaned. "I just got in from New York. It was a long flight."

"Too many ears," Admoni nodded. "Let's go for a walk."

Eban gulped down the last of his drink and followed Admoni out to the street. They walked together over to the lake and strolled along the shoreline. "When the committee convenes for its first session tomorrow," Admoni began, "Sandström intends to take up the issue of visiting the camps."

"Displaced-persons camps?" Eban asked.

"Yes."

"They've been talking about it awhile. Maybe they'll finally get around to doing it."

"Looks like Sandström is ready. He wants to visit several places. Thinks they need to go. But he has to get the committee to agree with him."

"That won't be difficult," Eban shrugged. "Iran and India will argue against it. Yugoslavia will vote with them. But that will be it. No one else will object strongly enough to vote against the proposal."

"Apparently he and Mohn are worried about Australia and Canada."

"That's Mohn talking," Eban chuckled. "He's been worried about them since the beginning."

"Mohn is still on our side, isn't he? I mean, he didn't sound too eager for this trip."

"He's been dragging his feet about it because he's worried that the people in the camps won't say they want to go to Palestine."

Admoni seemed concerned. "Do they want to go?"

"It's my understanding they do." But now Eban appeared unsure. "I sure hope so. We've been saying they do."

"Yeah," Admoni nodded. "And that's what bothers me. We've been saying they want to go to Palestine but no one has talked to them to see if that's actually true."

"Any possibility of finding that out before the committee makes its trip?"

"If you can get me a list of the camps they plan to visit," Admoni assured, "I can take care of it."

"I'll have it for you by lunch tomorrow."

"Good," Admoni smiled. "And maybe you should see if Canada and Australia really are a problem."

"I'll see what I can do, but I don't want to create an issue out of nothing by asking about it too much. One inquiry is an honest question. Two and you have a rumor."

"Ask, but be careful."

— • —

When they returned to the hotel, Eban went straight to Moshe Sharett's room and recounted for him the conversation he'd had with Admoni. Sharett wasn't as certain about Canada and Australia. "Mohn might be right," he grimaced. "They could be a problem."

"You've heard something?" Eban asked.

"Mohn keeps close watch over his counterparts with each of the delegations," Sharett explained. "He had lunch with an assistant on the Canadian team before they left Jerusalem. Apparently they didn't like the way the British handled things in Haifa, but they were even more upset when they learned we organized the protesters."

"We didn't tell the crowd what to do or say. We just told them what was happening and suggested they get down there. And besides, the crowd wasn't the problem. The British soldiers were and they did that all on their own."

"I know," Sharett agreed. "And Mohn told them that, but I'm not sure it did much good. I'm having lunch with Ivan Rand tomorrow. I'll see if we can get Canada back on our side. You take Australia. Hood shouldn't be much of a problem."

— • —

The following morning, Emil Sandström gaveled the committee to order for its opening session. As planned, the first issue on the agenda was that of visiting the displaced-persons camps.

Nasrollah Entezam, the representative from Iran, rose from his seat immediately. "Mr. Chairman, I object."

"On what basis?"

"Unnecessary delay. With the extra days spent in Haifa, we are behind schedule. A trip of this nature would require far too much time and deprive us of the opportunity for the kind of deliberation that our commission deserves."

Vladimir Simic, the representative from Yugoslavia spoke up. "Mr. Chairman, I must concur." He scooted his chair away from the table and stood. "Conducting a trip of this nature now, along with the necessary interviews and other evidence-gathering we would need, would make it difficult for the committee to reach its August deadline."

"On the contrary," Jorge Granados enjoined. "The General Assembly made this a part of our commission and we should get to it. We have discussed this trip from the very first day and we have tabled it every other time it's come up. I'm beginning to think some of our delegates have unstated reasons for not wanting to see the camps. And it makes me think the reasons for the delays have nothing to do with an honest effort to fulfill our obligations."

"Hear, hear!" someone shouted.

Sandström rapped his gavel on the tabletop. "Order! The delegate from Guatemala will address his remarks to the Chair."

"I fail to see what any of this has to do with Palestine," Entezam blurted out.

"It has everything to do with Palestine," Granados responded. "This question of the interest of the Jews who are now in the camps in returning to Palestine is the central issue of this problem. Thousands of Jews are living in camps across Europe. We are told they want to immigrate to Palestine, their ancestral homeland. That is the driving issue we face and it's precisely why the General Assembly included the issue in its directions to us. They want us to find out—do these people really want to go to

Palestine and, if so, can we find a way for it to happen?"

"Let them find another place," Simic scoffed as he returned to his chair. "The Arabs have lived there for thousands of years and the United Nations has no authority to displace them. The charter guarantees the security of every country as it now exists."

Ivan Rand, from Canada, spoke up. "That might be true under other circumstances, but there is no country in Palestine." The answer gave a glimpse of Rand's thinking on the question of Palestine, and the implication did not escape Sandström's attention. He shot a knowing look at Mohn but did not interrupt as Rand continued. "We have now only an area in that region that is under the control of a UN mandate. A mandate that existed at the time the charter was enacted and one that was expressly continued by the UN after that charter was adopted. One may wish otherwise, but as of right now, there is no recognized country of Palestine, Arab or Jewish."

Simic shook his head. "I still say let them find some other place where their presence would be less disruptive."

Granados turned to Simic. "Your country would take them?" He paused as if awaiting an answer. "Yugoslavia is ready to do such a thing? To accept the Jews as full and lawful citizens?" Simic did not respond but instead waved him off with a dismissive gesture. "I did not think so," Granados continued. "And that is the problem we and the Jews face. There is no other place. There is no other time. We have explicit directions from the General Assembly to find a workable solution and to do that we must know if the Jews in the displaced-persons camps really want to go to Palestine. If they do, we must find a way to send them. If they do not, we must find a way to address the hundreds of thousands of Jews already living there as a minority."

Dr. Blom, the delegate from the Netherlands, spoke up. "How many of these camps are we going to visit?" he asked in a dry, emotionless voice.

Sandström seized on the question and the manner in which it was asked as an opportunity to move the discussion forward. "We are to visit fifteen locations," he said matter-of-factly. "All of them are located in either Austria or Germany."

Abdur Rahmam, the delegate from India, now joined the argument.

"Already you have this trip planned and scheduled," he complained. "You would drag us from country to country without so much as a vote? Travel alone will consume vast amounts of the committee's time and energy. There would be interviews at every site. Pictures. Notes. Transcripts. It is simply too much for us to undertake now."

"This is Europe, Mr. Rahmam," Sandström explained tersely. "The distance between the locations is quite short, I assure you."

"There is another issue with which we must concern ourselves regarding this proposed trip," Simic interjected. "And that is the issue of fairness. The camps hold very few Arabs. Most of the residents are Jewish. We've already heard far too much from the Jews and far too little from the Arabs. To add even more Jewish voices would be grossly unfair."

"And I would remind you," Alberto Ulloa argued. "The Palestinian Arabs chose to ignore our requests for comment and testimony. They refused to participate in our hearings and refused to submit documentary evidence. They cannot now complain of the result their own decisions have produced." He turned to Sandström. "Mr. Chairman, I call for action on the question of whether we tour the displaced-persons camps. We've avoided this decision long enough. We need to vote."

"Very well," Sandström said. "The question has been called on whether the committee will tour the displaced-persons camps, conduct interviews, and gather such evidence as may be necessary and helpful regarding whether the residents at those camps desire to immigrate to Palestine. All in favor of making the trip and conducting the necessary work there will signify by saying 'Aye.'" A loud "aye" went up from the committee in response.

Sandström noted the vote and said, "All opposed?"

Rahmam, Simic, and Entezam shouted their response in the negative but they were obviously outnumbered. Delegates from Canada and Australia formally signified their abstention and the measure passed.

When the vote was concluded, Ulloa spoke up. "Mr. Chairman, I would suggest that you prepare a list of sites for us to visit on this trip, rather than spending more committee time arguing over each one. This trip is important but we don't have a lot of time."

"Second," Dr. Blom droned without waiting to be asked.

Sandström nodded his assent, apparently glad for the suggestion and the encouragement to proceed. "All in favor of so authorizing the chair signify by saying 'Aye.'" Before anyone could speak he rapped the gavel on the table and declared, "The ayes have it." He spoke rapidly, without waiting for a response. "Let's recess for lunch. We'll reconvene in two hours." Then he pushed back his chair from the table, rose to his feet, and walked quickly from the room.

Simic rose from his chair in a halfhearted attempt to object, but before he could speak Paul Mohn called out, "We'll have a list of the sites for you after lunch. See me when you return this afternoon." By then members of the committee were already making their way toward the door. Simic, realizing the issue had been resolved against him, slumped into his chair and slowly shook his head.

— • —

As noon approached, Abba Eban took a seat on a bench in the hall outside the committee meeting room. He'd been seated there perhaps ten minutes when the door opened and delegates emerged on their way to lunch. Not long after that, Mohn appeared holding an envelope. He turned up the hall and started in Eban's direction.

Mohn seemed to pay Eban no attention but kept his gaze focused straight ahead. As he passed the bench, he stumbled as if tripping over Eban's foot. He caught himself with a hand on Eban's shoulder and, at the same time, let go of the envelope. It landed in Eban's lap just as Mohn righted himself, apologized for the sudden intrusion, and continued down the hall. A moment later he turned the corner and disappeared from sight.

When he was gone, Eban rose from the bench, envelope in hand, and walked in the opposite direction. As he did, he opened the envelope and looked inside to see a list of fifteen displaced-persons camps scattered throughout Austria and Germany. He slipped it into the inside pocket of his jacket, then took the elevator downstairs to find Nahum Admoni.

CHAPTER 17

FOR THE NEXT TWO WEEKS, UNSCOP traveled across Austria and Germany, visiting displaced-persons camps. At each site, committee staff and members interviewed hundreds of detainees. And at each location the interviewees repeated with enthusiasm their singular desire to travel to Palestine and make it their home.

As they had with the committee's prior travel, Abba Eban and Ralph Bunche accompanied members on each stage of the journey. Bunche used the time to collect notes for work on the committee's final report. Eban used the occasion to focus attention on the delegations from Guatemala and Uruguay. As potential swing votes on the committee, he made certain they met detainees and soldiers at the camps who had ties to their respective countries.

Advance notice of the sites from the list provided by Mohn allowed Nahum Admoni and a team of Shai agents to travel ahead of the committee, preparing detainees for the committee's arrival. Convincing detainees to talk of their desire to immigrate to Palestine took no coercion—most of them genuinely wanted to relocate there—and that portion of the interviews went as expected even from the first stop, but that wasn't all the committee members learned.

When the group reached its second site, a camp outside Salzburg, Karel Lisicky, the delegate from Czechoslovakia, struck up a conversation with Aviv Gronich, a detainee from Austria. In the course of Lisicky's interview he asked Gronich about his experiences during the war.

"I was a tailor," Gronich said with a hint of pride. "My shop in Vienna was filled with wonderful fabric." He closed his eyes and tipped his head at an angle. A smile turned up the corners of his mouth and stretched across his face. "I can feel it even now." He paused for a moment, remembering, then his eyes opened and he continued. "People of every kind came to me for clothes. I made suits for men, and my wife made dresses for women. Our clients included politicians of every party and members of the Austrian and Netherlands royal families. We lived in a house with many rooms and our children filled it with laughter." His eyes clouded over and his voice dropped to an ominous tone. "And then the Germans came."

"What happened after they arrived?"

"They took the shop from me and gave it to someone else—a man from Poland with ties to the Nazi Party." Gronich shook his head in disgust. "His fingers were so fat he could barely thread a needle. Such a klutz. No talent for handwork." He took a deep breath and let it slowly escape. "Then they took the house. Herded us into the ghetto to live like animals."

"Your wife is here with you?" Lisicky asked expectantly.

Gronich shook his head sadly, "They murdered her at Auschwitz."

"Oh," Lisicky said reverently. "I didn't—"

"My son died at Buchenwald," Gronich continued, taking no notice of Lisicky's attempted sympathy. "Our daughters were forced to work as housemaids for Amon Goeth at Plaszow." He looked over at Lisicky, his eyes heavy with sadness. "You know about Plaszow?"

"I know the Germans had a camp there, but I do not know much about it. We were struggling to survive in our country, too."

"Horrible camp," Gronich continued. "One of the death camps. Built solely for the purpose of exterminating Polish Jews, then they decided to kill Austrian Jews there, too. Many of my friends from Vienna died there."

"Your daughters died there?"

"Yes," Gronich nodded. "But not in the gas chambers. Goeth was the camp commander. After each killing in the gas chambers his workers sorted through the bodies and extracted gold and silver fillings from the teeth of those who died. Goeth was supposed to turn it over to the German treasury but he kept most of it for himself and sold it through a dealer in

Krakow. The Nazis found out about it and had him arrested. One of the SS men tipped him off and I'm sure he planned to escape. Before he did, he took our daughters out to the garden behind the house and shot them."

Lisicky's jaw dropped in horror. "He shot them?"

"Goeth enjoyed shooting Jews. Said it helped him relax and cleared his mind so he could concentrate. Each morning before breakfast he walked outside with his rifle. He could see the camp from his front yard and he would raise the rifle to his shoulder, sight down the barrel toward the camp or along the road where the workers walked, and select one or two unsuspecting Jews for murder. All of them killed with a single shot to the head. Apparently he was an excellent marksman."

Lisicky stood there a moment in silence as the color drained from his face. Then he turned away and vomited.

Bunche and Eban had been seated nearby and when Lisicky became ill they walked over to where he stood to see about him. Gronich said quietly, "They still are proud of what they did."

Eban had a puzzled frown. "The Nazis?"

"Yes," Gronich replied. "We see them here from time to time. At first they worked in the camp, doing menial labor, but we objected and they were removed. But while they were there, some of us talked to them, thinking they might wish to repent, but they insisted it was their duty to treat us as they did. We were the enemy, bent on ruining their lives. Some of them went so far as to tell us again how worthless we were and an even greater blight on society now than before."

— • —

That evening, Bunche and Eban had dinner together at a Salzburg restaurant. Bunche picked at his food with a fork and pushed it around on his plate. Then finally he said, "That was quite a story we heard today from the Austrian tailor."

"It was no story," Eban replied. "And there are millions more just like it buried all over Europe."

"I didn't mean it was fiction, just that it was quite an account."

"It was arresting," Eban sighed.

Bunche moved his plate aside. "And sobering. I can't eat with those images in my head."

"Good," Eban said, laying aside his fork. "No one should be able to eat and think of those things at the same time." He called a waiter to the table and ordered coffee. When the cups were filled and they were alone again, he continued. "Gronich spared you the worst of it."

"The worst of it?" Bunche asked in disbelief. "It gets worse than that?"

"He didn't tell you about the bodies that were skinned."

"Skinned?" Bunche put the corner of his napkin to his mouth. "Now I *will* be sick."

"Their skin was tanned like animal hide and used for upholstery." Bunche swallowed hard. Eban kept going. "And he avoided telling you about the babies they used as targets. Tossed them out a window to see who could shoot them before they hit the ground."

"Stop," Bunche protested as he reached for a water glass. He took a long drink and set the glass aside, then wiped his mouth on the napkin. "I can't even drink coffee. Let's go out for some air." Without waiting for a response, he scooted back from the table, rose from his chair, and started toward the door.

Eban found the waiter and paid for their dinner, then walked out to the sidewalk. Bunche was waiting near the curb. "Sure you're all right?" Eban asked when he caught up.

"Yes," Bunche nodded. "Sorry about that."

"It's okay. I wasn't interested in eating anyway."

"How can we be so cruel to one another?"

"The heart of man knows only darkness."

They walked in silence up to the corner, then turned and started toward the hotel. Finally Bunche said, "It's from Jeremiah."

"What is?"

"That line you quoted. The heart of man is desperately wicked."

"I suppose that's one of our jobs, we Jews. To remind you Christians that evil really is a problem."

Bunche glanced over at Eban and changed the subject. "Listen, before we get back to the hotel, I've been meaning to tell you, I had an interesting conversation with one of your generals, Aharon Hartman."

"Oh?" Eban was concerned but did his best to hide it. "When did you see him?"

"When we were in Palestine."

"Oh. Yes," Eban nodded. "That night at Ben-Gurion's home. I was there. That was a rather strained conversation."

"Yes, it was," Bunche acknowledged. "Strained and strange, but that's not the visit I'm talking about."

Eban arched an eyebrow. "You saw him again? Since then?"

"Yes. He came to the hotel just a few nights before we left."

"Did he try to solicit your help in locating munitions for the army?" Eban spoke with a sarcastic tone but inside he was angry at Hartman for such a reckless breach in protocol. Bunche was a diplomatic officer. Hartman should not have approached him without a formal invitation.

"No, he told me about his plan for governing Palestine."

"His plan?"

"Yes."

"And what was this plan?"

"That the country should be unified under majority rule, which would mean Arab rule for the time being. That there should be provinces, arranged so that they are ethnically oriented to the way people are living now, Jewish provinces and Arab provinces, with each able to determine their own local affairs."

"He wants to have an Arab state?"

"I think he wants to *govern* an Arab state," Bunche emphasized.

"He wants to take Ben-Gurion's place."

"He didn't say so exactly, but I don't think he has much confidence in Ben-Gurion's ability to control the military. From what he said, it appears he wants to scrap the framework created by the Jewish Agency and govern from a different direction. That's what he was trying to talk about that night at Ben-Gurion's house, when he was ushered from the room."

"He was out of place," Eban said flatly. "Have you told anyone about this conversation you had with Hartman?"

"No," Bunche replied with a shake of his head. "And I don't intend to report it. Telling you is all I want to do with it. But I was wondering whether Hartman's idea of how to govern is merely his personal opinion or also the official position of Haganah. And if it is Haganah's position, then I would have doubts—or at least questions—about whether you'll be able to effectively defend the country, should the committee recommend partition."

Eban smiled wryly, "I can assure you, whatever Hartman told you were only his views, not the opinion of Haganah. All the general staff support Ben-Gurion."

"With the exception of Hartman," Bunche noted.

"Yes," Eban agreed. "With the exception of Hartman, who is now in question."

"I only ask because this work we are doing in Palestine is the United Nations' first. It would be terrible for the UN as an entity if we voted for partition only to watch the Jewish state disintegrate. Something like that would be bad for everyone—the Jews who have endured so much already and the UN which is still trying to prove itself and win credibility among the nations."

— · —

Eban continued with the committee to the next camp, then broke away and returned to Geneva. Alone in his hotel room, he prepared a detailed report of his conversation with Bunche about the discussion Bunche had with Aharon Hartman. When the report was finished, Eban placed it in a diplomatic pouch and sent it back to Tel Aviv through a Shai courier traveling on a French diplomatic passport. The report landed on the desk of Walter Eytan at the Jewish Agency's political department. He read it quickly, then walked down the hall to Ben-Gurion's office.

Eytan dropped the report on the desk, "You might want to read this."

"I'll look at it later," Ben-Gurion replied.

"I think you should read it now," Eytan suggested.

"I'm in the middle of something," Ben-Gurion scowled, "and you're interrupting me."

"You better stop what you're doing and read this. It's from Abba Eban."

Ben-Gurion gave a frustrated sigh. "Why didn't you say that in the first place?" He set aside the document he was reading and picked up the report. He scanned it quickly, then leaned back in the chair and read it slowly. When he finished, he tossed the file on the desk and shouted toward the door, "Get me Gedaliah Cohen!"

"On the phone?" the secretary called from her desk in the hall.

"Tell him to come over here!" Ben-Gurion shouted. He looked up at Eytan and pointed to a chair near the desk. "Have a seat," he lowered his voice. "This might be interesting."

Ten minutes later, Cohen arrived at the office. Ben-Gurion tossed the report to the corner of the desk. "Have a look at that."

Cohen glanced over the report, then took a seat next to Eytan. "This could be a problem."

"*Could* be?" Ben-Gurion growled. "If he's talking to Bunche, he's talking to everybody. This guy is plotting a coup."

"I wouldn't go that far," Cohen cautioned.

"I don't think it's an exaggeration. An army officer, criticizing my ability to lead, suggesting he would be better for the job. Now he's lobbying UN diplomats for support." He lifted his hands in the air in frustration. "We should at least hear what he has to say about it," Cohen argued. "And, David, I wouldn't push the general supreme commander idea very far."

"Why not? Are you with him on this?"

"I'm not with him," Cohen said coldly. "But you aren't the supreme commander of anything yet. You aren't a head of state. We have no head of state."

"So it's a free-for-all brawl. Is that what you're saying?"

"Listen to me," Cohen slid forward in his chair. "We are in a very ill-defined moment right now. You are head of the official liaison agency between the Jewish settlers and the United Nations Mandatory Authority—the British—but we have no nation-state status." He eased back in the chair. "That's all I'm saying. So don't overstate your case." Cohen rose from his chair and started toward the hall. "I'll get him and be back in few minutes."

"Gedaliah!" Ben-Gurion called after him. "Don't tell him about the report."

Cohen frowned. "Why not?"

"That report was written as an official communiqué to this office. It wasn't written for general dissemination. I don't think he should know all the details."

"Very well," Cohen conceded, then walked up the hallway.

Twenty minutes later, Cohen returned with Hartman. Ben-Gurion and Eytan were waiting when he arrived. Ben-Gurion stood as they entered the room and came from behind the desk to face Hartman. "I want to know every detail of your conversation with Ralph Bunche," he said between clenched teeth.

Hartman took a step back. "What conversation are you talking about?"

"You went to Bunche's hotel to tell him how you would run Palestine if you were in charge." Ben-Gurion jabbed with his finger to emphasize each word. "I want to know what you said."

Hartman's eyes darted away. "I don't think that conversation is any of your business."

"Let me make something perfectly clear to you," Ben-Gurion said without raising his voice. "When a general officer of Haganah talks about policy to an international diplomat, without prior approval from this office, it's my business."

Hartman squared his shoulders. "I wasn't speaking as a member of Haganah and certainly not as a general officer."

"Well, it didn't come across that way. Ralph Bunche thinks you speak for Haganah and he thinks what you told him is Haganah's official position." Ben-Gurion wasn't exactly forthright about Bunche's perception but he didn't want to talk about what Bunche really said or the doubts he'd raised.

Hartman shook his head. "Impossible. I made it clear to him that I did not speak for anyone other than myself. There's no way he could have misunderstood."

"What did you tell him?"

"The same thing I've told anyone else who cared to listen. That partition is wrong. It will only lead to permanent war. Our forebears were here before the Arabs but our forebears left and the Arabs moved in. Displacing the Arabs now would be at least as disruptive as bringing us back. Instead of carving up the region, we should work to create a unified Palestine controlled by a government elected by a majority vote in a fair and open election. Right now that would be Arab. We could balance that by creating provinces that would govern at the local level. Bunche says they would be small and not more than two or three, but that's all we need to cover the majority of Arab and Jewish areas as they are populated now. Then we could move forward into the future."

"There's only one problem with that," Ben-Gurion replied. "The Arabs would be in the majority and they don't want us here. They certainly don't want any more of us. Immigration would end."

"Perhaps," Hartman conceded. "But they might change their minds when they see that having us here makes a difference—a positive difference that benefits them."

Ben-Gurion turned away and stepped behind the desk. "That's not what we've decided to do."

"And that's not an acceptable answer." Hartman was angry and it was evident in his voice. "War will destroy everything we've worked for to this point."

Ben-Gurion dropped onto his chair. "War will give us our nation."

"But it would be a—"

"They hate us!" Ben-Gurion shouted. His face was red and the veins in his temples throbbed. "Don't you get it? They hate us. They hate us because we're here. They hate us because we succeed. But most of all, they hate us because we're Jews! They hate us because of who we are! And that's never going to change. If we don't have our own country where we can control our own destiny, we will always be subject to people who hate us. It was that way in Poland, Austria, Hungary, the Netherlands, Germany. They all hated us. Not because we had done something wrong, but because of who we are. Because we are Jews. And it will always be that way. The only way we can be safe and free is to have our own country. And if that means a country always at war, then so be it."

"But thousands will die," Hartman protested. "Maybe more in the coming years."

"Millions died by submitting to European rule," Ben-Gurion countered in a calm and steady voice. "And we are not going to let that happen again." He paused a moment, then continued. "General Hartman, if you wish to speak your mind about our policy positions at any time in the future, do so after you have tendered your resignation to this office. Otherwise, I shall expect no further statements from you, either public or private, regarding alternate plans for governing the region. You're excused."

"You can't—"

Cohen took him by the elbow to guide him away from the desk. "Let's go, Aharon."

"But I'm not finished."

"Yes, you are," Cohen insisted. "Let's go."

Reluctantly, Hartman left the office and stepped out to the hallway. Cohen escorted him downstairs. When they were gone, Ben-Gurion turned to Eytan. "That is what I face every day."

"I understand," Eytan nodded. "And I think people will always question our legitimacy. At least during our lifetime."

"I'm not giving up," Ben-Gurion said in a determined voice.

"I'm glad."

A few minutes later, the door opened downstairs and the sound of footsteps came from the stairway, then Cohen appeared in the office doorway. "I got him calmed down but I don't know for how long."

Ben-Gurion leaned back in his chair. "Can he follow orders?"

"I don't know." Cohen entered the office and stood near the desk. "But I don't have anyone else with his experience."

Ben-Gurion banged his fist on the desk. "We need a real army!"

Cohen folded his arms across his chest. "David, we're doing the best we can."

"I know you are," Ben-Gurion admitted softly. "It's just frustrating, always piecing things together, always choosing the least-disruptive course of action rather than the best."

"You should try leading them in battle like that," Cohen commented.

"I should have fired him on the spot," Ben-Gurion grumbled, "but I can't because we don't have anyone who can take his place."

"And that's why you're the political leader and he's not," Cohen said with a tight smile. "You can make a tough decision when you'd rather do the more comfortable thing. He can't. He's a general, not a politician."

Ben-Gurion nodded. "Make sure he knows that."

"I will."

CHAPTER 18

AS HE HAD THREATENED after the Night of the Bridges attacks, Alan Cunningham, the British High Commissioner for Palestine, deployed troops across Palestine in a region-wide roundup of Jewish leadership. Soldiers raided homes, private businesses, and the Jewish Agency's offices in Jerusalem and Tel Aviv. Ben-Gurion avoided capture only because he was away on a previously arranged trip, but Cunningham's men took into custody many of the agency's key players. Somehow Golda, back from an extended stay in Paris, was not taken but they seized boxes of documents, maps, and carefully compiled directories of settlers dating back to the 1800s—all in an effort to cripple the Jewish organization.

At the same time, British units struck Haganah headquarters in the Red House and carried away senior officers and even more records. When it was over, almost three thousand Jewish leaders were in British custody. Irgun and Lehi commanders, however, went unscathed by the crackdown, primarily because their covert nature and loose organizational structure made them difficult to locate. With Haganah reeling from the loss of key general staff, the smaller paramilitary organizations stepped up to provide both protection and a response.

For several days, no one knew where the British had taken many of the most notable figures. But Yitzhak Jeziernicky, head of Lehi, the smallest but most radical of the Jewish paramilitary organizations, had an efficient network of contacts and informants. Within the week he learned that those arrested were imprisoned at Latrun, a fortified British outpost along the highway from Jerusalem to Tel Aviv. Jeziernicky gathered his men at a safe house near Haifa to plan a response. They met around the kitchen table.

"Okay," Jeziernicky began. "Our men are being held at Latrun."

"You're certain of it?" Mischa Katz asked.

"I have it from a good source," Jeziernicky replied.

"A trustworthy one?"

"He's never been wrong before."

"Latrun was an ancient stronghold," Arie Talmi noted. "They called them strongholds for a good reason. It sits on a hilltop. The Romans used it and they were never defeated there."

"They aren't there now," Katz replied.

"Only because they abandoned it when they left Palestine," Talmi countered. "The site is virtually impregnable, especially with the improvements the British have made."

"Are you suggesting we shouldn't attempt to rescue the prisoners?"

"Not at all. I'm just saying this won't be easy."

"It won't be easy," Jeziernicky agreed, "but we don't have to seize it. We only need to free the prisoners." He took out a map of the area and spread it on the table. "We can work our way up this wadi," he traced a route with his finger. "Come in around this way and up the back side of the hill. It's not as steep as the front."

Noam Shalev spoke up. "Any idea in which part of the place they're being held in?"

"They're housing them in a building over here." Jeziernicky pointed to the map. "Inside the central compound."

"Isn't that the part inside the wall?" Talmi asked.

"Yes," Jeziernicky nodded. "The ancient wall. They've extended the wall with a new part that runs over this way." He pointed to a spot on the map. "But we can go through over here." He moved his finger to the right. "It's strong but not as strong as the reinforced concrete they used for the new construction. If we hit the wall here we can open a gap large enough to move in and out quickly."

Mati Ziffer spoke up. "What do we do about the Arabs?"

"What Arabs?" Talmi asked.

"They have prisoners there besides ours," Ziffer explained. "Many of them are Arabs we helped the British capture. If we open a gap in the wall, and breach the building where our guys are being held, everyone is going to make a run for it."

"All the better," Shalev suggested. "The more confusion they create, the better our chances."

"And if the Arabs storm out of the place," Katz added, "we'll get in their midst and use them as shields."

"But do we shoot them?" Ziffer asked.

"Shoot them?" Shalev asked with surprise. "Why would we shoot them?"

"That's been our standard method," Ziffer replied. "When we raid a place, we shoot them all. They would shoot us if the circumstances were reversed."

"No," Jeziernicky interjected, not waiting for a response from the others. "We're not going to shoot them. In fact, we need as little shooting as possible, so don't fire unless fired upon. We are going in there for one reason and that is to free as many as we can."

"Okay," Shalev smiled. "So, when do we go?"

"Tomorrow night."

"Why not now?"

"We need to gather the explosives to blow the wall."

Talmi grinned with anticipation. "*That* we can do tonight."

"And all the more easily," Shalev added, "with Haganah still recovering."

— · —

Sometime after midnight, Shalev, Talmi, and Ziffer entered a Haganah compound outside Tel Aviv. Dressed as Haganah soldiers, they encountered little difficulty entering the central warehouse from which they stole three containers of C-4 explosive, along with a handful of detonators and timers.

The following evening, Jeziernicky led a six-man team up the wadi to a ledge behind the Latrun outpost. They waited there while Shalev and Talmi placed explosive charges near the base of the wall that surrounded the compound. Within minutes, the roar of an explosion shook the hill, creating a gap five meters wide in the wall. Before the dust settled, Jeziernicky and the team were inside the compound and making their way to the building where the men were being held.

Awakened by the explosion, British guards rushed to the wall. Jeziernicky and his men avoided the first group by hiding in the shadows, but a second group arriving moments later spotted them and opened fire.

The original plan called for Shalev and Talmi to breach the wall and make their way to the building where Remez was being held. Working together, they would then either force open the door or blow it open with a small explosive charge. However, in the confusion that followed the initial explosion, Shalev and Talmi were separated. Alone and with no support, Talmi reached the building but was unable to force open the door. At the same time, two British soldiers fired on him and forced him to retreat around the corner of the building. Huddled there as bullets whizzed past his head, he abandoned the original plan and set a small charge near the back wall, hoping to create an opening without causing bodily injury to those inside. The explosion that followed was much stronger than he expected and collapsed a large section of the wall. A dozen prisoners escaped but none of the Jewish leaders were among them.

Facing an obvious attempt to free their prisoners, British troops poured into the rear area of the compound, laying down a withering barrage of gunfire from their automatic weapons. Overwhelmed both in numbers and weaponry, Jeziernicky and his men were forced to retreat. They fought their way back to the wall where Shalev and Talmi rejoined the others. Under cover of three more blasts from Talmi's explosives, they made their way through the gap and down the hill to safety. When they gathered there, they realized that two men, Ziffer and Katz, were missing.

— • —

Three days later, Jeziernicky learned that the British had captured them. Both men were scheduled to hang at the earliest possible opportunity. Once again, Jeziernicky gathered his men to plan a response.

"We left two men behind," Jeziernicky growled. "We have to go get them. Anyone have any suggestions on how we do it?"

"We could go up the hill the same way as before," Talmi suggested. "Go through the same gap. I'm sure they haven't repaired it yet."

"That didn't work so well last time," Shalev quipped.

"We could try it again," Talmi continued. "Maybe we'd do it better this time."

"We can't just let them swing."

Isidor Gechtman, who had not been part of the raid, spoke up. "What if we grab two of theirs?"

"British soldiers?" Talmi frowned.

"Yes."

"And do what?" Shalev asked.

"Offer to trade them for ours," Gechtman suggested.

"That only works if we threaten to kill them," Jeziernicky observed.

"Right," Gechtman nodded. "We offer to swap their two soldiers for ours. And we tell them, if they don't release ours, we'll hang theirs."

Shalev cut his eyes in Gechtman's direction. "You're serious?"

"Yes. Absolutely serious."

"You would hang a British soldier?"

"No," Gechtman said with a shake of his head. "I would hang two."

"You don't think they'll come down even harder on us for that?"

"I don't care if they do. They aren't helping us now."

"Good point," Shalev nodded.

"Okay," Jeziernicky said slowly. "Where do we get these soldiers?"

"They patrol the roads by vehicle," Talmi offered. "They ride two men to the vehicle. Usually only a single vehicle for each patrol. No backup. No support of any kind. Just two men in a jeep. I say we snatch them while they're on patrol."

— • —

The following day, Shalev parked a truck along the coastal road in a desolate area near Netanya, south of Haifa. He raised the hood and propped it open, then disappeared into the brush where Talmi and Gechtman waited. Half an hour later, a jeep approached and as it drew near the men could see two British soldiers seated in front. The jeep came to a stop alongside the truck and both men got out. "See anyone?" the driver asked.

"No," his companion replied with a wary glance. "Wonder what happened?"

They stood near the truck's front bumper and leaned over to check inside the engine compartment. As they did, Talmi and the others darted from hiding and charged toward them. Before the soldiers could react, Gechtman and Shalev had them in their grasp. Talmi bound their hands behind their backs. When they were secured, Gechtman and Shalev gagged them and placed a hood over their heads. Then they lifted the two men into the back of the truck and drove away.

— • —

A few hours later, a young boy approached the main gate at the Latrun outpost and handed the guard an envelope. It was addressed to Lieutenant Colonel Forbes Adair, commander of the Latrun post. The guard glanced at it just long enough to note the name, then handed it to a private standing nearby and ordered him to deliver it at once.

Adair came to Palestine after serving at outposts in India, the Persian Gulf, and more recently in North Africa. Similar to Latrun in size, they'd been surrounded by an unfriendly local population that Adair had won over with humanitarian projects. Held in high esteem by the troops he commanded, he was often seen as weak by his fellow officers. His opposition to the recent roundup of Jewish leaders only exacerbated that perception. He was seated at his desk when the envelope arrived. With a quick swipe, he opened it and inside found photographs of two British soldiers, each with a name scrawled on the back—Clifford Martin on one, Mervyn Paice on the other. A note with the photos read, *If you hang ours, we'll hang yours.*

Adair was incensed. "Get me the High Commissioner's office!" he shouted. An aide seated just outside the door placed a phone call to Alan Cunningham's office. Moments later, Cunningham came on the line.

Adair stood at his desk as he read the note aloud. Cunningham listened politely, then said in a dismissive tone, "It's only a ploy. I assure you, they only want to bargain. And as I have told you and the others on numerous occasions, we are not negotiating with these Jews. I simply will not permit it."

"Sir," Adair said in a sober voice, "I think they're serious."

"Don't be ridiculous," Cunningham sniped. "They wouldn't dare follow through on such a thing."

"That might have been a logical conclusion before they blew up a dozen bridges, sir, but now I don't think we can so easily dismiss such an obvious threat."

"Nonsense!" Cunningham answered sharply. "How long have you been in this country?"

"Eleven months, sir."

"Well," Cunningham said in a parental tone, "when you've been here as long as I you'll understand these people. They talk, but they rarely follow through. No, the accused have been duly tried before a military tribunal and they've been convicted. You are authorized to execute the sentence. Do your job." And he hung up the phone without waiting for a response.

The following morning, a little before nine, Adair assembled his troops in the courtyard at Latrun. Ziffer and Katz were led from the prison and guided up the steps of a well-constructed wooden gallows. A hangman awaited them and he carefully fitted the noose of a rope over the head of each, then pulled it snug against their neck. When all was set, he glanced in Adair's direction. Adair nodded his head slowly.

The hangman stepped to one side of the platform where a lever protruded from the floor. He grasped it with both hands and gave it a shove. Instantly, a trapdoor beneath Ziffer and Katz swung open. Both men plummeted a distance of eight feet, where the rope reached its full extension. When they reached the end of the rope, the force of their weight caused their heads to snap backward, breaking their necks. They dangled in midair together, swinging gently from side to side, their bodies lifeless.

— • —

The following morning, Salman Aruri, a farmer who lived near Netanya, sat atop an oxcart as he rode toward town. Behind him in the cart were four goats that he planned to sell. Fat and ready for slaughter, he estimated the price of each and calculated the total in his head. This would be a fine day for his family. Perhaps he would buy them all a treat before he returned home.

As Aruri crested a low hill, he came to spot where the road passed through a grove of cedar trees. Tall and majestic, they had been there since before he was born. He remembered riding past them with his father and grandfather when he was a small boy. The memory of those trips brought a pleasant smile and he gazed up at the branches as he drew near. But the smile faded quickly and he brought the cart to an abrupt halt as he came to the middle of the grove.

Suspended from the branch of a large cedar, hanging a few meters in the air, were the bodies of two young men. Flies circled them and the smell of death filled the air. Aruri became sick to his stomach but he worked the ox diligently and carefully brought the cart closer. Then he stood on the seat for a better look.

Both men were dressed in British army uniforms and as they turned in the breeze he saw their names stenciled in black above the pocket of their shirts. "This one is Martin," he whispered. "And that one," he said, glancing at the other body, "is Paice." He bowed his head and whispered a prayer for the dead.

CHAPTER 19

IN RAMAT GAN, NOGA SHAPIRO received news of Lehi's attempted rescue at Latrun and of its subsequent failure with deep sorrow. He had often derided their leadership as both unimaginative and shortsighted. He was stunned by the deaths of the two British soldiers, but was impressed by the courage of the attempted rescue mission.

Yet in spite of the rhetoric, Shapiro had avoided suggestions from his men that he should follow through with an equally bold move by Irgun. He was concerned about the escalation of violence at a time when international support seemed to be in their favor and although he differed with Ben-Gurion and the Jewish Agency on which course of action to pursue, he was sensitive to the political repercussions that more aggressive actions might bring. Indeed, international reaction to the hangings had been strong and many in London were suggesting the UN might wish to reconsider Palestine's future. Only a strong denunciation from Ben-Gurion as he remained in Paris staved off a collapse of support for UNSCOP's continued work.

But for Shapiro's assistant, Tuvia Megged, that all changed when he learned that during their raid of Haganah headquarters, British soldiers seized documents that implicated Irgun in several incidents that directly involved the deaths of British troops. That was a serious matter, one that threatened to expose Irgun's most sensitive covert operations—some of which Megged had authorized without Shapiro's knowledge.

A few days after the hanging, Megged located Gil Benari in a Jerusalem coffee shop. They sat across from each other at a table near the back of the store while Benari sipped coffee from a tulip cup. "I think we should revisit that plan of yours," Megged said quietly.

"Which plan is that?" Benari asked with a puzzled frown.

"The one involving destruction of the occupational authority's headquarters."

Benari's lips moved as he repeated the phrase to himself, then his eyes opened wide in a moment of realization. "The King David?" he whispered.

"As soon as possible," Megged said cryptically.

"We are ready to go now."

"You are ready now?"

"We have all that we need," Benari assured him. "I knew we would come back to this so I had my men move forward with planning *and* procurement."

"Good."

"We should do it?"

"Yes," Megged nodded. "Do it."

— • —

Two days later, Yoni Shalit backed a truck up to the loading dock at the service entrance behind the King David Hotel. Riding with him were Shlomo Avital and Dover Kastner. All three were dressed as deliverymen and when the truck came to a stop they climbed out to unload it.

Using a cart from the hotel, they wheeled six milk cans from the truck and pushed them down the hall to La Regence Café, a coffee shop located in the hotel basement beneath the south wing of the building. Inside the café, a large concrete column stood near the bar, another was located at the center of the room, and a third stood along the wall to the left of the door. While Shalit watched the door, Avital and Kastner positioned two cans at the base of each column and connected them by wire to a single timer. When everything was set, they walked back to the loading dock, and casually climbed into the cab and drove away.

As the truck moved across the city, a young recruit sat in a telephone booth at a coffee shop ten blocks from the hotel. He glanced at his watch to check the time, then picked up the receiver and placed a call to the switchboard at the King David Hotel. "There is a bomb in the building," he said when the operator answered. "It's set to go off in twenty minutes." He hung up abruptly and glanced down at his watch.

One minute later, he telephoned the *Palestine Post* and told the operator, "A bomb has been planted in the King David Hotel. It's set to go off in the next twenty minutes."

Finally, he telephoned the French Embassy, which was housed in a building across the street from the hotel. The warning he left there was taken seriously and everyone inside evacuated safely.

At the hotel, several staff members made a cursory attempt to check the obvious locations—the main lobby on the first floor, a café that faced the street at the corner, the basement laundry—but no one took the warning seriously. A bellman delivered the warning from the operator to the British occupation headquarters in the hotel's south wing, but no one there thought much of it, either. "We get one of these a week," Robert Worthington groused. "If we evacuated every time, we'd never—"

Just then, shards of glass flew across the room as the concussion of the blast shattered windows up and down the street. The floor trembled beneath their feet and seconds later a scream was heard. Dust filled the air and the floor gave way as chairs, tables, bookcases, and people tumbled toward the basement five floors below, Worthington and those in his office among them. In less than a minute, the south wing of the building lay in a heap.

CHAPTER 20

MEANWHILE, FAR TO THE NORTH at kibbutz Degania, a communal Jewish farming settlement on the shore of the Sea of Galilee, Yaakov Auerbach sat on the ground beneath a clump of bushes near a well-tended field. American by birth, he traveled to Palestine alone from his home in Chicago on a mission to find peace and fulfillment in the homeland of his ancestors. Not quite twenty years old, he had lofty dreams that he couched in even loftier rhetoric about the wonder and beauty of a collective lifestyle, the regenerative effects of an agricultural environment, and the reward of hard labor applied to a collective goal.

That rhetoric carried him from Illinois to Palestine, but when he first arrived all he could talk about was his family—a brother who was a writer in New York, a sister who was a housewife in Atlanta, and a cousin in Detroit who worked in the automobile industry. Those with whom he worked at the kibbutz understood it as an expression of homesickness and waited patiently for him to settle into the rhythm of farming life. Then about three weeks after arriving at Degania he saw Suheir Hadawi, an Arab girl who lived with her family on a neighboring farm. After that, he no longer talked of the communal dream, or of his family back home. He only talked about her.

Suheir sat beside him that day as they cuddled together beneath the clump of bushes. He squeezed her close and gazed into her eyes. "We should just run away," he said dreamily.

"They would find us," she said with a hint of resignation. "And besides, where would we go?"

"Far, far away." He pressed his lips against hers and kissed her deeply. After a moment she pulled away. "I am not sure that would work."

"We could go somewhere no one fights or argues anymore," he said in his most coaxing voice.

"That would be a long way from here," she said sadly. "Much too far away."

"We could go to America," he suggested with a smile.

"But that would mean leaving my family," she lamented.

"We would be together," he countered.

"But we would be alone. And besides, I have—"

Just then, Ahmad, Suheir's older brother appeared. "Papa is coming," he gasped.

Suheir leapt to her feet, her eyes wide with fright. She gestured desperately to Auerbach with both hands. "You must go quickly."

"Perhaps I should stay and talk to him," Auerbach said casually. He was still seated on the ground where he'd been before and leaned back on his elbows. "I'm sure we could sit and talk things over. Come to a reasonable solution."

"No," Ahmad insisted with a shake of his head. "That would not be a good idea."

"I can reason with him," Auerbach argued.

"No," Ahmad said firmly. "You can't."

"Why not?"

"Because he is coming to kill you." Ahmad spoke through clinched teeth. "Don't you understand anything?"

"Why would he want to kill me?" Auerbach protested. "I have done nothing wrong."

"To him you have defiled the honor of his daughter and of our family," Ahmad said in an exasperated tone.

"I haven't defiled anything."

"To him, you are an infidel, the most godless of people alive. Just being with her is cause enough."

The sound of footsteps drew nearer. "Run," Suheir pleaded. "Please! I beg you. Run!"

"I will do my best to stall him," Ahmad said, tugging at Auerbach's arm. "Get up and go."

Reluctantly, Auerbach rose from his place on the ground and kissed Suheir once more. "I will see you tomorrow," he said, then walked quickly away. When he'd taken only a few steps he heard the angry voice of a man shouting from behind him. "Suheir! If you are with that Jew, you will get the same thing I'm going to give him! I have warned you. You must not ..."

Auerbach didn't wait to hear the rest but broke into a run and sped toward the kibbutz compound as fast as his legs would carry him.

— • —

Natan Shahak was outside the shop at the kibbutz, his head bent low over the engine compartment of a truck, when the sound of Auerbach's footsteps caught his attention. Unlike Auerbach, Shahak was born in Palestine to an Austrian couple who moved there in 1935. Last year, when he turned nineteen, he left home to make his own way. A childhood friend told him about the farm at Degania and he applied for admission. The kibbutz admitted him because he had farming experience and he knew how to work on the equipment.

Shahak glanced up to see Auerbach, out of breath and gasping for air, as he stumbled into the compound. Shahak came from the truck and caught him just before he hit the ground.

"Take it easy," Shahak said as he moved Auerbach toward the shade. "Why are you running? What happened?"

Auerbach pulled free of Shahak's grasp and bent over, his hands on both knees, trying to catch his breath. "I was with Suheir," he panted.

"Then why were you running so hard?" Shahak asked.

"Her father didn't like it."

Shahak's expression turned serious. "I told you this wouldn't work out. This is not Chicago. Arab families will never accept the American way of life."

"Relax," Auerbach cooed. "It's nothing."

Movement at the compound gate caught Shahak's eye. "I don't think it's nothing to him," Shahak said with a nod in that direction.

Auerbach glanced over his shoulder to see Suheir's father at the gate. "Walk with me," Auerbach said, and he took hold of Shahak's arm, positioning himself with Shahak blocking the line of sight from the gate. "Don't let him see me," he continued as he pulled Shahak with him past the corner of the building.

"Why are you hiding from him?"

"I was with Suheir this morning. In that clump of bushes where we like to meet."

"What did you do to her?"

"Nothing," Auerbach insisted.

"He didn't chase you away for nothing. What did you do?"

"Nothing," Auerbach said with a sheepish grin. "I just kissed her. That's all."

"This isn't going to be good," Shahak warned.

From behind them came the sound of angry voices, but neither of them dared peek around the corner of the building to see what was happening. Then Hanoch Keret, the leader of the kibbutz, arrived. "Rashid Hadawi and his son are at the gate," he said with more than a hint of irritation. "He's demanding to see you, Auerbach. Were you with that girl again?"

"I just kissed her," Auerbach protested. "That's all. Just one kiss."

Keret sighed. "We warned you to leave her alone."

"I can't," Auerbach whined. "I love her."

Keret shook his head in disbelief and started back toward the gate. Shahak went with him. When they arrived, Keret said with a polite smile, "I'm afraid he's not here right now. No one seems to know where he is."

Rashid pointed an index finger at Keret. "You tell that American Jew I'll be back. I'm not going to forget about this. I will have my revenge. No stupid American Jew is going to defile my daughter and live to talk about it!" he shouted. "Allah will give me his life." Then he turned and walked away.

Ahmad, who had been standing quietly to one side, waited until his father was a few paces away, then turned to Shahak. "I will fix this with Papa," he said in a voice that was little more than a fearful whisper, "but Yaakov must not see Suheir again. Ever."

"I understand," Shahak nodded. "You'll explain it to your sister?"

"She already knows," Ahmad said grimly.

— • —

At dinner that evening, Shahak sat with Auerbach and told him what Ahmad said. "Keret is not pleased with you either. Neither is the leadership council."

"What do they care about my love life?"

"They care nothing of your love life, as long as it does not threaten the community."

"I just love her," Auerbach said with a moon-eyed expression. "That's all."

"That's not all," Shahak snapped. "You aren't thinking. This is Palestine, not Chicago, or New York, or Atlanta, or any of those other places in America you used to talk about. This is the Galilee. Arabs do not tolerate us. They will not accept our marrying their daughters. They would kill us."

Auerbach had a pained expression. "But I can't live without her. I love her."

"You'll have to get over it. Learn to love someone else." He pointed to a woman across the room. "What about her?"

"She's seeing Benny Goldstein."

"Not anymore," Shahak said with a grin. "She moved back to her room two days ago."

Auerbach studied her a moment, then shook his head. "Not really my type."

— • —

A few days later, Auerbach was working in a field away from the compound in the opposite direction from where Suheir lived. Shahak was there, repairing a belt on a tractor. As he glanced up to reach for a wrench, he saw Auerbach staring into the distance. A moment later, Auerbach tossed aside the hoe he'd been holding and hurried toward the road that ran along the edge of the field. Shahak started after him. "Hey," he called. "What's the matter?" Then he saw Ahmad Hadawi, Suheir's brother, walking up the road a few meters away. At the sound of Shahak's voice, Ahmad glanced back over his shoulder and saw Auerbach coming behind him. "You shouldn't be seen with me," Ahmad cautioned.

"*You* came by the field," Auerbach smiled. "This is our field. I didn't come to you. You came to me."

Ahmad smiled. "I didn't realize where I was."

"Tell Suheir I miss her."

"She is not here," Ahmad said, lowering his voice. "I came by here hoping to see you so I could tell you."

"Where is she?"

"Papa sent her to Jerusalem to live with our uncle."

"For how long?"

"Until she is properly married."

"I would marry her," Auerbach offered.

Ahmad frowned. "A Jew married to an Arab? I do not think that will happen for a long time to come."

"What's the uncle's name?" Auerbach asked.

"You cannot find her." Ahmad wagged his finger. "And you should not try."

"Why not?" Auerbach shrugged.

"They will never allow you to see her and if you try you will only cause trouble for everyone." Ahmad turned to leave, then glanced back once more. "But I will tell her you asked about her."

Auerbach stared after him, watching as Ahmad walked away. When he was gone, Shahak came to Auerbach's side. "You aren't seriously thinking of trying to find her, are you?"

"How can I go on if she isn't here?" Auerbach gestured to the fields around them. "This only means something because of her."

"What about the dreams you had? Joining us as we build a Jewish state with our own labor and all that?"

"Labor means nothing compared to love," Auerbach sighed.

"You're sick," Shahak chuckled. "Really sick."

"Yes," Auerbach laughed. "I am sick. Sick with love."

— • —

When Ahmad returned home that evening he found his father, Rashid, waiting outside the front door. "First your sister. Now you," he said with an angry scowl.

Ahmad was puzzled. "What do you mean?"

"You were seen talking to that Jew," Rashid fumed. "The one no one could find when we went to the compound."

"I was passing by the field where he works," Ahmad explained. "He did not come to me."

"All the worse. You went to him."

"He is not so bad."

"Every Jew is bad for us."

"He's not really much of a Jew," Ahmad smiled. "He's an American."

"Even worse still," Rashid growled. "A Jew who doesn't follow his own religion."

"He means no harm." Ahmad glanced away, hoping to deflect his father's anger.

"Listen to me. American Jew, European Jew, French Jew, German Jew—they all share a common purpose. They intend to take control of this country. It's our country and they intend to steal it from us and if that doesn't work, they mean to take it by force."

"By force?" The words sounded more argumentative than Ahmad intended, but he did not apologize as he continued. "No one forced the emirs to sell them the land they now farm."

Rashid's eyes narrowed. "War is coming and there will be blood on every hand."

"I do not think it will come to that."

"Have you heard the news?"

"No," Ahmad replied. "What news?"

"They blew up the King David Hotel."

"That makes no sense," Ahmad frowned. "Where did you hear this?"

"Ismail heard it on his radio and told me." Rashid stepped closer and his voice softened. "War is coming, Ahmad, and all the Jews will be killed.

The mufti is making plans for it now. If you are associated with the Jews, even the nice ones, you will be killed. You must have nothing to do with those people."

That night, Ahmad lay on his bed thinking of all his father had said—blowing up the hotel in Jerusalem, the mufti making plans to kill them all. Ismail might be right, that the Jews did it, but he was certain all the talk of war and killing them all was nothing more than the dreams and fears of an older generation. Still, he wondered what might be happening elsewhere that gave life to such wild rumors, and he wondered what Suheir was doing in Jerusalem. "There is one way to find out for certain," he whispered to himself. He could go there and see with his own eyes. Then he would know if his father was telling the truth. He could stay a few days, visit with relatives, check on Suheir, and still get back by the end of the week.

When everyone in the house was asleep, he slipped from beneath the covers and dressed. Moving quietly, he took clothes from the chest by the door and stuffed them into a canvas bag, then slipped on his sandals. As a last thought, he scribbled a note telling his father where he was going and left it on the bed. Then he tiptoed from the house and started toward the road. Hopefully, a truck would pass by before long and he could get a ride, maybe even one that would take him all the way to Jerusalem.

CHAPTER 21

HAJ MOHAMMAD EL-HUSSEINI, the grand mufti of Jerusalem and de facto leader of Palestinian Arabs, sat in his Jerusalem home, propped on a cushion before a low table. Next to him was Wasif Sarid, a Muslim academic whose writings held great sway with teachers in the madrassas, and beyond him was Anis Aburish, a Muslim cleric from a mosque near the center of the city. Across from them were Mourid Dajani and Mahmoud Beidas, merchants and partners with shops in Jerusalem, Haifa, and Ashdod. All of them were leaders of the fledgling Palestinian nationalist movement and they had gathered to consider their next course of action in the long effort toward ridding the country of both the Jews and the British.

"I am certain you all will agree," Husseini began, "British indifference has emboldened the Jews to ever more aggressive attacks."

"They are true infidels," Dajani groused, "and know no bounds of decency."

"I still cannot believe they blew up the hotel," Beidas said with a slow shake of his head. "Their offices are located there. It's as if they're attacking themselves."

"But," Dajani noted, "They blew up the south wing. Jewish Agency offices are in the north wing. Only the British are in the wing they hit."

"Very clever," Beidas agreed. Then turning to Husseini he said, "However, the heart of the matter is as you have said. The failure of the British to impose discipline has emboldened the Jews. Now they are engineering prison breaks, killing British soldiers, and destroying even the oldest and best-established businesses. This is nothing short of an attack on the economic heart of our existence."

"But what can we do?" Sarid asked. "If the British with all their military might cannot contain them, what could we do to rein them in?"

"There is only one solution," Husseini's gaze moved around the table, falling on each of their faces. "We must make them pay. The Jews. The British. All of them. We must make them pay dearly."

"This is good," Sarid agreed. "The only way they will ever leave is if we make it too costly for them to stay."

"But this would require more military resources than we currently have. It would help if we had the full support of all our neighbors," Beidas suggested.

"And who does not support us?" Sarid asked.

"I am concerned that King Abdullah does not freely provide the arms we need," Beidas said. "I expected more from him."

"It is true he talks freely with the Jews," Aburish observed. "Some say he favors them over us and does not want another Arab state in the region. But we are not totally devoid of arms. We have grenades that were seized from the truck that overturned."

"And King Abdullah will eventually come to our aid," Dajani reassured. "But it will take time. Once the British are gone and he no longer has to concern himself with them, he will provide all that is lacking."

"I agree," Sarid nodded. "By the time this is over, he will bring the British to our side. They will be with us as we conquer the Jews and drive them into the sea."

"In the meantime," Husseini interjected, bringing the conversation back to the moment, "we must take the initiative and strike on our own."

"Where do we begin?" Dajani asked.

"We should begin by making the Jewish Quarter a living hell. We have plenty of grenades and many disconsolate youth who would be glad to vent their boredom by lobbing them into the Jewish neighborhoods."

"Yes," Dajani agreed, "but I think we must not view this solely in terms of Jerusalem. We must make Haifa and Tel Aviv unlivable as well."

"And how would you do that?" Husseini asked. "All of us live here in

Jerusalem."

"We have local leaders who will organize it for us," Dajani replied. "All they would need from us is the arms—ammunition and some of those grenades."

Aburish glanced at the others, "We can steal that from the British. Actually, I think they're glad for us to take it."

"And we should take this war into the countryside," Sarid noted. "To the Jewish farming settlements. That would strike terror in their hearts to know that the vaunted Haganah cannot protect them because Allah has blinded them to our presence."

Husseini nodded in agreement as he glanced around the table once more, "You can get this word to our people? That they should rise up against the Jews."

"Yes," they said, nodding as one.

"How soon shall we strike?" Sarid asked.

"If you leave from this house on your way home," Husseini answered, "and your car should strike a Jew along the way, it would not be too soon."

"They had their Night of the Bridges," Aburish said. "We shall respond with a lifetime of jihad."

— · —

Two nights later, the Arab uprising envisioned by Husseini began when three men recruited by Wasif Sarid entered the Jewish Quarter carrying explosives taken from an unguarded British stockpile. They set charges near a pump station for the sewer system and also next to an exposed water pipe in two places. Minutes later, powerful blasts rocked the neighborhood, leaving gaping holes in the city streets and tearing apart water and sewer pipes. Water spewed into the air and raw sewage filled the bomb crater, then oozed along the gutters.

That same evening, on the road just west of the city, a band of Arabs from a mosque led by Anis Aburish attacked an approaching bus filled with Jewish commuters on their way home to Tel Aviv. They stopped the bus, forced everyone out, and shot them at point-blank range. Then, in a frenzy, they hacked the bodies to pieces and set the bus on fire.

The following Friday evening in Haifa, at the urging of Mourid Dajani, an Arab gang barred the doors and windows of a synagogue, set it on fire, and danced around it while it burned to the ground. Other Arabs joined in singing and dancing, while a squad of British soldiers looked on. And so it went in almost every town and village of Palestine, violence building on violence, as Husseini's followers stoked the fears of local Arabs and goaded them to rise up in arms against their Jewish neighbors.

— · —

Back at Degania, Natan Shahak stood watch in the night thirty meters beyond the perimeter fence that encircled the main compound. Outbuildings beyond the fence loomed eerily in the moonlit shadows and he studied them closely, trying to see through the shadows, searching for the slightest sign of suspicious activity. Reports of increased violence from all across Palestine had everyone on edge and though violence was long an accepted way of life for them, this latest wave of terror was different, more pronounced, more evil than before. In response, the settlement leaders had redoubled their security effort, assigning everyone to a three-hour watch that continued around the clock.

As Shahak stood there in the darkness, a rifle cradled in his arms, he thought of Palestine, the conflict between Arabs and Jews, and the vitriolic rhetoric both sides used against one another. Taken like that, in the abstract rather than the personal, it was easy to fall into the widely accepted characterization of hatred and the resulting angry reaction, but when he thought of the Arabs he actually knew the language of conflict seemed overdone. Most of the Arabs he knew were quite friendly and seemed tolerant of his Jewish heritage. Some he even counted as friends. Ahmad certainly was. And his father, Rashid, had been cordial until Yaakov Auerbach noticed his daughter. Yaakov Auerbach…remembering him put a smile on Shahak's face.

After the incident in the field when Ahmad came to tell them Suheir had been sent to Jerusalem, Auerbach had spent a restless several days alternately working at a manic level then skulking about in a deep depression. Then Shahak arrived at breakfast one morning to learn from Auerbach's roommate that he had left the kibbutz. No one seemed to know exactly when or how, but most speculated he was on his way to Jerusalem in search of Suheir. Others suggested they should take wagers on how long it would be before Auerbach turned up dead. Shahak wondered, too.

Although he felt certain Auerbach had gone in search of Suheir, Shahak was not so convinced that he would meet the painful end others suggested. Like most that came from America to live in Palestine, Auerbach was woefully ignorant of life there and shamefully devoid of any understanding of Islam, but he had a way of getting through tough situations unscathed. No matter how the odds were stacked against him, he always seemed to come out in a better position than he started.

Suddenly, a noise from one of the outbuildings interrupted Shahak's thoughts. He took a flashlight from his belt and shined it in that direction. Someone darted from behind a building. "Hey!" Shahak shouted. "Stop!" As he raised the rifle to his shoulder, a muzzle flashed and with it came the sound of gunfire. Bullets whizzed past his head. He dropped to a knee and shot back in the direction from which the attack had come.

Behind him, he heard footsteps as men raced from the dormitory to join him, each hurrying to their assigned positions. A moment later, Keret crouched at his side. "What is it?" he asked alertly.

"A man ran from the shed and ducked behind the pump station," Shahak said. "But gunfire came from that direction." He pointed to the right. "I'm not sure how many there are."

"Well, let's see if we can find out," Keret drew a flare pistol and pointed it to the sky. There was a loud bang as he fired the gun and seconds later a flare lit up the night.

"I see three behind the shed!" someone shouted.

"Two more at the pump station!" another added.

"Don't let them blow it up!" Keret called, then leaned toward Shahak. "Stay right here. Hold this position. No one gets past you. Got it?"

"Yeah," Shahak replied. "Where are you going?"

"We need to flank them from the left," Keret explained. "I'll get some men and work our way in that direction." Then he turned away and disappeared.

Shahak stretched out flat on the ground and scanned the area around the buildings. Nerves on edge, heart pounding, he wondered what would happen next. Then he heard the sound of an automobile engine and lifted his head to see. Just then, a car turned from the road and barreled toward the front gate of the perimeter fence. A voice shouted from behind him, "Car! Car! Car!"

As the car passed Shahak's position, he raised the rifle to his shoulder and shot at the front tires, jerking the trigger as fast as his finger would work. The report of the gun rang in his ears and he fired without knowing whether his aim was even close to the target, but at the last moment the car veered, struck a utility pole, burst into flames, and exploded, sending shrapnel into the air.

— · —

Traveling to Jerusalem to find his sister took longer than Ahmad Hadawi expected, but after two days on the road he arrived at their uncle's house where he found Suheir safe and well. At first he spent the days searching for work but when that proved fruitless he simply wandered the streets.

One day, as he sat on the curb outside a store, a young man took a seat next to him. About Ahmad's height, he was perhaps ten years older with a wiry frame and a winsome smile. His name was Khalid Suleiman, a follower of Anis Aburish, the Muslim cleric who helped Haj Mohammad el-Husseini foment the recent Arab uprising. "We see you walking these streets every day, but today you are not walking. Why is that?"

Ahmad was taken aback that someone had noticed him. "I have been searching for work. But there is none to be found and now I am bored." He looked over at Suleiman. "How do you know me?"

"Ah, Mohammad el-Husseini has many eyes."

"Well, if you are so smart, then tell me my name."

"You are Ahmad from Degania in the Galilee. Your sister was sent here to live with her uncle because she was in love with a Jew. And you have come here under the guise of checking to make certain she is safe."

Ahmad did not like the tone of voice but did not want an open confrontation, so he tried to change the subject. "And who are you?"

"I am a man of many names, but you may know me as Khalid."

Ahmad nodded slowly. "Khalid Suleiman," he said with a smile.

"Oh," Suleiman said with pride. "I see my reputation has preceded me."

Even with few friends and contacts in the city, Ahmad had heard of Suleiman's reputation. He was known on the street as a brutal and vindictive person but seeing him now, with his slender physique and disarming charm, he did not seem such a bad person. Still, he was not someone to be trifled with and Ahmad took care in how he responded. "You are known to many," he said cautiously.

"So tell me, Ahmad from the Galilee, if your sister loves one Jew, how many Jews do *you* love?"

Ahmad did not like the implication of that question. "I hold no grudge against anyone," he said, hoping Suleiman would go away.

"That is correct," Suleiman noted. "And your amicable disposition, commendable under other circumstances, has allowed this Jew to defile your sister."

"She was not defiled," Ahmad argued, "and anyway, she wants nothing more to do with him."

"That is not what I heard," Suleiman said with an unsettling smile. "I heard she was sad to leave him and came here under protest."

"Nonsense," Ahmad scoffed. "She is glad to be here and relieved to be away from him."

Suleiman's voice grew serious. "If you had been with us from the beginning, instead of squandering your friendship on Jews, this would never have happened. We never would have let that American Jew defile her. And if he did, we would not have allowed him to live or permitted her to bring such shame on your family."

Ahmad wanted to leave but he felt intimidated. "Father can take care of it," he said, once again attempting to deflect the discussion.

"But he isn't here," Suleiman countered, "and your uncle is weak."

"My father will arrive when his presence is necessary."

"How can we be sure?" Suleiman's voice was no longer friendly at all. "Her relationship with this Jew is casting a cloud over your family and over us all, bringing shame to everyone. And here, outside her father's protection, she is only a young, beautiful, vulnerable woman."

"I told you," Ahmad repeated. "She doesn't want to see him anymore."

"We must—"

"Leave my sister out of this," Ahmad snapped, no longer able to hide from his duty to defend her.

"Perhaps if we knew you were with us that might be possible."

"Why am I so important to your cause?"

"If you are with us, your friends among the Jews will know that our cause runs deep. Deeper than friendship. Deeper than anything. Your father would know this, too. He is an influential man in the Galilee and with your encouragement he could be a mighty force in turning the region in our favor."

Now Ahmad realized there was more to Suleiman's approach. "So, you think you can get to him through me."

"We are offering you an opportunity to join us," Suleiman explained, avoiding the issue. "After the fight is over and the Jews are gone, it will be too late. Too late for you. For your father. Your sister. Too late for your entire family. Perhaps even too late for your uncle."

Ahmad felt trapped. Suleiman was not going away and now he was threatening the entire family. Resisting seemed the worst possible course of action, so he said, "And what does it mean to be with you?"

"Come." Suleiman stood and gestured with a wave of his hand. "We will show you."

— • —

That afternoon, Suleiman led Ahmad and three others down a Jerusalem street in a quiet neighborhood. Not far from the mosque where Aburish presided they came to an alley. Suleiman led them about fifty meters farther where they reached a house with freshly laundered clothes hanging from a line that had been haphazardly strung along the back of the building. The four men crouched there and Suleiman turned to Ahmad. "You see those pants and shirts hanging on the line?"

"Yes," Ahmad nodded.

"Those are British army uniforms. The woman who lives here does laundry for them." Suleiman grinned. "We need four of each."

A frown wrinkled Ahmad's brow. "Four of what?"

"Four shirts. Four pants." Suleiman patted him on the back. "Go get them."

"But they're right there by the back door. Anyone could see me."

"You will find a way," Suleiman chuckled.

"What about the sizes?"

"We don't care about the sizes," Suleiman said in a stern voice. "Quit stalling. Get the clothes. We'll find the men to fit them later."

Ahmad crept from hiding and made his way from the alley to the clothesline. Moving quickly, he snatched the clothes—four pants and four shirts—then darted back to the others. Suleiman grinned with pride. "See," he said laughingly, "that wasn't so tough, was it?"

"We better get out of here," Ahmad said. "She'll come out to check on them before long."

"You didn't know it was that easy to become a criminal, did you?"

"I'm no criminal."

"Whose clothes are you holding?"

Ahmad glanced down at the bundle in his arms. "This is different. I'm just…"

"Yes," Suleiman interrupted. "It is different." He pointed to the clothes. "Those are British army uniforms. Government-issued property of England. They catch you with that they'll shoot you on sight."

"What are you talking about?"

"I'm talking about keeping it a secret," Suleiman said without a smile. "You stay with us, no one will ever know. If you try to leave, you never know who we might tell."

Stealing army uniforms from a clothesline didn't seem like a treasonous offense to Ahmad, but he didn't know much about British law or how their soldiers operated. The things Suleiman said might be correct, or they might not. But he knew one thing for certain: His father would not approve and neither would his uncle. And so, reluctantly, he kept his objections to himself and went along with the others, if for no other reason than to avoid yet one more argument with his father.

As they walked up the alley toward the street, Ahmad moved closer to Suleiman and asked, "Why do we need uniforms?"

"You will see," Suleiman assured him.

"Where will we find someone who fits them? I have no idea what sizes I grabbed."

Suleiman turned to him and his eyes roamed over Ahmad. "I'd say one of them will fit you."

"Me? I'm not putting one of these on."

"Yes, you will," Suleiman nodded confidently. "Yes, you will."

— • —

The next day, dressed as a British soldier, Ahmad steered a truck loaded with explosives down a Jerusalem street. Accompanying him that day was Ibrahim Abbas, one of the men who'd been with him in the alley the day before. The other two men who had been with them were used the night before to steal the explosives. One of them was dead. The other was missing.

Ahmad's palms were sweaty as he gripped the steering wheel and brought the truck to a stop in front of the *Palestine Post* newspaper office. Using both hands for leverage, he set the front wheels sharply to the right, opened the driver's door, and climbed from the cab. Ibrahim got out on the opposite side.

As casually as two men on an afternoon stroll, they walked up the street to a car parked at the end of the block. Suleiman was seated behind the steering wheel. Ibrahim got in back. Ahmad took the passenger seat. When the doors were closed, Suleiman steered the car from the curb, made a U-turn in the center of the intersection, and drove in the opposite direction, away from the parked truck. "You set the detonator before you left?" he asked.

"Yes," Ahmad nodded.

Suleiman glanced around warily. "It should have gone off by now."

"I turned it on," Ahmad insisted.

Suleiman was startled. "Turned it on? You were supposed to—"

Suddenly a loud noise erupted behind them. Suleiman glanced in the rearview mirror and grinned. Ahmad turned in time to see a giant fireball rolling into the sky. Even though he knew it was awful and many were dying from the blast, the sight of the explosion was somehow rewarding.

CHAPTER 22

IN THE EARLY EVENING, Lord John Marbury gathered with a group of men for dinner at Ravenwood Hall, the main house of his family's estate near Chelmsford in Essex County, about sixty kilometers northeast of London. A member of the royal family and the House of Lords, Marbury was an influential man in UK affairs, particularly among sub-cabinet government officials. "That is where the real governing takes place," he often said, "among the less-visible appointees and permanent civil service. That is where one controls the flow of paper and with it the direction of millions."

His ancestors had occupied the grounds of Ravenwood from the time of the Anglo-Saxon invasion and were well known across the region and through the centuries not only for their interest in politics but also for their kind treatment of tenants, their disposition toward benevolent societies, and their devotion to family and friends. Less well known, however, was the family's anti-Semitic predisposition—the few who knew of it would say hatred—which Marbury embraced with zeal and exercised through his leadership of an organization known as The Link.

Founded in England the year Hitler came to power by Lord Arthur Williams, Marquis of Claxton, The Link's stated purpose was that of encouraging positive relations between England and Germany. But the real purpose had been to drum up support for Hitler and to pave the way for a smooth Nazi takeover following the much-anticipated collapse of the British government. Agents from MI5, the United Kingdom's domestic security service, caught wind of that underlying purpose and arrested many of the key members, including Lord Williams. He spent the war in an internment camp and was later sentenced to prison.

Lord Marbury, however, avoided arrest and took over the group, which continued to meet in secret. Now that the war was over, they were working through less obvious means to further the dual Nazi dreams of racial purification and global fascist domination. Though Hitler's demise had dealt them a setback, members of The Link still held out hope of achieving their goal through an emergent, though poorly defined, Fourth Reich.

Most recently, they'd focused on derailing the Jewish drive for statehood and spent much time contemplating ways to defuse the postwar "backlash of Western guilt," which they felt was tipping global policy decidedly in favor of the Jews. To that end, members of The Link gathered quarterly at Marbury's estate for dinner, drinks, and discussion. They ate much, consumed vast amounts of liquor, and engaged in endless discussions but thus far had done very little actual work toward any of their aims. And so, while Palestine descended into chaos, Lord John Marbury once again gathered his guests around the dining table at Ravenwood for yet another meeting.

Seated at the far end of the table opposite his father was Marbury's son, Richard. At the age of thirty he was a graduate of Oxford but unmarried and unambitious, save for the singular desire to inherit his father's title and fortune and take command of the family estate. To Richard's right was Anthony Morrison, undersecretary for Middle Eastern affairs at the UK Foreign Office. Morrison and Richard were roughly the same age and, like their parents before them, lifelong friends, though not of the same station in life. Morrison's family lived as tenants on Ravenwood and he obtained a start in the Foreign Office with Lord Marbury's help. His resulting undying loyalty was but one more example of Marbury's approach to manipulating governmental policy through sub-cabinet officials. Morrison was one of many young men he'd so situated.

Joining them that evening, in addition to the regular attendees, was John Hammersmith, a colonel on active duty in Her Majesty's army. Hammersmith had been invited to the meeting by Leland Coatsworth, the Earl of Chevonshire. They were seated across from each other about midway down the table.

As the first course was served, conversation turned to UNSCOP and the latest news about its work in Geneva. "I hear they are tending now toward partition," someone offered.

Edward Hastings spoke up. "The Jews are manipulating committee members at every turn."

"I hear," Michael Felding, seated closer to Marbury, began, "they have compiled a dossier on every delegate noting all their weaknesses."

"It really makes no difference whether they partition or not," Hastings said rather dourly. "We are withdrawing and that is that. Sometimes I think the prime minister would give the Jews the entire region if they would just let him out politely, but instead he might just be giving it to the Arabs."

"The prime minister hates the Jews as much as we do," Coatsworth countered. "He's getting out because he is weak, personally, not because he's being run out by the Jews."

"Leaving on our own or under duress is the worst possible solution," Hammersmith commented sullenly. "We shouldn't be leaving. We should be fighting." Coatsworth's chest swelled with pride at the contribution of his guest. Hammersmith continued. "The Jews have us acting like Frenchmen instead of like true subjects of the king."

"Hear, hear!" someone said in approval.

"The world needn't wonder why we favor the Arabs," Richard noted. "I mean, purely from a practical matter, we can't survive without Arab oil."

"And under those terms," another added, "it's our survival or the Jews'." He cast a glance around the table. "You all know which side I would choose."

"We certainly are not responsible for the Jewish situation," Coatsworth said with disdain. "They put themselves in this position. Trying to take over the world. I should rather think they got what they deserved."

"And though I loathe him so, the prime minister has now exposed their Jewish conspiracy for what it is," Marbury suggested. "By leaving Palestine abruptly he has placed them at the mercy of those who can perhaps finally finish what Hitler set out to do."

"If the Americans don't come to their rescue," Felding added. "That is perhaps our most pressing problem. The Jews have the Americans under their spell."

"That much is correct," Hammersmith agreed. "However, when we are gone, the armies of Egypt and Transjordan will sweep across Palestine and drive the Jews into the sea before the Americans or anyone else have time to react."

"Egypt and Transjordan?" someone asked. "I should have thought we'd see local Arabs take the lead. After all, it's their land at stake."

"The local Arabs couldn't arrange a daily bath," Hammersmith chortled.

"Then I say good riddance to them all. Let King Abdullah have it. And the Egyptians, too."

"But I sometimes fear the British government is relying too much on the Arabs to solve this problem," Coatsworth added. "I am concerned that if the Jews receive enough outside assistance to put up a stiff resistance, the Arabs will fold their tents and run away."

"Then we should find a way to help the Jews lose," Felding quipped. Those at the table laughed in response.

"What is their source of strength?" Richard asked when the laughter died away. "Perhaps if we could identify that, and put the ax to its roots, we might be able to end this rather quickly."

"Their population is rather young and they don't mind working," someone observed.

"Jewish money from America is propping them up," Felding commented flatly. "Take away the cheap financing from New York and their settlements would crumble in a fortnight."

"Truman's administration is backing them, too."

"I thought Marshall was against the Jews," Richard said.

"He is," Felding noted, "but Truman tends to favor them."

"The Arabs aren't running away," Hammersmith offered. "They're actually seizing the initiative. Indigenous violence is on the rise."

"It's about time," someone noted. "Their country has been invaded. They shouldn't just sit around and watch while the Jews take over."

"They've been taking it away from them for a long time, and right from under their noses."

"Well, they're making them pay dearly now," Hammersmith added. Then to the delight of those seated at the table, he recounted details of several recent Arab attacks, embellishing the parts he knew and imagining the rest. "Jerusalem," he concluded, "is hell for the Jews right now. The road to Tel Aviv, already too treacherous to travel at night, is now a death-trap during the day. Hundreds of Jews have died trying to make the trip."

Felding raised his glass in a toast. "May there be more, and soon." The others lifted their glasses in response. "Hear, hear!" they called. "Hasten the day."

— • —

Later that evening, after guests took their leave, Richard Marbury and Anthony Morrison were alone in the study. Richard was seated behind an oak desk, his feet propped on the desktop, a glass of brandy in his hand. Morrison was sprawled in an armchair nearby, nursing a glass of Scotch.

"Father is right, you know," Richard observed. "The prime minister is weak. Too weak to deal effectively with the situation in Palestine."

"I don't think he could do more," Morrison responded. "There are no real solutions for us to the problems of Palestine, short of all-out war and total occupation by our troops."

"There is one," Richard said with a mischievous smile. "One solution everyone in that room tonight understood but no one wanted to mention."

"What's that?"

"Ben-Gurion."

"Ben-Gurion?" Morrison paused to take a drink. "You think he's the solution?"

"I think Ben-Gurion is the key. He is their real strength. Their only strength. No one else among the Jews has the temerity for such an endeavor as nation building. Without him, the dream of statehood will wither and die. If we eliminate him, we eliminate any possibility of a Jewish nation— at least for the remainder of our lifetime."

"That would be a great relief to many," Morrison sighed.

"Yes, it would," Richard nodded. "But the men in that dining room tonight will not take that action. They are too old, too restrained by convention to even mention it."

"What about that Hammersmith fellow? Think he has the fortitude to do anything daring or creative to effect a good result?"

"No," Richard slowly shook his head. "Hammersmith is just like the others. All talk and that's about it." He looked over at Morrison. "You and I shall have to do it for them," he said quietly.

"You and me?" Morrison chuckled. "Are you out of your mind?"

"I've never been more in my mind." Richard moved his feet to the floor and hunched over the desk. "No one else will act. You and I must do this. For our own sakes, for country, for the king."

Morrison's eyes darted away. "I've never killed anyone in my life," he said nervously.

"But you have contacts," Richard said with a smile.

"Yes," Morrison nodded. "I have contacts."

"And some of them would be glad to do just such a thing as this," Richard continued.

"Yes," Morrison nodded. "They just might."

"And you could put me in touch with them."

"Yes," Morrison nodded again. "I suppose I could." A frown wrinkled his forehead. "But isn't that a bit risky?"

Richard set aside his glass and laced his fingers together, resting them on the desktop in an almost reverent pose. "Listen to me, Anthony. The events of history always come down to the actions of a few who are willing to do what needs to be done to make things turn out right. This thing we are talking about is good and right. For the past two thousand years, the Jews have visited nothing but misery on us all, and for what?" he shrugged. "Because we believe in the Christ? Because we accuse them of His murder? No." He moved his hands apart and shook his head. "Because we have money and they want it."

"They *are* greedy. I'll give you that."

"And that greed at the core of their nature has caused nothing but misery. Because of that, the world has been dragged into countless wars with one group of Jews financing one side, and another financing the opposite. They get rich regardless of who wins while everyone else is left destitute." He leaned forward again, his gaze focused on Morrison. "But we can end it. You and I." He pointed with his finger for emphasis. "We can end it. You with your contacts. Me with the color of royal authority."

Morrison shifted uneasily in his chair. "I wouldn't know where to begin."

"I hear reports of Waffen SS soldiers still living in hiding in Germany and Belgium," Richard suggested.

"I hear those reports, too."

"Perhaps one of them would like a handsome salary, a new identity, safe passage to a place of residence where no one could bother them."

"They might." Morrison sat up straight. "But there are numerous logistical details to address," he cautioned.

"Let's take this one step at a time," Richard smiled. "Locate such a person and put me in touch with him. I'll take it from there," he beamed. "We Marburys have a way of cutting through the clutter."

CHAPTER 23

THE NEXT DAY, Anthony Morrison telephoned Kurt Eckert, a German scientist who'd been captured at the end of the war and brought to England where he worked in aeronautical research. Morrison was in charge of the rescue program—Operation Surgeon—and had become well acquainted with Eckert. They agreed to meet at Kensington Park and went for a walk near the Italian Garden fountain.

"You said it was urgent," Eckert said with a note of concern. "Are we in trouble?"

"No," Morrison replied, unsure how to begin. "No trouble."

"Good. You sounded so ominous I thought perhaps the Soviets were making another inquiry about why I wasn't on that train."

"Don't worry about the train. That was years ago."

"If you knew what happened to the men that were on that train, you'd know why I still worry."

"I know what happened to them and I understand fully." Morrison guided their walk around the back side of the fountain and when they were obscured from view he said in a hushed tone, "I wanted to ask you about something that must be kept absolutely secret."

"Okay," Eckert nodded.

"I'm serious. This must be between only the two of us."

"Sure. I understand. I will tell no one."

Morrison glanced around warily before continuing. "I would like for you to put me in contact with Odessa."

Eckert gave him a blank stare. "I haven't the faintest notion of what you're talking about."

"Look," Morrison said with a hint of frustration, "I know the organization exists and I know you know about it."

"If I don't know what you're talking about," Eckert shrugged, "how can you be so sure that I do?"

"I've read your files," Morrison said in a resolute voice. "I know that you know about Odessa. And you know how to contact them." They walked a moment in silence, then he said once more, "I need you to put me in touch with them."

Eckert began with the careful precision of a scientist, "If such an organization existed, why would you want to contact them?"

"We need their help."

Eckert had a playful smile. "We?"

"We," Morrison repeated flatly. "People at the highest levels of government."

"Anyone could say that. How can I be sure the request you make is legitimate? How can I know that what you are telling me is the truth?"

"You can ask that after all we've been through?"

"I ask that precisely because of what we have been through." Eckert had a serious expression and his voice took on a deeper, studied tone. "If someone wanted to manipulate me for a nefarious purpose, you would be the perfect person they would turn to. No one knows me as well as you do. And there is no one else in the British government whom I trust but you."

"You've never doubted me before. Do you doubt me now?"

"You never asked me to do anything like this before. Never to go back. Always it was about going forward, getting away." The expression on Eckert's face changed to one of curiosity. "But tell me something I never understood. Why were you assigned to me? You're from the Foreign Office. Most of my colleagues were assigned to people from the Defense Ministry. How did I get you?"

Morrison's eyes focused on the ground as they continued to walk. "We all ran many programs back then. Many of them not directly in our normal port-folio." He glanced over at Eckert. "Get in touch with them, Kurt. We need it."

"But what would I tell them—" Eckert caught himself—"if such an organization existed. What would I tell them? You want to talk? You want to have tea? This isn't a group with an office and a telephone and you call them up and say, 'Can I come over?'"

Morrison gestured with his hand. "Tell them we need to meet regarding a solution to the Jewish question in Palestine."

"If this organization existed," Eckert conceded, "and if I knew how to reach them, what reason would they have to trust you?"

"They don't have to trust me. They just have to help."

"And why should they help you? After all, you were the ones who destroyed their beloved homeland, assuming of course such a clandestine organization actually exists."

Morrison turned abruptly to face him. "Look, you can cut the game about whether they exist or not. We think Eichmann is still in Germany and we know that all the remaining SS officers live every day in fear of his capture and what he might say about SS operations."

"I'm sure many of them would like to kill him."

"So," Morrison continued, "tell your Odessa contacts that we can deliver Eichmann to them. They can execute him or send him on his way or do whatever else they want with him. If they want to relocate him, we can get him into South America."

"That would help Eichmann," Eckert nodded.

"It helps everyone."

"How so?"

"By getting him out of Europe, there would be much less chance anyone else would find him. If he can't be found, he can't testify."

"That's a good start, but I think you will need a little more than that to get anyone of standing to meet with you."

"A little more?"

"Yes," Eckert nodded. "Something to sweeten the pot, as you English sometimes say."

"Okay." Morrison gave a reluctant sigh. "A number of German officers are interested in keeping the gold they hid in Swiss bank accounts. The Americans are on the verge of locating it. We can help move that gold to a location where it will be out of American reach."

Eckert appeared skeptical. "You are offering to betray your closest ally merely for the sake of a meeting with someone from this organization you call Odessa?"

"Yes," Morrison readily agreed. "For the sake of a meeting with a legitimate Odessa representative. Someone who can make a commitment and who I know can deliver on it."

"Someone *you* can trust?"

"Someone I know."

"And how will they know who that someone is? They can't possibly know which German officers you know."

"You ask them for the meeting," Morrison explained. "Tell them I need to meet with someone I know has the ability to follow through. They'll understand who to send and what to do."

— • —

Later that week, Morrison returned to his office from a meeting to find his assistant, Julie Benson, waiting with a message from Kurt Eckert. "He phoned right after you left," she told him. "Said he had a question about his status here. Wanted to know if you could help."

"Status?" Morrison replied, trying to appear perplexed. "Why didn't he call the Home Office?"

"I don't know," Julie shrugged. "I'm just delivering the message."

"Very well," Morrison replied. "Did he leave a number?" She handed him a note with the number and turned away. He glanced at it, then walked into his office and closed the door. Using the phone on his desk, he placed a call to Eckert. They arranged to meet at a café a few blocks away.

Eckert was seated at a table in the corner when Morrison arrived. He slid onto a chair opposite Eckert and flagged down a waiter to order coffee.

"You talked to them?" Morrison asked when the waiter was gone.

"My friends tell me there is a conference in Paris next week. Something about a new agreement on tariffs." Eckert forced a bewildered expression. "They called it *gat* or something like that."

"Yes," Morrison nodded. "G-A-T-T. It's an acronym for General

Agreement on Tariffs and Trade. It was signed last year. Most businesses still haven't sorted out what it all means. There's a meeting in about two weeks in Paris to help explain it. But why are you talking about that?"

Eckert ignored the question. "Do you plan to attend that conference?"

"I haven't decided." Morrison was perturbed. "Why are you asking about this? Did you talk to your friends?"

The waiter appeared with a carafe of coffee. He set it on the table with cups and then moved away.

When they were alone again, Eckert gave Morrison a knowing smile. "You should go to the conference."

"Oh," Morrison said, suddenly aware. "That might be a good trip after all."

"Perhaps you will meet an old friend," Eckert suggested.

"Does this old friend have a name?"

"No. But you should be prepared to deliver on the offer you mentioned, just in case."

"Which offer?"

"The one involving safe travel."

"Ah," Morrison nodded. "That one. And how will I meet this old friend?"

Eckert leaned closer and hunched over the table. "He will approach you," he said quietly. "You won't have to search for him."

"How will I know it's him?"

"It will happen like this," Eckert began. "One day you will be walking along the street, perhaps alone, perhaps with others, and a car will come alongside. Someone will call out to you, calling you by name and suggesting you are an old friend—as if they are an acquaintance from high school or university on a trip and surprised to see you. They will invite you for a ride. Do not hesitate to go with him."

— · —

Ten days later, Anthony Morrison arrived in Paris for the GATT conference. While walking back to the hotel from dinner one evening a car pulled alongside. The rear passenger side window lowered and a man seated in back smiled at him. "Need a lift?" The door opened and Morrison crawled into the back seat as the man who'd spoken to him scooted over. When the door was closed, the driver steered the car away from the curb and they started forward.

Morrison wanted to ask a thousand questions about where they were going, but the man beside him in back stared straight ahead with a demeanor that did not invite conversation. Each time he had the courage to open his mouth, Morrison felt apprehensive and so he sat quietly, hands folded in his lap, and stared out the window as the driver negotiated downtown traffic.

In a little while they reached the far side of the city and came to a narrow driveway that led through a gate that appeared to be the entrance to a large estate. The car idled beneath a thick canopy of ancient oaks and followed the drive as it wound in gently-sweeping curves set in an irregular manner until the pavement opened to a wide parking court in front of a five-story mansion. There the car came to a stop.

Built of stone blocks, each one neatly cut and stacked with evenly spaced joints, the house seemed to go on forever in all directions, towering above to the sky and stretching left and right to the horizon. Though solid and majestic, the texture and patina of the stones hinted of their ancient origin, as if they'd been carved by the Romans thousands of years ago, or even by some earlier civilization long since forgotten. Morrison sat in the back seat, staring up at the mansion until the man beside him tapped him on the arm and gestured with a smile toward the door. "This is where you get out. He's waiting for you inside."

Morrison groped for the door handle but before he could get the door open a footman came from the front steps of the house and opened it for him. "He is expecting you," the footman said. "Please follow me." Morrison climbed from the car and dutifully followed up the steps and through the front entrance of the house.

Beyond the door was an entryway that opened into a broad vestibule with a soaring ceiling that stood probably twenty feet above a stone floor. As he paused to take it in, a man dressed in a butler's uniform greeted him. "This way, sir," he said. Morrison followed him down the central hall to a parlor on the left. "Wait here," the butler instructed. "Someone will be with you momentarily."

A portrait of a woman hanging on the opposite wall caught Morrison's eye. He moved closer and stood in front of it, gazing up at the exquisite detail, and wondered how anyone could create such a magnificent work of art. He was still standing there, lost in the moment, when the sound of footsteps approached and Martin Bormann, Hitler's former secretary and confidant, appeared in the parlor doorway. Thought to be dead by most reliable sources, he stood strong, fit, and confident in his German uniform. Morrison recognized him immediately.

"I assume you know who I am."

"Yes," Morrison replied.

"And you are confident I can make good on whatever we discuss here today? They said that was important to you."

"Yes," Morrison smiled politely. "It is and I am sure you can accomplish whatever we might reach an agreement on."

"Good." Bormann's voice was pleasant, almost jovial. "So, tell me, what is this about eliminating the Jewish problem in Palestine?"

"They are on the verge of establishing a state. We would like to prevent that."

"A commendable aim," Bormann noted, "but you've done a shamefully poor job of limiting their ambition so far. How would you propose to succeed at it now? Your American friends are in favor of it. The Russians are in favor of it. The international community is shifting to the Jews. And, as I said, you've failed miserably in allowing things to get this far. So, how do you propose to deny them their precious national state at this late hour?"

"By removing Ben-Gurion."

Bormann arched an eyebrow. "You think that will do it?"

"Ben-Gurion is the key. If he is no longer with them, the effort will die."

"And you come to me for this?"

"You have contacts. Perhaps one of your Waffen SS soldiers would like a new life."

"And you can give it to him?"

"Yes."

"His new life in exchange for Ben-Gurion's old one?"

"That would not be a problem."

"You do realize, don't you, that with what you've told me just now I could bury you? Report it to the right authorities and attempt to exchange it for my own freedom and anonymity."

"We're willing to take that risk."

"Interesting."

Morrison had grown impatient with the cat-and-mouse game. "The person we want must be capable, experienced, able to slip in and out undetected. Once the arrangements are made and the deal struck, he would be on his own to complete the task."

"You've never done this before, have you?"

Morrison ignored him. "Will you arrange a meeting with such a person?"

Bormann seemed concerned. "You wish to talk with someone directly?"

"Yes."

"Hmm," Bormann mused. "I will see what I can do."

"Very well," Morrison replied and turned toward the door. "You know how to get in touch with me when you've set it up."

"You brought the documents for Eichmann?"

Morrison stopped a few paces from the door, reached to the inside pocket of his jacket, withdrew an envelope and then handed it to Bormann. "Everything he needs is in there."

Bormann opened the flap of the envelope and glanced at the contents. He nodded approvingly, "This is good. Except for one thing."

"What's that?"

"I need one more set of documents."

"We had a deal for Eichmann."

"One more set," Bormann insisted. "Or you never hear from me again."

"For whom?" Morrison sighed impatiently.

"For me."

— • —

Two days after returning to London, Anthony Morrison arrived at his office to find an envelope with his name on it sitting on his desk. He opened it and took out a note that read simply, *Pera Palace Hotel, Istanbul. One week from today.*

Five days later, under the guise of attending a meeting with Kemal Ataturk's foreign affairs assistant, Morrison departed for Istanbul, where he checked into the Pera Palace Hotel. Early in the morning of the appointed day, he rode the elevator to the lobby and took a seat at a location near the front entrance from which he could be plainly seen by anyone entering or leaving. He'd been there less than five minutes when a bellman approached. "This way," he said, as if Morrison were expecting him. Without even a hint of hesitation, Morrison rose from his chair and followed the bellman across the lobby and down a hallway to a conference room where the bellman left him.

The room was small with a table large enough to seat four. A floor lamp stood in the corner near a window with a shade that was lowered halfway. Morrison wandered over to the window and gazed out at an empty court-yard at the center of the hotel. He'd been standing there a few minutes when the door opened and a man entered.

"I am Otto Keppler," he said in a businesslike tone. "I understand you wish to see me." He had handsome features, carried himself with discipline and purpose. He spoke perfect English, though with an accent—German, Morrison thought, or perhaps Austrian. "Our friends in Paris seem to think you are a man who can get things done."

Morrison turned from the window and stepped toward him, unsure whether they should shake hands. By the time he was near enough, Keppler had moved his hands behind his back and so Morrison said simply, "We are interested in engaging your services."

"And for what purpose would those services be needed?"

It was all so like a commercial transaction, which suited Morrison fine. He had never done this kind of thing before. "We would use them to apply pressure to the Jews of Palestine," Morrison explained in the efficient, sterile dialect of a diplomat.

"We?" Keppler asked expectantly.

"The British government." There was no point in being coy now. If he was going to do this, then let it be done.

"No," Keppler said with the indulgent smile of a seasoned veteran addressing an amateur. "You mean *elements within the British government.* That's how you say it. Elements. Remember that next time. Otherwise, if this came from the top, I would be talking to someone else and you would be back in London, seated at your desk, wondering what you might have for dinner when the day is over."

"I assure you," Morrison said, unwilling to yield to Keppler's invitation for self-deprecation. "I speak for those in positions of authority in London."

"Very well," Keppler shrugged. "We'll do it your way. What kind of pressure are *we* interested in asserting?"

"We were envisioning a world without David Ben-Gurion."

"Ah," Keppler nodded. "You got that part correct. Envisioning. Imagining. Couch your ideas in language as obscure as possible so it will be deniable later, should you need at some point to reconstruct this moment to put yourself somewhere else." He moved slowly across the room and glanced out the window from the side, as if checking. "You present a most interesting proposition. How much of this task are you prepared to execute yourself?"

"None. That's why we are coming to you."

Keppler glanced back at him. "And what would I get out of this?"

"Ah," Morrison said with a playful smile. "I see at some point we all must show our hand."

"How much?"

"One million pounds deposited in a Swiss account. Half now and half when you finish the job."

"Two million pounds," Keppler said without so much as a glance.

"That's a lot of money."

"Then perhaps you would like to continue searching for someone cheaper." Keppler turned toward the door.

"Okay," Morrison sighed. "Two million. But half now and half later."

Keppler turned back to face him. "And a new identity in a country where no one will bother me."

where no one will bother me."

"Yes," Morrison readily agreed. "So long as you eliminate Ben-Gurion. He is the key."

"Very good," Keppler smiled. "But I do not want the money in a Swiss account."

Morrison looked puzzled. "Why not?"

"Too much attention from the Americans," Keppler explained. He took a pen from his jacket and scribbled a note. "Send it to this account at the Deutsche Bank in Berlin."

"Berlin?"

"Yes."

Morrison was skeptical. "You're sure of this?"

"I am certain."

"All right. Berlin." Morrison glanced at the note and tucked it into his pocket. "How soon can this be done?"

"Hopefully, within weeks."

"That would be good. But I want to be certain you understand, he must be eliminated."

"Consider him gone already."

CHAPTER 24

FOR THREE DAYS AFTER WALKING AWAY from the British detention center, Jacob and Sarah Schwarz made their way across the British sector of occupied Germany, trekking south from Bergedorf, near Hamburg. No one seemed to notice them or pay special attention, but they found sparse assistance, mostly from local churches that offered a cot for the night or a cold meal.

On the fourth day, with the help of a ride from a farmer and a day spent as stowaways on a freight train, they crossed into the state of Hesse. By then, Sarah, normally energetic and active, was exhausted. "We have much farther to go than this," Jacob said as her pace grew slower and slower.

"I know. But I need to rest. To sleep. And I need something filling to eat."

When they left the detention center, Jacob had put aside many fears—of British patrols who might send them back to the camp, thugs who might take advantage of them, or the rumored roving bands of disgruntled Nazis who might shoot them on sight—but the one worry he'd been unable to shake was that of traveling with a woman. Sarah was smart and tough, but to get back to Palestine they needed to get to Paris, where the Jewish Agency had an office. There, he was certain they would find help in making a fresh attempt at immigration and he was aggravated with himself for not thinking of that sooner. They could have ignored the warnings onboard the ship and simply gotten off in France the first time around—on their way to the detention center. Now, reaching Paris would be difficult, even for a man who wouldn't mind sleeping in the open and scrounging for food. Making the trip with Sarah would be another matter, but he hadn't counted on it being this difficult. He'd hoped they would be in France by the fourth day but they were still in Germany.

When they arrived in Kassel, a town in the German province of Hesse, they found a large green tent standing in the center of the town square. A line of townspeople stretched from it in two directions and the smell of food wafted through the air.

"An army kitchen?" Sarah asked expectantly.

"I don't know," Jacob replied warily. "Maybe we should keep going."

Sarah came to a stop. "Think they will give us something to eat?"

"I don't know. Men in uniforms are standing beneath the tent. They appear to be soldiers. I think we should avoid them."

"I'm hungry," Sarah grimaced. "Can't we just see who they are?"

"If they are British soldiers," Jacob worried, "they might recognize us and send us back to the camp."

"How would they recognize us? There are so many wandering the roads just like us."

"But not so many who were on the *Exodus* and sent to a detention center. Perhaps they have posters with our pictures. The Nazis would do that, and they would find us. They found almost everyone who escaped."

"The British are not the Nazis," Sarah replied without shifting her gaze from the tent.

"I am not so sure."

Sarah looked over at him and gave his arm a playful tug. "You are so handsome when you worry like that. Trying to protect me." She gestured with a nod and a smile. "Come on. Let's go see who they are. Then we will decide what to do. It will only take a few minutes. Besides, I don't think I can go much farther without eating."

Reluctantly, Jacob acquiesced and with Sarah holding tightly to his arm they made their way along the edge of the crowd, studying the men standing beneath the tent, watching, listening. They were soldiers—that much was certain—but Jacob couldn't tell whose. Like the canvas tent, their uniforms were green but they didn't appear to be British. These were different, less kept, less fussy. Then one of the men turned to the side and

Jacob saw a patch on his shoulder. A broad grin spread over his face. "Look," he directed Sarah's gaze. "He has an American flag on his shoulder."

"This is good," Sarah grinned. "This is very good."

"Yes," Jacob nodded. "The Americans will not turn us away hungry." He led her to the end of the nearest line and they shuffled ahead with the others, hoping for their first hot meal since Tel Aviv.

When they reached the tent they found serving tables filled with bins of food. A soldier handed them both a metal plate and fork. Farther down the line they received a generous helping of potatoes, green beans, roast beef, and a thick slice of bread. At the end, someone set a small piece of cake on top. It was more food than they'd eaten in weeks.

A church stood on the far side of the square with a stone ledge that ran the length of the building beneath beautiful stained-glass windows. Jacob and Sarah found a seat on the ledge, rested their plates in their laps, and began to eat.

"Go slowly," Jacob cautioned. "You don't want to get sick." Sarah gave him a questioning look, but with his head bent over the plate he didn't notice.

When they finished eating, Jacob returned the plates and utensils to the tent, then came back for Sarah. "I don't think I can travel any farther today," she said. "I need to rest."

Jacob wanted to keep moving and tried his best to persuade her to continue but she insisted on staying, so they wandered inside the church in search of a place to spend the night. A priest met them as they came up the center aisle. He was friendly and seemed genuinely interested, so when he pressed for details Sarah told him of their saga. When he learned they had been passengers on the *Exodus* he was intrigued, and when she told him they were trying to reach Paris, his face lit up. "I am going there tomorrow. You can ride with me."

That evening, the priest took them to the church parsonage where they once again had a hot meal. Afterward, Sarah had a warm bath and slept with Jacob in a real bed.

The following morning, Jacob awakened at dawn to find Sarah in the bathroom, bent over the toilet with nausea. "Perhaps it was the food we ate yesterday," she suggested.

"Perhaps it is that we finally had some food. My stomach isn't doing so well, either."

Sarah nodded politely but said nothing more.

After a breakfast of bread and jam they departed for the ride to Paris. Four hours later, they reached the French border. The priest had German identity papers, which satisfied the guard, but when they searched the trunk of the car they found only his suitcase.

"Three people," the guard said with a curious twinge of an eyebrow. "But only one suitcase."

With the defeat of Germany, the exiled French government returned, bringing with them a reluctance to admit refugees from other parts of Europe. Allied agreements called for the free movement of displaced persons from country to country as a way of helping those who'd been left homeless by the war to find a place to begin again. France, however, being occupied by the German army, had not been a party to those agreements and thus wanted to accept only its former residents. Sarah and Jacob were Polish citizens, a fact readily discernible from the papers they carried.

Still, the priest had a way with words and after an hour at the border convinced the guards that Jacob and Sarah were legitimate refugees attempting to reach Paris for the purpose of leaving Europe for Palestine. Then a bus arrived at the checkpoint with thirty passengers awaiting his attention and reluctantly the guard stamped their papers with entry permission and sent them on their way.

Five hours later, they arrived in Paris. It was dark by then and the priest invited them to stay with him at the home of a friend.

The following morning Jacob once again found Sarah in the bathroom struggling with nausea. This time there was no meal to blame, so he said nothing but in his heart he knew what was wrong.

Later that morning they walked a dozen blocks up the street to the Jewish Agency. A bewildered receptionist listened to an abbreviated version of their story, then scurried off to find someone to help. At first no one seemed to know what to do, but finally they were ushered into Jules Stavisky's office. He listened quietly as Jacob and Sarah once more recounted the story of surviving the war, the displaced-persons camp, their attempt to reach Palestine aboard the *Exodus*, their escape from the detention center, and their desire to return to Palestine. When they finished he took a note pad from the corner of his desk and scribbled a message, folded it in half, and handed it to Jacob. "I have a friend at the French Foreign Office. Pierre Schuman. Ask for him by name and give him this note."

"You are certain it is safe? We do not have French papers."

"Don't worry," Stavisky smiled. "It is absolutely safe."

"How far away is the Foreign Office?" Sarah asked.

Stavisky rose from behind his desk "Not far. But don't worry. I will call a cab to take you there." He came around the end of the desk and walked with them toward the door. "Ask for Pierre by name and remember to give him the note." He stepped aside while they moved into the hall, then led them down the steps to the front entrance.

Outside, a taxi waited at the curb. The driver opened the rear door for them and as Sarah slid into the back seat, Stavisky reached in his pocket and handed Jacob a business card. "This is the card of Golda Meir," he said in a hushed tone. "She works at our office in Tel Aviv. When you get to Palestine—and I'm certain you will—go see her. Tell her I sent you. She will help you."

Jacob had a questioning frown. "A woman?"

"Palestine is not Europe," Stavisky smiled. "She is becoming one of the most powerful people in the region. She will help you find a job and get settled."

"I want to join the army to fight the Arabs."

"She can help you," Stavisky repeated with an indulgent pat on Jacob's back. "Just ask for her and tell her I sent you."

A few minutes later they arrived at the French Foreign Office and, as instructed, asked for Pierre Schuman. When the receptionist on the first floor was reluctant to admit them, Jacob added, "Tell him Jules Stavisky sent us."

Ten minutes later an assistant came for them and escorted them to Schuman's office. He was seated at his desk when they entered the room but rose and offered them a chair when he saw Sarah. After they were seated he looked over at Jacob and asked, "How do you know Jules Stavisky?"

"We met him at the Jewish Agency," Jacob replied.

"Oh," Schuman replied in a less-than-enthusiastic tone. "I thought perhaps you were old friends." He gave a heavy sigh but mustered a polite smile. "Then tell me, what brings you to the Foreign Office?"

For the next ten minutes Jacob recounted again their saga about the war, the camps, and traveling aboard the *Exodus* to Palestine. Schuman, who began as merely an indulgent listener, now sat with rapt attention as Jacob told of all they'd endured, then he excused himself from the office and disappeared.

Jacob turned to Sarah. "Should we leave now?"

"Let's see what happens," she replied in a tired voice.

"Are you okay?"

"I think we both know what my condition is."

A grin spread over Jacob's face. "Our baby will be born in Palestine."

"I've been wondering about that."

"What about it?"

"Is that the best place to deliver a child?"

"You can think of another? You would rather have the child in Poland?"

"No. But I would not mind having the child here."

"We can't stay here," Jacob whispered. "We have no papers."

They talked quietly while they waited and in a little while Schuman returned carrying a large envelope. He closed the office door and took a seat at the desk. "These are your papers," he said quietly. "From this point on, you are French citizens. That is okay?"

"Yes," Sarah replied without waiting for Jacob to speak. "That is good."

Schuman opened the envelope and removed the contents. "This is your ID card." He handed one to Jacob and to Sarah. "Identifying you as citizens."

"French citizens?" Sarah asked.

"Yes. You will be traveling on French documents." He sorted through the papers and handed them both a passport. "And you have a visa from the British government for entry as tourists. It's good for use anytime during the next thirty days." He propped his elbows on the desktop and gave them a satisfied smile. "That will take care of it?"

"Yes," Jacob nodded. "That will take care of it quite nicely."

"Those documents will get you into Palestine and once you are there," he shrugged, "who will find you and send you home?"

Jacob rose from his chair. "You are a true gentleman," he said, then he leaned over the desk and shook Schuman's hand.

— • —

While Jacob and Sarah were at the Foreign Office, Stavisky checked the *Exodus* manifest to make sure they'd actually been passengers. When he confirmed that they had, he made arrangements for them to travel by air to Tel Aviv. "We've made it a priority to return as many *Exodus* passengers as possible to Palestine," he said. "You will be traveling by air day after tomorrow."

"Then we should find a place to stay," Jacob said.

"Do you have a place?"

"No," Sarah replied. "We have nothing."

"Not to worry," Stavisky smiled. "I've taken care of that, too."

That evening, as they ate in the hotel's downstairs restaurant, Sarah returned to the topic they'd discussed earlier. "I've been thinking about this pregnancy," she said softly.

Jacob's eyes opened wide with concern. "Are you not well?"

"I am fine. Except for the morning nausea."

"Then what is the matter?"

"I am concerned about what we will face in Palestine. It is a place of turmoil and uncertainty."

"But we can't stay here. We must go somewhere."

"We have French identity cards and passports."

"But if we stayed here in France, what would we do? How would we live?"

"You could get a job making shoes, as you did before."

"Yes," he nodded. "I suppose I could, but we have no place to stay and the Jewish Agency is only helping us because we were on the *Exodus* and told them we were returning to Palestine."

"I know. But I remember what it was like there before, and though we only saw a glimpse it seemed quite harsh."

"I'm sure it will be challenging but it would also be exciting to be there from the beginning. To work and build a country."

"Do you think there will really be a country? A Jewish nation?"

"Yes," he nodded with a broad smile. "'I will increase the number of men and animals upon you, and they will be fruitful and become numerous. I will settle people on you as in the past and will make you prosper more than before.'"

"Ezekiel again."

"These are the promises God has given us."

"You know, not everyone believes those are still true."

"It doesn't matter what others believe. It only matters what God believes. And what you and I believe."

"What do you believe, Jacob?"

"I believe the words of the prophets are coming true in our lifetime. Israel is being born again."

"Will they call it that?"

"What else could they call it? It will be the nation of Israel."

Sarah smiled. "I suppose so. But they don't call it that right now."

He knelt beside her. "This is important, Sarah. First the nation is reestablished, and then the messiah will finally come."

"I doubt that happens immediately."

"Perhaps not," he conceded. "But without the nation of Israel, it can't happen at all. *With* Israel reborn, we are one step closer to the day."

CHAPTER 25

AS STAVISKY PROMISED, air travel was provided and two days after arriving in Paris, Jacob and Sarah boarded a flight for Tel Aviv. They landed there late in the afternoon and were greeted by an assistant from the Jewish Agency who drove them into town.

When they reached the office, staff members from the political department interviewed them, trying to determine job skills and where they might best be put to work. In the course of that, Jacob showed them Golda Meir's business card and asked to see her. A few minutes later, he and Sarah were escorted into Golda's office, where they found her seated at her desk.

By then, Golda had heard about Jacob and Sarah's trek through Europe and their determination to return to Palestine, but she wanted to hear the story in detail. Staff members were concerned about finding them a place to stay, at least for the night, but Golda seemed not to be concerned at all. Instead, she brought chairs to her desk for Jacob and Sarah and placed them in front of her desk. "Please, tell me about your journey and all that happened."

For the next hour, Sarah and Jacob told their story, some of it for the first time to anyone. Golda was moved to tears. "You are the first passengers from the *Exodus* to make it back to Palestine," she said when they were finished.

"We got a head start," Sarah suggested. "I'm sure the others are still in the camp in Germany."

"Well, we're glad to have you and want to help you get settled," Golda smiled. "What kind of work can you do, Jacob?"

"I want to fight in the army."

"Haganah?" Golda asked with obvious skepticism.

"Yes."

Golda frowned. "I do not think that is such a good idea."

"Why not?"

"I think your wife might object to sending the father of her child into battle so soon after arriving."

"We have no children."

"No," Golda glanced in Sarah's direction, "but you have one on the way, do you not?"

"It would seem so," Sarah chuckled.

"How do you know?" Jacob asked.

"Women know these things," Golda smiled.

"But how?" Jacob insisted.

Sarah patted him on the knee. "We can talk about it later."

Golda pressed again on the issue of work. "What were you doing before the war, Jacob?"

"I was a student. I wanted to be a lawyer but I was a student before the war. And I worked in a shop making shoes."

"We don't have many jobs for cobblers. Most of the work we do is manual labor. Primarily farming."

"I prefer to fight," he said. "To join the army. To defend our new state."

Golda rose from her desk and smiled. "We don't have a state yet, but come on. Let me see if we can find you a place."

Golda led them down the hall toward Eyal Revach's office and along the way stopped to introduce them to several people in the adjoining offices. Revach overheard them talking and came out to listen and when he heard of Jacob and Sarah's ordeal, he led them farther down the hall to see Ben-Gurion.

For yet another time, Jacob and Sarah recounted their journey through the war to Palestine, back to Europe, and then to Paris.

"So," Jacob said at last, "here we are in Palestine, ready to make a new life."

"And so you are," Ben-Gurion replied. "What do you plan to do?"

"My original plan was to work and build a great nation for our people," Jacob beamed, "but with things changing and after the experiences on the ship, I think I would like to fight."

"Fight?" Ben-Gurion seemed not to understand.

"For Palestine," Jacob explained. "For the new state."

"Oh. Yes," Ben-Gurion nodded indulgently. "Hearing someone else talk about it with such enthusiasm and candor is…refreshing."

"War is coming," Jacob argued with zeal. "The British are leaving. The Arabs want us to leave as well. Our people will not go voluntarily. So the Arabs must fight to make us leave. And then there will be war."

Ben-Gurion looked over at Revach, who stood near the door. "This guy knows his stuff," he said with an amused smile. "Can't we find room for him here in the office, with the couriers and messengers?"

"Sure," Revach nodded. "Come on. I'll take you downstairs."

As they started toward the door, Golda took Sarah by the arm. "You come with me. We need to find you an apartment or a room, and you haven't told me what kind of work you do."

— • —

With Jacob trailing behind, Revach led the way downstairs to a large holding room at the back of the building. A dozen young men were sitting there, reading the newspaper and napping. Revach called to an older man who was standing at a bulletin board on the far side of the room. "Hey, Gavriel. I have one more for you."

"I got no room for one more," Gavriel called in reply as he turned to face them.

"Sure you do," Revach cajoled. "There's always room for one more good man." He put his hand on Jacob's shoulder. "This is Jacob Schwarz. He was on the *Exodus* when it arrived here. Broke out of the British detention camp in Europe. Just made it back to Palestine today. Ben-Gurion wants him as a courier and aide." Without waiting for a response, Revach turned to Jacob. "His name is Gavriel. Most of the time we call him Gabby. He can be a little difficult at times but he's a good man and he works hard. Whatever he tells you to do, that's what you do, got it?"

"Yes. I'll do my best."

"Good." Revach patted him on the shoulder. "I know you will." Then he turned away and left the room, leaving Jacob to face Gavriel and the others alone.

— • —

"You get a place to sleep and plenty to eat when you're on duty," Gavriel growled. "And they pay you a few Palestinian pounds a week for your trouble."

"Okay," Jacob nodded, not knowing what else to say.

Gavriel pointed to one of the men seated along the wall. "That guy on the end is Yehuda Geller. He's been with us the longest. He'll show you what to do."

Geller rose from his chair and walked across the room to Jacob. They shook hands, then Geller gestured with a nod. "Come on. I'll show you where to put your things." He led the way across the room to a hallway and into a room with rows of cots. "This is where you sleep. Yours is over there next to the wall."

"Hottest place," Jacob observed.

"And the coldest," Geller added. "But after you've been here awhile you can move up to a different spot."

"How's that?"

"We lose one or two men a month, so when they're gone everyone who came in after them moves up."

"Where do they go?"

The question caught Geller off-guard for a moment, but he recovered quickly to say, "They die."

"Oh." Jacob was embarrassed. "I'm sorry. I didn't realize."

"Yeah. It's a dangerous job. So keep your eyes open and your mouth shut." Geller pointed. "We work three days on and one day off, but sometimes we just work straight through and nobody knows what the schedule is. The main point is that whatever we're told to do, we have to get it done. This isn't a job with a time clock." He pointed to a wooden footlocker at the end of Jacob's cot. "Put your stuff in there when you come on duty, but don't bring a lot of stuff. You won't need it and somebody might borrow it while you're out on a run."

"What exactly do we do?"

"Deliver messages, mostly. Sometimes we drive the car for officers and dignitaries. But mostly we deliver messages, letters, envelopes, that sort of thing." Geller pointed to a door. "That leads outside where the bikes are parked."

"Bikes."

"Yeah. Bicycles. You can ride, can't you?"

"Yes. I can ride a bicycle. That's what we use to deliver messages?"

"Most of the time. Unless it's just up to the Red House, then we walk. Quickly. And we have a couple of motorcycles."

Jacob had hoped for something more challenging. "I never imagined I would have a job in Palestine delivering messages."

"Hey," Geller replied defensively, "it's a great job and we do a lot more than just deliver messages. You'll see. This job puts us at the heart of all the great events. Whatever happens, we know about it before anyone else and we get to have a hand in determining the outcome."

"I like that. And I'm glad to be here."

"Good. Let's hope you feel the same way after your first run."

— · —

With Golda's help, Sarah and Jacob settled into a small apartment not far from the Jewish Agency headquarters. Jacob's work, though not what he had planned to do, proved more interesting than he'd expected. It soon occupied most of his attention and kept him away from home for days at a time. Sarah went to work in Golda's office.

At first her tasks were simple—typing records, proofreading press releases, and filing correspondence—but very quickly she moved on to work with newly arrived immigrants and help organize relief for those who'd suffered loss from Arab attacks. A few weeks into the job, she accompanied Golda with Diana Ladenburg and two others to a meeting in Haifa to discuss conditions at a local school. Diana drove and Sarah sat in back.

They had a pleasant ride up the coast and received a warm welcome when they arrived. Sarah sat to one side and did nothing all day, which left her wondering why she'd been brought with the others.

When the meeting concluded, they rode over to the waterfront. From the street she could see the warehouses where they'd been forced to stay after the British removed them from the *Exodus*. The sight of it sent a shudder through Sarah's shoulders, but no one seemed to notice either her reaction or the buildings.

A moment later they turned down a quiet street just across from the docks. Sarah glanced out the window to see a residential neighborhood. "We have another appointment?" she asked, still wondering why she'd been told to accompany them.

"Yes," Golda replied from her place in front. "This one is for you."

"For me?" Sarah asked, now more concerned than ever. "I did not know I had an appointment. What am I to do? I am not prepared."

"You will do fine," Golda assured. "Don't worry."

A little way farther, they turned off the street onto a driveway that led into a cemetery and a moment later Diana brought the car to a stop. Golda threw open the front door of the car. "Come, you will want to see this."

Sarah rose from the back seat and followed Golda. The others trailed behind as they made their way past rows of graves to one with a simple plain marker. "There," Golda quietly pointed at the marker. "This is what we wanted you to see."

Tears filled Sarah's eyes as she whispered the name. "Avi Livney. A martyr for the cause aboard the *Exodus*. July 18, 1947."

Golda moved beside Sarah and put her arm around her waist. "I am sorry they did not allow you to attend his service. We tried our best. Ben-Gurion himself argued with the High Commissioner about it, but they would not relent." She gave Sarah a hug. "We wanted to bring you here so you could at least see where he was buried."

Tears streamed down Sarah's cheeks. "It was awful." Her top lip quivered as she spoke. "I tried to be strong for Jacob's sake, but it was awful," she sobbed. "One minute he was there, and the next he was dead. Lying there on the deck of the ship with blood ..." She looked over at Golda.

"Why did they do that? Why did they do that to him? To me? To Jacob? To all of us. Why?"

"We have been asking those questions for a long time," Golda replied calmly. "And still we do not have the answers. But we know a way to prevent them from doing it again."

"How is that?"

"We will create for ourselves a country where justice for our people truly reigns. Where no one chooses our destiny except we ourselves."

"But there is violence all around us," Sarah countered.

"Yes," Golda nodded slowly. "And I think we shall always be subject to attack from our neighbors. But not from ourselves and not from the government that rules us. Not ever again."

CHAPTER 26

AFTER VISITING THE DISPLACED-PERSONS CAMPS in Austria and Germany, UNSCOP members returned to Geneva and entered again into deliberations amid tight security. From their room on the fifth floor, Shai operatives listened to the formal discussions in each session. In addition, using strategically placed listening devices and a large network of agents posing as hotel employees, they monitored informal conversations that took place among delegates and their advisers in the halls and rooms after hours. Information gleaned from each day's events was methodically summarized, analyzed, and disseminated through a memo that was delivered to Jewish Agency participants and Haganah operatives the following morning.

From the opening session, even before they toured the camps, committee members agreed that the British mandate should end. Beyond that, however, they disagreed on almost every other point and over the next several weeks the committee meetings quickly moved from examination of evidence to a battle over whether to partition Palestine into two separate states—one Jewish, the other Arab—or allow the Arabs to control the entire region. As that nexus of contention became clear, Abba Eban and Moshe Sharett discussed their options.

"If the choice is partition or nothing," Sharett opined, "then we have no choice but to take partition."

"Absolutely," Eban agreed. "Ben-Gurion and the others in Tel Aviv have already indicated that is their preference as well."

"Are they still receiving summaries of the daily memos?"

"Yes," Eban nodded.

A quizzical smile turned up the corners of Sharett's mouth. "Think we should contact anyone for direction or clarification?"

"Who else would we contact?" Eban shrugged.

Sharett arched an eyebrow. "We could arrange a meeting with Weizmann."

"I don't think so," Eban said, shaking his head. "He's much too academic for this and we can't afford to waste time with another of his cerebral exercises. It's decision time. I think we should proceed with the direction we already have."

"Okay," Sharett nodded. "I do, too." He sat up straight in his chair. "So, what do we need to achieve to ensure that the committee produces a report favoring partition?"

"I see two basic elements. First, we need a majority of delegates to support the idea and then favorable language in the report."

"I suppose—other than the question itself of whether to partition or not—we'll have a fight over where to draw the boundary lines."

"Maybe," Eban nodded. "But the Arab High Committee has been categorically opposed to partition and decidedly unengaged in the discussion of alternatives to their demand for total control of the region. If the committee decides to partition, we might see the Arabs refuse to participate further. They might see a discussion of boundary locations as acquiescing and I don't think they're going to acquiesce to anything other than a gun and a sword."

"That's probably correct," Sharett agreed. "So then it comes down to delegate counts. Where do we stand?"

"I think we play it just like we did on the earlier vote about visiting the camps," Eban suggested. "In fact, I think that vote gave us a glimpse of where everyone stood in general. Iran, India, and Yugoslavia will vote against partition and there's no way we can change that. If we can't convince Canada and Australia to vote in favor of it, then we need them to abstain. The Netherlands, Czechoslovakia, Sweden, and Peru will support whatever is most favorable to us. Their support is solid. So if we can get Canada and Australia to remain neutral, then Guatemala and Uruguay will put us over the top."

"Bunche will be writing the report?"

"Yes."

"Is he in favor of partition?"

"He's a practical guy. I think he sees it as the only viable alternative."

"Okay," Sharett sighed. "I'll take the delegates from Guatemala and Uruguay. You take Canada, Australia, and Bunche. Keep the delegates at least neutral and make sure we see Bunche's report before he gives it to the committee members."

For the next four weeks, Eban and Sharett spent every waking hour lobbying, cajoling, and coaxing the delegations from Canada, Australia, Guatemala, and Uruguay. At the same time Eban met regularly with Bunche to keep tabs on his work in developing the committee's written report. Gradually, Uruguay and Guatemala joined the regular session discussions and threw their support behind a proposal for partition.

With that development, Sharett and Eban were comfortable they could attain the necessary support for the committee to adopt a report favoring partition. As a consequence, they turned greater attention to the text of the report. Shai operatives on the hotel housekeeping staff regularly searched Bunche's room. Trash from the room was collected and analyzed for every possible scrap of information that might indicate his thoughts on the matter. Admoni and those working in the room on the fifth floor stepped up their efforts to electronically monitor Bunche's conversations, both personal and by telephone. All the while, Sharett continued to meet with delegates in an effort to keep them focused on the issues at hand.

Then one morning as Sharett ate breakfast in the hotel restaurant, Jorge Granados, the delegate from Guatemala, stopped by. "I understand Peru has yet to declare its position on this matter of whether to divide the region."

"Yes," Sharett nodded.

"No doubt you are counting on their support."

"Ulloa is a conscientious man. I think he is merely trying to be deliberative."

Granados was worried. "I am not so sure."

"Oh?"

"I noticed the Arab delegation has been paying him much attention since we returned from visiting the camps."

Sharett arched an eyebrow. "The usual enticements one might expect under these circumstances?"

"No," Granados replied. "Ulloa is above reproach. He would never yield to temptations of the flesh. He is, however, very much a man of Peru, having held many offices in the government there, both elected and appointed, as I am sure you already know. I understand he is genuinely concerned about his country's economic development. The Arabs seem to be interested in it also."

In their analysis of potential support, Sharett and Eban had counted Ulloa as solidly in their favor, a position supported by his earlier comments and votes regarding other committee action. That he had not yet publicly declared his support for partition had been of no particular concern. The Czech delegation had also not yet made its position public. Now news from Granados called all of that into question.

Ulloa was known as a man who took his work seriously and who would want to reserve public comment until after he had reviewed the evidence, even if he had already made up his mind beforehand. But if his delay in reaching a decision indicated a true wavering of position, the Jewish cause would be in trouble. If they lost Ulloa, they might very well get a report from the committee that denied them a Jewish state.

With the delegate count hanging in the balance, Sharett walked down the street to the apartment of a friend and placed a phone call to Weizmann in New York, using a phone line not monitored by Haganah or any of the other delegations. The call was short and to the point. Critical developments had occurred. Sharett needed to talk in private. Weizmann readily agreed and, to shorten the travel time, suggested they meet in London the following day.

— • —

Sharett and Weizmann arrived tired and beleaguered as they huddled in a hotel room near Buckingham Palace.

Weizmann listened carefully as Sharett outlined the problem, then said, "I think Czechoslovakia is the key for us."

"Czechoslovakia?"

"If my perception is correct, Karel Lisicky has not yet voiced direct support for the plan, right?"

"No. He hasn't," Sharett acknowledged. "But he's supported us all along. We weren't concerned about him."

"And rightly so," Weizmann smiled. "But I think he has purposefully delayed voicing that support, perhaps in hopes of making a dramatic announcement at the end, perhaps for other reasons not related to his ultimate decision."

"I'm not sure I follow you," Sharett replied. "Do you want him to go public now?"

Weizmann shook his head. "It doesn't matter when he announces his support. Now or later is fine. But I think the real issue is that Czechoslovakia is acting as proxy for the Soviet Union in this matter."

Sharett seemed puzzled. "What makes you think that?"

"You remember the speech Gromyko made earlier, supporting a Jewish state?"

"Yes."

"I think he signaled the Russian position on the matter. They aren't really interested in us as much as they are in getting the British out of the Middle East, so I think they will support us if for no other reason than that. Now, they can't very well give us aid directly without confronting Great Britain and, perhaps, the United States. So I think they have decided to work through Czechoslovakia."

"We don't have a problem with Lisicky. Our problem is with Peru."

"Exactly," Weizmann nodded. "And to get Ulloa back in our corner, you should approach Lisicky about helping Peru. Economically."

"You mean ask him to ask the Soviets about it?"

"No," Weizmann said with a frustrated shake of his head. "Don't ask him for Soviet help. Just tell him there is an opportunity in Peru that might be of benefit to us all—Czechoslovakia, an emerging Jewish state, our friends. Use that language. Our *friends*. Lisicky will know what to do."

— • —

When he returned to Geneva, Sharett arranged to meet with Lisicky at the Czech Embassy where they could talk away from other committee members and beyond the reach of Haganah operatives. The two men talked for an hour with Sharett sticking close to the topics suggested by Weizmann and never once mentioning the Soviet Union, the committee, or the pending report. Three days later, a press release from Moscow announced that a joint delegation of Soviet and Czech economic advisers would be meeting with their counterparts in Peru to discuss development of Peruvian mining resources.

Eban, who had been deliberately left in the dark, was taken aback by the sudden development and worried that the timing might somehow unravel all their work. Sharett, unwilling to disclose all that had happened, decided to trust Weizmann's advice. He would leave the outcome to Lisicky's discretion and use his senior position with the Jewish Agency to restrain Eban's curiosity.

— • —

As the summer wore on, committee delegates continued to sort through the evidence they'd gathered in Palestine and at the displaced-persons camps, often digressing into needless arguments that reflected delegate vanity rather than serious deliberation. At the same time, the weather in Geneva turned warm, making lengthy daytime sessions more problematic. With the committee's work stalling, Sharett and Eban turned their attention to the language of the report and the process necessary to bring matters to a vote.

"We need to see a copy of it," Sharett worried as they gathered in his hotel room. "And we need it before they submit a draft to the committee. Notes from the trash in his room are helpful, but we need to know exactly what Bunche is writing before he gives the final product to the delegates."

"I've tried to get a draft from him, but he doesn't seem to take the hint."

"We could always get someone to procure one from his room. You keep him occupied. Our guys go in and do a serious search."

"No," Eban objected. "That is far too risky. If one of them got caught, the whole thing could blow up in our faces. We need to keep working and stay patient."

"This can't take much longer. Time is running out. Have you tried to prod Bunche on getting a vote?"

"I've suggested it. That's a little easier than asking for the report. We've actually had frank discussions about the process."

"When does he think they'll bring this to an end?"

"He won't say for certain."

"You need to get him to do it. This thing has dragged on long enough."

"They're coming to a deadline," Eban noted. "Pretty soon, they won't have much choice but to vote."

A few days later, Elia Strauss, listening to Sandström and Mohn as they met in Sandström's suite, learned that the written report was ready and would be introduced by the end of the week. Strauss sent for Eban and briefed him on the conversation. That night, Eban had dinner with Bunche.

"I understand your report is finished."

"How do you know so much about what we're doing?"

"I get around."

"No," Bunche said as he rested his fork on the edge of his plate. "I'm serious. How do you know so many details about what goes on around here?"

"The future of our state hangs in the balance," Eban replied in a frank manner. "Did you really expect us to sit on our hands and let others decide our destiny?"

"I suppose not."

Eban took a bite and swallowed. "So, any chance I could see a copy of that report before you give it to the delegates?"

Bunche reached down to a satchel that was propped against the leg of his chair. He opened it and took out an envelope. "I brought this copy for you. We plan to introduce it later this week. I'd like your comments by morning."

"Okay. I'll meet you for breakfast. Will that be soon enough?"

"Yes. That will be fine."

Eban wiped his mouth on the napkin and laid it beside his plate, then stood and scooted his chair away from the table. "I'll see you in the morning."

"You aren't going to finish your dinner?"

"Not now," Eban replied. "I have work to do."

Working together, Eban and Sharett spent the night dissecting the proposed report. When Eban met Bunche for breakfast the next morning he was still wearing the same clothes he'd worn the night before.

"You look a mess," Bunche commented.

A waiter filled their cups with coffee and Eban took a sip. "I'll feel better after I have a second cup of this coffee."

"What did you think of the report?"

"You'll get some push-back on location of the boundaries."

"Oh?" Bunche frowned. "How so?"

"Ben-Gurion wants all of the Negev for the Jewish state and the lines as drawn give the Arabs a state with over ninety percent Arab. Ours would be only fifty percent Jewish. He'll give up some of the Galilee to get the Negev and a state with a stronger Jewish majority."

"You talked to him?"

"Not about the report but about what he wants."

"Okay."

"Don't get me wrong," Eban continued. "We'd love to have control of the entire region and there are some who would want to hold out for it, but those who make the decisions agree that having a Jewish state is far better than not having one."

"Is this going to be a problem?"

"Boundaries?"

"Yes."

"The question about the boundaries will come up."

"In a bad way?"

"In a respectful way."

"And if you don't get an adjustment?"

"We'll live with what we get."

"Good," Bunche took a deep breath to relax.

"But there is one more thing."

"What's that?"

"The vote. We need to get this to a vote."

"We're about there now. They'll have a few days to review the text and then they'll vote. Sandström won't let it drag on much longer. He's ready to bring things to a close."

"Good," Eban nodded. "Let's eat."

— • —

Two days later, Sandström ordered the draft report distributed to the committee. As expected, delegates from the Netherlands, Canada, and Czechoslovakia voiced support for the draft as written, a position clearly favored by Sandström and the remainder of the Swedish delegation. The approval process, however, required formal committee sessions and an opportunity for comments and debate on the record. Early the following week, the committee gathered for the first of those sessions. Once again, Nasrollah Entezam, the representative from Iran, led the opposition.

"Mr. Chairman," he announced loudly as he rose from his chair. "I object to the draft report."

"On what basis?"

"On the basis raised by Mr. Simic earlier which is that of the United Nations' limited authority. Arabs have resided in Palestine for thousands of years, building homes, businesses, schools, and places of worship there. Generations of Arabs have lived and died there and were living there when the United Nations was formed. Consequently, the UN has no authority to displace them. The charter guarantees the security of every country as it existed at the time of the UN's formation. That guarantee includes the Arab majority in Palestine."

"That might be true under other circumstances," Sandström replied, "but as Mr. Rand from Canada has already pointed out, there is no country in the area of Palestine currently under review. We have only an area that is under UN control pursuant to a mandate that existed at the time the UN charter was enacted. Your objection is noted and overruled."

Vladimir Simic, representative from Yugoslavia, spoke up. "Mr.

Chairman, I understood our focus was to be that of arriving at a solution that was not only acceptable to a majority of the committee, but also to the parties involved—namely, Palestinian Arabs and Jews. The notion of partition, as reflected in the draft report, might be acceptable to the Jews, but it is completely unacceptable to the Arabs and thus, it cannot become the report of this committee."

"It can if it gets enough votes," Sandström droned. "Overruled."

"But if I may, Mr. Chairman," Simic continued. "As our committee has seen, the region we are discussing is quite small. Even this draft report recognizes that it cannot survive economically as two totally separate states. That's why the report recommends a unified economy. Now, if the economy of the region must be unified to remain viable, the logical thing to do is to create one unified country—politically and economically—with a democratically elected government, and let the vote of the people sort out the problems of how that is reflected in the daily lives of those residing in the region."

"Mr. Chairman, if I may," Alberto Ulloa leapt to his feet. Sandström nodded his approval and Ulloa turned to face Simic. "Are you suggesting that Yugoslavia is prepared to dispatch troops to ensure the safety of all residents in Palestine?"

"I am not …" Simic glanced down at the table, cleared his throat, and said, "I am sure we would be willing to participate in a multinational peacekeeping force."

"Peace-keeping," Ulloa scoffed. "How many troops would you send? Better yet, how many soldiers does Yugoslavia currently have in its military?"

"I am not prepared to divulge that information," Simic replied in an arrogant tone.

"I don't suppose you are." Ulloa turned to Sandström. "Mr. Chairman, during my time of service on this committee, I have found that it is easy to speak glibly about solutions for the region of Palestine, but the reality of conditions there is much harsher than would yield to glib solutions. Far more difficult than my friend from Yugoslavia is willing to admit. At present, the British government has over two hundred thousand soldiers on station in Palestine and today unrest is at an all-time high. To quell that unrest would easily require a force twice as large as currently deployed. Think of it. That's four hundred thousand men. No country whose representatives are seated at this table could send and sustain a force like that. Even the United Kingdom can no longer maintain a presence of that nature, which is why we are here."

"No one is arguing for a continuation of the mandate," Simic retorted.

"No one is saying so, directly," Ulloa countered. "But if we did as you suggest, and create a single country subject to democratic rule, the Jews of Palestine would face yet another holocaust, this one at the hands of the Arabs."

"I resent that remark," Entezam shouted.

Sandström rapped his gavel and called for order while Ulloa continued. "A democracy only works if the elected government protects the minority. The Arabs constitute an overwhelming majority in the region, yet they have shown no penchant for doing that. Indeed, they have shown quite the opposite in attempts to follow through on their oft-spoken desire to drive the Jews into the sea. Any vote in favor of a unified government for the region is a vote in favor of the elimination of the Jewish population of Palestine."

Sharett, listening from the room on the fifth floor, had a satisfied smile. The overture to the Czech delegation had worked. Peru was onboard. As Ulloa continued to talk, Elia Strauss, the Shai agent who supervised the monitoring program, looked over at Sharett.

"Did I miss something, or did Ulloa just say he was voting for partition?"

"Yes," Sharett nodded. "And not just a vote, but *the* vote."

"*The* vote?"

"Delegates from the Netherlands, Canada, and Czechoslovakia have already indicated they would vote for partition. Guatemala is with us but hasn't said so publicly yet. And now—"

"Ulloa brings Peru," Strauss interrupted.

"And that is enough. Especially if Australia abstains as it did on the earlier vote about visiting the camps."

"We are one step closer to having a Jewish state."

"In a sense, we have witnessed it here today."

— • —

When the final vote was taken, UNSCOP approved Bunche's draft report, with minor revisions, and transmitted it to UN headquarters in New York. Shortly after receiving it, the General Assembly convened as an ad hoc committee on the Palestinian Question to explore the possibility of finding an amicable resolution that would satisfy both sides. Representatives of the Arab High Committee and the Jewish Agency for Palestine were invited to appear and offer their respective views. Walter Eytan, who'd been moved from the Jewish Agency's political department in Tel Aviv to the office in New York, took over the Agency's approach, which was simply to accept the report and request a few modest adjustments to the boundaries. Representatives from the Arab High Committee rejected the report in every respect and refused to accept anything short of full Arab control of Palestine.

In the end, the boundaries were adjusted more or less along the lines requested by the Jewish Agency, and the ad hoc committee recommended a resolution to the full General Assembly dividing Palestine into separate Arab and Jewish states consistent with the terms of UNSCOP's report. A vote was scheduled for final approval on November 29, 1947.

CHAPTER 27

ON THE EVENING OF NOVEMBER 29, staff and officials at the Jewish Agency in Tel Aviv gathered with Ben-Gurion in the downstairs room used by the couriers. Jacob and Sarah Schwarz joined them.

A radio sat on a table in the corner and everyone stood with rapt attention, listening in silence to news reports from New York. It was noon over there and the UN General Assembly was ready to vote on a resolution partitioning Palestine. As voting started, Sarah sat near the radio and kept a running tally of the vote, marking each one on a note pad. When the final vote was announced, people in the room broke out in shouts and laughter. On the streets outside, people were dancing and singing at the top of their voices.

Inside the room, however, Ben-Gurion had a sober look. He did his best to force a smile and respond to well-wishers with cordial remarks but anyone could see his joy was tempered by something serious. Golda looked much the same and when Jacob asked Sarah why, she explained, "They all know it doesn't mean peace or the end of conflict."

"Zion is in travail," Jacob replied.

"Not more of the prophets," Sarah said, shaking her head. "Not tonight."

"Why not tonight?"

"This is only the beginning." Sarah gestured to the others in the room. "And they all know that's all this is. A beginning."

"Yes, but it's the beginning we've all hoped and prayed for," Jacob said. "The fulfillment of all that has been promised and foretold and we are here to see it. How could we not remember the prophets on a night like this? People for thousands of years have longed to see this day," he grinned, "and we are here to see it."

Sarah gave him an indulgent smile. "I love you, Jacob Schwarz."

He leaned over and kissed her on the lips. "I love you too, Sarah."

— · —

Later that evening, as the city-wide party continued, Ben-Gurion convened a meeting with the Jewish Agency leadership council at his home. It was long after midnight when they gathered. In spite of the late hour, all the regular members were there, plus several extra people.

"War is coming with the Arabs," Ben-Gurion began. "The UN can pass a resolution, but in the end we will have to fight for the right to exist."

"When do you expect it will start?" someone asked from the back of the room.

"We've been fighting since we first returned here," Ben-Gurion said with a wry smile, "and, as you are all aware, we've been enduring a renewed wave of heightened Arab attacks the past few months. But as to full-scale war, the British are scheduled to leave by May 15. I expect our Arab neighbors will attack us soon after."

"Regardless of the exact date, we should be ready to defend ourselves by then," someone else suggested.

"Our first step," Golda offered, "is to seize the moment and declare our independence. The UN has authorized it. We should respond by declaring it."

"But not until the British are gone," Ben-Gurion cautioned. "I think we should wait until then. I don't want to give them any provocation that would permit them to attack us."

Gedaliah Cohen spoke up. "Do you really think Syria and Transjordan will attack? I know what they've been saying, and the reports we get and all that, but when it comes down to actually doing it, will they follow through?"

"Without a doubt," Ben-Gurion responded.

"And not just them," Golda added, "but the entire Arab League. I just returned from a meeting with King Abdullah a few hours ago. He will stay out of the fight—at least that's what he's saying right now—but he assured me the others are ready for war. They're just waiting for the British to leave before they do it." An uneasy twitter rippled through the group.

"So," Ben-Gurion continued, "we're outnumbered maybe three or four to one in terms of soldiers. And they have far better equipment than we do. And you might as well know right now, if Abdullah goes back on his word and joins the fight, we could very easily lose."

"Better to lose in a fight than wait to be slaughtered," Cohen chuckled.

"Is that army humor, Gedaliah?" Golda asked.

"So, if the British leave," someone spoke up, "who will be in charge? From a UN point of view. How do they see this working out?"

"I don't think they've seen that far," Ben-Gurion responded.

"There's supposed to be a transition period," Revach explained. "To give both sides time to form their respective governments. And the text of the resolution and accompanying documents allude to an international monitoring force, but so far no one has taken steps to actually establish that force."

"When the British leave," Ben-Gurion went on, "we will be in charge of our own destiny. National defense, maintaining order, all of it will be left up to us. No one is going to solve this problem or address our concerns for us. We will have to do it for ourselves."

"What does that mean?" Baruch Riskin asked. "How do we translate that into action?"

"It means we need to take steps now to make certain we are ready." Ben-Gurion turned to Revach. "Eyal, I want you to take charge of procuring men and matériel for war. Get a team together, maybe Ehud Avriel and Teddy Kollek would be good. Send them to wherever they have to go to find the weapons we need to defend ourselves. Talk to Gedaliah. Come up with a list."

"There's lots of surplus out there," Gedaliah commented. "Left over from the war. Surely someone will sell some of it to us."

"What about Munia Mardor?" Revach asked. "Can I use him?"

Ben-Gurion glanced in Golda's direction. "Can you spare him from your office?"

"Yes," she nodded.

Ben-Gurion turned back to Revach. "Use him, too."

Rami Fehr was seated on the far side of the room. "How are we going to pay for it?"

"I'm going to the United States to raise the money," Ben-Gurion replied. "I'm not sure they will help us, but I'm going to ask."

Several in the group groaned their disapproval. "I don't think that's a good idea," Golda chimed in. "You need to be here, coordinating things on the ground."

"Then whom would you suggest?" Ben-Gurion asked, his voice betraying a hint of irritation.

"Me," Golda replied with a smile. "What you do here, I can't do. But I can raise money."

"No." Ben-Gurion shook his head. "I need you here."

"I think we should vote," Golda offered, unwilling to give up. "Let the council decide who should represent us to the Americans."

"Yes," someone added.

"I'm for that," another said.

"Let's take a vote."

"Very well," Ben-Gurion reluctantly conceded. "We'll vote. All in favor of Golda going to the U.S. to raise the money, lift your hands." Everyone in the room voted in favor. A wisp of a smile flickered over Ben-Gurion's face. "Well, then," he said softly. "Golda it is."

They talked awhile longer, but with only a few hours remaining until dawn the meeting soon broke up. As people began to leave, Ben-Gurion took Golda aside. "Okay. By my count, we need twenty-five million dollars."

Golda was unfazed. "I'll get the money."

Ben-Gurion grinned, amused at her confidence. "I'll call Henry Montor and tell him you're coming. He'll be your best source of information. It'll be tough raising that kind of money. Jews in America think they've found the Promised Land. They don't want to come over here and they don't understand why we do. I don't know if you can get twenty-five million out of them, but do your best."

"I'll get it," she reassured him once again. "Don't worry."

"And one more thing." Ben-Gurion took an envelope from his pocket and handed it to Golda. "I scribbled a note a while ago. It's in here. There's a guy in Washington, D.C., named Mickey Marcus. He's at the War Department. I need you to find him and give this to him."

"I'm not sure I'll be in Washington," Golda said, not quite catching the tone of his voice.

"Make a special trip if you have to," Ben-Gurion insisted. "But give him the envelope personally. Don't leave it for him or give it to someone else to deliver. Deliver it from your hand to his."

"Okay."

— • —

After he left the meeting with Ben-Gurion, Gedaliah Cohen knew that time was of the essence. Ben-Gurion was right. War was coming, and every hour, every minute, counted. He was tired from a long and exciting day, but instead of going home to bed he drove straight from Ben-Gurion's house to Ehud Avriel's apartment. The door was locked but he let himself in with a key that was hidden under the doormat.

Once inside, he went up to the bedroom where he found Avriel and his wife asleep in bed. Cohen reached over and gave Avriel a shake. "Get up," he whispered. "We need you to take a trip."

Avriel, not quite awake, squinted in a pained expression. "Where am I going?"

"Europe."

"Europe?"

"Yes. Get up and get dressed."

Avriel pulled himself up to a sitting position. "Why am I going to Europe?"

"We need arms. Planes, weapons, ammunition."

"Arms?" Avriel took Cohen by the sleeve of his shirt. "Am I really awake, or is this a dream?"

"You're not dreaming," Cohen said sharply. "Now stop asking so many questions and get out of bed."

Anna, Avriel's wife, looked up at him. "Gedaliah, you've barged in here in the middle of the night. Don't expect too much."

"It's not the middle of the night. It's almost dawn."

"It's okay," Avriel said to her, then turned to Cohen. "What are you talking about? What is this about?"

"The UN voted. They've agreed to partition Palestine into an Arab and a Jewish state."

"I know. I was in the room with everyone else, listening on the radio. Where did you go? I couldn't find you."

"Never mind about that," Cohen said in a hurried voice. "Listen, war is coming and there's no time to lose."

Avriel's eyes opened wide. "We're under attack?"

"No. Not yet. But we will be soon."

Avriel threw back the covers. "How much time do we have?"

"A few months."

"A few months!" Avriel exclaimed. He fell back on the bed with a groan. "Then why are you waking me up now to tell me this? We've known the Arabs would attack for a long time."

"Yes. But now we know when and we know where."

"When?"

"The mandate will end at midnight May fourteenth. They will attack on the fifteenth."

"You know this for certain?"

"Yes."

"And where are they going to attack?"

"Here, in Tel Aviv. Haifa. Jerusalem. The Galilee. Everywhere. Do you know where we can get some serviceable fighter planes?"

"Yeah," Avriel sighed. "I think so."

"Good. Get moving." Cohen grabbed him by the ankles and rolled him out of bed. He hit the floor with a thump. "There's no time to waste." Cohen stepped over him and moved to the door. "I'll go downstairs and make a pot of coffee. You get dressed and get moving."

— • —

A few hours later, Cohen met with Moshe Dayan, a hero of earlier

Jewish struggles with the Arabs. They met in Cohen's office at Haganah headquarters, just up the road from the Jewish Agency offices.

"Our latest intelligence indicates the Syrians are preparing to amass troops and equipment on our northern border with the Lebanese."

"The Lebanese will allow them to do that? To encroach on their territory?"

"To attack us, I think they would permit most anything they thought might lead to success." Cohen reached behind his desk for a map and unrolled it on the desktop. "We expect Syrian troops to cross the Jordan in a two-pronged attack. One headed toward Masada and the other toward Sha'ar Hagolan."

"If they do that, their real goal would be Degania," Dayan offered.

"That's our thought, too."

"Degania is the key to the eastern half of the Galilee. If they take it, they can roll all the way to Tiberius."

"We think it would be worse than that. We think almost the entire Galilee would fall under their control."

"Who do we have to direct the Degania defense?"

"No one."

"Then I must go there at once and help them prepare. I was born there. I still have friends and relatives in Degania."

"Not now. We've briefed them on what we expect will occur and what they should do to prepare. You can go there when the time arrives. Right now we need you here to prepare a mechanized unit for combat against the Egyptians in the Negev."

"Against the Egyptian army?"

"Yes."

"They have the best-equipped military of all our neighbors," Dayan noted. "The Transjordanians are the best trained, but the Egyptians are by far the best equipped."

"We are aware of that," Cohen responded. "We expect the Egyptians to attack in two areas, as well, using their tanks and armored cars with the infantry transported in trucks. One thrust will strike toward Beersheba, the other will move up the coast through Gaza. Unless we can stop the column in Gaza, they will roll right up the coast toward us."

"We will need tanks," Dayan nodded grimly. "And lots of them."

"We have dispatched buyers to find them."

Dayan's eyes opened wider. "We have money to pay for tanks?"

"Someone is addressing that problem, too," Cohen said with a dismissive tone. "You should concentrate on what a mechanized unit will need, not on what it doesn't have."

"We'll need armor. There's no substitute for it."

"You must improvise until it arrives."

"Anything I improvise," Dayan said with an ironic grin, "won't be a match for Egyptian tanks."

"Then come up with a strategy that minimizes their strengths and maximizes ours."

"You have seen the inventory reports on our munitions?"

"Yes."

"And our mobile equipment?"

"Yes."

"And our troop readiness?"

"I've seen all of those reports," Cohen said in an exasperated tone.

"Then you should know there is only one strategy that could help us resist such an attack."

"What is that?"

"Prayer."

"I'm already doing that," Cohen replied. "You should add that to your preparation list, too."

CHAPTER 28

THE FOLLOWING DAY, Daniel Agee, an assistant secretary for Middle Eastern affairs with the US State Department in Washington, D.C., received a phone call from Alex Berkman, a friend from New York City.

"I have some information for you," Berkman said.

"Okay," Agee replied. "What is it?"

"Not over the phone."

"I don't have time to come to New York."

"I'm here. In Washington. Meet me at the usual place." Berkman ended the call without waiting for a response.

He was eccentric, which occasionally made him difficult to deal with, but Berkman had many friends, most of them well placed in the Jewish community, and more than once he'd provided Agee with crucial information. Half an hour later, Agee found him on a bench near the Lincoln Memorial. "So what's this important information?"

"Golda Meir is coming to town," Berkman said in a matter-of-fact tone.

"Here?" Berkman frowned. "To Washington?"

"No. To New York. A guy in Henry Montor's office told me."

"Why is she coming?"

"To raise money."

"For what?"

"No one will say but they think it's for something big."

Agee seemed perplexed. "Is that it?"

"Yeah," Berkman nodded. "They think she'll be here sometime in the next two weeks. They weren't specific. Can't you track that down through her visa application?"

"She has diplomatic status. She doesn't need a visa."

"Well, that's what I know." Berkman gestured with a wave of his hand. "You leave first. I'll wait here until you're gone. I don't want anyone to notice us leaving together."

"Okay," Agee grinned. "But you know no one talks like that. Just in the movies."

"Whatever," Berkman shrugged. "I just don't trust guys who keep secrets for a living."

"But you don't mind sharing information with us."

"You're different. I know you. Now go on before someone gets suspicious."

With further conversation pointless, Agee stood and walked over to Constitution Avenue where he hailed a taxi and rode back to the office. When he arrived at his desk he telephoned Howard Hicks, a friend at the CIA's domestic intelligence section. The two arranged to meet for lunch that day at a café just off E Street, not far from Hicks' office at the CIA head-quarters building. They sat at a table in the corner.

"So," Hicks said after they'd ordered, "your phone call sounded important. What's up?"

"I have a source," Agee said in hushed tones, "who tells me that Golda Meir is traveling to New York from Palestine. She has a diplomatic pass-port, so we don't have a visa application for her, which means I don't have a lot of specifics, but our source thinks she'll arrive sometime in the next two weeks."

"Is she still using a British passport?"

"Yes," Agee nodded. "The British are still in control of the region until May."

"Your people don't have any better details?"

"This is all I have and I just learned this a few hours ago. I haven't written a report on it and I'm not sure I will. I'm just giving you a heads up. You guys can use your own people to find out exactly when she'll arrive."

"You don't know why she's coming?"

"They think she's coming to raise money."

"Those Jews are good at that," Hicks said with a chuckle.

"This could be big. No one will say what, exactly, but the word from Henry Montor's office is it's important."

"Any way to stop her before she gets here?"

"I don't think so," Agee said with a questioning glance. "That would cause a major international incident if we tried. Why do you ask?"

"We don't really need to get sucked into this Palestinian mess. I know you don't want to turn this over to the FBI, but the president has been rather frank with the director about keeping our hands off."

"I'm not trying to suck you into anything," Agee countered. "It's just that with tensions high in Palestine and Secretary Marshall's position on events there, we thought you might want to keep tabs on her. We aren't equipped for that sort of thing. And no, I don't want Hoover and the FBI involved at all. They'd turn routine surveillance into an international fiasco."

"I'd be glad to take it on, but I'll have to check. Like I said, we've been told to keep clear of any of it."

"That's from an operational perspective," Agee suggested. "No under-cover operations. No attempts to influence events and governments. But this isn't like that. This would be strictly surveillance. Nothing covert, except it'll work better if she doesn't know your people are there. You aren't going over to Palestine. This is right here on our soil."

"I'll pass on the information. We'll see where it goes from there. Thanks for the tip."

After lunch, Hicks went back to his office and requested a meeting with Doyle Pittman, his boss. Surprisingly, Pittman thought shadowing Golda was a good idea. "The State Department follows Marshall's lead, but Marshall tends toward anti-Semitic views. President Truman does not. When the situation in Palestine finally forces a decision, Truman will side with the Jews. We should be ready with the best intelligence assessment we can give him. I'll authorize a team. Put Charles Barlow in charge. He can report to you. You keep me apprised of any big developments."

— • —

Not long after the UN vote approving the partition resolution, Golda Meir arrived in New York City. She was met at the airport by her sister Clara and Bernard Lowenstein, an assistant from Henry Montor's office. "Henry is in Chicago," Lowenstein said as they came from the arrival gate. "He's attending a meeting of the Council of Jewish Federations."

"Oh?" Golda said with curiosity. "Perhaps I should have flown straight there."

"Well," Lowenstein continued, "it's probably better that you didn't. Henry said to tell you there was no need to come out there. In his words, they're all ardent anti-Zionists anyway. He seemed to think you'd be better off to stay here and get ready to work with potential donors in New York."

Golda wasn't comfortable with that suggestion, but Ben-Gurion had made a point of telling her to rely on Montor's advice, so she kept her misgivings to herself.

Lowenstein accompanied Golda and Clara from the airport to their hotel, then left them there to wait for Montor's return on Monday. When they were alone, Clara wasted little time expressing her opinion. "He's wrong," she blurted out. "Just plain wrong."

"What are you talking about?"

"That kid," Clara continued. "Lowenstein. He's wrong."

"About what?"

"You shouldn't sit around here waiting, Golda. You should go to Chicago, as fast as possible."

"That was my initial reaction, but Ben-Gurion suggested I follow Henry's lead. Do you really think I should go?"

"I know so. You have to get to Chicago," Clara insisted. "David Ben-Gurion is a great man and a wonderful leader and I know you think a lot of him. But he's not an American. He doesn't understand Americans. And most Americans who've met him don't understand him. You know these people. You know how Americans think and how to reach them. All the leading people in our movement are out there in Chicago right now. And they are all rich. This is the crowd you came to see."

They continued to discuss the matter, and the more they talked, the more convinced Golda became that Clara was right. "Well," she said at last, "let's go over to the office and see if we can reach Henry."

"Wouldn't it be better just to get on a plane and fly out there?"

"Maybe. But to raise the kind of money that will help us, we are going to need Henry's help. I don't want to offend him the first day."

With Clara along for support, they took the elevator to the lobby, hailed a cab, and rode over to the Jewish Agency office. From there, Golda placed a phone call to Montor at his hotel in Chicago. When her call went unanswered, she tried the Chicago Athletic Club, where the council was meeting. Before long, she had him on the line.

"Henry," Golda began, "I think I should come out there. They might be a cantankerous crowd but those are our people. My people. And I need to talk to them."

"Well," Montor said slowly, "if you insist, I suppose it wouldn't do any harm. But let me see if I can get you on the schedule so you can address one of the sessions. That's the way to talk to them. Not one-on-one."

"Should I simply show up?"

"No. You don't want to come all the way out here if it's going to be a flop. Let me check. I'll call you back."

Rather than return to the hotel, Golda and Clara waited in the office. An hour later the phone rang. "Okay," Montor sounded more upbeat than before. "They'll let you speak, but you'll have to get here quickly. They've added you to the schedule for tomorrow afternoon, near the end of the conference."

With a hastily arranged flight, Golda arrived in Chicago the next day and went straight to the Athletic Club. About eight hundred were present. Montor introduced her and when he gave her the podium, she spoke straight from the heart, recounting the long struggle many had endured in Europe, Palestine, and the need for a Jewish state where they could determine their own destiny. At the beginning, attendees, weary after a weekend of meetings, were little more than courteous listeners, most out of respect for Montor, but as Golda continued they warmed to her and to her subject. By the end of her speech, they were on their feet, clapping and cheering in support, and when she left the Athletic Club that evening, she had received pledges of support that totaled twenty-five million dollars.

Golda spent the next two weeks crisscrossing the United States, giving speech after speech, none of them written in advance, all of them delivered from her heart—a heart devoted to the Jewish cause and the Jewish people. Assistants from the Jewish Agency accompanied her and kept account of the pledges and donations, all of them astounded at her eloquence and proficiency. As the trip drew to a close, the total raised reached fifty-five million dollars, more than twice the sum Ben-Gurion said they needed.

As requested, on her way back to New York, Golda stopped in Washington, D.C., and located Mickey Marcus at the newly formed Department of Defense, still in the old War Department building on C Street. With little fanfare, she delivered Ben-Gurion's note, still sealed in its envelope. She never asked about the contents and Marcus never offered to tell her. They talked awhile about Palestine in general, the newly adopted resolution specifically, and what partition might mean for the immediate future of the region. The conversation lasted about twenty minutes, then Golda said good-bye and headed off to New York for one last round of fund-raising and the long trip home.

CHAPTER 29

CHARLES BARLOW WAS SEATED IN A CAR outside the War Department building. As Golda Meir walked out, Ray Seals came to the car. "She went to see Mickey Marcus."

"About what?"

"I don't know. The meeting was brief. Our guy in the office said she handed Marcus an envelope, they talked awhile, then she left."

"Okay," Barlow mused. "There aren't many things she could discuss with an army colonel that don't have serious implications."

"Except that she walked into the building in broad daylight. She wasn't even trying to be clever about it."

"Maybe she doesn't know what was in the envelope."

"Probably not."

Seals reached for the handle to open the door. "I gotta go. They're leaving to follow her and I need to catch up."

"Tell Darnell to come here. You take his place."

"Right."

A few minutes later, Horace Darnell approached the car and got in on the passenger's side. When he was seated, Barlow started the engine and pulled away from the curb.

"Where are we going?" Darnell asked.

"She just visited Mickey Marcus."

"Yeah. Seemed a little strange but there apparently wasn't much to it."

"That's the part that bothers me," Barlow replied.

"What are you saying?"

"I want you to see what you can find out about Marcus. Pull his service record, check the usual sources, and then put together a team and follow him awhile."

Darnell raised an eyebrow. "You want me to follow an army colonel?"

"I want you to follow this one."

"We didn't follow anyone else she talked to."

"We know all those people. We don't know much about Marcus."

"But, Charlie, this guy's an officer."

"Which is all the more reason for us to find out about his connections to Meir. Maybe we've stumbled on to a secret operation that no one's told us about. Maybe it's a friend stopping by to see a friend. I don't know, but our job is to find out things like this."

"Okay," Darnell sighed. "But this seems a little too much to me."

"Just do it, and let's see what we find," Barlow insisted. "If it doesn't turn up anything soon, we'll drop it."

— · —

Marcus first became acquainted with Ben-Gurion several years earlier during one of Ben-Gurion's trips to the United States. A mutual friend introduced them at a dinner given in Ben-Gurion's honor by a Washington socialite. Later, Eyal Revach came to see him and the two had remained in contact with each other through the years. Marcus kept an eye on subsequent events in Palestine and as the UN moved toward approval of the partition resolution he knew the struggle for independence and statehood would only get worse, but he hadn't expected the note that Golda gave him.

The note from Ben-Gurion was short and to the point. The goal of establishing an independent Jewish state was within their grasp, but they needed help. Could he find someone who would help shape Haganah into a national army on a par with others in the region? Marcus read it and reread it, and each time he did he had the sense that though the letter asked him to find someone, he was being asked to take the job himself.

Three days later, Marcus traveled to Fort Campbell, Kentucky, and talked to Homer Perkins, a fellow colonel in the army. Perkins was a devout

Christian. Marcus was hoping that meant he was pro-Jewish. When Marcus showed him the letter he received from Ben-Gurion asking for help, Perkins was intrigued, but not enough to say yes.

"I just can't, Mickey. My wife has been counting the days until retirement and we're almost there. She made it through the war with me and that took a lot from her. I can't ask her to go through any more."

From Fort Campbell, Marcus traveled to Fort Hood near Killeen, Texas. His former West Point classmate Dewey Payne was stationed there. Payne listened sympathetically as Marcus made his pitch but turned him down, too. "We just got here," he said. "And this is my last stop before I get a general's star. I can't bail on it now."

Marcus made four other stops in his search for help but received a similar response at each of them. Everyone was sympathetic to the cause, but no one was willing to take the job. It was understandable. Official policy required the United States to remain neutral out of respect for British involvement in the region, but that didn't make rejection any easier.

Marcus arrived back home feeling tired and dejected. He came in from the airport and flopped down on a chair at the kitchen table. Catherine, his wife, took a seat across from him. "You've been through this before— a project that everyone recognized as valuable but no one wanted to get involved with." She reached across the tabletop and took hold of his hand. "You'll find a way to make it work."

"I can understand why they said no," Mickey sighed. "It's a big risk and most of them are late in their careers. This would take them out of the regular rotation. While they're in Palestine, someone else will move up and take their place here."

Catherine let go of his hand and leaned back in her chair. "The Jews in Palestine have done well so far. What more do they need? From what I've read, I can't imagine the Arabs have much of an army."

"The Palestinian Arabs don't. If that's all they faced, Ben-Gurion would be in good shape. But the countries around them have professional, well-equipped armies. Ben-Gurion is certain they will invade as soon as the British pull out."

"Is that right?" she asked. "Will they invade?"

"Yeah," Marcus nodded. "I checked with some of our people. The Syrians are already amassing troops on the border. Egypt is moving its forces across the Suez. The only country that hasn't mobilized is Transjordan and if the others attack, they'll be forced to participate."

"Forced?"

"Strategically. If one goes, they all have to go. Otherwise, one or the other of them would take control of the entire area and that would at least double their size. Overnight they would become the dominate nation in the Middle East. King Abdullah can't let that happen."

"Sounds like you've already given this some thought."

"A little," Marcus nodded. "I mean, it's Israel. These are the Jews, many of them are people we rescued from the German camps. Forming a new country." He looked across the table at her. "How could I not be interested in that?"

They sat in a silence a moment, both of them looking away. Then Catherine said quietly, "Do you want to do it yourself?"

"I don't know," Marcus shrugged. "Helping them would do nothing to advance my career."

"That's not what I asked you."

Marcus focused his gaze on her. "Yeah," he said with a wan smile. "I think I do."

"Then you should go."

"But how will we manage? I can't imagine they would be able to pay me for it."

"They could pay you something. They have to know that no one is going to take the job for free. The rest we would just…find a way to make do."

"That's the part I don't like." Marcus tapped the tabletop with his finger. "You've been making do a long time."

"And I can make do some more."

"But I might have to resign my commission."

"Then, you'll resign. And you'll do this and after you finish we'll do something else. Maybe something even more exciting."

Marcus had a twinkle in his eye. "I guess I never thought of it that way."

Catherine rose from her chair, took a seat in his lap, and then leaned over and kissed him. "That's why you have me. But you have to tell Macon Talbert."

"Think he'll be upset?"

"I don't know, but he's your commanding officer. You can't slink off in the night and try to do this in secret. You have to talk to him about it."

— • —

Macon Talbert was a brigadier general in charge of the civil affairs unit to which Marcus was assigned. The next day, Marcus went to see him and told him about the note from Ben-Gurion.

"I want to do it, sir," Marcus said. "They can't survive without some help. No one else wants to do it. I want to go."

To Marcus' surprise, Talbert didn't say no. "If you want to do it, I'm okay with it, but we'll have to get it approved all the way up the line. You don't want to do something like this and then come back to find you've lost your citizenship."

"I was worried about my pension. I didn't think about my citizenship."

"If they approve your assignment, you won't have to worry about either one. You want me to put in the request?"

"Yes. I do."

"You've talked this over with Catherine and she's okay with it?"

Marcus nodded. "She's okay with it."

— • —

After talking with Marcus, Talbert went to see Ralph Horn, the major general in charge of his section. He was surprised to find out that Horn already knew about Marcus' interest in the job with Ben-Gurion.

"I received a report about Marcus' activity yesterday."

Talbert frowned. "A report from whom? The guy's in civil affairs. I'm surprised anyone outside the building knows he's here."

Horn sighed, "Apparently the CIA knows him. They've been following him."

Talbert was incredulous. "Why?"

"Golda Meir arrived in the country a few weeks ago. She's been traveling around raising money for the Jews in Palestine. I suppose to pay for building an army. That's what I'd be using it for. She's gone now but before she left she went to see Marcus. While she was here, the CIA followed her. That led them to Marcus and they were curious about the connection."

"Did you know about this beforehand?"

Horn opened a desk drawer and took out a folder. "No. I didn't know anything about it until they sent me a report. Said they were giving it to me as a courtesy." He tossed the file across the desk. It landed in front of Talbert. "Have a look. There's not much to it."

Talbert scowled as he scanned the report. "This is ridiculous. Marcus is an outstanding soldier. A brilliant officer."

"That's what I told them."

"You talked to them?"

"This morning."

"What did they say?"

"They said they'd back off."

"Good." Talbert closed the file and laid it aside. "So, what do I tell Marcus? Can we approve his request?"

"It's okay with me, but maybe he should travel under an assumed name or something. We don't want any trouble with the British. And no fanfare. Tell him to slip quietly out the door, stay awhile, get things in shape over there, and report on it when he comes back."

"We're keeping him on the payroll?"

"Yeah. I don't think he'll be gone long. That thing will be over quickly, one way or the other."

CHAPTER 30

EHUD AVRIEL ARRIVED IN PRAGUE, Czechoslovakia, and made his way to the Hotel Druzba, not far from the Vltava River. He checked into a room and went downstairs to the hotel bar for a drink. A few minutes later, he was joined by Antonin Gottwald, assistant to Vladimir Clementis, the Czech foreign minister.

"Perhaps we should go for a walk," Gottwald suggested.

Avriel took one last sip from his drink. "Certainly, the fresh air will do me good."

They crossed the lobby and stepped out to the sidewalk, then strolled toward the river. When they reached it, they turned and walked slowly along a scenic pathway that followed the riverbank.

"I trust you had no trouble getting here," Gottwald began.

"None," Avriel replied.

"You did as we suggested?"

"Yes. I think I lost them in Paris."

"But just to make sure, you went through the safe house in Bratislava before coming here?"

"Yes."

"Good. We use that route sometimes ourselves, but not too often. Only for special trips. We don't want them to find the house."

"Between the British and the Americans, it's difficult to go anywhere without being seen."

"You should try living under the nose of the Soviets," Gottwald chuckled.

"I can only imagine.. Did you get my last telegram?"

"The one about needing much?"

"Yes."

"I have been instructed by Foreign Minister Clementis to inform you that we shall supply as much as possible to aid in your effort."

"That is good news," Avriel grinned.

"And," Gottwald continued, "to that end, Clementis has put at your disposal an airfield near Zatec for your use. You can recruit the necessary pilots?"

"Yes," Avriel nodded. In truth, he had no idea where he would find pilots. The Jewish Agency had only one light unarmed plane and a single pilot to fly it, but Gottwald was offering to help in ways he had never imagined possible and had no intention of turning him down. "We need aircraft. What kind of planes do you have?"

"We have 23 Avia S-199s we can deliver immediately." Gottwald glanced in Avriel's direction. "Those are our version of the Messerschmitt 109. You are familiar with that aircraft?"

"Yes," Avriel nodded. "That would be wonderful." But once again, he had no idea how they would get them to Palestine, let alone how they would pay for them. "What do you have in small arms and ammunition?"

"Actually," Gottwald replied, "we have about ninety million rounds for you and an assortment of weapons to shoot them with."

Avriel was overwhelmed by the offer, but the logistics of transporting it back to Palestine was now a serious issue. "Any idea how we can get it to Palestine?"

"Oh, yes," Gottwald laughed. "We have air transport planes for some of it and ships to take the rest."

"Are you supplying pilots for the transports or are we?"

"It will work better if you supply all the people," Gottwald explained. "You have people who can fly the transports?"

"We're getting them."

"What about ground crew?"

"For the cargo planes?"

"Yes. And for the fighters as well."

"We have people who can crew the cargo planes."

"What about the fighters? And I must explain, we would send them to you in crates. Someone would have to assemble them."

Avriel frowned. "How much assembly?"

"Bolt the wings on and make certain the flight controls are attached properly."

"That part might go better for us if you sent mechanics who know what they're doing. That way we could get up and running immediately. Time will be of the essence. Do you have people who can help?"

"Yes," Gottwald nodded. "You can pay for their services?"

"Certainly."

"And what about for the merchandise? Are you prepared to make arrangements now?"

"I don't think that will be a problem."

Gottwald's eyes opened wide with concern. "You are uncertain about payment?"

"No," Avriel lied. He was more concerned than ever but he wasn't about to let Gottwald know it. "Just make the arrangements," he said with feigned confidence. "They were working on the details when I left but I thought it was more important to see you and get things moving rather than waiting. Let me make a call to confirm what they have arranged."

"Certainly," Gottwald replied. "But be careful. People at the hotel will listen to calls from your room, and the telegraph service is an open system of manual relays. Hundreds of people would be able to read your communications."

"Right," Avriel nodded. "I'll be vague."

They continued along the river a little farther and had dinner at a restaurant before returning to the hotel. When Gottwald was gone, Avriel walked down the street to the telegraph office.

By then, Golda had concluded her fund-raising effort in the United States and was back in Tel Aviv. Avriel had been gone for weeks and had not seen her since she left for New York. He'd heard her meetings were successful but he didn't know how that translated into dollars. To confirm that money was available, he sent a telegram to her office that read, *Found the items. Money to pay?*

A few hours later a bellman knocked on the door of his hotel room and handed him Golda's reply. *Call me. Payment on the way.*

CHAPTER 31

ALTHOUGH THE UNITED STATES VOTED IN FAVOR of the partition resolution—at the president's personal direction—Truman continued to refuse to meet with any delegation from Palestine, either Jewish or Arab. Because of that, Abba Eban remained in the United States after the vote, dividing his time between the Jewish Agency offices in New York and Washington, D.C. With independence on the horizon, official recognition of the Jewish state by individual countries would be important. Recognition by the United States was crucial and he tried every possible means to assure that recognition was forthcoming after the British withdrawal in May. After every alternative approach had been explored and proved unsuccessful, he went to see Chaim Weizmann to ask for his help. They met at Weizmann's apartment in Manhattan.

Weizmann, who had been relegated to the sidelines in the push for adoption of the resolution, was cool at first but as Eban caught him up on the latest events he began to warm up. "I understand you've been trying to see Truman," Weizmann offered with a knowing smile.

"Yes," Eban nodded. "But I haven't had any success."

"He isn't seeing anyone on the question of Palestine. Still won't talk about it with Marshall."

Eban looked over at Weizmann. "We need his support. When the British leave in May, we'll be on our own."

Weizmann had a thoughtful expression. "Independence. I never thought it would happen this fast."

"Many think you're against the idea of an independent Jewish state."

"That's one of the drawbacks of being outspoken." Weizmann spoke as one wizened by years of experience but in a tone bordering on arrogance. "I've been in favor of a Jewish state my entire adult life. I just didn't think this was the time. I had hoped we would gain control of the entire region, and I think we might have done so if we'd taken a broader view of things, but there just wasn't time for it." Even now, after the obvious success they'd had, he could not quite hide his lingering contempt for Ben-Gurion.

Eban ignored the comment and pressed on to the topic at hand. "Any ideas on how we could get a meeting with the president?"

"You've kept me out of the loop on this," Weizmann complained.

"I know," Eban replied, hoping to avoid a confrontation.

"Why?" Weizmann could no more hide the hurt in his voice than the contempt.

Eban shrugged. "I think you know the answer to that."

"Ben-Gurion has never trusted me."

"He sees himself as taking the lead and views some of your comments as undercutting him."

"I thought we were engaged in a dialogue. I never meant to undercut anyone."

"Well," Eban leaned back in his chair, "we can't resolve that now. We have to move forward, and the path forward requires a meeting with the president."

Weizmann noted thoughtfully, "There is one way to reach him."

"What is that?"

"Eddie Jacobsen."

Eban frowned. "Who is he? I've never heard of him."

"Truman's former partner from Kansas City," Weizmann explained. "They were in the clothing business together before Truman entered politics. If anyone can change Truman's mind, it's Eddie."

"He might be a good man," Eban conceded, "but I don't know him and he hasn't been involved with our work. I doubt he knows the history of what we've done. Not in any detail. Are you sure we could brief him well enough to make our case?"

"We don't need him for that," Weizmann smiled. "We just need him to convince the president to see us."

"To see *you*," Eban replied. He understood Ben-Gurion's frustration with Weizmann and had agreed with the policy of cutting him out in dealing with UNSCOP, but approaching the president was a different matter, one for which Ben-Gurion was woefully unsuited. "There's only one person who can take this to the White House," he pointed to Weizmann. "And that person is you."

"I'm not sure that will go over well in Tel Aviv."

"They have no choice. We can't send anyone else. I don't have the stature for it. None of the others have the weight of personal presence or the sense of polish for it. It's you or no one."

"Well, if you put it that way, I would be happy to meet with him," Weizmann agreed. "In fact, as you know, I've been trying on my own all year to do that very thing."

"So, how do we get to Jacobsen?"

"I know him," Weizmann said with a smile. "I'm seeing him next week. He's coming to New York to visit his daughter."

— • —

The following week Weizmann had lunch with Jacobsen. While they ate, he outlined the circumstances in Palestine.

"I've followed some of it in the newspapers," Jacobsen said when Weizmann finished. "And we were all listening to the radio at home when the UN voted. Exciting times," he smiled. "A new Jewish state. The rebirth of Israel. I know you and David have worked a long time for it."

"We've had the help of many," Weizmann added.

"We've all done something for the effort," Eddie continued. "Our federation hosted Golda when she came through."

"And that was much appreciated," Weizmann commented. "But there's one other thing I need you to help us with," Weizmann said, finally turning the conversation to the topic most on his mind. "When the British leave Palestine, we will be on our own. An independent nation among the nations of the world. Official recognition by other countries will be important. We need your help convincing Truman to give me a few minutes to discuss Palestine."

"If you're wondering whether he'll recognize you, I don't think there's much question about that. I mean, the United States voted for the resolution at the UN."

"We aren't so sure it's that clear when it comes to official recognition. The State Department has its doubts about us. Marshall and many others in the administration aren't on our side."

"Why don't you just ask his secretary for an appointment?"

"We have. I have. But he won't see me."

Jacobsen glanced away. "Oh, I didn't realize that."

"Would it be a problem for you to ask him to meet with me?"

"I don't know," Jacobsen sighed. "It's just that since we closed the business and he went into politics, I have never asked Harry for anything. And I made a point of not asking. I've even told him I wouldn't ask."

Weizmann hadn't expected that. "So, you've never been to the White House?"

"Oh, I've been there, all right. I've visited him at every office he's ever held. When he was vice president we saw each other frequently for dinner and our wives met about every week. But what I mean is, since the day he entered politics—when he ran for judge back in Missouri—I haven't asked him for a single favor. Not one."

"Well," Weizmann said in an upbeat voice. "I can't think of a better cause to ask him about."

"I know. It's just…I don't know."

Weizmann waited for Jacobsen to look at him. "Eddie, we need the president's support. And we need your help to get it."

Jacobsen had a wry smile. "I thought you were against the formation of a Jewish state."

"No," Weizmann shook head. "Everyone thinks that, but I was never against a Jewish state. I just had reservations about the timing."

"And now?"

"Events like this require an enormous effort. They don't simply occur. This is as close as we've ever been and we may never have another opportunity. We have to take this chance now, while we can. We need the president's help to do it."

Jacobsen relaxed against the back of his chair. "What do you want me to ask him?"

"Ask him to see me."

"Is that all?"

"That's it. Just ask him to see me."

"Well," Jacobsen shrugged. "Okay. If you have to see him, if it's that important, I'll ask."

— • —

Weizmann waited in his apartment all the next day, one moment pacing the floor, the next seated in his favorite chair, staring out the window at the Manhattan skyline. Finally, a little after six that evening, the phone rang. The call was from Jacobsen. "President Truman will see you tomorrow morning at ten. Weizmann phoned Eban to let him know. But don't tell a soul," he warned. "Not even Ben-Gurion."

CHAPTER 32

AFTER WEEKS OF SEARCHING, Yaakov Auerbach located Suheir at her uncle's house in Jerusalem, but instead of rushing right in to talk to her, he watched from the roof of a nearby building. Each morning, a little before ten, she left the house with a large earthen jug and walked three blocks to an alley that took her to a neighborhood well. There she filled the jug with water, then retraced the same path for the walk home.

For three days, Auerbach followed her from above, moving from rooftop to rooftop, watching each day to see who might be following her. After the encounter with her father at the gate in Degania, he was wary of approaching her boldly as before. When he was convinced she made the trips unguarded and alone he left the rooftop and positioned himself in an alley that led from the street to the well. As she passed by, he came alongside her and kissed her on the cheek.

Suheir snapped around to face him, her eyes blazing with anger. "What are you doing!" she exclaimed. Then she recognized him and her mouth fell open. "What are you doing here?" Her eyes were wide with surprise. "You cannot be here." She lowered her voice and glanced around quickly. "This is very dangerous. Someone will see you."

"I don't care about the danger. I couldn't stay away any longer."

"But how did you find me?"

"I'm good," he grinned and he kissed her on the lips.

She grinned, then swatted him playfully. "You are good. This is why you must leave immediately. If they find you here with me they will kill you and drag your body through the streets. Then they will beat me."

"Who would do such a thing?"

"My uncle. His friends." She spoke rapidly, her voice just above a whisper. "There are roving bands of boys all too eager to impress the elders by killing people like you. Even Ahmad has joined them. You must leave at once."

"Ahmad?" Auerbach frowned. "He is here? In Jerusalem?"

"Yes. He came the—" A sound from the next street caught Suheir's attention, then a dog barked. Her eyes were alert as if sensing danger. "Go," she said. "Go quickly."

"Okay." Auerbach took a step back. "Do you come by here every day?"

"Yes," she said impatiently. "You must go."

"I will be waiting for you." He stepped quickly toward her and kissed her on the cheek. "Do not disappoint me." Then he hurried up the alley in the opposite direction.

— • —

The next day, Auerbach returned to wait for Suheir in the alley. A little before ten, she appeared at the corner by the street and came toward him. As she passed by where he was hiding, he stepped out to follow her. Dressed as a Muslim this time, he walked alongside her and she paid him no attention, then she realized who he was. "This is even more dangerous than I thought," she said.

"Not seeing you is worse."

"My uncle asked why it took longer than normal yesterday."

"But I have to see you," Auerbach pleaded. "I have to."

"You cannot see me," Suheir insisted. "You must leave. Go back to the kibbutz. This is my home now, but it is not safe for you. Go back there and forget about me."

"But I can't forget about you. Don't you understand? I love you."

She stopped and pressed her finger to his lips. "Hush! You are speaking nonsense. A Jew cannot love an Arab …" Almost unconsciously, and with her eyes focused on his, she set the jug on the pavement and slowly leaned toward him. He pressed his lips to hers and she was lost in his arms as he kissed her deeply.

After a moment she pulled away. "I love you, Yaakov," she whispered, "but you must go at once."

"You could leave with me."

"And where would we go?"

"We could take the bus to Amman and from there go anywhere we like."

"And how would we pay for this fanciful journey you've dreamed up?"

"Getting to Amman is easy," he suggested. "And from there, my brother in New York will see that we get to America."

Suheir's eyes lit up. "America?" she said with a smile.

Over Auerbach's shoulder she saw a woman turn from the street into the alley. Suheir drew away from Auerbach's embrace. Without another word, she picked up the jug and walked away. Auerbach, sensing danger, retreated from the alley through an open doorway and waited in the shadows while the stranger passed. When she was gone, he stepped back to the alley, hoping for one more glimpse of Suheir, but by then she was gone.

— · —

The next morning, Auerbach intercepted Suheir as she entered the alley, coming alongside her much closer to the street so that he could walk the length of the alley with her and they would have longer together. She greeted him with a broad smile. "I thought about what you said yesterday."

"Which thing was that? The part about my loving you, or the part about leaving with me?"

"Both."

"And?" he asked expectantly.

Suheir leaned near him as they walked. "I will go with you," she whispered. Auerbach grinned from ear to ear and turned to kiss her but she leaned her head away. "Not here," she protested. "Someone will see us. I fear they are talking even now."

"Then we should go now."

"No," she said. "Tomorrow."

"You want to wait another day?"

"My uncle will be busy tomorrow," she explained, "and we will have all day to get farther away before he realizes I am gone. Meet me here as usual. I will leave with you then." They were at the opposite end of the alley and she kissed him gently on the lips. "Now go quickly wherever it is you go when you are not with me, and don't let anyone find you."

— . —

Suheir's father, Rashid, was waiting for her when she returned to her uncle's house. Ahmad was there, too, sullen and angry. She smiled and hurried toward him. "Father, I didn't know you were coming." She put her arms out to embrace him but he pushed her away.

"I am told the American Jew has found you," he glowered. "Didn't you hear me when I forbid you to see him?" he shouted.

"But, Father," Suheir replied, "I didn't search for him. He searched for me. He came to me. I did not go to him."

"And what did you do? Did you tell him to go away?"

"I told him, repeatedly," she argued, "but he would not."

Rashid shook his head. "I do not know what has become of you two." He cast an angry gaze in Ahmad's direction. "And you," he growled. "How could you associate yourself with Khalid Suleiman?"

"He is a courageous leader," Ahmad snapped.

"He is a charlatan and a fraud, out to profit from other people's bravery. It's a wonder you aren't both dead. One child fraternizing with a Jew—and an American at that—the other has become a terrorist."

"I am not a terrorist," Ahmad countered. "I am only defending our people. And you are the one who said the Jews want to take over."

"They do want to take over. They want to rule us all. And that is precisely my point. This is not—"

"You don't understand," Ahmad shouted. "We're just trying—"

"No," Rashid roared, flush with anger. "*You* don't understand! This is not a game. This is real. The Jews plan to take over and they will kill all of us to do it."

"The mufti means to defend Jerusalem and our country," Ahmad argued, "and he will kill all the Jews to do it, too."

Rashid threw up his hands in frustration as he turned away from Ahmad and back to Suheir. "If you continue to see the Jew," he said, his voice calmer than before, "both you and he will be marked for death. The Mufti's Army of the Righteous, your own brother and his gang of thieves, will hunt you down and kill us both." He turned to Ahmad. "Am I not right? Would Suleiman spare your sister's life if he knew she was seeing this infidel?"

"The infidels seek to defeat us by every means possible," Ahmad kept his gaze from Suheir. "If they cannot defeat us with the sword, they will seek to do so by contaminating our lineage with their impure blood. We have sworn to defend their every attack."

"There," Rashid said, turning once again to Suheir. "You heard it from his lips. He will kill you, his own sister, if he has the chance."

"Ahmad," Suheir exclaimed, on the verge of tears. "How can you say such a thing? We are family."

"My family is out there," Ahmad said with a sweeping gesture, "among those who are faithful to Allah."

"Come." Rashid took Suheir by the arm and gently guided her to a chair. "Sit here."

"You would let him do such a thing?" she asked.

"I would do everything in my power to prevent it, which is why we must talk." Suheir took a seat on the chair and Rashid knelt beside her. "Now tell me everything you have promised this American Jew."

Her eyes darted away. "I have promised him nothing."

"Your eyes tell me different."

"That is between us, Father."

"Has he persuaded you to leave with him? To go away somewhere, on the promise that you will be safe with him?"

"Papa—"

"Has he?" Rashid insisted.

Tears trickled down Suheir's cheeks. "We are going to America."

"How? How is it that he could promise such a thing?"

"We can travel through Transjordan to Amman. From there, his brother will pay to bring us to America."

Ahmad was wide-eyed. "You can't possibly mean that!"

"What do you care?" she retorted. "You are planning to kill me. Why should I listen to you?"

"You would not only run away with a Jew, but to America? Is this not going from one infidel to many?"

"If I am already marked for death, then what does it matter?" she said defiantly.

Rashid held up his hand for them to stop. "He is not going to kill you, and you are not going to America."

"Yes, I am."

"You can't," Rashid said calmly. "It is impossible. Since the adoption of the UN resolution, all bus service to Amman has been suspended. Only military vehicles are allowed on the road. King Abdullah is repositioning his troops near the Jordan River in preparation for the defense of the city after the British withdrawal. The only way out of the country is through Syria and that you must do on foot."

Suheir was crestfallen. "It is a lie," she sobbed.

"No." He stood and put his arms around her. "What I say is the truth." His voice was soft and tender. "If the road to Amman was open," he whispered, "I would go with you, but sadly it is not."

— • —

At noon the following day, Auerbach entered the alley but Suheir was not there. He found a doorway where he could wait in seclusion and made himself as inconspicuous as possible. In a few minutes, she appeared at the street end of the alley, worried and tentative. She glanced to the left and right, moving haltingly, whispering his name as she went. "Yaakov? Yaakov? Are you there?"

Auerbach stepped from the doorway and walked toward her. "You came after all," he said with a smile as he reached out to wrap her in his arms.

"Yaakov." Her eyes were sad and she was on the verge of tears. "I cannot go with you."

"What do you mean you can't go?" He pulled her close. "Yesterday you said you would. I have made the arrangements."

Her eyes focused on his. "Please believe me. I do not mean to hurt you."

Just then, two men jumped him from behind, pinning his arms to his side. He twisted to the right and caught sight of Ahmad holding fast to his arm. Khalid Suleiman was with them and while Ahmad and the other man held him, Suleiman hit him in the stomach. Pain shot through him and he collapsed, hanging by his arms.

Then a voice came from a doorway to the right. Auerbach could not understand what was said but he recognized the sound of it and turned to see Rashid Hadawi, Suheir's father, coming toward him.

Rashid drew a knife from the waistband of his robe and held it menacingly close to Auerbach's neck. "I should slit your throat from ear to ear right now for the misery you have caused my family."

"If I have harmed your family," Auerbach gasped, "I apologize. I only meant to—"

Suleiman jerked the knife from Rashid's grasp. "By your own words you mock us!" he shouted and lunged toward Auerbach.

At the same time, Suheir darted between them. "No!" she shouted. "Don't kill him!" Suleiman thrust the knife toward Auerbach but instead he sank it into Suheir's abdomen. Rashid watched with horror as she collapsed to the ground.

"She was a whore," Suleiman snarled. "Better that she is dead than to bring shame on your house." He glared defiantly at Rashid. "I have done what you were too weak to do for yourself. Now you owe me your—"

Suddenly, Rashid snatched the knife from Suleiman's hand and with one flick of his wrist sliced the blade across Suleiman's throat. He staggered backward and fell to the ground, gasping for breath and writhing in pain as blood poured from the gash.

In anguish, Rashid tossed aside the knife and knelt over Suheir. He gathered her in his arms, held her close, and cried.

Ahmad knelt too. "How badly is she injured?"

"She is dead," Rashid whispered.

With tears streaming down his cheeks, Auerbach crawled to Suheir and kissed her forehead. Rashid looked over at him. "You must go and never come back."

"I wanted her to go with me," Auerbach sobbed. "I love her."

"I know," Rashid nodded. "And she loved you. And that is the only reason you are alive now. But she is dead and you must leave before someone sees you. Go to Tel Aviv. Go back to America. Go anywhere you like but do not come back here."

Auerbach stood as Ahmad wrapped his arms around Rashid and both men wept aloud. He stood there watching for a moment, then finally turned away and hurried toward the street at the end of the alley.

CHAPTER 33

WHEN AUERBACH WAS GONE, Rashid picked up Suheir's body. "Come," he said with urgency. "We must get her to the hospital."

"They cannot help her if she is dead," Ahmad replied.

Rashid replied in a matter-of-factly. "She's not dead. The knife passed through her side but missed her heart. She is still breathing, but not well."

"But Yaakov ..." Ahmad was bewildered. "The things you said...you knew even then?"

"I made sure he could not see it."

"Why did you do such a thing?"

"So he would leave and not try to return. He means well but these are dangerous times and he is not a careful man."

— · —

At the hospital a British policeman asked for details about how Suheir was injured. "She was on her way to the well for water," Rashid explained. "When she did not return as expected, we went looking for her and found her lying in the alley."

"She had already been stabbed?"

"Yes."

"Did you see who did it?"

"No. But the neighbors who lived there told us that a Jew attacked her. One of the men tried to stop him but the Jew drew a knife and slit the man's throat."

"Slit the throat of the man who tried to help her?"

"Yes."

"You saw this man?" the policeman asked. "You saw the one who helped?"

"He was lying in the alley when we arrived."

"Was he dead?"

"Yes," Rashid nodded. "He was dead. Suheir was breathing very lightly, but the man who attacked her was dead." He glanced at Ahmad and the two exchanged angry glares, but Ahmad remained silent.

The policeman seemed not to notice the exchange between them but made a note of what Rashid said, then gave a satisfied nod. "Very well. I hope your daughter recovers fully." Then he closed his note pad, slipped it into his pocket, and disappeared up the hallway.

Rashid and Ahmad sat together, quietly waiting for word of Suheir's condition, but they were alone for only a short time when Samih Nuri appeared in the doorway. He glanced around as if searching for something or someone, then caught sight of Ahmad and came to sit beside him. "We have new leadership," he whispered.

"Already?" Ahmad asked.

"Yes. Hatoumi took charge as soon as we heard the news. You have no objection?"

"No." Ahmad shook his head. "I have none."

"He wants to know what happened to Khalid. They are having a meeting now to decide what to do." Nuri stood. "Come. You must go with me."

As Ahmad slid forward in his chair to stand, Rashid took hold of him by the arm. "Ahmad," he implored, "do not go. Stay here with me."

"I must," Ahmad retorted, then he pulled free of his father's grasp and started toward the door.

— · —

From the hospital, Ahmad followed Nuri back to the neighborhood near his uncle's house. A few blocks from the alley where Suleiman had been killed, they joined others in their gang who were gathered inside an abandoned warehouse.

Yezid Hatoumi, a young man with dark, intelligent eyes, was seated on the floor with a circle of followers clustered around him. When Ahmad appeared he looked up at him with a somber expression and said, "Come. Have a seat next to me." He patted the spot with his hand. "Let us hear what you have to say about this terrible thing that has happened."

Ahmad took a seat beside him and glanced around nervously. "I am not sure how much sense I can make of it."

"We are all sorry for the injury to your sister, and saddened at the death of Suleiman, and we want to hear what happened in the alley, but first we must pray for Khalid's soul and for his entrance into paradise." Hatoumi rose on his knees and bowed his head. The others followed suit and then they all began to pray the Salat al-Janazah, the Muslim funeral prayer for the dead.

"O Allah, forgive our living and our dead, those who are present among us and those who are absent, our young and our old, our males and our females. O Allah, whoever you keep alive, keep him alive, and whoever you cause to die, cause him to die with faith. O Allah, do not deprive us of the reward and do not cause us to go astray after this. O Allah, forgive our friend and leader Khalid Suleiman and have mercy on him, keep him safe and sound and forgive him, honor his rest and ease his entrance to Paradise and protect him from the torment of the grave and the torment of Hell-fire; make his grave spacious and fill it with light."

When they finished, Hatoumi shifted from his knees to a sitting position and waited while the others did as well. Then he turned to Ahmad and said, "Tell us what happened."

"Well," Ahmad began slowly, "my sister went to fetch the daily water from the well in our neighborhood." He concentrated hard, trying to remember the story his father told the policeman. If Hatoumi shared Suleiman's contacts, he might already know what the policeman had reported. "When she did not return at her usual time, we searched for her and found her in the alley. She had been stabbed and was bleeding."

"How did it happen?" Hatoumi asked. "Do you know?"

"People from the neighborhood were there when we arrived and told us the attacker was a Jew. Khalid saw the attack and tried to intervene. In the process, his throat was slit. When others from the neighborhood came to help, the Jew ran away."

"They told you a Jew attacked your sister and when Khalid tried to intervene, the Jew attacked him, too?"

"Yes," Ahmad nodded. "That is what they said. Khalid was already dead when we arrived."

Hatoumi let his eyes move slowly around the circle gathered before them, his index finger raised in a professorial pose. "You have heard from Ahmad what happens when Jews are allowed to walk the streets at will. If they are free for any purpose other than to go to work, this is what happens." Those seated with them nodded in agreement as Hatoumi continued. "If the Jews worked more, they would have no energy for anything else. But if they do not devote themselves to labor, they do things like this. The world outside does not understand them. The British do not understand them. Nor do the Americans, or anyone at the United Nations. But we do, because we have lived with them all these years." Once again the group nodded their agreement to the things he said. "Our people have a long history with them and understand the mind of a Jew, an understanding passed down to us. If a Jew can make a pound by working but half a pound by sitting still, he will do both and convince you he's done neither. They are masters at the art of deception, which is why we can never live under Jewish authority. It would be an affront to Allah to submit to such dishonesty. Jews must live under our authority, under the authority of truth revealed through Allah, and for that to happen we must convince the British that it is in their best interests to withdraw. Once they are gone, we will be free to establish ourselves as rulers of the land. And so it is our task to teach the British a reality they refuse to face—that they can no longer solve the problems of Palestine. And to teach them, we must increase the violence even more. If Palestine descends into chaos, some of the nations that voted for the plan of partition will change their minds and will delay its implementation. But we have to make trouble for both the Jews and the British. And we must avenge Suleiman's murder."

"For Suleiman!" someone shouted.

"For Suleiman!" they all repeated.

— • —

Later that evening, Ahmad, Nuri, and the others carried a mortar to a hilltop just outside the Jewish Quarter. They set it in place on a level spot and Nuri dropped a shell down the tube. It made a blast that startled them all as the projectile shot into the air. They laughed in response and watched as a thin contrail arced across the night sky and disappeared from sight. Moments later, a red flash erupted from two kilometers away, followed by the report of a violent explosion.

"That was too long," someone said.

"It went beyond the quarter."

"What if it hit a house of our people?"

"We will blame it on the Jews," Nuri quipped, and they all laughed. He knelt beside the mortar and adjusted the angle, then picked up another shell and dropped it down the tube. "Cover your ears!" Again there was a loud report as the projectile shot into the air. Seconds later an explosion erupted, this time about a kilometer away.

"Much better," someone said.

Near the heart of the Jewish Quarter, a blaze rose from the house that had been struck by the mortar round. Nuri lifted his hands and shouted, "Allah Akbar!" The others joined him, dancing around the mortar and repeated the phrase like a chant while flames in the Quarter leaped higher.

While they still were celebrating, Hasib Bahour joined them. One of the newest members of the group, he was eager to prove his worth and since joining them had made a point of finding new things for them to do. "Look down there," he pointed. "Along the road that leads from town."

"What of it?" Nuri was aggravated at the interruption.

"A bus full of Jews," Bahour said excitedly, "on their way to Tel Aviv."

"Are you sure?"

"Yes," Bahour nodded. "I am certain. I was following them earlier. See if you can hit them."

Nuri picked up the mortar tube and turned to Ahmad. "Grab one of those shells and come with me. Bahour, you come, too." Ahmad did as he was told and as he turned to follow, Nuri called back to the others, "Stay right here. We'll be back soon."

From the hilltop they ran down a narrow street that skirted the Jewish Quarter, then cut through an overgrown patch and came out on the road ahead of where they'd seen the bus. Out of breath and gasping for air, Hatoumi stood with his hands on his knees and said to Ahmad, "Set that mortar at the lowest angle. Quickly. Before the bus arrives."

Ahmad adjusted the angle of the tube and set it on the ground. "I do not think it is low enough. The angle is still too steep."

By then Nuri had recovered enough to move about and checked the angle of the mortar. "We'll prop it against a rock. Maybe that will do." They searched frantically for something large enough to lean the mortar base against but nothing was found and the bus was drawing near. "Forget that," Nuri snapped. "Give me your shirts."

They all removed their shirts and Nuri wrapped them around the base of the mortar, then gripped it with both hands and tucked it beneath his arm. His eyes glued on the approaching bus. "Okay, drop the shell in the tube."

"Are you certain this will work?"

"Just do it before the bus goes by."

Ahmad lifted the shell from the ground, fitted one end into the mouth of the mortar tube, and shoved it with all his might. When the shell hit the bottom it ignited with a bang, sending the projectile straight toward the bus. It struck near the rear wheels and the bus burst into flames.

"Ah!" Nuri screamed and he dropped the mortar on the ground. Smoke rose from the shirts he'd wrapped around it and he danced around, slinging his hands. "That was hot!"

With the rear half of the bus on fire, it careened from the pavement and tumbled down the hill. Partway to the bottom, it tipped on its side, rolling over. Bahour shouted with glee, "Die, you stinking Jews! Die!"

As the flames lit up the night, Ahmad saw people inside the bus, groping and staggering about in search of the door, then the fire burned hotter and they disappeared in the mass of orange and red that consumed the bus.

— • —

It was well past midnight when Ahmad returned to his uncle's house, but he found Rashid waiting.

"How is Suheir?" he asked, hoping to avoid a confrontation.

"Never mind about your sister," Rashid shouted. "I told you to stay away from them!"

Ahmad replied with a sullen tone. "How do you know where I have been?"

"I saw you with the mortar. They will kill you if they find you!"

"The Jews will never find us," Ahmad smirked.

"They are finding people every day. I found you. You think they will have a more difficult time than I did? The Jews are not stupid. There are hundreds of mortars just like the one you and your friends have. All of them shooting into the Jewish Quarter. And every night the Jews are out in the streets and alleys searching for them. Going house to house to find them. When they find you, they will kill you. No questions. No inquiry. Just a bullet to the head or a knife to your throat."

"I don't care. I must stand with my countrymen and defend our families."

Rashid lowered his voice. "I thought you liked the Jews. That's what you told me before."

Ahmad turned away. "I was wrong."

"No," Rashid countered. "I was wrong. I do not like the idea of them taking control of the country, and it is abhorrent to Allah for them to touch our women, but I do not hate them personally."

"That is the opinion of someone too old to oppose them by force. We are not hampered by such limitations. We must fight."

Rashid stared at him in silence a moment, then said with a heavy voice, "If that is your decision, then so be it. You are old enough to bear the conse-quences for yourself. But I will not stay to watch what you make of it. I am taking Suheir home. She will be safer there with me than here with you. I never should have sent her here in the first place."

"Is she able to travel?"

"We will make do the best we can," Rashid replied. "She cannot stay here." He squared his shoulders and looked Ahmad in the eye. "If you want the life of a warrior, then you shall have it, here, in Jerusalem, but do not bring it to my house. I do not want this near my family."

— • —

In the night, while Ahmad slept, King Abdullah's army arrived from Transjordan with heavy artillery pieces. The next morning, the booming sound of the cannon and the constant explosion of shells jarred him awake. From the room where he slept, he made his way downstairs and took a seat in a chair in the courtyard behind the house. Rashid was already gone with Suheir and a sense of loneliness swept over him. When he tried to put it from his mind, images of the burning bus from the night before took its place and all he could see were the passengers stumbling about in the flames.

Before long, Nuri arrived and the misery Ahmad felt was replaced by a sense of dread. He no longer wanted to launch mortar rounds into the Jewish Quarter or inflict misery on anyone, but he was afraid to turn down the suggestion he knew was coming.

"You are missed," Nuri said with a broad grin. "Everyone is asking about you."

"What are you doing?"

"Come with me," Nuri urged. "You will see."

Reluctantly, Ahmad pushed himself up from the chair and followed Nuri as he led the way back to the hilltop where they'd been with the mortar the night before. Everyone was gathered there again, laughing and singing as they took turns lobbing shells onto the houses below. They laughed and joked about the misery each would cause, then shouted for joy as shells exploded in a hail of fire and smoke.

Ahmad dutifully took his turn, dropping a mortar shell down the tube and shouting angrily at the Jews as it flew into the sky. His heart was no longer in the fight, but he was afraid something might happen to his father and sister if he refused to participate. Suleiman would know without being told that he had—

Suddenly Ahmad remembered Suleiman was dead and no longer a threat. A sense of liberation and freedom came over him with a rush of excitement that put a genuine grin on his face. Suleiman was dead! He was free! Free to say no, to do whatever he wanted, to leave the city and never return.

The rumble from the artillery continued to shake the ground as round after round was launched into the city. So heavy was the barrage that it seemed to Ahmad as if all the Muslims in the world had joined in attacking the Jews. But instead of elation, he thought of Yaakov Auerbach, Natan Shahak, and the Jews he knew from the kibbutz near his home at Degania. Shahak and the others didn't want trouble. They only wanted to farm and live in peace. Ahmad wanted the same thing, to work the family farm and live in peace. He was proud to be an Arab but not proud to fight the Jews and had only been caught up in the struggle out of fear. Now that Suleiman was gone, that fear no longer controlled him and the desire to return home welled up inside.

While others in the group continued to launch shell after shell from the mortar, Ahmad drifted away and returned to his uncle's house. He went upstairs to his room and stuffed his things into a backpack, then slipped from the house and started up the street. Home was a long way off but if he continued walking north he would reach Degania in a few days.

CHAPTER 34

WHEN MICKEY MARCUS ARRIVED in Tel Aviv, Ben-Gurion assigned him an apartment near the Jewish Agency office and met with him there to talk in private. The evening he arrived they talked for two hours, beginning a conversation that continued off and on for the next week as Marcus learned the history of Haganah and how Irgun and Lehi had broken away to become separate fighting units.

"Now," Ben-Gurion said, "we need to bring all of these organizations together as a single army. A unified national fighting force."

"That might not be possible without a messy confrontation," Marcus noted. "Each of these units has its own sense of mission. From what I can tell, leaders of these groups have serious differences of opinion with you about which direction to take the country."

"They do and that's a problem, but the central issue," Ben-Gurion stressed, "is how to bring them under a single commander. Lehi is smaller and less organized. We could add most of its men to our existing units without much trouble. Irgun is a different matter. It's larger and more tightly organized with a distinct identity."

"I assumed as much from the way you described them earlier," Marcus nodded. "But resolving this situation now might be so disruptive it detracts from the overall military purpose."

"There is no purpose except the establishment of a Jewish state," Ben-Gurion countered. "And that requires an army subject to the authority of its supreme commander." He pointed to himself. "I'm that commander. If we let them persist in their differences, they will eventually grow bold enough to attempt a takeover by force. We'll face a coup d'état. I cannot allow it. President Truman wouldn't allow such a thing in America. No national leader would."

Ben-Gurion returned to his earlier theme. "It's true that in the United States we have a single military organization," Marcus explained, "all of it accountable to a civilian authority. But that organization is broken into a number of components. Army, navy, and now the air force. And within each of those we have several different units we call commandos or Special Forces. And the navy has the marines, which has a history different and unrelated to all the others. If an American president ever tried to merge the marines into the army we'd have a brawl in Washington at every level. But the accountability flows up the chain of command to a single military leader, who is subject to civilian authority."

"You have the luxury of viewing these matters from the perspective of a long history. And you have the benefit of having endured the organizational struggles already. We do not."

"That's true. And there was certainly internal conflict in the beginning as George Washington asserted control over the Continental army."

"There can only be one force for us, and if establishing that means an armed confrontation, then so be it. I need you to review the troops and tell me how to fix this. And I don't want your insight limited by political considerations. I want the raw truth."

"I'll do my best," Marcus replied.

"I know you will. That's why I came to you for help."

— · —

While Marcus conducted a detailed readiness review of Haganah and the other fighting units, Ben-Gurion convened the Council of Thirteen—the heads of the Jewish Agency's departments—to address civilian readiness.

"As we are all aware," he began, "Jewish independence in Palestine is fast approaching. The British will be gone by May fourteenth, and we must be ready to assume responsibility for our own affairs. That independence will almost certainly involve war with our neighbors. So I would like for us to discuss today, and at daily meetings for the next several days or however long it takes, our level of preparedness to assume that responsibility."

"To me," Eyal Revach began, "one of the most important things we lack is a single national military. We have a number of small Jewish forces operating in Palestine, but only Haganah is directly within our control. Somehow, we have to bring all the paramilitary organizations into a single cohesive national army."

"Yes," Ben-Gurion agreed. "That is a problem and the American, Mickey Marcus, is reviewing this issue. He will help us figure out those military questions. What we need to focus on is the question of what we, as a government in waiting, must do to be ready to meet the challenges of independence, beyond the military questions."

Cohen spoke up, "I know you want to take this discussion in a different direction, but I worry about whether we can resolve all of our military organizational issues now and, at the same time, avoid a civil war."

"I'm not sure we can solve that problem now, either," Golda argued. "Perhaps it would be better if we continued to let them function separately until after we've gained our independence and established ourselves. Once the British are gone, all the neighboring countries will invade and we need to focus on defeating them before we turn on each other."

"You sound rather pessimistic," someone in the back of the room suggested.

"I'm not pessimistic at all," Golda replied. "I am certain we will win, but my point is we don't really know how difficult the war will be. Our assessments indicate it could be quite difficult."

"I think there is a marked difference in the resolve of Palestinian Arabs and those from surrounding countries," Cohen offered. "Palestinian Arabs have a stake in the outcome that is quite different from that of Transjordan or Egypt. How that plays out, no one yet knows."

"Well," Yitzhak Rutenberg began dryly, "as far as military readiness goes, we have no armor to speak of. No cannon. Only rifles and sidearms, and half enough ammunition for any of them, which won't provide much resistance for the well-equipped armies we will face."

Haim Edri spoke up, "Some are suggesting we should postpone a declaration of independence. Perhaps we should consider that option."

"We have no choice but to declare our independence as planned," Ben-Gurion responded, hoping to steer the conversation away from military issues. "We can't wait. It's now or never."

"And besides," Golda added, "the British will be gone and we will have no one to turn to except ourselves anyway."

"This is as close as our friends and allies can get us," Ben-Gurion said solemnly. "We have to do the rest ourselves. They have helped us to this point, a point from which we can see independence. A point from which we can see a Jewish state. From here, we must do the rest ourselves, which is what I wanted—"

Phineas Ben Zvi interrupted, "Do you realize we don't even have a flag?"

"This is the kind of thing I wanted to discuss," Ben-Gurion chuckled.

"Then let's adopt one," Golda suggested. "Let's adopt a national flag."

For the next thirty minutes they discussed the design of a flag and settled on a blue Star of David resting on a white field. Then they turned to the matter of a name.

"Is there really any choice?" Zalman Shazar asked. "Do we even need to vote?"

"The answer seems obvious to me," Zvi shrugged.

"We are a Jewish state in Palestine," Shazar continued. "History demands that we take the name of Israel."

"Let's have a show of hands," Ben-Gurion said, pressing for a vote before anyone could suggest another option. With little fanfare, every hand in the room went up. Almost immediately, someone started clapping and soon the room was filled with the sound of clapping and cheering. Ben-Gurion let them continue a moment, then slowly brought them to order. "Now we have a flag and a name," he said when the room was quiet. "And that brings us to the crucial question: When do we declare our independence to the world?"

"Should we do that?" Yosef Brenner asked from the far side of the room. "Or should we wait and let the UN dictate the terms of the new state's existence? They created a transition process in the resolution that takes us to independence. Would it be better to wait for them to enforce it?"

"I think independence, by definition, means we decide our own course," Zvi argued. "An independent state does not wait around for someone else to determine its destiny. It is true, if we declare our independence, the Arab nations will invade us. But even if we remain silent, they will invade as soon as the British leave. So if we must fight anyway, we might as well fight for our own freedom."

"We should declare our independence on the day the British mandate ends," Shazar added. "May fourteenth. That way we have a seamless continuity of government."

"Are we in agreement on May fourteenth?" Ben-Gurion asked, unwilling to let the opportunity for a decision pass.

"We should vote," Golda interjected. "We need a clear record of how we arrived at this decision."

Ben-Gurion had a questioning look. "A vote on which?"

"On both," Golda replied. "A vote on declaring our independence and on doing so on the fourteenth."

Ben-Gurion smiled indulgently. "All in favor of declaring our independence and announcing it on May fourteenth say, 'Yes.'" The council responded with a resounding shout and again the room erupted.

As the noise faded, a voice from the back of the room spoke up. "If I understand things correctly, the British mandate won't actually end until midnight of the fourteenth."

"That is correct," Ben-Gurion nodded. "And at that moment we shall become a sovereign nation."

"The fourteenth is a Friday. The Sabbath begins at sunset. It will be the Sabbath at midnight. Conducting a ceremony to declare our independence on the Sabbath will be a problem with the rabbis."

The room fell silent. Ben-Gurion, taken aback, seemed to fumble for a response before recovering enough to say, "Then we will announce our declaration in the afternoon, before the Sabbath begins, and note that it will be effective at one minute past midnight on the morning of the fifteenth."

— • —

A few days later, Ben-Gurion met with Mickey Marcus to review Marcus' findings. "I talked to Gedaliah Cohen about consolidating control over Haganah," Marcus reported. "That won't be a problem and I think you've already done most of that. But you have one unit you didn't tell me about."

"Palmach," Ben-Gurion said with a sheepish smile.

"Yes," Marcus nodded.

"They report to me, though."

"If it's part of Haganah, it needs to report to Cohen. You need to make them accountable to Cohen and Cohen accountable to you."

"You think Cohen will be able to control them? Is he the right man for the job? I meant it when I said I wanted the raw truth."

"I think if he can't control Palmach, you're in very serious trouble. He's the best leader you have. Do you really doubt his ability?"

Ben-Gurion shook his head. "No, I have confidence in him. I just want your analysis—of everyone."

"I understand your desire to consolidate control with a civilian at the top, but for this to work you'll have to exercise your authority through a single military commander. You don't have anyone other than Cohen who can fill that billet."

"You talked to him about this?"

"Not about his ability but about the necessity of establishing a clear chain of command."

"What about integrating Lehi and Irgun?"

"Cohen understands your intention and he agrees with it, but he thinks integrating both units right now would be very disruptive and ultimately counterproductive to the immediate goal of defending against the Arab threat. I think he's probably right."

"We can't have separate Jewish armies running around the country fighting under their own policy and strategy."

"No," Marcus nodded. "You can't. But you can't fight a civil war right now, either. Cohen suggested incorporating Lehi now and addressing Irgun later. That makes a lot of sense."

"A two-step process."

"Yes."

Ben-Gurion seemed receptive to the idea. "What kind of timeline?"

"Address the Lehi issue immediately. Perhaps delay incorporation of Irgun until after the war."

"I don't think the situation will wait that long."

Marcus had a puzzled frown. "What do you mean?"

"If we bring Lehi under our control but not Irgun, they will see it as authorization to exert them in whatever way they choose."

"You may be right," Marcus acknowledged. "And if that happens, you'll have to face it. But I wouldn't go looking for trouble internally. Not now. You've got enough trouble elsewhere. You have some significant gaps in your defense."

"We've identified Egypt as our primary threat."

"That's true in the Negev. And they have the best-equipped army. But Transjordan has the best-trained army. Abdullah will take the West Bank."

"Can we stop him?" Ben-Gurion asked.

"You won't need to. He'll take the West Bank and go no farther."

"We have wondered the same thing, but can we be certain?"

"I think so. He will take it for much the same reason as you would let him have it."

Ben-Gurion had a knowing smile. "Abdullah is smart."

"Taking the West Bank makes obvious strategic sense for him. It's contiguous to Transjordan and has a strong Arab majority. Taking it makes sense from his perspective, but it makes sense from yours, as well. If he takes that area, it relieves you of a large bloc of Arab population. He knows this and is banking on you not resisting his advance in that region. He won't go any farther because if he does he would occupy areas that are majority Jewish, which would shift his population mix too far away from an Arab supermajority and invite unrest."

"It's a little unsettling to trust him."

"I don't think you have any realistic option," Marcus said flatly.

Ben-Gurion seemed to agree. "What about the others? Syria, Lebanon, and Iran."

"Iran is too far away to be a serious threat. Lebanon and Syria are too weak. You can stave them off in the Galilee. The key for you is to address threats from the north with the least force possible, control Jerusalem—which means maintaining control of the Jerusalem-Tel Aviv highway—and concentrate the bulk of your forces on the Negev."

"To whom do you suggest we give that responsibility?"

Marcus sighed. "Aharon Hartman is your best field commander. He has experience, knows tactics and strategy, and he has an intangible gift for field operations—all of the leadership qualities that are absolutely crucial for mounting a credible defense against the Egyptians."

"But?" Ben-Gurion asked expectantly.

"He's not convinced war is necessary."

"And he thinks we're being shortsighted by pushing things in that direction," Ben-Gurion added.

"You've talked to him about this?"

"He has doubts about me," Ben-Gurion replied.

"In his estimation, you're not a military man."

"I served during the Great War."

"But not with a regular army and not for very long. He thinks of you as a politician."

"Can he follow orders?"

"I don't know," Marcus shrugged. "I think he probably can, but his doubts about your ability are big issues for him."

"I should have fired him," Ben-Gurion sighed in disgust.

"I don't think so," Marcus countered. "You don't have anyone else you can put in charge of the Negev defense."

"What about Moshe Dayan?"

"Moshe is a great leader. A natural leader with many of the same gifts as Hartman. One day he'll be better than Hartman. But not right now. Even with your largest force concentrated on the Negev, you'll be stretched thin to meet an Egyptian attack. A younger leader might give you the brashness necessary for a stunning victory, but he also might give you the blunder that sinks an entire battalion. You don't want to lose your southern army."

— • —

After meeting with Marcus, Ben-Gurion decided to follow his advice and make consolidating Lehi a priority. Incorporation of Palmach into Haganah's command structure would be handled as an internal Haganah issue with Cohen taking the lead. Addressing military issues through Cohen was new for Ben-Gurion and left him uncomfortable, but he was certain the approach was correct and was eager to see how well it worked. Talking to Yitzhak Jezand-Gurion took for himself. They met to discuss it the following week.

"Yitzhak," Ben-Gurion said from behind his desk, "as you know, we will become an independent nation in May. We're preparing the necessary political apparatus now."

"The Arabs will never accept that peacefully."

"You're right," Ben-Gurion nodded. "Independence will mean war and we're preparing for that, as well. Haganah will become the national defense force."

"Everyone already knows that," Jezing replied.

"We need your men to join it."

"You want us to dissolve?" It was an obvious question but Jezing seemed not at all off-guard.

"Yes," Ben-Gurion nodded. "We do."

"And if we do not?"

Ben-Gurion kept a straight face. "You'll be outlawed as our first official governmental act."

"Well," Jezing shrugged, "if we have no alternative, then we will disband."

"But we need your men to become part of Haganah."

"I will tell them and give them that option, but I can't force them to join."

Ben-Gurion pushed back his chair and stood. "Okay, but we will appreciate their cooperation." Then the two men shook hands and Jezing left. The meeting had been cordial and brief, more amicable than Ben-Gurion expected, and he sat at his desk thinking long after Jezing was gone, wondering what would happen next.

— • —

A few days later, Ben-Gurion met with Noga Shapiro. Though he had decided to forego a formal integration of Irgun into Haganah, he nevertheless wanted to discuss the matter with Shapiro to avoid the implication that Irgun was free to operate totally on its own. Ben-Gurion began the meeting as he had all the others. "As you are aware, war is coming," he said.

"War is already here," Shapiro corrected.

"And it will get worse when the British leave."

"But now we are hampered by their presence from fully responding. When they are gone, we will be free to defend ourselves without concern for their interference."

"And that is what I want to discuss. You and I have not always seen things the same way."

"No. We have not."

"But when the British leave," Ben-Gurion continued, "I will be head of the provisional government, at least until we hold elections."

"You have guided us for a long time," Shapiro remarked.

"We don't need a fight among ourselves."

"No." Shapiro shook his head. "We don't."

"But we do need a single fighting force, controlled at the top by a single commander."

"What does that mean for Irgun?"

"You may continue to command Irgun, but you must coordinate your strategy through me."

"You mean I must be accountable to you."

"Yes. You and all of Irgun."

"But to you. Not to Gedaliah." Shapiro said it as a statement, not a question.

"No. Not through Gedaliah."

"I cannot submit to him," Shapiro continued.

"I understand."

"He means well, but he has no sense of how hard we must strike our enemies."

"Casualties worry him," Ben-Gurion explained.

"I understand that," Shapiro countered. "But sometimes, pressing forward vigorously is the best way to reduce casualties."

Ben-Gurion turned the conversation back to the original topic. "If you will agree to account to me—coordinate your plans through my office, subject to my review, and follow orders—then we can move forward."

"And if not?"

"Do we really need to discuss that now?" Ben-Gurion asked.

Shapiro stared at him for what seemed like a long time, "No. I suppose not."

CHAPTER 35

OVER AT HAGANAH HEADQUARTERS, across the road from the Jewish Agency offices, Moshe Dayan reviewed the latest intelligence reports from Shai. Photographs and personal reports indicated the Syrian army was gathering along the Syrian and Lebanese frontier. Farmers in eastern Galilee reported seeing small numbers of Syrian troops on the Palestinian side of the Jordan River. Dayan was concerned about what he saw and went to see Gedaliah Cohen. He found Cohen in his office, seated at his desk.

"Have you seen these reports?" Dayan asked as he strode through the doorway.

"Which ones?" Cohen asked as he looked up from the documents that lay before him.

"About Syrian troop movements."

"Yes," Dayan replied. "I saw those this morning."

"If they are sending out patrols on our side of the river, they may be on the verge of crossing in large numbers."

"You think they are probing with force to see what resistance is like?"

"Yes." Dayan was worried. "I do."

Cohen opened a drawer and took out a folder, then tossed it onto the desktop. "We've had similar reports from French operatives living in Syria and Lebanon. They think the Syrian army will occupy the Galilee as far west as Tiberias before the British withdraw."

"Then we should reposition some of our forces to that region now," Dayan insisted. "Have them engage in large-scale exercises. Patrol the area in numbers large enough to be obvious."

"Can't do that," Cohen said with a shake of his head.

"Why not?"

"You know the strategy. Hold the north with local resistance. Commit the bulk of our forces to defending the Negev."

Dayan squared his shoulders. "Well then, I think it's time for me to go to Degania."

"Yes," Cohen replied. "I agree." The expression on his face turned grim. "But I'm serious about our overall strategy. Degania will have to defend itself with what they have on hand. We don't really have anything to give you in support. You'll be pretty much on your own, at least for now."

"Then we'll rely on what we do best—making do with what we have."

— · —

Early that afternoon, Moshe Dayan procured a car from the Haganah motor pool, packed a bag with a few clothes, and prepared to leave. On his way out of town he stopped by a Haganah base near the outskirts of town and cajoled a clerk into giving him three World War II–era bazookas, which he placed in the trunk of the car. Three hours later he arrived at the Degania farm compound and brought the car to a stop near the cafeteria building.

For Dayan, coming to Degania was like returning home. His parents, some of the first settlers to arrive at the kibbutz, arrived there from the Ukraine in 1909, not long after the settlement was established. Dayan was only the second child born there and he remained of special interest to the settlers, many of whom continued to follow his career closely.

As he exited the car, Hanoch Keret, the leader of the kibbutz, appeared. "We are honored to have you here with us," he said proudly.

"I should like to have come under less dire circumstances."

"Oh?" Keret seemed concerned. "Has something happened?"

"The Syrians have moved much of their army to the border. We hear reports of patrols operating as far west as Tiberias."

"We have seen soldiers," Keret confirmed, "but quite frankly no one knew whose they were."

"Most likely, they were Syrians. Haganah has no active patrols out here."

"Well," Keret said with a determined smiled. "At least we have you."

Keret escorted Dayan across the compound to a tractor shed where Yosef Fein was busy showing a new arrival how to operate the equipment. Fein was startled to see Dayan but excited to meet him. "We have heard a lot about you."

"I hope some of it was true," Dayan replied with a laugh.

"Yosef is in charge of the settlement guard," Keret explained. "He can show you what we have done so far to prepare our defenses."

"Certainly," Fein said with a gesture toward the door. "Right this way."

From the tractor shed, Fein led Dayan to a perimeter wall that encircled the central portion of the compound. Constructed of brick and mortar, it stood slightly taller than Dayan's head and was half a meter thick. Dayan made note of its solid construction, then said, "If we are to stop the Syrian army, we'll need more than this."

"It is not strong enough?"

"It's as strong as a wall could be," Dayan replied. "We just need more."

"What do you suggest?"

"We need an antitank ditch and berms placed farther out, well beyond the wall, to slow their tanks before they get close. This wall would slow them down, but eventually a tank could break through and there's nothing behind it to prevent them from taking the compound. If we can slow the tanks while they are farther out, we can perhaps have a chance to disable them out there, before they get inside."

"We have only small arms and a few explosive charges," Fein explained, "but no heavy arms capable of stopping an armored vehicle."

"Perhaps we can make our own," Dayan said with a smile.

The following day, Fein assembled a crew with heavy equipment and assigned them the task of digging a ditch, five meters wide and five meters deep, all the way around the compound. While they did that, Dayan gathered several farmhands at the shop. Natan Shahak joined them.

"Today," Dayan began, "we are going to prepare one of the simplest but most effective weapons available." He held up an empty glass bottle. "The Molotov cocktail."

For the next hour, he walked them through the process of preparing the hand-thrown bombs. First showing them how to mix the correct proportions of gasoline, diesel fuel, and motor oil to fill the bottle, then attaching a cork in the open end and a cotton cloth to the outside to serve as a wick. Natan Shahak was included in that group and was taken with Dayan from the moment they met.

With a number of empty bottles prepared, Dayan took them outside to the refuse pile located beyond the perimeter wall. A steel drum stood there among the mound of trash, and Dayan lined them up a few meters from it. "The trick to using one of these is to hold it long enough for the wick to catch fire but throw it before it explodes in your hand. To do that, you simply light it, pause for a few seconds, and throw it. When the bottle strikes a hard object the glass will break, releasing gasoline vapors. As soon as those vapors reach the flaming wick, it will erupt."

To show them how it worked, Dayan filled one of the bottles from a can of petrol. When it was full, he placed a cork in the mouth of the bottle and carried it a safe distance away. Shahak was standing nearby and Dayan said, "Light it and step back quickly."

Shahak took a match from his pocket, struck it against the leg of his pants, and lit the cloth attached to the side of the bottle. Dayan hesitated a moment, allowing the cloth to fully catch fire, then hurled the bottle toward the steel drum. It struck the side of the drum with a bang and instantly erupted in flames. Everyone gasped at the sight of it.

"That, gentlemen," Dayan said proudly, "is a Molotov cocktail."

Under Dayan's tutelage, they took turns filling a bottle, lighting the wick, and throwing it toward the steel drum. Most of the bottles exploded on impact. "When the tanks attack us," Dayan said as they continued to practice, "they will be forced to slow to negotiate the antitank ditch. While they are doing that, we will attack."

Someone spoke up. "These glass bottles will stop a tank?"

"The steel tracks on a tank travel across rubber rollers," Dayan explained. "If you aim for the tracks, the fire from the gas in the bottle will melt the rubber. With the rubber rollers gone, the tracks will come off and the tank will be unable to move."

"Will we actually do battle against a tank?" Shahak asked eagerly.

"Yes," Dayan replied. "Several."

"Who's going to attack us?" another asked in a derisive tone. "We're a farming community."

"The Syrians," Shahak answered.

"The Syrians? Are you crazy? They wouldn't waste time with us. They'd just go around."

"We're too large to ignore," Shahak explained. "If they go around us, they have to worry about us attacking them from the rear."

Dayan looked over at him. "You've studied tactics?"

"No. But my father fought against the Arabs during the revolt. I learned many things from him."

"He has prepared you well."

"I hope to have an opportunity to use that preparation."

"I think you will."

"Are the Syrians really that close?" another asked in a skeptical tone.

"Yes." Dayan pointed to the east. "They are just over the next hill."

CHAPTER 36

IN KEEPING WITH HIS CONVERSATION with Ben-Gurion, Yitzhak Jeziernicky ordered Lehi to disband. It was a bittersweet moment for him—Lehi had been formed with the notion that one day the Jewish state would become a reality, which was now on the verge of happening, but he had misgivings about the training and effectiveness of Haganah and misgivings about the decisiveness of Jewish Agency leadership. Primarily, he doubted Haganah would be ready for the challenges of independence. *Before long,* he thought, *Ben-Gurion will wish he had an organization like Lehi to do the toughest jobs.*

Most Lehi members immediately volunteered for service in Haganah and were assigned to regular units. Jeziernicky was appointed to a position on the general staff. But secretly, a group of two dozen former Lehi members continued to meet, planning covert operations and searching for ways to carry them out. When Jeziernicky learned of it, he contacted Nahum Halevy, one of Lehi's best leaders and one of the few who had refused to join Haganah. They met for coffee at a café in Tel Aviv.

"I understand some of you are still together," Jeziernicky said, getting straight to the point.

"Do you really want to know these things?" Halevy asked.

"I am always concerned for the safety of my men."

"You should be worried for your own safety."

"How so?"

"Surely someone has seen us together." Halevy gestured to their surroundings. "This is a public location."

"I am not worried."

"You are not concerned that they might think you have encouraged us to continue, even after the official order to disband?"

"You are the one who should be worried," Jeziernicky cautioned. "I am merely having coffee with an old friend. No one will deny me that. But if you do anything to bring attention to yourselves, they will send troops to find you and you will be executed."

Halevy's eyes were alive with passion, "Listen, you and I both know that Gedaliah Cohen will never order the kind of decisive and bold military action our defense demands. And even if he would, Ben-Gurion will never let him do it. The Arabs know it, too, which is why they continue to attack our villages and towns."

"You are proposing your own action? Based on your own policy?"

"I'm not telling you what we're doing," Halevy replied. "You don't want to know the details, you don't need to know the details, and if I tell you, you will eventually have to tell someone else. So, I'm not saying."

"You're probably right," Jeziernicky shrugged.

"You know I am."

"If you were planning to conduct one of these undisclosed, nonexistent operations, what kind of undisclosed, nonexistent materiel would you need to pull it off?"

Halevy's eyes were serious. "Are you sure you want to ask that question?"

"Old habits are hard to break."

"To do almost anything we would need everything. Haganah took all our equipment and supplies when we officially disbanded."

"That should not be difficult," Jeziernicky replied. "You still remember where we got the things they took?"

"Yes."

"I think you'll find most of what you need there."

"Won't that cause trouble for you?"

"Not if they think it was taken by the Arabs," Jeziernicky replied.

"You think you can do this?"

"I'm not doing it."

"Not that. We can do that. I mean, live the double life."

"I am merely having coffee with a friend," Jeziernicky replied with a sly smile.

CHAPTER 37

ON THE AFTERNOON OF MAY 14, 1948, Ben-Gurion stepped onto a raised platform in the main hall of the Tel Aviv Museum. All thirty-five members of the People's Council were seated behind him as he strode to the podium and gaveled the council to order. Several hundred invited guests, crammed into every space in the room, settled into their seats. On the back row, Jacob Schwarz dropped into a chair next to his very pregnant wife, Sarah.

Outside, a crowd of thousands filled the street, listening to the meeting as it blared through loudspeakers. They'd started gathering after lunch as word spread around the city of what was about to transpire. Ben-Gurion had issued strict orders, copies of which Jacob had delivered along with the invitations, specifically instructing those who received an invitation to keep the matter confidential so as not to alarm or provoke the British before their scheduled withdrawal. But news of an event like this proved difficult to contain and word had spread quickly.

Standing at the podium, Ben-Gurion reached up to adjust the height of the microphone. When it didn't move he glanced off-stage, in a plea for help. A technician from Voice of Israel Radio, self-conscious and nervous, came to his side and made certain the microphone was in the proper place. Across the region, those who didn't already know about the gathering were about to learn of it as Ben-Gurion's address was carried live through the Voice of Israel Radio station. Both men wanted to be sure every word reached the airwaves.

By then the room was silent. Ben Gurion, standing erect and confident, cleared his throat and began to read. "'The land of Israel was the birthplace of the Jewish people. Here their spiritual, religious, and political identity was shaped. Here they first attained statehood, created cultural values of national and universal significance, and gave to the world the eternal Book of Books.'"

With rapt attention the audience listened as he continued, word by word, line by line, through the document to the final paragraph. "Accordingly we, the members of the People's Council, as representatives of the Jewish community of Israel and of the Zionist movement, are here assembled on the day of the termination of the British mandate over Palestine and, by virtue of our natural and historic right and on the strength of the resolution of the United Nations General Assembly, hereby declare the establishment of a Jewish state, to be known as the State of Israel.'" He paused a moment before saying, "Let all those in favor of adopting this declaration of independence signify their assent thereto by standing." At once, the council stood to its feet.

Enthralled by the reading and lost in the moment, Jacob stood, as well. Sarah grabbed the sleeve of his jacket and gave it a tug, but before he could turn to her everyone in the room was on his feet, applauding. Jacob clapped even harder and shouted a cheer. Others whistled and shouted. Some cried openly.

After a few minutes, Ben-Gurion called them to order once again and said triumphantly, "It is done. Effective as of one minute past midnight, we shall join the nations of the world as the State of Israel."

There was another round of applause as Ben-Gurion stepped out of the way and Rabbi Fishman came forward. He waved his hands once or twice to quiet them and when the audience was silent he recited the Shehecheyanu blessing. As he concluded the prayer, the Tel Aviv symphony, seated on the mezzanine above, began playing "Hatikvah," the de facto and soon-to-be official Israeli national anthem. Those gathered in the hall began to sing along and soon the room was filled with the sound of their voices.

Tears streamed down Jacob's face as he sang at the top of his voice. Then suddenly he felt a fist punch him on the thigh. Startled, he looked down to see Sarah doubled over, clutching her abdomen in pain. His mouth fell open and his eyes were wide with fright. "What's wrong?" he blurted out as he knelt beside her.

"It's time," she gasped.

"Time?"

"I've been having contractions since before we got here."

"Why didn't you say something?"

"I wanted to be here for this." She clutched her stomach even tighter and groaned. "Jacob, I can't hold back much longer."

Jacob was near panic. "What do we do?"

A hand touched his shoulder and he glanced around to see Eyal Revach standing behind him. "Take my car." He handed Jacob the keys. "And get her to the hospital as fast as you can."

Jacob slipped an arm around Sarah's waist and helped her to her feet. Then, with Revach making a way through the crowd, they hurried outside to the car.

— • —

At the Jewish Agency's office in Jerusalem that evening, Felix Rosenblueth and his staff sat around his desk listening to Ben-Gurion on the radio. They had been involved in final negotiations of the text and had an advance copy of the approved version, which they followed as he spoke. Still, it was an emotional moment and even now, as the Tel Aviv Symphony continued to play, several seated in the office wiped tears from their eyes.

While the others listened to the broadcast, Rosenblueth rose from his chair, crossed the room, and wedged a chair at an angle beneath the doorknob. No one paid him much attention. Then he made his way to the opposite side of the room and unlocked a cabinet that contained a cache of automatic rifles, handguns, and ammunition.

Discussion around the desk turned to speculation about the world's reaction and what they might expect from the major powers. Most were counting on the United States giving immediate support. Others thought Russia might, as well.

While the others talked, Rosenblueth gathered an armful of guns from the cabinet and brought them to the desktop, then returned for ammunition. With it piled on the desk, he switched off the radio. "Each of you should take one of these," he instructed. "A handgun and a rifle. And plenty of ammunition for both."

Beryl Steinberg rocked his chair on its back legs. "You really think this is necessary?"

Rosenblueth handed him a pistol. "Yes. Make sure you keep a side arm with you at all times. Have the rifle with you in the office. If you want another for your home or the trunk of your car, let me know and I will arrange it."

Moran Brosh appeared puzzled. "Has something happened we didn't hear about?"

Rosenblueth pointed toward the radio. "You just heard the most important and the most dangerous statement of your life."

"The most dangerous?" Brosh frowned.

"We are now the Jerusalem office of the provisional government for the State of Israel, Rosenblueth explained. "Many people in this city will not like that. Some will attempt to respond against it in force. We will be the object of those attempts."

Steinberg crossed the room to a file cabinet and opened a drawer. "Well, if that's the case," he said as he took out a bottle of champagne. "Anyone have a glass?"

Someone went down the hall to the storeroom and returned with half a dozen water glasses. Steinberg divided the bottle between them and they all raised their glasses in a toast. "To the new State of Israel," Steinberg proclaimed, "may God grant her peace, a long life, and citizens with the courage to make it so."

"Hear, hear!" they all said in response.

When they'd finished their drink Rosenblueth set aside his glass. "We must be vigilant," he said, returning to his earlier theme. "The next days could be our best yet, but they could also be the deadliest we've ever encountered."

"But we are free," someone argued. "Shouldn't we be happy?"

"The declaration made us independent," Rosenblueth corrected. "But we will only be as free as we are able to make ourselves." He held up a rifle. "A pen may be the instrument of our political independence, but this will be the instrument of our freedom."

— • —

In Washington, D.C., Eliahu Epstein lingered in his office, listening to the crowd at the Tel Aviv Museum as they sang with the symphony. He'd dreamed of this day since he was a child and worked for it all his adult life. Now the moment was at hand and he had participated in making it happen. Perhaps not as much as others, and certainly not as long, but he'd been a part of history nevertheless. From here on out he would play a more vital role.

On his desk was a leather satchel and in it were two documents. One was a request from Ben-Gurion as head of state asking the American president for diplomatic recognition. The other was a statement from the president acknowledging Israeli independence and granting the requested status. Epstein's palms were sweaty as he came from the behind the desk and picked up the satchel.

By a prearranged plan, Epstein arrived at the White House and was escorted to the office of John Steelman, President Truman's chief of staff. Steelman was waiting and without a word extended his hand for the documents. Epstein took a blue folder from the satchel and handed it to him. "Everything is in here."

Blue folder in hand, Steelman disappeared into the Oval Office. A few minutes later he returned and motioned for Epstein to join them. "He wants you in here for this," Steelman said.

Epstein followed him into the office and stood near the president's desk. Truman glanced up at him and in unemotional fashion said, "This is a big moment for you and your country."

"Yes, Mr. President, it is."

"Then I am glad we could share it together."

With quick strokes, Truman signed the document that read, *This government has been informed that a new Jewish state has been proclaimed in Palestine, and recognition has been requested by the provisional government thereof. The*

United States recognizes the provisional government as the de facto authority of the new State of Israel.

With his signature complete, Truman laid aside the pen and stood, then shook Epstein's hand and gave the document to Steelman. "I'm sure you'll know what to do with that."

"Yes, Mr. President," Steelman turned to Epstein and gestured toward the door. "Come with me and we'll prepare a copy for you."

Twenty minutes later, Epstein left the White House and hurried back to his office. When he arrived, he placed a phone call to the Jewish Agency office in Tel Aviv. Someone answered the phone but noise in the room was so loud Epstein could not hear. Frustrated, he ended the call and placed a second one to Golda's residence. A crowd was gathered there and he had to wait while she quieted them before telling her, "He did it."

"Who did what?"

"President Truman," Epstein said as emotion welled up inside and he struggled to swallow the lump in his throat. "I was in the Oval Office when he signed it…the document recognizing the provisional government as the de facto government of the new State of Israel."

Tears rolled down Epstein's cheeks as the sound of cheering and laughter echoed through the phone. He stood there a moment listening to his friends celebrating from the opposite side of the world. A sense of sadness swept over him that he was not there with them to join in the celebration of a goal they'd all worked so hard to attain, but he was also happy. Happy to be a part of it and to participate in making the Jewish dream a reality, but he was unable to communicate any of that over the phone. Finally, when he could contain himself no longer, he dropped the telephone receiver onto the cradle, collapsed in the chair behind his desk, and wept.

CHAPTER 38

THE DISTANCE FROM THE TEL AVIV MUSEUM on Rothschild Boulevard to Hadassah Hospital on Balfour was only four blocks, but the streets were jammed with people dancing, singing, and cheering wildly in celebration of Israel's independence. Negotiating through that sea of humanity took Jacob longer than he expected. Sarah, lying in the back seat, groaned and cried in pain all the way. "I'm doing the best I can," Jacob called from the front seat.

"This child will be born in a car if you don't hurry," Sarah shouted.

When they finally reached the hospital, nurses lifted Sarah onto a gurney and wheeled her down the hall. Jacob tried to follow but was pushed aside. "Wait here," he was told. "We'll come get you when it's time."

Reluctantly, Jacob took a seat on a chair in the hall and hoped time would pass quickly, but minutes seemed like hours and he grew more anxious with every passing second. When he could stand it no longer, he walked outside for a breath of air. Sounds of celebration from the crowd near the museum wafted toward him and he imagined them still gathered on the street. No doubt in larger numbers than before.

As he stood there listening to the city reveling in the arrival of the new state, he thought about all he and Sarah had endured to get to this moment. Life in Poland as children, the ghetto, the horrors of the Holocaust. They'd survived all of that, found each other again, and made not one but two treks to Palestine. And then he thought of Sarah's cousin, Avi Livney.

The notion of Israel reborn from ruins had come to Jacob from the prophets but the idea of making the trip to Palestine, to join those reset-tling the land, was Livney's. When they were in the displaced-persons camp he talked about it constantly and his chatter eventually drew Jacob out of a postwar malaise and won him over to the idea of actually doing it. But Livney was no ideologue. He wanted to come to Palestine solely for the personal benefit of living somewhere other than Europe, to escape the European cycle of anti-Semitic violence, to live in a place where no one would categorize him solely on the basis of his heritage. Very quickly, Jacob came to see that was a dream that existed only in Livney's mind. Reality in Palestine was quite different. Thinking about that sent a smile over Jacob's face. "This place is all about ethnic strife," he whispered to himself. "And there is more to come before it gets better."

But those dreams—Livney's of finding a place of peace and safety, Jacob's of seeing the prophets' visions come true—were enough to bring them to Palestine, and he remembered his grandfather's words from long ago. *"God can fulfill His promises by any means He chooses."* And so He had and now they were in Tel Aviv, about to give birth to their first child, and Livney was dead, having never set foot on the land he longed so much to see.

At once Jacob's eyes opened wide as it occurred to him, *This may be the first child born in the new state of Israel.* They had discussed many things about the child—how they would care for the baby with their busy sched-ules, where she would go to school, and what she might become as she grew up—but they had not yet settled on a name, primarily because Sarah refused to discuss anything but girls' names. "We don't even know if this child is a boy or a girl," Jacob kept saying. But Sarah just smiled and said, "Until a boy is born, we shall discuss her as if she's a girl." Now they were perhaps only minutes away from the child's arrival and they still had no name.

"I can see it now," Jacob muttered. "A headline in the newspaper. Nameless First Child Born in New State."

Just then, a voice called to him. "Mr. Schwarz." He turned to see a nurse standing in the doorway behind him, smiling and gesturing for him to come. He made his way toward her and when he reached the door, she said, "You have a new baby boy."

Jacob felt his heart leap against his chest. "A boy?" he gasped.

"Yes," she said, smiling and nodding. "Come with me. I will show you."

Jacob followed her down the hall to a room where Sarah lay in bed. Cuddled beside her was a baby wrapped in a blanket, his eyes closed, a peaceful expression on his face. Jacob looked over at Sarah. "A boy? What shall we call him?"

Just then, Yechiel Diskin, the rabbi who intervened with the British when the *Exodus* arrived, stood at the foot of the bed. Jacob recognized him from their meeting at the warehouse. "I can tell you his name," Diskin said. He moved alongside the bed and reached over with his hand, holding it just above the baby's head. Instinctively, Jacob stood beside him, unsure of what was about to happen next and ready to pounce at the first sign of trouble.

Diskin ignored him and said quietly, "His name shall be Benzion, for he is the Son of Zion, the firstborn of the new nation. He shall grow up to be strong and wise and will lead his people twice, once through a difficult time and once through a time of great prosperity. And when he is old they will say of him, 'The son of Zion grew up to lead us and we have become his children.'" Diskin's eyes met Jacob's. "You shall not pass away before these words have been fulfilled."

Jacob and Sarah stared at each other, neither knowing what to say. Then, without more, Diskin turned away, crossed the room, and disappeared down the hall.

A moment later Eyal Revach appeared. "Did I just see Rabbi Diskin?" he asked. "Was he in here?"

"Yes," Jacob replied.

"What brought him to see you?"

"I'm not sure."

"Interesting man. One of the Karaites. You know him?"

"Sort of. He was at the ship, the *Exodus*, when they removed Avi Livney's body."

"Yes," Revach nodded. "He was the one responsible for getting those bodies from the British." He looked past Jacob to Sarah. "How are you?"

"Tired but happy," Sarah replied.

"Glad to have delivered your baby, no doubt."

"Very much," she nodded.

Revach stepped around Jacob to take a peek. "Have you chosen a name?"

"We were just now discussing that," Jacob said. "I thought Avi would be good."

"After your friend?" Revach asked.

"Yes. Sarah's cousin."

"But I think we've settled on Benzion," Sarah said with a glance toward Jacob. "It seems like a good, strong name for a boy with a wonderful future ahead of him."

"Yes," Revach grinned. "That's a good name. 'Son of Zion.'" Then his eyes opened wide with excitement. "You know, this child may be the first child born to the new nation."

"He is," Jacob nodded proudly. "I believe he is Israel's firstborn."

"Wow," Revach replied, his eyes even wider. "This child could do great things."

"He will," Sarah said confidently. "I am certain of it."

CHAPTER 39

THE FOLLOWING MORNING, as the sun broke the horizon, the Syrian army crossed the Jordan River en mass. Two hours later, the forward columns arrived within sight of the compound at Degania. A guard standing along the inner wall sounded the alarm. "They're here!" he shouted. "I see them."

Moshe Dayan climbed the wall and squinted against the morning glare. "There," the guard said, pointing to the east. "A little to the left."

"Yes," Dayan replied as he looked in that direction. "I see them." Binoculars hung from a strap around his neck and he lifted them to his eyes for a better view. "I count six." He lowered the glasses and turned away. "But that is only the first wave of their armor. They will have many more coming behind it, I am certain." He climbed from the wall and shouted for the others to gather around.

Men and women assembled in the open space at the center of the compound. Dayan stood atop the hood of a truck and addressed them. "As you heard last night, we are now citizens of the world's newest country, the State of Israel. Our neighbors, however, are unwilling to accept that decision and they have assembled their armies against us. Just now, to the east," he said, pointing, "the Syrian army is preparing to attack us. The first of their armored units have arrived and are parked within sight. If they do not attack today they will most certainly do so tomorrow. You should prepare to defend yourselves and be ready to do so in hand-to-hand fighting. This may get rough before it's over."

When he was finished, Dayan climbed from the hood of the truck and went to work directing last-minute preparations. A team was assigned to fill the Molotov cocktails and bring them to a distribution point. Weapons were checked and ammunition issued with strict orders not to fire until ordered to do so. "We don't have much," Dayan cautioned, "so we must be careful how we use it." Then he patrolled the perimeter wall and antitank ditch. Workers were just finishing the last sections of a barbed wire fence that stood beyond the ditch and he watched them while they worked.

Keret came alongside him. "Think we can survive?" He spoke with a calm, quiet voice.

"Some of us will," Dayan replied in an equally even tone.

"How many?"

"Not nearly enough."

A few hours later, the line of tanks along the horizon advanced forward and the men of Degania lined the perimeter wall to meet them. As the tanks came within range they began to fire. The first shells landed in the compound. They made a loud noise and sent dust into the air but caused little damage. Then they began falling on the buildings. Chaos descended on the compound as men ran in every direction, some dodging the shells, others trying to put out fires caused by the explosions, and still others tending to the wounded.

— · —

In the days since Dayan arrived at the compound, Natan Shahak had been filled with excitement over the prospect of fighting alongside a national hero. But now that shells from the tanks were exploding around him, Shahak was filled with fear. Ten minutes later, when the shells began landing near the wall and body parts flew through the air it was no longer a romantic exercise. Shahak retreated behind the shop building and hoped the next rounds would come nowhere near him.

As the tanks moved forward, ranks of soldiers marching behind them came into sight followed by yet another line of tanks not far to the rear. Shahak leaned around the corner of the building and saw them in neat rows, tanks, soldiers, and more tanks. The men marched as if in a drill, rifles at the ready, bayonets attached. Suddenly he understood their plan. They would pummel the compound with shells from the tank cannons, then push through the wall and create gaps for the soldiers to rush inside. "That must never happen," he said to himself. "They will kill us all."

Suddenly the fear that drove him to hide behind the building melted away and in its place courage once again rose up. "If I must die," he said through clenched teeth, "then let me die fighting for a chance to live." He came from the corner of the building and rushed toward the wall just as the first line of tanks rolled over the barbed wire fence and plunged nose first into the ditch. Engines revved as they struggled to pull themselves up the other side and Shahak realized they were vulnerable to an attack. Molotov cocktails sat at his feet and he grabbed one in each hand, then nudged Gilad Tamir, who stood beside him. "Come on. Let's take out a tank."

Tamir seemed startled. "Are you crazy?"

"If we stand here and wait, we die," Shahak growled. "Come on."

With Tamir following, they scrambled over the wall and ran toward the nearest tank, sitting nose down in the trench. Its engine revved and the tracks churned the ground wildly in an attempt to move forward. Without hesitating, Shahak held the Molotov cocktail in his right hand and shouted, "Light it!"

Tamir struck a match on the side of his pants and a flame came to life. He held it against the cotton rag tied to the outside of the bottle and in spite of his shaking hand the rag caught fire. Shahak glanced at it to make sure it was fully aflame, then threw the bottle at the front edge of the tank track. The bottle shattered against the steel of a hub and burst into flames.

Shahak shifted the second bottle from his left hand to the right and once more shouted, "Light it!"

Tamir lit the wick just as the hatch of the tank popped open. "They're coming out!" he cried.

Shahak threw the second bottle toward the turret. It landed near the hatch door, bounced backward, and tumbled through the opening into the tank compartment. Seconds later the bottle exploded, sending smoke and flames spewing out top. Screams filled the air as the men inside were consumed by fire. So loud were their shrieks that the soldiers walking fifty meters behind came to a sudden halt, then slowly backed away.

Along the wall in both directions others followed Shahak's example and scrambled over with Molotov cocktails in hand. Ignoring the danger, they ran toward the ditch and tossed the bottles against the tank tracks, destroying all six machines that attempted to cross the defense. The sight of its mighty armor reduced to flames and the shrieks from inside as the crew burned alive caused the second line of tanks to stop, then retreat, leaving the foot soldiers that were with them exposed to small arms fire. Men along the wall mowed them down in a slaughter that made even the toughest flinch.

With the Syrians in retreat, Shahak and the others climbed back over the wall to find the compound littered with the bodies of their fallen friends. Only one building, the cafeteria, escaped damage from the barrage of shells. Others were reduced to nothing more than the walls, their roofs crumpled and broken. Two were in flames. Keret organized a detail to bury the dead, and others manned the buckets to control the fires.

Meanwhile, Dayan took stock of their defenses. "We should restring the barbed wire fence," he said. "And drag those tanks from the ditch."

"We don't have anything that can pull them out," Keret replied.

"If we leave them," Dayan warned, "the next wave of tanks will use them as a bridge and come straight across without stopping."

Shahak was standing nearby and heard them talking. "Do you think they will return?" he asked.

"In the morning," Dayan nodded. "They will come at us in the morning. That's what I would do."

"Then why should we wait for them?"

"You would retreat?" Dayan asked with a hint of disgust.

"No," Shahak insisted. "Never. But we shouldn't just sit here waiting for them, either." He glanced up at the sky. "It will be dark before long. We should go out and meet them in the dark. Surprise them."

Dayan grinned. "You are a good soldier."

"I am a good Jew," Shahak replied. "I need no more than that to succeed."

"Come with me," Dayan said with a wave of his hand. "I have something to show you." He led the way across the compound and behind the cafeteria building where his car was parked. When they reached it, he opened the trunk to reveal the three bazookas he'd brought with him. "I've been saving these for just such a moment as this." He lifted one to his shoulder. "Simple to operate. You just point and shoot."

"Are they armed?"

"Yes," Dayan nodded. "Armed and ready." He handed the bazooka to Shahak. "So be careful."

— • —

After dark, Dayan, Shahak, Keret, and two dozen men from the compound assembled in the cafeteria building. On a table before them were a few rifles and handguns, the three bazookas, and two dozen Molotov cocktails.

"Here's the plan," Dayan said when they were all together. "The Syrians are camped about a mile east of here. There's a low hill on the north and south sides of their position. When we get there, we'll divide our force in half. I'll take twelve men and one of the bazookas around to the north side. Natan Shahak will take the other twelve along the southern hill and we'll attack from both sides."

"With what?" someone asked.

"With this," Dayan replied. "The bazookas will take out three tanks first, from our positions on the ridges. Then half of each team will charge the camp and attack with the cocktails. The other half will remain on the ridges with the rifles to cover their exit."

"Will they come after us?"

"Not if they follow their training. If they do as armies are instructed, they will give chase to the hill but no farther."

Dayan looked over at Keret. "Position the remaining men at the fighting places along the perimeter wall. Have them ready to cover us as we retreat. I'm not sure what we will encounter, but if they come after us you'll need to hold them off until we can get inside the compound."

"Through the gate?"

"Yes. There would be no way to scale the wall fast enough."

Then Dayan, Shahak, and the twenty-four with them came from the cafeteria and made their way toward the gate to leave.

— • —

As Dayan had said, a mile from the compound they came to a low hill. They crawled up to the crest and lay flat for a view of the area below. At the bottom of the hill was a large, flat area two miles across that stretched all the way to the river. The Syrian army was camped at the western end of it with their tanks parked in clusters of three or four. The crews were camped near them with the infantry soldiers in tents not far away.

Dayan whispered as he glanced around at the men, "Remember, sound carries in the night air. Any noise you make will travel a long way, so be quiet." Then he leaned near Shahak. "This is where we split up." He gestured to a man holding a bazooka. "I'll take him and the weapon with me. You take the others. Work your way farther down this ridge to the east." He pointed with his thumb. "We'll attack from the opposite side, so keep the angle of your fire away from us. Aim the bazookas at the tracks of the tanks, just like you did with the Molotov cocktail. Wait until you hear us fire before you begin. Got it?"

"Got it."

"Good luck."

"We don't need luck. We are like Gideon's army. God is with us."

"May He be with us all."

While Dayan and his men moved off to the left, Shahak retreated down the backside of the hill and repositioned his men farther to the east. When they were in the correct location, they moved up to the top of the hill and spread out along the crest. Half the men carried rifles, the other half held a Molotov cocktail in each hand.

Twenty minutes later, they heard gunfire from across the way. At the sound of it, Syrian soldiers roused from their tents. Suddenly a shot from the bazooka struck one of the tanks on the far side of the camp. The tank exploded, sending a fireball into the night sky. Syrian soldiers surged toward Dayan's force.

"Okay!" Shahak shouted. "It's our turn now." He rose up on his knees with one of the bazookas resting on his shoulder and aimed it at the closest tank, then squeezed the trigger. Instantly, a projectile shot from the end of the tube, streaked through the air, and exploded against the tank's track. Farther down the crest a second bazooka shot hit a tank in the next group.

While six of his men remained on the crest with rifles at the ready, the others, with Shahak in the lead, slid down the hill toward the encampment. Molotov cocktails in hand, they ran through the darkness straight toward the tents. When they reached them, they continued to run rather than stand and fight, and tossed the lighted Molotov cocktails as they sped by. Explosions from the handmade bombs ripped through the night, followed by screams of soldiers set ablaze by the fuel.

CHAPTER 40

FAR TO THE SOUTH OF JERUSALEM, near the Egyptian border, Baruch Zada commanded the Israeli troops defending the southeastern portion of the Negev, a vast, sparsely populated area that lay between Beersheba and the Jordan River. For two months prior to the British withdrawal, he'd been scouting the territory, preparing defenses at key locations, and monitoring Egyptian patrols that continually operated in the region. All day long he worked with his men at Dimona, the first settlement of any size north of the border, digging antitank ditches, putting up berms, and creating tank traps. And every night he sent teams into the desert to spy on the gathering Egyptian forces.

Late one evening, as Zada met with his officers at his tent, a patrol returned with news that Kamal al-Aziz had been spotted among the forces assembling east of Hasna. "He appears to be in command."

Zada clapped his hands and shouted, "God is with us!"

Uri Dushinsky, his assistant and newly arrived from Europe, seemed perplexed. "You know him?"

"Years ago we met at a conference in Cairo, when the British still thought they could negotiate a peaceful resolution between us and the Arabs. I have studied him ever since, thinking we might one day meet in the field."

"Is he capable?"

"Very much so," Zada nodded. "But he is lazy and not a little bit vain."

"So you think he will give up?"

Zada shook his head. "No, I think he will always choose the easy way."

"Then maybe we should withdraw to Beersheba and fight there. Concentrate our forces for greater effect. Put up a stronger resistance. We have no hope of defeating them here."

"This isn't a fight for Dimona," Zada replied.

"Then what are we fighting for?"

"Jerusalem."

Deep furrows wrinkled Dushinsky's brow. "I don't understand."

Zada strode to a table and pointed to a map that lay on it. "This is the route they must take," he said, tracing with his finger. "North from Hasna, across the border to Dimona, then on to Beersheba."

"You are certain of it?"

"Without a doubt. We already know the main attack will come along the coast, led by General Muwawi. He is hoping to sweep north through Gaza to Tel Aviv. That is the crucial area for them."

"Right," Dushinsky nodded. "Greatest population center. Cuts us off from the sea."

"The units at Hasna will enter farther to the east, where we are, in order to protect Muwawi's flank." Zada pointed again to the map. "If Aziz takes Dimona, he will move on to Beersheba. From there he has two choices, toward Beit Shemesh, in keeping with the obvious strategy, or through Hebron and into Jerusalem from the south. I'm betting he chooses the route through Hebron to the big prize of this war—Jerusalem."

"Why?"

"We need him to take that route because it puts him in the least defensible position."

"That's why *you* want him on that route," Dushinsky argued. "But why would *he* want it?"

"The western route through Beit Shemesh exposes both of his flanks. He would have to work to negotiate it successfully and if he does, Muwawi reaches Tel Aviv and gets all the glory. The Hebron route exposes only one flank, is much easier, and if he is successful in reaching Jerusalem, he will be the Arab hero."

"Interesting," Dushinsky nodded. "The army of Transjordan would lie to his east."

"Exactly," Zada smiled. "His only exposure is from the west, making the route through Hebron the easiest and the quickest, especially for an armored unit like his with tanks and trucks. But it puts him in the least defensible position." He tapped the map with his finger. "That is where we want him."

"Then we should force him in that direction."

"That's what we're going to do," Zada grinned. "If we can make them fight every step of the way, and leave open the route through Hebron, he will take it."

"And by fighting, we weaken them enough in the process to stop them before they take the city."

"See," Zada laughed. "Only a few days with me and already you're smarter."

On the evening of May fourteenth, Zada and his men gathered around a radio, listening as Ben-Gurion read the declaration of independence. When the ceremony ended, many of the men broke into a rendition of "Hatikvah." Zada gathered his reconnaissance teams at his tent for one last mission. "This is the most important night of your lives," he told them. "If the Egyptians do as I expect they will, they will slowly advance on our position tonight and attack at dawn. I need you to determine their exact locations and report back to me as soon as possible." Two hours later, radio transmissions from the recon teams confirmed what Zada suspected, the Egyptians were north of the border moving toward Dimona at a steady pace.

— • —

To the west, along the coast, Aharon Hartman commanded the Israeli troops defending the coastal road through Gaza to Ashdod and on to Tel Aviv. He'd been there since the confrontation with Ben-Gurion months earlier, planning, strategizing, and waiting. He knew war was coming, but he didn't want to fight. "We should spend our effort getting along with the Arabs and working out a peaceful coexistence," he argued to anyone willing to listen. "They should never have let Ben-Gurion go this far. He should never have been placed in charge." But as events moved toward independence, Hartman's training and experience came to the forefront and he prepared for the conflict that was rapidly approaching.

Primary units from the Egyptian army were assembled at Arish, a city on the Mediterranean coast about fifty kilometers south of the border. Ahmed al-Muwawi was in command. Known for his slow, plodding pace, Muwawi was nevertheless an experienced commander and one of Egypt's best.

During the first week of May, Mickey Marcus arrived to review conditions in the Negev. He met with Hartman at his headquarters near the settlement of Yad Mordechai.

"You are prepared for an invasion?"

"Yes. As ready as can be expected."

"What does that mean?"

"It means we have none of the things modern armies use to fight a war. No armor. No trucks. No artillery."

"I understand you are conceding Gaza from the beginning."

"It's an Arab city with a very small Jewish population, making it indefensible from our perspective. We have evacuated everyone from there and have repositioned them here to defend Yad Mordechai."

"That's a lot of territory to give up."

Hartman explained, "Under normal circumstances, yes, it is a lot to give up, but these are not normal circumstances. If they go through with the declaration announcement as planned, we'll be facing the best-equipped army in the region. They have armor and an air force. We have rifles, rocks, and Molotov cocktails."

"You have a little more than that, don't you?"

"Not much. Hand grenades. One or two armored cars. Some trucks. But no artillery and no planes of any kind."

"I understand most of that is on the way and should be arriving as soon as the declaration is issued."

"But that takes time," Hartman replied. "And that is our job. To give them time. They've made that abundantly clear at every meeting. Which is why we can't hold Gaza and there's no point in trying. If we attempt to do that, we would not only face the Egyptians but local Arab militia as well.

We can't hold out against both of them. The key for us is delay. The longer we can delay them here, the more time Tel Aviv has to prepare and, hopefully, get the equipment we need. The best place to do that is here, at Yad Mordechai, where there are no Arabs." He sighed. "Maybe in the meantime someone in Tel Aviv will get their act together and actually do something that matters."

— · —

Early on the morning of May fourteenth, reconnaissance teams reported Egyptian units had reached Rafah in the night and were now in central Gaza. "But I don't think they're staying long. They've made no attempt at establishing an encampment."

"They've advanced their tanks that far?"

"Yes, sir. Tanks, armored vehicles, and artillery pieces. The infantry arrived with them, traveling by truck."

Hartman was worried. "And they haven't erected tents for the infantry?"

"No sir. Most of them are sleeping beside the trucks."

Hartman paced back and forth as he thought about what this news meant. Perhaps he'd underestimated Muwawi and been too brash in not resisting him at Gaza. "This could be bad," he mumbled. "Really bad."

Elazar Karelitz, one of Hartman's younger officers, spoke up. "I thought we knew they would take Gaza."

"Yes," Hartman replied, "but the Egyptians are prepared to move quickly. Much quicker than we thought. If they make a lightning dash up the coast, instead of following Muwawi's usual plodding pace, they could bypass our current position in favor of a direct assault on Ashkelon. Holding Ashkelon would provide a forward base for Egyptian aircraft that would allow them to attack almost any location in the region."

"Then we'll have to convince them to fight us here," Karelitz replied.

"Exactly," Hartman answered. "Take three units over to Karmia. When you get there, make your presence known. Send out patrols, put men in the trucks and ride around, do everything possible to create the appearance that you are much larger than you are."

"Won't that attract attention?"

"Yes. And that is precisely what we want," Hartman explained. "We'll do the same here. Hopefully, Muwawi will notice our presence at both locations and decide that he must fight us here first, rather than bypass us and risk leaving a large force behind him to attack from the rear. Get moving. There's not much time to make this work."

That afternoon, Muwawi's forces took up positions just south of Yad Mordechai. Not long after that, artillery shells began to fall. As they exploded around him, Hartman held a radio microphone near his lips and shouted to Karelitz, "Can you hear that?"

"Yes," Karelitz replied from his post at Karmia. "It worked!"

CHAPTER 41

AFTER THE INCIDENT IN THE ALLEY, Auerbach wandered the streets of Jerusalem in a daze. With every step, images of Suheir played over and over in his mind—lying on the pavement, blood oozing from her chest. He had wanted to save her, yet she had died saving him. If only he'd stayed in Degania she would be safe now. He could have found her later, after things settled down, and they could have left then. She'd been willing to go with him now, surely she would have waited a little longer and all would have been well. But he'd insisted on rushing off to find her and when she tried to tell him to wait he'd insisted on pressing ahead. Now she was gone.

Gradually, as the weeks passed, he came to grips with what had happened. She wasn't coming back, Rashid had given him a chance to live in her place, and he should try to make the most of it. Images from the alley slowly receded, and as they did he thought of home, his family in America, and the life he'd wanted to lead before deciding to come to Palestine. Perhaps he could find that life again if he just kept trying. Maybe things would make more sense then.

No longer interested in returning to the kibbutz and afraid to go to Tel Aviv for fear he would be forced to fight with the Haganah, Auerbach was relegated to sleeping in doorways and scrounging for food wherever he could find it, usually in a garbage can or from an open window to someone's kitchen. As the emotional fog continued to lift, he remembered his original plan—to cross into Transjordan and contact his brother from Amman, then make his way to New York and get on with his life, whatever that might hold. It was a good plan when he proposed it to Suheir and it was still a good one now. All he needed was a way out of the city and across the river.

Traveling at night, he moved slowly toward the southern edge of town. From the bits and pieces of conversation he'd heard through open windows and at the market, he learned that units of the Transjordanian army were there already with the eastern routes from the city under their control. He hoped to find a bus or truck bound for Amman.

One day early in May, just at dusk, he came from an alley and rounded the corner of a building. Suddenly, the sound of gunfire erupted in the next block. Bullets whizzed past his head, some so close he heard a sucking sound as they zipped passed his ear. Instinctively, he dropped to the pavement as bullets ricocheted off the buildings to his left and right. Desperate to avoid them, he crawled on his hands and knees back to the alley and huddled close to the building.

A few minutes later, three men appeared on the street just a few meters across from him. Dressed in green uniforms with shiny black boots, they walked forward with hesitant steps, rifles at the ready, as if they sensed danger ahead. *They're going to get shot,* Auerbach thought. *Don't they know this is crazy?* Seconds later, a burst of gunfire came from up the street and all three men fell to the ground.

In his mind, Auerbach knew he should run but right then he could think of no place to go that assured him any greater safety than where he was. *Darkness,* he thought. *That is my only hope. In the nighttime no one will see me.* So he scooted farther into the alley, huddled in a nook beyond the corner of the building, and waited for darkness to fall.

Slowly the shadows that covered the alley stretched out into the street. Two hours after the soldiers had been shot the street was blanketed in shade, and an hour later it was totally dark. Auerbach could wait no longer. He crawled from his hiding place intending to run, but the bodies were still lying in the street right where they'd fallen. Cautiously, he crept toward them, expecting at any moment to hear the report of a rifle and feel a bullet rip into his flesh. Instead, all he heard was the rustling of a breeze as it blew between the buildings.

In the street, he knelt by the bodies and checked their pockets for money, finding a few silver coins and three one-pound British notes. Then he noticed again the shiny black boots and a plan came to mind. Without a moment's hesitation, he grabbed the arm of the man nearest his size and pulled him into the alley. He stripped off the man's boots, pants, and shirt, and put them on. When he was dressed, he darted into the street for a cap and scooped up a rifle before returning to the alley.

Dressed as a soldier, he slung the rifle over his shoulder and made his way down the alley to the next cross street. From there he worked his way around the location from which he'd heard the gunfire and started toward the western edge of the city.

Late that night, he stumbled across a group of Transjordanian soldiers camped in a field not far from the Jordan River. He skirted them and came around to the opposite side where a group of open-top trucks were parked. Men worked in the dark unloading boxes from one and he watched from a distance. When they finished unloading it, the driver prepared to leave.

"This is what I've been looking for," Auerbach whispered to himself. He came from hiding and made his way toward it, walking in front of the parked trucks to obscure himself from view of the others. As the empty truck pulled away, it came past Auerbach's position. As it did, he jumped in back. If he'd guessed right, he would be out of the city in a short while and arrive in Amman in a couple of hours. *If I guessed wrong, I'll be dead before morning.*

CHAPTER 42

IN THE NEGEV, the strategy of delaying the Egyptian army's progress by fighting and gradually withdrawing slowed the pace of advancement on both fronts. Muwawi's blitz through Gaza and up the coast soon bogged down in a meter-by-meter contest as Hartman fought to buy time for better equipment to arrive. It did and, with the help of newly arrived Czech aircraft, his forces stopped the Egyptian advance just north of Ashdod.

To the east, Zada kept Aziz occupied at Dimona for so long that the Egyptian general gave up and went around it. But by the time he reached Beersheba, Zada's men had regrouped and were in place to continue fighting there even harder than before. Aziz added reinforcements and took the town, then veered east for the easier route through Hebron where he was met by fresh Haganah forces, and his advancement faltered.

More problematic, however, Transjordanian troops, with the help of local Arab militia, seized control of large portions of Jerusalem. They also took the stronghold at Latrun, a fortified hilltop that they used to control the highway from Jerusalem to Tel Aviv. From it they rained down artillery shells on passing vehicles with deadly accuracy, making use of the roadway impossible. Jews living in Jerusalem were cut off. Food supplies quickly ran low.

In an effort to relieve that condition, Ben-Gurion ordered numerous attempts to dislodge the Arabs and retake Latrun. All of those attempts met with defeat. Heavy losses were sustained in the process. Desperate to get help to Jews living in Jerusalem, Ben-Gurion turned to Mickey Marcus, hoping the West Point graduate could somehow capture the site.

With the focus on Latrun, Jacob Schwarz spent much of his time delivering messages back and forth between Tel Aviv and Marcus' field headquarters. In order to make the round trip quickly, he used a motorcycle. Riding on the open road was not without risk but it also afforded him time to think and gave him a panoramic view of the Palestinian countryside. One day, as he traveled up the road from Tel Aviv with yet one more message, he noticed a trail leading from the pavement to the south, away from the highway and away from the hilltop at Latrun. As he came past it on the return trip, he slowed to give it a more careful inspection.

On the off chance the obscure trail might offer a useable alternate route that avoided Latrun altogether, he took a detour and followed it to see. A little way off the highway he found the trail opened into what must once have been a well-traveled road. Unkempt and overgrown, it was little more than a faint outline across the barren ground, but it gave him the idea that there might be a better solution to the highway problem than continually assaulting the Arab position.

When he reached Marcus' position with his next delivery, he told Marcus what he'd found. "I was wondering if it might be a route that was out of range from Latrun."

Marcus had a puzzled expression. "Is it serviceable?"

"I could get through on my motorcycle, and a truck could probably make it most of the way, but for regular use it would need some work. At least as far as I could see. I didn't go all the way."

"Interesting idea," Marcus nodded. "Actually, I'm not sure why we didn't think of that earlier. Building an alternate route around this stronghold would be quicker than taking it." He gestured with a wave of his hand. "Ride with me and let's take a look."

With Jacob at his side, Marcus took a jeep and drove to the location. The transition from the paved highway to the dirt trail was rough but once they were off the pavement the unused roadway opened up. "There are a few obstacles to using it," Marcus observed. "We'd have to cut the brush and all of it could use a grader."

"There's a wash farther up, and a ravine, too."

"We should get an engineer out here to see if it's feasible." Marcus took a note pad from his shirt pocket and scribbled a message, then handed it to Jacob and said, "Take this to Gedaliah Cohen when you get back to Tel Aviv. We'll see what he says."

— • —

Later that day, Marcus came to Tel Aviv and met with Ben-Gurion about their overall strategy for getting help to Jerusalem. Gedaliah Cohen was there, along with Revach, and discussion soon turned to the question of opening an alternative road.

"I like the idea," Cohen commented said. "Far more acceptable than expending more lives trying to take the location by force."

"It would be like our own Burma Road," Marcus suggested, referring to the Chinese road built as an alternate route during the Japanese occupation.

Ben-Gurion glanced at Revach. "What do you think, Eyal?"

"It's certainly worth a try. We haven't been able to dislodge them from Latrun and I don't think we can do it until we get better artillery and air power. Jerusalem won't last that long. I say we get to work on the road and see if we can make it operable."

"Okay," Ben-Gurion decided. "Let's do it. We should have thought of it from the beginning."

"Actually," Marcus added, "the idea came from your courier."

Ben-Gurion was taken aback. "A courier? Which one?"

"Jacob Schwarz."

"He's a good guy," Revach grinned. "Maybe we should include him on the project. Give him a little more responsibility."

"Fine with me," Ben-Gurion concurred.

"It would do him good. But we'll need someone with construction experience to supervise."

"Amos Horev," Revach suggested. "If anyone can get it done, he's the man. And I think he'll get along well with Schwarz."

— • —

That evening, Amos Horev was placed in charge of the Latrun road project. Jacob was assigned to work as his aide and assistant.

"The first thing we need is a bulldozer," Horev directed.

"I know where we can get two," Jacob replied.

"Two?" Horev said with surprise.

"The British left them at the port in Haifa. We can send trucks up to get them first thing in the morning."

"Do they work?"

"I saw them when I was up there last week and the guy at the docks told me they did. The British were going to take them back when they withdrew, but the last ship was too full so they left them."

"We don't have any trucks here that can haul them, but get up there and see if you can get them down here."

The following morning, Jacob rode the motorcycle to Haifa. He arrived before sunup and found a number of trailer trucks at the docks waiting to receive tanks and armored equipment from a ship that was due in port that afternoon. He cajoled two of the drivers into hauling the dozers down to Latrun, and before the sun was an hour above the horizon they were loaded and on their way. By noon, the equipment was busy smoothing out the old roadway.

"This is the way the highway used to go," Horev observed as he and Jacob stood together watching the dozers work. "But that was a long time ago."

"Were you here when it was in use?"

"No," Horev laughed. "This was the road the Romans used."

— · —

Over the next two days, Haganah engineers put the old road in passable condition as far as the ravine near Bayt Susin. Three days later, it was open on the other side to Jerusalem. Negotiating the ravine, however, was a problem. "This will delay use," Horev worried. "It will take a while to break the grade down and make it useable by vehicles all the way to the bottom and up to the top on the other side." He ran his hands over his head as he thought. "I'm not sure we can get it ready in time to make a difference for the people in Jerusalem."

"Maybe we could find a way to make it work for the short term," Jacob suggested. "While the dozers continue to fix it."

"You have something in mind?"

"Well," Jacob began slowly, "if we packaged the loads in small enough containers we could bring them this far with the truck, unload it by hand on this side, carry the packages across the ravine, and reload them in another truck on the opposite side."

"Yeah," Horev sighed. "I thought about that, but it would require twice the number of vehicles and lots of people. It would also be very slow."

"It would get us up and running, though. And it would be better than what we have right now for resupplying Jerusalem."

"That's a lot of manpower," Horev sighed as he stared down at the ravine. "Where could we get that many people?"

He smiled, "I think I know just the place."

When they returned to Tel Aviv, Jacob went to Golda's office at the Jewish Agency. Sarah was there with little Benzion asleep in a crib that sat in the corner.

"Shouldn't he be at home?" Jacob asked in a whisper. "He's not even a month old."

"He's fine," Sarah replied. "And I was bored. I can't sit around that apartment all day while everyone else is doing something for the war."

Jacob tiptoed over for a look and Sarah came to his side. "How's it going out there?" she asked.

"We need your help."

Sarah gestured with a nod of her head for him to follow and she led him to Golda's office. "We can talk in here," she said as she closed the door. "That way Ben can sleep."

"You call him that?"

"If you said Benzion as many times as I do," Sarah smiled, "you'd find a shorter way to say it, too. Believe me." She leaned against the desk. "What do you need our help with?"

"Maybe we should talk to Golda about it. Where is she?"

"She won't be back until tomorrow."

"Oh. Well, in that case …"

"What is it?"

"We have most of the road open," Jacob began, "but there's still a ravine that has to be crossed."

Sarah appeared perplexed. "How could we possibly help with that?"

"We need volunteers to hand-carry the loads over to the other side."

"A portage."

"Yes."

Sarah folded her arms across her chest. "We'll have to figure out how to package everything in manageable sizes. The people we can get are mostly older. And it'll be mostly women."

"Okay," Jacob nodded. "But this will take a lot of people. Maybe a hundred or more."

"That won't be a problem."

"You can get them?"

"Yes," Sarah nodded confidently. "We can get people. You'll just have to be ready to adapt to them. They won't be soldiers or anything like that. This won't be people who are used to working all day in the heat."

"We'll work with whoever you bring."

— • —

Two days later, the road was open on both sides of the ravine. Trucks were placed at staging areas on either side with volunteers to man them. Teams on the Tel Aviv side unloaded trucks that carried supplies to the ravine, then walked the packages across the ravine to the opposite side. Crews on that side placed the packages on trucks for the remainder of the trip to Jerusalem. Transfers on the first day didn't go as smoothly as Jacob had hoped, and the process was more physically taxing than he'd anticipated, but by sundown the initial load of supplies reached Jerusalem and the work continued through the night.

With each passing day, construction crews smoothed the road into the ravine and lessened the grade, placing the staging area closer to the bottom with each day's work. Transfer times improved and the number of volunteers doubled, which allowed hourly deliveries into Jerusalem. After two weeks, a temporary bridge was laid over the roughest parts of the ravine and trucks from Tel Aviv began making the round trip all the way to Jerusalem and back without stopping.

CHAPTER 43

AT THE FAMILY ESTATE OUTSIDE LONDON, Richard Marbury sat with his feet propped up on his father's desk in the study. Slouched in a chair across from him was Anthony Morrison. They sipped from glasses of brandy while listening to an evening broadcast of news from the BBC, much of it devoted to reports about the growing international interest in a UN truce for Palestine. Though he did not say it aloud, Marbury hoped, as he did every evening, to hear a report that an assassin's gunshot had ended Ben-Gurion's life. It would have made for the kind of dramatic moment he relished and one that would have signified the death of the Jewish obsession with establishing a homeland.

When the broadcast ended with yet one more excerpt from Ben-Gurion's address at the Tel Aviv Museum, Richard switched off the radio and leaned back in his chair. "The Americans," he sighed. "If they weren't so weak this would have never gotten out of hand." He looked over at Morrison. "They never once offered to help us solve the Palestinian problems. Not once."

"And then they were the first to recognize them."

"Stabbed us in the back," Richard fumed. "Stabbed us in the back."

"And now, after a month of dealing with their Jewish friends, they come to the Security Council wanting a truce."

"I think they just want to give the Jews a chance to resupply."

"You may be right," Morrison shifted in the chair. "Their analysts say that if the fighting goes on like this without a break, the Jews might lose and Truman doesn't want that to happen."

"Truman," Richard scoffed. "Stabbed us in the back. Stabbed Marshall in the back. His own secretary of state." He took another sip of his drink. "I'm sure all their liberal friends are behind the truce idea. They will rue the day he signed that arms embargo. Do our people realize the United States has boxed itself in?"

"I'm not sure. Our people don't mind having a brokered deal as long as Egypt and Transjordan are amenable to it, which means the Arabs have to come out on top."

"Not much chance of anyone else agreeing to that."

"No," Morrison replied. "I don't suppose so."

They sat in silence a moment, then Richard said, "We haven't heard any news from our contacts, have we?"

"No, we haven't."

"And so far as one could tell from the reports, Ben-Gurion remains alive."

"Yes," Morrison nodded, "unless the BBC has joined the global Jewish media conspiracy, I'd say he's very much alive."

Richard thought for a moment, then cut his eyes in Morrison's direction once more. "We should send someone to find out why the job has not been completed."

"No," Morrison said with a slow shake of his head. "That would be a big mistake."

"But what if our man simply made off with the money?"

Morrison gave him a look. "If he did, would you want to be the one to ask for it back?"

"No, I suppose not." Richard took another sip before saying, "What about that Hammersmith fellow?"

"Wouldn't touch it," Morrison said with a wry smile.

"He's a military man."

"And a good one, they say," Morrison agreed. "But I wouldn't touch it."

"Any possibility he could be assigned to Palestine to find out what happened?"

"I don't know," Morrison shrugged. "Maybe. But we just spent a lot of money getting everyone out of there. I think if he went back, someone would start asking questions about why."

"You could make up a good cover story for him. Isn't that the sort of thing you do?"

Morrison was suddenly alert, "Look, once these things are set in motion, they have a way of staining anyone who gets involved. Right now, no one knows you had anything to do with it. If we touch this thing again, someone will find out."

"But we don't even know if anything's been set in motion. For all we know, the man you talked to in Istanbul is lying on the beach somewhere counting his money." Richard's eyes opened wider. "No, *my* money!"

"Wouldn't touch it," Morrison repeated, settling back in his chair. "Wouldn't touch it at all."

Richard, however, was unable to let the topic pass and took another tack. "What is the Foreign Office doing about this push for a UN truce?"

"Our people are working toward it. They think a truce now, this early in the conflict, would still leave the Jews with a state too small to survive. And when it collapses, the Palestinians can step in and take over, either by agreement or force, and that will be that."

"How are they doing that without offending the Americans? We don't want to lose them. They're still our economic lifeline."

"They're using others to make the argument for them. Getting close to agreement on a plan for a truce with a mediator to try and resolve things."

"What names are they suggesting for the mediator?"

"The usual suspects," Morrison replied. "Our office is trying to convince the Dutch to propose Count Folke Bernadotte."

"The Swede?"

"Yes."

"He has lots of wartime service in a similar capacity."

"Jews love him," Morrison added. "Helped several groups avoid the death camps."

"Think the Security Council will agree to him?"

"Probably. But first they have to agree to the truce."

"What are the chances of that?"

"Pretty good."

"Think my father could help?"

"Not with the truce, but he might help get Bernadotte approved once the truce passes."

Richard set his glass on the desktop. "I'll speak to him about it. If we can get Bernadotte approved, I think he'll accept Hammersmith as an advisor."

"Wouldn't touch it," Morrison repeated as he folded his hands in his lap and closed his eyes. "Wouldn't touch it at all."

— • —

A few days later, the UN Security Council ordered a truce in Palestine. With all the major international powers behind it, both Israel and the Arab League readily agreed to a cessation of hostilities. Folke Bernadotte was appointed to mediate a long-term settlement. Ralph Bunche was named as his assistant and, with Anthony Morris prodding and Lord Marbury suggesting, the British offered John Hammersmith as an advisor. Bernadotte, a personal friend of Marbury, accepted him with pleasure.

Hammersmith's plane was scheduled for immediate departure for Tel Aviv where he was to meet Bernadotte and Bunche before beginning their work. Prior to leaving, however, Morrison met with him for a briefing on the latest events. As they neared the end of that meeting, Morrison rose from his chair, crossed the room to the door, and pushed it closed.

"There is one more thing," he made his way back to the chair.

"I'm not sure how much more we can do here," Hammersmith said, checking his watch. "My plane is set to leave this afternoon."

"You'll want to hear this." Morrison took a seat behind the desk and took a moment to gather his thoughts, "Earlier this year, plans were set in motion for an alternative solution to the Jewish situation in Palestine."

"Oh?"

For the next ten minutes, Morrison outlined for Hammersmith the steps he and Richard Marbury had taken to contact a former SS assassin and arrange for him to make a hit on Ben-Gurion.

"Interesting idea," Hammersmith said when Morrison was finished. "I like the reasoning. Ben-Gurion is by far their most able leader. How long has this been afoot?"

"We began working on it the night you dined with us at Marbury's residence."

"Why are you telling me this now?"

"We want you to find Keppler or Gebhardt or whatever his name is and learn what he's doing to fulfill his agreement—assuming he's even in Palestine."

"Is that why Marbury was pushing for my appointment on Bernadotte's staff?"

A smile turned up the corners of Morrison's mouth. "Lord Marbury saw the value of having you in this position."

"Well," Hammersmith said as he stood. "You should have contacted me about his. I would have been glad to do the job for you."

Morrison stood to shake his hand. "At the time, we didn't know you quite that well."

Hammersmith stood, "Well, perhaps I'll finish the job while I'm there. Is there a bonus if I beat your man to him?"

CHAPTER 44

WITH THE ROAD AROUND LATRUN OPEN, supplies reached the Jewish Quarter of Jerusalem daily. Conditions there improved dramatically. Jacob Schwarz returned to the office in Tel Aviv, where he continued working as a courier and aide. He was there when the UN truce took effect and was present when Bernadotte and his mediation team arrived to meet with Ben-Gurion and Revach. Gedaliah Cohen joined them and the meeting lasted most of the day. Jacob was assigned as an aide and spent the time running errands. In between trips he sat in the corner and listened.

Late in the afternoon, after the meeting concluded, Bernadotte took Revach aside. "I think it might be helpful if we had someone assigned to us who knows the area and can act as a liaison between our mediation team and you. Someone who can steer us through the maze of local relationships and help us communicate the various positions in ways that make everyone's intentions clear."

"That might be helpful," Revach nodded. "We don't always do a good job of understanding each other. You're going to Jerusalem tomorrow?"

"Yes," Bernadotte answered. "In the morning."

"I don't know," Revach grimaced. "Jerusalem is a dangerous place. We can't really spare any of the generals for duty there. They'd be too tempting a target."

"I wasn't really talking about someone of that rank. I was thinking of someone who could function more like a body man."

Revach was perplexed. "A valet?"

"No. Not that much. But if I need something—a drink perhaps but more importantly an office item, something of that nature—it would help to have someone who knows where to find it. None of my team will know that." Bernadotte pointed to Jacob. "What about him?"

"You know him?"

Bernadotte shook his head. "No, but he's been with us all day and he seems like a good man."

"He is." Revach grinned. "He's an excellent man, actually."

"Very well," Bernadotte nodded. "We'll take him with us."

"He will join you in the morning?"

"Yes. We're spending the night here, then leaving first thing tomorrow."

"He'll meet you at the hotel."

When they were gone, Revach took Jacob aside. "Bernadotte wants someone to act as liaison between him and us."

Jacob thought it odd that Revach would ask for his opinion but he was always glad to be on the inside of key conversations. "You have someone in mind?"

"Yes, you."

Jacob's mouth fell open. "Me?"

"Don't get excited. They'll have you running errands and who knows what, but the thing I need is for you to keep your eyes and ears open."

"Right."

"I want to know everything that happens."

"Yes, sir," Jacob agreed. "I'm suspicious of Colonel Hammersmith already."

"Yeah," Revach sighed. "Me too." He patted Jacob on the shoulder. "Pay attention. See if you can figure out why."

— · —

The next morning, Jacob was waiting in the lobby at the Dan Hotel when Hammersmith and Bernadotte came down. Bernadotte introduced him to Hammersmith and the others, then they made their way to the car and started for Jerusalem.

For most of the day, Bernadotte and Hammersmith met with Haj

Mohammad el-Husseini, the grand mufti of Jerusalem. They talked about the Arab majority, how the Jews were interlopers in Palestine without the approval of Palestinian Arabs, and how they had conned the Turks in Istanbul into selling them land.

"The Europeans don't want them," Husseini argued. "The Americans don't want them. No one wants them. So why are they willing to impose them on us? Only because we are small and cannot make trouble for them … yet. But when trouble comes to us, it will come to you, too."

"And what does that mean?"

"It means, how will the world survive without Arab oil?"

"How will you survive if you can't sell it?"

"We've been doing very well for thousands of years without selling a drop to anyone."

"You want to—"

"Listen to me," Husseini snapped. "We will never accept a Jewish state."

"You expect them to leave?"

"The ones who are here now can remain here so long as they do so peaceably. They can have their enclaves with their streets and schools and museums. We will not bother them. But they cannot live in this land outside the reach of Arab rule. You did not allow them to live in Europe outside of European rule. It must be the same here. It defies the charter of the United Nations for you to impose them on us."

— • —

That evening, Bernadotte and company stayed at the King David Hotel. The south wing of the building was still in ruins from the previous attack. Other parts, however, were up and running. Jacob was assigned a room on the floor with Bernadotte and he was certain they meant for him to remain there, waiting to dash off on another errand. But the room afforded him no chance to see what everyone else was doing, so he went downstairs and found a bench near the front desk from which he had a clear view of the lobby and the entrance.

In a little while, Hammersmith appeared and made his way out to the sidewalk. Jacob waited a little longer to give him time enough to get ahead, then went outside to follow. He saw Hammersmith already in the next block and started after him.

At the next corner, Hammersmith turned onto a narrow street and went inside a small café. Jacob found a place across the street from which he could see through a window in front and had a clear view of the tables inside. Hammersmith took a seat at a table along the wall near the door. He sat opposite a man with a light complexion and blond hair. Jacob was certain he was European. Probably not English. Perhaps German or maybe French.

— • —

As Hammersmith took a seat, the man looked up at him and smiled. "Ah, Colonel. We meet again."

"Yes," Hammersmith replied. "But this time you are not shooting at me."

"What can I say? It was a war. These things could not be avoided."

"What name did you use this time?"

"Does it matter?"

"I prefer to know."

"Your government knows me as Otto Keppler."

"The people you met with before are concerned you have not upheld your end of the bargain."

"They should practice patience."

"Have you seen Ben-Gurion?"

"Yes," Keppler nodded. "Many times. But he is always with too many people."

"A crowd is not a problem. In fact, the men who are paying you would probably be glad if he died in a crowd. The more dramatic the better."

"They might not mind, but I do."

"And why is that?" Hammersmith wondered.

"I prefer to execute my responsibilities under conditions that provide me with a means of escape. I don't mind sacrificing someone else for your cause, but I don't care to join them by sacrificing myself."

"Where have you been?"

"His office. Haganah's office. His residence. They are all constructed with men like me in mind."

"I overheard something that made me think he must have a second location."

"That would make sense. I see him going to one location but then he comes from a different."

"Follow the couriers."

"I would if I had the manpower, but I am working this assignment alone."

"I'll see that you have all the help you need."

"You will make certain they are discreet?"

"Yes."

"I do not need a blunder."

"No. But we need to get this mission completed soon."

"We? You are now part of this conspiracy?"

"If they had come to me first the job would already be done."

"But they didn't."

"No, and the Jews have held on too long. If they last much longer they'll begin to believe they can actually win."

"I think they might already be convinced of that."

"You don't get paid to think about that," Hammersmith said tersely. "You get paid to do one job. Now finish it."

— · —

Jacob watched from across the street as Hammersmith rose from his chair at the table and strode to the door. As Hammersmith came from the café and started back toward the hotel, Jacob waited to see what the European did. Moments later, the European came out and walked down the street in the opposite direction. Before he was out of sight, a man slipped from the shadows at the far corner of the café building and followed. Jacob lingered a little longer, waiting to see what happened but soon they were gone. As he turned to leave, a car entered the alley and rolled slowly toward him. He squeezed back in his hiding place, doing his best to become invisible, and waited while the car idled past. Two men were in the front seat. Jacob watched them as they went by, but they did not seem to notice. When they were out of sight, he came from his hiding place and hurried back toward the hotel. He'd been gone too long. By now Bernadotte would have noticed he was missing, and Jacob thought about what to say when he returned.

CHAPTER 45

TWO DAYS LATER, Bernadotte returned to Tel Aviv and holed up with Ben-Gurion in the office. While they met, Jacob walked down the hall to Revach's office. From the doorway, he caught Revach's eye and gestured with a nod of his head for him to follow, then moved downstairs and out to Bernadotte's car.

A few minutes later, the door opened and Revach stepped outside. "Everything all right in there?"

"Best I can tell," Jacob replied. "But I've only been in with them a few times."

"How'd it go in Jerusalem?"

"Bernadotte seems to be interested in understanding the Arab argument. Looking for an opening. Trying to actually find a solution. Hammersmith is pushing him toward dividing the place, suggesting proposals with greater and greater territory for the Arabs. Less and less for us."

Revach nodded. "We'd heard he favors partition."

"But he doesn't seem to favor us," Jacob shrugged. "Why would he want to give us anything?"

"The British don't want to give us anything," Revach explained, "but they know international opinion favors us. So rather than oppose us openly, they are trying to give us the smallest state possible."

"So that we will fail?"

"Yes," Revach nodded. "They are trying to give the Arabs enough to satisfy them and get the approval of the international community. By making our part too small to survive, we collapse and the Arabs get it all. To them, all these talks are just part of the process to get us out of the way. That's why Hammersmith is on this trip."

"El-Husseini hasn't accepted anything they've suggested, and every time Bernadotte tries to broaden the discussion, Husseini keeps saying they will never accept a Jewish state."

"And he means it. They will never accept us. Husseini wants us all dead." Revach glanced around warily. "You'd better get back upstairs before they miss you."

"There's one more thing," Jacob replied. "The first day we were in Jerusalem, after the talks concluded and we all went back to the hotel, I sat in the lobby. While I was there, Hammersmith came out in civilian clothes and went down the street to a café where he met a European. Rather tall man, blond hair, military deportment. I'd say he's German but that's just my opinion."

"Any chance they were old friends?"

"They might have known each other, but it was a serious discussion. No handshakes or laughter."

"Okay."

"And another thing. Someone else was watching."

Revach's eyes widened. "You saw this person?"

"Yes," Jacob nodded. "I waited while Hammersmith and the European left. Hammersmith walked back toward the hotel. The European went in the opposite direction and a guy followed him."

"Are you sure he was following him?"

"Yes. And about the time they were gone a car came by with two men inside. From the expression on their faces I'd say they were with the man on foot."

"Did you get a good look at any of them? Could you see who they were?"

"The men who followed him?"

"Yes."

"I'm not sure I could identify them, but they were some of us."

"Us?"

"Jews. Definitely not Arab," Jacob explained. "And not European. You know. They were some of us."

"Okay." Revach gestured toward the door. "You really should get back upstairs. We don't want anyone to—"

Just then the door opened and an assistant from upstairs appeared. "Mr. Revach," she called. "They need you."

Revach turned to go back inside. Jacob followed after him. When they reached the doorway, the assistant turned, "There's a ship in port at Haifa carrying weapons and refugees."

"Great," Revach smiled. "Let's get it unloaded. You don't need me for that."

"It's the *Altalena*," she explained.

Revach pushed past her. "I don't care about the name. Get it unloaded."

"It's an Irgun ship."

"Irgun?" Revach paused. "This could be a problem."

"This is why they need you upstairs."

"I thought Irgun no longer existed," Jacob noted. "Wasn't that the point of the order at the first session?"

"Well," Revach growled, "now we get to enforce our order."

"They didn't work this out ahead of time?"

"Ben-Gurion thought it would be better this way."

On the second floor they found an irate Ben-Gurion in his office, standing behind his desk, shouting into the telephone receiver. "We are the provisional government of Israel! We issued an order." The veins in his neck throbbed and he pounded the air with his fist as he continued to shout. "You are a citizen of Israel and obligated to follow the law!" He paused briefly as if listening, then continued again. "No," he snapped. "Not just one more. There is no one more. The State of Israel has decreed that Irgun cannot exist as a military unit. You are defying the law of this nation!"

Ben-Gurion slammed down the phone and yelled to no one in particular, "Get me Gedaliah Cohen!" He took a deep breath and lowered his voice as he turned to Revach. "Irgun has a ship full of weapons and ammunition approaching Haifa. Tuvia Megged says the cargo was purchased before our decree. It's just now arriving. They want to distribute it to Irgun soldiers, then give us what is left."

"We knew it could come to this if we didn't confront him before," Revach reminded.

"But this puts us in a much stronger position to deal with them," Ben-Gurion replied.

"They won't back down."

Ben-Gurion's eyes flashed with anger. "They can surrender the cargo or we will take it by force."

In a moment Cohen was on the phone. "Don't let that ship leave port," Ben-Gurion ordered. "Take some artillery pieces to the dock. If they won't surrender the cargo, we'll sink the ship." He listened a moment, then began shaking his head. "No. We're not doing that, Gedaliah. We aren't risking lives to board their ship." Ben-Gurion dropped the receiver onto the cradle and came from behind the desk. "Come on," he growled. "Let's get up there. They aren't getting away with this."

— • —

When Ben-Gurion and Revach arrived at the docks in Haifa, the *Altadena* was less than a kilometer off shore. News of its arrival spread quickly and a crowd had gathered to watch the ship unload. Cohen was there, too, standing with his troops, behind the crowd, nearer the coastal road.

Members of Irgun, armed and ready, were stationed along the pier. Shapiro's assistant, Tuvia Megged, stood with them, hands behind his back, appearing confident and self-assured.

Revach gestured in that direction as he turned the car from the road. "I think they've been waiting for us. Do you want to talk to him?"

"Where's Shapiro? I don't see him."

"You want to talk to Megged?"

"I guess so. But pull up there next to him," Ben-Gurion pointed with disgust. "I'm not walking to meet with an Irgun assistant."

Revach threaded the car through the crowd and brought it to a stop a few meters from Megged's position. As it came to a halt, Ben-Gurion opened the car door and stepped out. "Where's Noga?"

"He went to make a phone call. We didn't know you were coming."

"You must surrender the cargo from that ship," Ben-Gurion said in an authoritative voice.

"We own this ship and its cargo," Megged replied. "You have no right to take it or to stop us from unloading it."

"The provisional government issued an order outlawing all paramilitary groups," Ben-Gurion countered as he stepped closer. "You know that. I know that. That's the law."

The two men stood face-to-face. Megged lowered his voice. "You should have talked to Shapiro about this ahead of time."

"I *did* talk to him," Ben-Gurion replied. "Months ago."

"He says you never mentioned issuing an official order."

"I don't have to get his approval before orders are issued. We've created a single fighting force. All others are illegal and I'm not arguing with you about it." Ben-Gurion had an odd smile. "That ship is carrying war materiel. We are in a state of war. I am the head of the provisional government acting under a lawful government order. Irgun can surrender the cargo to the government of Israel, or lose it. The choice is yours."

Megged struck a defiant pose. "I can't do that."

"Very well. Have it your way." He returned to the car, dropped onto the passenger seat, and slammed the door. "Drive over to Gedaliah."

Revach put the car in gear and backed away. "What did he say?" he asked as he turned the car around.

"They won't surrender the cargo."

Once again, Revach steered the car carefully through the crowd and came to a stop behind Cohen. Three artillery pieces were arranged there with a crew prepared to fire them. Ben-Gurion came from the car and started in that direction.

Ben-Gurion ordered, "Sink the ship."

"You really think we should do that?"

"We have no option," Ben-Gurion replied. "They have defied the government's order. If we give in to them now, they'll take over. Irgun will be the government."

"Maybe we should—"

"Gedaliah!" Ben-Gurion shouted. "Sink the ship or go stand with Irgun!"

"I was going to say," Cohen continued calmly, "maybe we should move the crowd out of the way before we start firing."

Ben-Gurion glanced around. "Remove them from in front of your position but don't bother moving the entire group. That will take too long. They aren't in danger anyway. Get this over with quickly."

Moving the crowd a safe distance from the artillery pieces took a few minutes. Megged stood with his soldiers at the dock and watched but gave no hint of changing his mind. Half an hour later, Cohen's artillery fired its first salvo. The shells dropped into the water on the far side of the ship. Megged grinned at the sight of it. A second round put the shells in the water on the near side. "Merely warning shots," Megged clarified. Even from a distance Ben-Gurion could read his lips.

The crowd fell silent as Cohen's soldiers loaded a third round, then his voice echoed across the water. "Fire!"

With a deep, thudding boom three shells shot from the artillery, whistled through the air, and arced toward the ship. Moments later, they plunged into the center of the ship, directly above the cargo hold, where they exploded in quick succession. Smoke billowed from the ship, followed by a secondary explosion as the cargo detonated, sending a giant fireball into the sky.

Just then, a car screeched to a halt on the street and the front door flew open as Shapiro came from it. "Are you crazy?" he shouted as he pushed his way through the crowd. "My men were on that ship!"

"Noga," Ben-Gurion said in a steady, even voice. "I gave you a chance to do the right thing. And I gave Megged the same opportunity. Both of you refused."

"But how could you do such a thing?" Shapiro fumed.

"Tell your troops to join units of the Israel Defense Forces, as every other security group has done, or they will be arrested."

"We had rifles and ammunition on that ship." Shapiro was beside himself with frustration. "We needed them."

"Noga," Ben-Gurion said, still not raising his voice, "the only reason you and Megged are free right now is because we are at war and need every able man to defend our nation. Otherwise, you would both be arrested this very moment. Tell your men to join IDF and find a place in our army. And if you ever try this again, I'll put all of you in prison."

CHAPTER 46

LATE THAT AFTERNOON, Revach walked over to IDF headquarters and found Jeziernicky at a table, studying a map. "Let's take a walk," Revach suggested.

Jeziernicky laid aside the map he'd been reviewing and followed Revach from the room. They walked out to the shaded side of the building and stood facing away from the street. "I hear Shapiro wasn't too pleased with the way things turned out," Jeziernicky said when they were alone.

"No," Revach chuckled. "He wasn't. Think he'll cause any more trouble?"

"I don't think so. You need me to help with that?"

Revach shook his head, "No, I need you to help with something else."

"Sure. What's that?"

"I hear things," Revach said. "And I know that some of your Lehi members are still together."

"I don't know anything about that," Jeziernicky said, waving his hands in protest. "I'm doing my best to—"

Revach gave him a knowing look. "My cousin owns the café where you met with Nahum Halevy. But relax. I'm not trying to cause you any trouble. I need to meet with someone from that group."

Jeziernicky seemed puzzled. "For what?"

"For help."

"Help? That's an odd request coming from one of the key people behind the policy to eliminate Lehi."

"These are odd times in which we live," Revach replied.

"What's this about?"

"Someone spotted a man in Jerusalem. I want to know who he is."

"That's a little vague," Jeziernicky suggested. "Can you give me a little more detail?"

"Not now. Will you set up a meeting for me with someone who might know something about this?"

Jeziernicky stroked his chin, then folded his arms across his chest. "Okay, I'll set you up with someone. But if you try to arrest them, I'm done with the IDF."

"That won't be a problem," Revach assured him. "I just want to talk. The identity of who I talk to will go no further than me."

"How soon do you want to meet?"

"The sooner the better. Can you set it up for tonight?"

"Yes," Jeziernicky nodded. "I think so."

— • —

Late that night, Revach steered his car into an alley on the south side of Tel Aviv. As instructed, he brought the car to a stop midway down the alley and switched off the engine. A few minutes later, the passenger door opened and Nahum Halevy got inside.

"Yitzhak said you wanted to meet."

"There's a European in Jerusalem," Revach began. "John Hammersmith, the British colonel traveling with Folke Bernadotte, met with him last night. Some of your men were at that meeting."

Halevy reached for the door handle. "I agreed to talk to you. Yitzhak said it was about someone who'd been seen in Jerusalem. I'm not talking about anything else."

"I'm not asking about all of that. I want to know who the man was that Hammersmith met with. Your men were there?"

"I'm not giving you the names of our men. They aren't supposed to be operating separately anymore. We're all in IDF now. So if you—"

"Listen to me," Revach said with a hint of frustration. "You aren't hearing me." He took a deep breath and did his best to remain calm.

"The European," he said slowly. "Who was the European that met with Hammersmith?"

"Oh," Halevy said, suddenly realizing what Revach meant. "He usually goes by the name of Otto Keppler. That's his favorite alias. His real name is Ernst Gebhardt. Former Waffen SS assassin. Part of a special protection unit trained at a base outside Berlin. They were sent to locations throughout the world—London, New York, Paris. Killed most of the French army's best officers before Hitler ordered his Panzer divisions across the border. Tried to get Roosevelt and Churchill, too."

"Who's he here for?"

"Nobody knows for certain. I mean, none of the Arabs will talk about him. And believe me, the Arabs we asked would have answered by the time we were through with them."

"So he's not here for the Arabs."

Halevy shook his head. "Definitely not. He comes and goes at will without the slightest problem. And I'm sure he didn't come here for free. I'd say there's only one person anyone would spend that much time, money, and effort on."

A chill ran down Revach's spine. "Ben-Gurion." He'd thought many times since coming to work with the Jewish Agency about this very scenario—a professional assassin hired to kill Ben-Gurion.

"You'd better take measures to keep him safe," Halevy suggested.

"He won't like it."

"You don't have a choice."

— • —

The next morning, Revach summoned Gedaliah Cohen and Yisrael Galili, an IDF colonel, to his office. "We have a problem," Revach began as he closed the door behind them.

"I have lots of problems," Cohen replied. "And all of them need my attention. Will this take long?"

Revach ignored the tone of Cohen's voice and took a seat behind his desk. "We have determined that there is a credible threat against Ben-Gurion's life."

"A threat," Cohen frowned. "We've heard nothing of it."

"I have my sources."

"Your sources can't be better than ours," Cohen interrupted. "Certainly not better than Shai."

"What's the threat?" Galili asked.

"A German has been sighted in Jerusalem," Revach informed. "He goes by the name of Otto Keppler. His real name is Ernst Gebhardt. Former Waffen SS special unit member."

"I've heard of him." Galili appeared concerned and he took a seat across the desk from Revach. "He wasn't just an SS member and not just Waffen SS. He was a member of Leibstandarte."

"No one ever proved that unit even existed," Cohen said with disdain. He dropped onto a chair next to Galili. "I have a thousand things I should be doing besides this. We've been through this before. People see someone. Nothing comes of it."

"This was Hitler's own special unit," Galili continued, obviously wanting to pursue the subject. "It began as his personal protection detail, but went on to become a commando squad doing whatever he wanted them to do."

"We have to assign some protection for the Old Man," Revach said. "I need you two to come up with a plan that does everything we can possibly do to protect him."

"He's not going to like it," Cohen replied.

"We don't have much option," Galili offered. "He would be a big prize for el-Husseini, the Germans, the British. They all want him dead. And losing him would be devastating to us, both in strategy and morale. Not to mention the personal loss."

"He'll have to do most of the work," Cohen groused with a gesture toward Galili. "I've got a war to run."

Revach nodded to Galili. "Get busy on a plan to make certain nothing happens to him. I'll talk to him and smooth things over."

"Good luck with that," Cohen chortled.

When they were gone, Revach walked into Ben-Gurion's office and found him standing near the window, reading a document in the light that shined through the pane.

"We have a situation," Revach announced.

"Put it on the list," Ben-Gurion said dryly. "We have many situations."

"Look at me," Revach insisted.

Ben-Gurion turned to face him, obviously irritated by the interruption. "What is it?"

"Several people have spotted a German in Jerusalem."

"A German?" Ben-Gurion's forehead wrinkled in a frown. "Why would that matter to us?"

"This one is an assassin."

Ben-Gurion's shoulders slumped. "You *think* he's an assassin. We have heard these rumors before and nothing came of them."

"This one is the real thing."

"And does he have a name this time?"

"Yes. His name is Ernst Gebhardt. A former Waffen SS."

A hint of interest flickered through Ben-Gurion's eyes. "Leibstandarte."

"You know of them?"

"Yes. Of course I know of them. Everyone knows of them."

"I didn't know about them until this issue came up."

"You should pay closer attention to these things." Ben-Gurion turned back to the window and the document in his hand. "His presence here means nothing."

"No one knows for certain why he's here, but we think he's here for you."

"Nonsense," Ben-Gurion said in a dismissive tone. "No one would waste time on me."

"I think you're wrong."

"Well," Ben-Gurion sighed, his eyes focused on the paper, "you're entitled to your opinion."

Revach came to the window and stood next to him. "I want you to put that paper aside and think about this for a minute." He was respectful but insistent and when Ben-Gurion did not respond he lifted the paper from Ben-Gurion's hands and tossed it on the desk.

"I was reading that," Ben-Gurion protested.

"What do you think would happen if you were suddenly not here?"

"This is useless speculation," Ben-Gurion retorted. "You would carry on. Golda would carry on. But I don't want to think about it now. We have—"

"We have to think about it now," Revach insisted, this time more firmly. "After it happens, it will be too late. If you're gone, Golda and I would do our best to carry on, but there are many among us who would want to take your place. Weizmann, even as old as he is, would attempt to take control. Hartman would bolt with half the army. We would have chaos. The Arabs, the British, all our enemies know that if you aren't here, we will have no one to hold this thing together and the idea, the dream, of a Jewish state will wither and die."

"The state is bigger than any of us," Ben-Gurion argued brusquely. "Besides, no one deserves to have others put in harm's way just to protect him from danger. All of our soldiers face a bullet every day. Why should I be treated any differently?"

"No," Revach argued. "The state is not bigger than one person. Not right now. It will be. One day it will be bigger than all of us. But right now it's not. Right now you are the state, and those of us trying to make this work need you here with us." He paused and stood up straight. "I'm assigning men to guard you and I expect you to cooperate."

"I don't like it." There was a hint of resignation in Ben-Gurion's voice and he reached for the document from the desk.

"You don't have to like it. But you do have to cooperate. So get used to it."

CHAPTER 47

FIVE DAYS LATER, Bernadotte held a news conference at the King David Hotel in Jerusalem, where he announced his plan to partition Palestine. In spite of territorial gains made by Israel in the fighting during the initial month since independence, the plan he offered favored the Arabs with a much larger portion of the region than the UN partition resolution originally granted. The Arab League rejected Bernadotte's plan immediately, as did Ben-Gurion and the Israeli provisional government. Fighting resumed on all fronts the following day.

As Arab and Israeli armies turned once again to war, Bernadotte traveled to the airport at Tel Aviv and boarded an airplane bound for New York where he was scheduled to discuss his proposal and its failure with the UN Security Council. Hammersmith remained behind, a fact readily apparent to the former Lehi operatives who'd been following him. Oz Alterman, who was in charge of the surveillance detail, reported the situation to Halevy. They met in the back room of a coffee shop in the Jewish Quarter.

"You are certain he did not leave?" Halevy asked again.

"Like I told you," Alterman repeated, "he's over at the hotel right now."

"The King David?"

"Yes. He's in the same room he's been in the entire time since he arrived there with Bernadotte. He was there during the news conference and didn't even go with Bernadotte to see him off at the airport."

"So why is he still here?" Halevy mused.

"Supposedly to monitor things until Bernadotte returns."

"Bernadotte expects to come back?"

"That's what he said before he left."

"But all sides have rejected his plan." Halevy was frustrated. "Fighting has resumed already. Why would Hammersmith stay behind? And why would Bernadotte return? It makes no sense."

Alterman sighed heavily, "I'm only reporting what we hear on the street. The UN truce has not been lifted. Perhaps they plan something more. Some kind of enforcement."

"No, maybe that truce hasn't been lifted but it *has* been proved useless. It has been eviscerated." Halevy paused a moment as if thinking. "And maybe that's the issue. Maybe it's not so much about Palestine but about the United Nations. Their credibility is very much on the line here."

"Well, I don't know about all of that," Alterman shrugged. "All I know is, Hammersmith's here. What do you want us to do?"

"Follow him," Halevy answered. "Do you have someone with him now?"

"Yes."

"Good." Halevy put his arm around Alterman's shoulder and walked him to the door. "Stay on him. Follow him everywhere he goes. I think sooner or later we'll find out what he's really up to."

— · —

About an hour after sunset, Hammersmith met with el-Husseini at a house deep in the Arab quarter of the city. They sat on cushions in an upstairs room with only a candle for light. A hookah pipe sat between them and they took turns smoking from it.

"I have heard many reports of your activities," Husseini began. "So I was eager to meet you face-to-face."

Hammersmith took a long draw from the pipe and passed it to Husseini. "I understand you know Richard Marbury."

"Yes, but I have not talked with him in quite some time. You are acquainted with him?"

"Yes," Hammersmith nodded. "He arranged for me to be here so I could keep track of a project he helped put in motion."

"This business with Bernadotte was only a pretense for you?"

"From their perspective," Hammersmith nodded. "I don't think Bernadotte knew the real reason why I was added to his party. And I had hoped to make a difference, but the Marburys had me placed on his staff so I could check on the project."

"All of the Marburys are behind this…project, as you call it?"

"Richard. And a few other people."

"And by project, you are speaking of the German?"

Hammersmith arched an eyebrow. "You know about him?"

"We know about all important things that happen in Jerusalem," Husseini said with a smile. "I have met with him once or twice. He was very well known in Germany when I was there during the war. I remember his name but we had not previously met."

"Apparently he has maintained that reputation."

"But now you are experiencing some difficulty."

"They haven't heard from him since he arrived and the project has not been completed."

Husseini appeared concerned. "I am surprised that Lord Marbury did not think to contact me himself."

"This was not something Lord Marbury knew about," Hammersmith corrected. "This was Richard, his son."

"Yes. I understand," Husseini nodded. "But Lord Marbury and I have a means of communication that would have made this transaction much easier."

"I doubt Richard knew about that and probably didn't want to involve his father. They made several blunders along the way. He didn't contact me until after they'd already gotten things started."

"You question their judgment?"

"They are good people but they don't know about these things."

"You would have chosen someone different for the task?"

"No. I would have set this up in advance with greater attention to detail, though. Like I said, Richard is a good man." Hammersmith took pains to speak in a gracious tone. "But Richard lives in a world of tennis and tea. He knows nothing of these matters."

"So, what brings you to see me?"

"These truce negotiations with Ben-Gurion and the Jews will take you nowhere," Hammersmith said. "The only good that can come from them is a chance to resupply your armies and call up fresh soldiers. Peace will come only through victory, and for that you need help with training, tactics, and strategy."

"And you would be the person to help us with that?"

"Yes," Hammersmith nodded. "But I have a request. A price for my services, as it were."

"And what price would you require in exchange for these services?"

"We need help locating Ben-Gurion."

Husseini's eyes widened. "He is your target?"

"Yes."

"Excellent choice." Husseini made no attempt to hide his pleasure. "That takes the matter straight to the heart."

"Richard got that part correct."

"And obviously, you do not need help finding Ben-Gurion. You were with him not three days ago. Who is it that needs this help and why can you not show him yourself?"

Hammersmith had a sheepish smile. "The German," he said, lowering his voice.

Husseini laughed. "Your assassin cannot find Ben-Gurion? But the man is everywhere. If we were in Tel Aviv I could find him for you in less than five minutes."

"Yes," Hammersmith chuckled. "It sounds funny to us now, but he really does need help. He needs to locate Ben-Gurion at the right time and in the right place. These paid assassins aren't like you and me. They never want to die trying to kill their target."

"You know this German?"

"Yes," Hammersmith replied. "And he is very good at what he does. But what he needs is manpower to follow several key people. He's tracked him to all the known locations—office, residence—that sort of thing. None of those locations give him a suitable exit. From the way he describes Ben-Gurion's travel, I'm pretty sure Ben-Gurion has a second residence and that might be the best place to hit him. Think you could help him with that? Supply a few people?"

"This would be work in Tel Aviv?"

"Yes. Is that a problem?"

Husseini answered, "No, it is no problem. We would be delighted to assist you. And I may have someone who can do more than merely spy."

"Oh?"

"Check with me in a few days and I will let you know."

— • —

Before sunup, Alterman returned to Halevy with a report on Hammersmith's meeting with Husseini. An hour later, Halevy arrived at Jeziernicky's apartment. They stood in the kitchen and talked while Jeziernicky, dressed in pajamas and robe, made tea.

"I know this is dangerous meeting like this," Halevy said, "but I thought I should brief you as soon as possible."

"It's dangerous but I trust your judgment." Jeziernicky poured two cups of tea and handed one to Halevy. "What have you found out?"

"The Englishman, Hammersmith, met with el-Husseini last night."

"Where?"

"At a residence in Jerusalem."

"Any idea what they discussed?"

Halevy shook his head. "No, we don't know what they talked about, but we do know Hammersmith was with Husseini for almost two hours."

Jeziernicky took a seat at the kitchen table and gestured for Halevy to join him. "Certain to say they weren't talking about agreeing to a truce."

"No." Halevy pulled out a chair and sat. "But I don't like the look of this. Bernadotte leaves. Hammersmith stays behind. Now this meeting. And the German in town."

Jeziernicky frowned. "What German?"

Halevy realized he'd made a mistake. "Revach didn't tell you?"

"No."

"Interesting," Halevy smiled, pleased that Revach had kept his confidence. "Never mind about that," he said, discounting the blunder. If Revach hadn't briefed Jeziernicky on their conversation, Halevy wasn't about to, either. "It's nothing. The real problem is Hammersmith."

"Yes," Jeziernicky said slowly as he sipped from his cup of tea. "The man is a traitor. None of us have trusted him from the beginning."

"I don't think Ben-Gurion and the others understand the situation they face."

"No," Jeziernicky agreed. "I don't think so, either."

"Can we tell them?"

"I'm not sure. I...I'm not sure what would happen."

"Revach would understand. Maybe Golda," Halevy agreed, trying to communicate more without actually saying it.

"Yes," Jeziernicky nodded, apparently missing the implication in Halevy's tone. "But neither of them could stop Ben-Gurion from moving against you if that's what he chose to do. And if you come forward with this information," he warned, "you'll be exposing yourself and your men to arrest. Just what you've done so far violates the government order."

"And," Halevy shrugged, "if we act on our own to solve the problem, we'll be exposed to the same ordeal. It's an impossible situation."

"And ordeal, yes," Jeziernicky commented. "But not impossible."

"Oh?" Halevy took another sip of tea. "How so?"

"If you undertook to remedy the situation on your own, there would be consequences," Jeziernicky had a knowing smile. "But if you were successful, the threat would be eliminated."

They sat in silence a moment, each sipping his cup of tea, then Halevy said quietly, "And I assume anyone who would undertake such a mission would be on his own."

"That is the life of a hero," Jeziernicky sighed. He took another sip from his cup before saying sadly, "A life I gave up for the cloak of respectability."

Halevy reached over and patted him on the shoulder. "You put the good of your men first and that is the highest honor of all."

CHAPTER 48

AT THE JEWISH AGENCY, Jacob Schwarz was fast asleep on a cot downstairs in the back room when a hand shook his foot. "Wake up! It's your turn."

Jacob opened his eyes to see Yehuda Geller standing at his side. "Get up," Geller repeated with a smile. "The night is over. I'm done. It's your turn."

Tired and aching all over, Jacob swung his feet to the floor and rubbed his face with his hands. It had been days since he'd seen Sarah and little Benzion and he longed to do nothing but sleep. Still, the war was in full gear again and there was barely even time to eat. As Geller collapsed on a cot across the room, Jacob pushed himself up and staggered toward the bathroom to prepare for the day.

When he emerged a few minutes later, Eyal Revach came to the doorway of the back room where cots were located. "I need a minute." Geller pulled a blanket over his head. "You, too, Geller," Revach said in a stern voice. Geller rolled over to face them. Revach moved closer to his cot and Jacob followed.

"We're changing your assignments," Revach's tone was serious and authoritative but not demanding.

"I just got off duty," Geller groaned. "I need a few hours of sleep."

"I'm not talking about the schedule," Revach corrected. "I'm talking about your duties during your regular shift. You'll still be aides and couriers and still do whatever needs to be done, but now we're adding another responsibility. We need you to help supplement a security detail for Ben-Gurion."

Jacob looked concerned. "Has something happened?"

"Not yet, but it has come to our attention that there might be a credible threat against him."

"Might be?" Geller groused. "We're responding to the possibility that someone might want to kill him? We'll be some busy people."

Revach shot him a look. "Why do you say that?"

"There are a couple million Arabs out there. They all want him dead."

Jacob was irritated by Geller's attitude but did his best to focus on the issue at hand. "Who wants to kill him?"

"I can't tell you all those details. But we're not taking any chances. You'll receive some security training that will help you understand what to do."

Jacob nodded. "Just us?"

"You two and a couple of the others." Revach paused and turned to Geller. "Are you ready to do this, Geller? Because if you're not, I can find some other place for you to be."

"I'm in," Geller groaned. "I'm just tired."

"Someone will show you what is expected of you what to watch for and exactly how this will work."

"So, we're his bodyguards now?" Jacob asked.

"Not bodyguards. But we need you to act as if you are, to always be alert to your surroundings, to think in terms of his safety." Revach turned to leave. "We'll get you the training to do it right. I just want to give you a heads up that this is happening."

When Revach was gone, Geller rolled on his back. "What was *that* all about?"

"I'm not sure, but your attitude stinks."

"I've been up all night," Geller replied in a defensive tone.

"That was Eyal Revach," Jacob countered. "You can't talk to him like that."

"I had a tough night, okay? I had to go to Haifa once and Latrun three times. Then I had to go … Never mind. I did a lot. I'm worn out." Geller pulled the blanket over his head and in a few minutes was snoring lightly.

Jacob walked back to his own cot and picked up a clean shirt from his footlocker. He knew exactly what Revach was talking about. The German he'd seen in the café with Hammersmith was a serious threat. No doubt Revach had followed up on the few things Jacob had told him, and whatever they found, Revach was shaken. This was bigger than Jacob had imagined.

— · —

Later that afternoon, Tzvi Halutz, a major in the IDF, gathered Jacob, Geller, and six others in a room at IDF headquarters. For three hours Halutz and others lectured about basic security and protection procedures. Jacob hoped the time spent doing that counted as their regular duty and meant they would be free to go home for the night, but with others covering the work they would normally have done, he and Geller were required for the night shift.

The following day, they went to the firing range and learned how to shoot a pistol and rifle, then they practiced the things they'd been told about the previous day—basic self-defense maneuvers and techniques employed by protection details to minimize a subject's vulnerabilities.

Three days later, Jacob was summoned to Revach's office to pick up a message for delivery to a commander near Ashdod. When he arrived, Revach was seated at his desk, still working on the note. While he waited, Jacob glanced around the room and noticed the curtains on the windows were open. He stepped to the nearest window and drew them closed.

"Don't do that," Revach complained. "I like the natural light."

"The view is too wide," Jacob replied. "It's too easy to see inside."

"I like a wide view."

"So do snipers."

Revach gave him a smile. "You enjoyed the security training?"

"Yes," Jacob replied. "It was interesting and more in line with what I'd originally wanted to do when I came here." He pointed to the right. "You need to move that desk over there."

"Why?"

"It will change the angle of the sight line from the door." Jacob stepped to the spot he'd pointed to before. "If your desk is here, you can see out the door and down the hall to the stairway."

Revach leaned back in his chair. "Isn't it better if no one can see me from the hallway?"

"Only if someone is stationed between this office and the top of the stairs. Between you and anyone coming up. As it is, you won't know who's up here until they stick their head through the doorway. Move your desk over here and you'll see them as soon as they reach the top of the stairs. You'll catch them from your periphery vision."

Revach stood and gestured toward the desk. "Give me a hand."

Jacob had a blank expression. "With what?"

"Moving the desk," Revach said. "We took the time to train you, I'm not going to ignore the product of that. If you think it should be moved, let's move it."

"Oh," Jacob said, surprised to be taken seriously. A satisfied smile spread across his face as he grasped one end of the desk to move it.

CHAPTER 49

WITH THE SYRIAN ARMY CONFINED to an area east of the Sea of Galilee, and repairs underway at the Degania compound, Dayan gathered Natan Shahak and four key men in the cafeteria.

"IDF is stretched thin," he explained. "Volunteers are arriving every day and they are calling up every available person over the age of sixteen, but still they do not have enough men to cover every area of the country. Here in the Galilee, we are assembling our own force to take control of the region."

"You think we can do that?" someone asked.

"I've seen how you fought here, defending the compound with little more than your bare hands. You five men were selected for the bravery and leadership you showed during those firefights. I am confident we can take control of the Galilee in its entirety. But we have to do it now, while the Syrian army is bottled up to the east and before Iran or Lebanon can move in to take their place."

"Surely you don't mean just the five of us."

Dayan grinned. "No, not just the five of you. But you will be my leaders. We'll get the men we need from the villages and build our force as we go."

"Don't we need someone's permission?"

"We have permission," Shahak replied. "Moshe Dayan is standing right here in front of us. Telling us what we're supposed to do. Gedaliah Cohen sent him here to defend us. This is part of that duty."

"When do we leave?" another asked.

"We'll leave in the morning," Dayan replied. "Get your things together and get ready, but don't talk about what we're doing. We don't want word to get out."

The following morning, Dayan and the five men from Degania traveled through the southern Galilee, gathering forces and equipment along the way. Most of the villages they visited were Jewish farming settlements. Dayan and the others helped settlers build antitank defenses, strengthen their walls and fences, and instructed them on basic hand-to-hand tactics. Doing that exposed the best leadership and Dayan selected one or two from each location to add to his cadre. They also gathered foot soldiers, and the ranks began to swell.

Having strengthened his forces in the south, Dayan then turned north and marched to Tiberias. They met light resistance on the outskirts of town but subdued it without incurring casualties and used it as a base from which to exert control over the eastern half of the Galilee.

From there, Dayan and his army moved west to Rosh Hanikra on the coast, establishing outposts, training local militias, and removing the small pockets of Lebanese and Iranian troops they encountered. With the northern half of the Galilee under their control, they turned south toward Haifa.

At the same time, a separate force of regular IDF troops moved north from Tel Aviv, taking Netanya and Hadera, then joined with Dayan's unit outside Haifa. Fighting on the outskirts of town was the toughest Dayan's men had encountered, but after three days armaments purchased earlier with the money Golda collected in America finally arrived at the front. Czech airplanes flown by American pilots sortied overhead, strafing Iranian positions and bombing their artillery. Dayan's unit received its own artillery pieces, tanks, and trucks, as well as additional trained soldiers. Within the week, the region around Haifa was securely in their hands.

More like a regular army unit now, Dayan took his newly equipped force on one more campaign through the region, resupplying the outposts he'd established earlier, strengthening his forces with new recruits, and driving out lingering Iranian resistance. With only a month of fighting, all of the Galilee from the Mediterranean to the Jordan and north to the Lebanese border was under his control.

— • —

In the south, Hartman held the Egyptians in place below Ashdod but refused to engage his forces in an all-out push to drive them from the region. Rail bridges destroyed earlier by Lehi attacks were still out. Further advancement, he argued, required the Egyptians to use the coastal highway, which IDF troops held firmly in their grasp. Attacking them now in a frontal assault would only lead to a senseless loss of life.

Meanwhile, the flow of ammunition and equipment to Hartman's units steadily increased. Tanks arrived daily along with armored vehicles and additional artillery pieces. Air support from IDF's growing cadre of fighters and bombers was placed at his disposal, available on demand, and he had a good working relationship with Eli Broza, who coordinated their flights. Yet he would not engage the enemy.

Ben-Gurion, infuriated by Hartman's reluctance, demanded that he attack Egyptian positions and take control of the area. He sent Gedaliah Cohen to state his case. Revach met with him, too. But Hartman refused, using the time instead to bolster his army with still more weapons and fresh troops. And all the while, he met with his unit commanders, instructing, recruiting, and cajoling them in an effort to gain their support for his view of how the country should be run, subtly pointing them toward the person he thought could do that best—himself.

When he first began arguing for a different approach, Hartman had been content to do just that—argue. But as war approached he'd become more disenchanted with Ben-Gurion and had taken a more active role in mounting an opposition to him. Now that the war was upon them and, indeed, had gone on for several months, he was more belligerent than ever—and more open.

Not long after he rebuffed Ben-Gurion's demand that he take action, Hartman met with Ivry Haimovitz, a fellow general and commander of Hartman's strongest infantry unit. If things went as he expected, and an armed resistance to Ben-Gurion was required, Haimovitz's support would be crucial to their success.

Once again, Hartman explained his view on how the region should be governed and how his was the only plan that could succeed. "If we are to survive, we must have a unified Palestine. One national government for the entire region, divided into provinces based on ethnic majority. Some would be Arab provinces, others Jewish. Each ethnic group could control its own local destiny, even though the national government would be controlled by whichever group or whichever candidate gained nationwide majority support."

"This might have worked earlier," Haimovitz replied, "but things have changed now. Lives have been lost on both sides. Everyone's entrenched in their positions. The Arabs don't want us here and, frankly, I don't see how we can safely exist if they aren't totally suppressed."

"You sound like everyone else in Tel Aviv," Hartman chided.

"I'm just facing realities, Aharon. That's all I'm saying. I know you've got this all worked out in your head, but I'm a fighting man and I look at what we have on the ground—the facts and circumstances we face—and what you're saying just isn't going to work."

"Tell me one reason why it won't," Hartman demanded.

"I've given you one already. The Arabs aren't interested in it. They might have tolerated us before but the lines have been drawn. They want us out."

"We could work around that," Hartman said, unwilling to concede the point. "Give me another one. Give me one more reason aside from that one."

"All right, think about this: Palestine is a small place. You could drive the length of it in the morning and be back home for dinner. You could drive across it the other direction four times before lunch."

"So," Hartman shrugged, "what are you saying?"

"I'm saying it's not that big. This isn't Europe or America, where you have room for everybody to avoid each other. Here we're bumping into each other all the time, and dividing it into a dozen provinces, or even six, is going to be confusing. I don't think it will work."

"Maybe," Hartman said, pursing his lips. "But the provinces don't have to be traditional provinces. They could be some kind of other political subdivision. Something created just for this situation. All we need is a way for local people to control their everyday lives with a national government for the bigger issues. The regions are ethnically divided already. Maybe we only need three or four provinces. But this would put an end to the violence."

"Fighting this thing to a victory would put an end to the violence, too," Haimovitz argued. "And take a lot less time than you've spent going around politicking with everyone. Then we'd be the unifying government and could make room for the Arabs."

Hartman realized he was never going to convince Haimovitz with argument. "I can't stand the thought of Ben-Gurion in control," he seethed. "The man is an idiot."

"Like it or not, he's the leader of our country."

"He's fighting a war with no military experience. He doesn't understand these things. He has no sense of strategy or how to break it into tactics. He'll get us all killed chasing this dream of his."

"Actually," Haimovitz countered, "his strategy in the Negev is pretty good. Take control of the region to the east, bottle the Egyptians up along the coast in the west, and give them only one exit through Gaza."

"It sounds good on paper."

"It would work on the ground, too."

"But his approach won't solve the political problem," Hartman railed. "It won't address the overall situation. He will only leave us in a constant state of war with the Arabs."

"I think conflict is inevitable for the foreseeable future either way this breaks. If we win, they'll be rebelling against us. And if they win, we'll rebel against them. It's not going away."

"So you agree with Ben-Gurion?"

"Not on every matter. But he is the leader of our country right now and it's our job to follow orders. We get our say, but in the end we follow orders. Our orders are to defend our nation against invaders, which means we should be driving the Egyptians out of the east. Force them into a narrow area here on the coast and push them south through Gaza to the border."

"You've made that clear already," Hartman sniped.

"Most of the officers think we could do that with far fewer men and less equipment than we now have. Even the ones who've listened to you think we should be fighting instead of sitting here doing nothing."

Hartman glanced at him with a frown. "They do?"

"Yeah," Haimovitz said with an exasperated tone. "Some of them think we have so many men now they want to break off part of our force and liberate Beersheba. They would go today if you gave the order."

"And you?" Hartman asked. "What do you think?"

"I've told you what I think. We should be fighting. Not sitting here ranting about things in Tel Aviv. And I'll tell you something, Aharon." Haimovitz lowered his voice. "What you're talking about borders on insubordination, if not outright treason. I suggest you stop this and get on with what we were sent here to do."

Hartman's eyes narrowed in an angry scowl. He turned away, folded his arms across his chest in a defensive pose, and said coldly, "That's all, Ivry. You may return to your post."

CHAPTER 50

BERNADOTTE ARRIVED IN NEW YORK and went straight to UN head-quarters at Lake Success. An hour later he presented his report to a meeting of the Security Council, where he was grilled with questions about details of his proposal and the reasons for the Jewish and Arab reactions. When the meeting was over, he took a short break, then began a round of discussions with Ralph Bunche, Abba Eban, and representatives of the Security Council members as they worked toward acceptance and enforcement of his report. Bernadotte chaired the meeting.

Karim Sharif, a staff member from the Egyptian delegation, spoke up before the meeting had been called to order. "I think we can all agree the real solution—"

"Excuse me," Bernadotte said, cutting him off. He rapped the table with his knuckle. "This is a meeting of the Security Council working group on Palestine. This meeting will come to order." He glanced over at Sharif. "You may continue."

"I think we can all agree," Sharif started again, "the real solution to this situation is to withdraw the mediator's report and the General Assembly's resolution and issue an order respecting the will of the Palestinian majority."

"The real solution," Leslie Albiston, from Australia, replied, "is for Egypt to withdraw its army and use its position of influence in the region to bring the Palestinian Arabs to their senses."

"Gentlemen," Bruno Torres spoke up, "the United Nations declared a truce. We have little option but to enforce it."

Jorge Granados gestured down the table. "I think Mr. Bunche would like to speak."

"Ralph's not here as a delegate staff member," Sharif retorted.

"He's a UN staff member," Granados argued. "Let him speak. He's been involved in this situation since we took it over."

"Mr. Bunche," Bernadotte rapped his knuckles on the tabletop. "Please tell us what's on your mind."

"Gentlemen." Bunche rose from his chair. "If the Security Council, and indeed the entire General Assembly, won't stand behind the council's order for a truce, and make it work—or at least find a way to make it appear as if it worked—then this organization is finished as an international body."

"I agree," Albiston added. "We'll go the way of the League of Nations."

"But you can't simply impose the international will on us," Eban countered. "An arbitrary plan is no solution at all."

"Mr. Eban is out of order," Sharif called.

"This is an informal discussion," Bernadotte responded. "We can hear from Mr. Eban." He gestured with his hand. "You wish to say something?"

Eban rose to speak. "I think the question we should consider is that of the borders and territory. That was our primary objection to the mediator's report. And the question is this: Would the Arabs give us territory if they were the victors and had occupied part of the land originally granted to us?" He glanced around the table as if waiting for an answer before continuing. "You know they wouldn't. But we don't have to ask what might be. We can see what the Arabs have done. Since the day the first Jew from the diaspora returned to our homeland, a return sanctioned by the Ottomans who sold them the land, the Arabs have rejected every attempt to resolve this matter."

"This is a waste of time," Sharif huffed. "These speeches solve nothing. We do not need the international community to solve our problems."

"With all due respect," Eban interjected. "This is not an Egyptian problem. This is not a Transjordanian problem. This is not a problem of the Iranians who are thousands of miles removed from us, or the Syrians, or the Lebanese—all of whom have invaded the region for their own benefit. This is a problem between the Arab Palestinians and the people of Israel. And between those two groups, we are a nation. They are not."

"You are a nation only because the UN made you one," Sharif snarled. "We would crush you beneath our thumb."

"Ask General Muwawi about that," Eban retorted. "He's hunkered down near Ashdod hoping he can retreat with his life. You could reach him there yourself and ask him who's crushing whom. And we are not a country created by the United Nations. We were created by our sovereign declaration, just as the countries of many others who are seated at this table."

"Excuse me," Bernadotte interjected. "I believe you had a point you wished to make, Mr. Eban."

"The British offered the Arabs of Palestine a state after the Great War. The Palestinians rejected that offer and fought against the British who were in control of Palestine through a mandate from the UN's predecessor. The Arabs lost that fight. Then they sided with the Nazis against the Allies, on the promise that the Germans would give them complete control of Palestine. And they lost again. Last November, the United Nations offered them a state and they rejected that in favor of the Arab League's plan to invade. They defied this body's order and were joined in that defiance by some of the countries represented at this table. Nevertheless, they are losing again."

"We have lost nothing," Sharif shouted. "Nothing!"

Eban glanced around the table. "Mr. Sharif would have you see his anger as righteous indignation, but his country, Egypt, joined with Transjordan, Lebanon, Iran, and Syria in defying the UN's resolution passed in November and the truce order issued just weeks ago."

"We have not—"

"Yes," Bernadotte snapped. "You did. Let the man finish."

"Yet in spite of the Arab refusal to accede to UN resolutions," Eban continued, "in spite of their defiance, we are here today considering whether they should be rewarded for their defiance, and Israel penalized for its obedience."

"How is it we are rewarding them?" Bernadotte asked.

"The mediator's proposal gives the Palestinians even more land than they already had," Eban reiterated. "We chose peace. They chose war. We chose to comply. They chose to defy. Yet they are being rewarded for their conduct and we are being penalized merely for defending our homes and businesses, a right fully recognized by the United Nations' charter. The Arabs of Palestine should not be allowed to disregard the international community, plunge the region into war, and be granted additional land merely because they lost the fight. If they were the victors, if they had taken our land, they would not give us back one inch and none of you would force them to."

"Thank you, Mr. Eban." Bernadotte looked down the table. "Does anyone else wish to be heard with an opening remark?" Paul Van Valen raised his hand. "Very well, Mr. Van Valen."

"I understand the United States and Great Britain are refraining from direct involvement in this matter while they work out their differences over a solution they can both support."

Henry Wiggins from the United States answered, "That is correct. We thought it best to air our differences with each other in private rather than on the floor of the General Assembly."

"One can see why you would want to do that," Van Valen rejoined, "but it gives the appearance that you and your British cohorts feel this is *your* organization. That you can disregard or trump the decision of a General Assembly majority."

"Quite the opposite," Wiggins replied. "We know perfectly well we cannot do any such thing. Our countries have been allies for many decades. Even centuries. We've just fought a long war together. We're merely acting like responsible citizens of the international community in working out our differences without occupying the General Assembly with our internecine disputes."

"If the UN is merely an extension of British and American policy," Van Valen continued, "if it's just a way of getting the other nations to do their bidding, then we're doomed from that even as much as from failing to enforce our decisions in Palestine."

"But the reality remains," Albiston noted, "they are the only two major powers remaining."

"I think the Soviet Union would dispute that assessment."

"Yes," Dmitri Shuisky from the Soviet Union chuckled. "I think we might."

"In light of Israeli control of the Galilee," Wiggins continued, "land which I would note was previously given to the Arabs, the U.S. would suggest Israel should cede the Negev to the Arabs, to balance the areas."

Eban shook his head. "That will never work."

"Why not? You took something you weren't given. If you want to keep it, then you should give up something you received earlier."

"So," Eban said with a sarcastic tone, "Israel should sacrifice so the UN can save face?"

"We can't afford to look ineffective."

"You can't afford to look stupid, either," Eban retorted.

"Excuse me," Bernadotte spoke up. "Mr. Eban, you are here at the leisure of the chair. I suggest you refrain from similar comments if you wish to remain."

"I apologize, Mr. Chairman," Eban replied. "But the worst result for the United Nations—even more damaging than failing to support its order—is if the UN appears to favor the noncomplying country over the compliant. You'll be nothing more than a recent version of the League rather than the austere body you aspire to become. And you'll prove what your detractors say—that no international body like this can be effective in solving the world's problems."

"Excuse me," Shuisky spoke up again. "In this case I think Mr. Eban is correct. The Arabs did defy the UN order, and for us to return them to the condition they were in prior to that act of defiance would be rewarding them for their noncompliance. If we do so, we will be seen as surrendering to Palestinian demands. Then every nation will know it can defy UN orders with no repercussions. Every nation will know if it defies UN orders no one will do anything about it. Every person in the world will know the UN is an ineffective waste of time, money, and energy."

Discussion continued into the night, but during a break shortly after midnight, Wiggins and Eban met in the hall. "We are not unsympathetic to your situation," Wiggins informed. "But the world is tired of war, particularly the major powers. Most people just want to get on with their lives. They aren't interested in fighting again."

"Believe me," Eban responded. "We feel exactly the same way but the Arabs won't stop attacking us."

"Well, Truman is supportive, but this thing has to stop."

"If you don't try to move us back to the resolution boundaries, and if the British will simply abstain from further involvement, we can—"

"The British?" Wiggins was caught off-guard. "What involvement have they had in this? We thought they were out for good."

"They supply both Transjordan and Egypt with arms and advice. Their planes regularly support the Egyptian army, and several of their generals are leading the Transjordanian army."

The frown on Wiggins' forehead deepened. "You're certain about RAF support?"

"Several of our fighters—flown by American volunteer pilots, by the way—shot them down over the Negev and Gaza."

"Spitfires?"

"Yes."

"And what were *your* planes?"

"Avia S-199s."

Wiggins grinned. "The Messerschmitt?"

"Yes."

"Our boys in your Messerschmitts shot down their boys in Spitfires?" Wiggins seemed to beam with pride at the prospect.

"Yes. Haven't you heard?"

"Not a word." Wiggins patted Eban on the shoulder. "I'll see what I can do." Then he turned away and walked up the hall.

For the next two days, as argument continued among staff members, delegates meeting separately hammered out a Security Council resolution demanding a negotiated end to fighting between Israel and its neighboring countries, and threatening armed intervention if the truce was not respected. Noticeably absent was any reference to boundaries or territorial disputes. Great Britain raised no objection.

Bernadotte was ordered back to Palestine to implement the UN's latest measure. Two days later, he arrived in Tel Aviv and was joined by Hammersmith. Jacob Schwarz was among the party accompanying them as they left the airport to begin their work.

CHAPTER 51

WHEN AHARON HARTMAN LEARNED Bernadotte was in Tel Aviv, he traveled north from Ashdod in hopes of talking to him. He arrived unannounced at Rishon LeZion, a farming settlement about ten kilometers south of Tel Aviv, and made contact with Bernadotte's secretary through an intermediary. Bernadotte agreed to meet him at an apartment in Bat Yam, a town on the Mediterranean coast.

"I read your report on Palestine," Hartman began.

"I'm sure you object to it as strongly as Ben-Gurion."

"To the contrary. If one wanted to divide Palestine, your proposal might be an effective way to do it."

"You disagree with the idea of partition?"

"Partition sets us up for a future of conflict," Hartman said, moving the conversation to familiar ground. "If we divide the region between Arab and Jew, our offspring will be fighting until the end of time."

"You have a better solution?"

"Yes."

"What is it?"

"If we are to survive, there must be only one Palestine. Not two. One national government for the entire region, divided into provinces based on ethnic majority. Some Arab provinces, others Jewish based on where people live, not on geographic zones or topographic detail. This would give each ethnic group a majority at the local level and control over its own local destiny, even though the national government would be controlled by whichever group or whichever candidate gained nationwide majority support."

"You realize, don't you, that national government would be Arab?"

"Right now," Hartman nodded. "Yes. It would. But that might change over time."

"Assuming they would allow Jewish immigration."

"The question of Arab and Jewish immigration could be addressed in a unification document. And we could use the regions defined in the November resolution for initial provincial boundaries. My plan would not require many. The region is so small it could not support very many anyway."

Bernadotte was clearly intrigued. "Ben-Gurion would support this?"

"No, he would not. But I would. As would many others."

"You could deliver this?"

"Yes," Hartman nodded confidently. "I think I could."

— · —

The following day, Jacob Schwarz sat outside a room in the Dan Hotel, where Bernadotte and Hammersmith met with a delegation of Arabs from the Tel Aviv region. When the meeting concluded, Hammersmith left the building. Bernadotte was still in the room and Jacob went in to see if his assistance was needed. He found Bernadotte seated at a table, surrounded by stacks of files and a clutter of loose documents. "Give me just a minute. I'll have something for you to deliver."

"Certainly." Jacob glanced at the table and noticed several pages of notes, some of it written in German, some in English, much of it in Arabic and Hebrew. While Bernadotte continued to work on the document that lay before him, Jacob continued to scan the notes. As he read he realized the notes were from a discussion with General Hartman about ousting Ben-Gurion and taking the governance of Palestine in a different direction. He was engrossed in the notes when Bernadotte put down his writing pen and looked up at him. "Okay," Bernadotte said.

Schwarz was startled by the sound of his voice but Bernadotte seemed not to notice. He methodically folded the paper he'd been writing on and placed it in an envelope, which he sealed and handed to Jacob. "The French opened a temporary office in Tel Aviv a few weeks ago. It's not much, just one man on Ben Yehuda Street." He paused a moment. "I think that's the street. A couple of blocks off the water."

"I can find it. I've been there before."

"Good. Take this to them and ask them to send it to New York in their next pouch." Bernadotte turned the envelope face-up and pointed. "The delivery information is right there."

Jacob tried his best to appear nonchalant. "Very well."

From the hotel, Jacob rode his bicycle to the Jewish Agency building and walked to the holding room where the couriers gathered between jobs. A stove stood in one corner and he put on a kettle of water. A few minutes later, as steam came from the spout, he held the envelope over it to loosen the seal on the flap. When the flap came open, he removed the message inside and read it. What he found was a letter to the chairman of the United Nations Secretariat outlining a proposal that would steer Jewish matters away from Ben-Gurion, toward a federated, Arab-majority government—and do it with the support of key nonpolitical leaders. "This came from the notes I read," he said to himself. "This is what he and Hartman were talking about."

With the letter in hand, Jacob ran upstairs to Revach's office. He barged in without knocking and found Revach stuffing documents from his desk into a leather satchel. "Jacob," he said with surprise. "I didn't know you would be here today. Thought you'd be off with Bernadotte."

"I am." Jacob pushed the door closed behind him and moved to Revach's side. "I need to show you something."

"I don't have a lot of time."

"This will only take a minute."

"Okay. What is it?"

Jacob handed him the letter. "Bernadotte gave this to me to take to the French office. He wants them to send it to the UN in New York. I thought you should see it first."

Revach scanned the document with a frown. "Where did you get this?"

"Like I said, from Bernadotte. He gave it to me to give to the French, to send to New York."

"The French? In their diplomatic pouch?"

"Yes."

Revach was not happy. "And you opened it?"

"Yes."

"Why would you do such a thing?"

"While I was waiting for him to finish writing it, I read some notes that were lying on his desk. They were right there on the desk. I read them and that made me curious about what he was sending to New York. So I came back here, steamed the envelope open, and that was inside."

"This is a diplomatic transmission." Revach's eyes were deadly serious as he held the document with his fingertips. "It's supposed to be communicated by whatever country the sender requests, friend or foe, without delay and without interception."

Jacob reached for the letter, "Okay, I'll take it over there for the French to send."

Revach moved the letter out of Jacob's reach. "When did he give this to you?"

"Just a few minutes ago."

"I still don't understand why you wondered what it said."

"The notes I read indicated Bernadotte met with General Hartman last night." Jacob pointed to the letter in Revach's hands. "They discussed the proposal outlined in that letter. Hartman is one of the nonpolitical leaders he is referring to."

Revach's nostrils flared in anger. "Hartman was here?"

"According to the notes, he met with Bernadotte."

"Alone?"

"Yes," Jacob nodded. "I assume so. The notes didn't mention anyone else."

Revach turned away and walked to Ben-Gurion's office. Jacob followed him into the hallway and lingered near the door, unsure what to do next. Moments later, angry shouts came from inside the office. A fist pounded the desktop. Then the door burst opened and Ben-Gurion appeared. His face was red and his forehead damp with sweat. At first he seemed not to notice

Jacob as he yelled down the hall, "Someone get Gedaliah Cohen over here!"
Then he turned to Jacob and his voice softened. "I'm not sure how we'll get
you out of this. That letter was a diplomatic matter. Reading it was a viola-
tion of international law. But we won't let them take you. So just relax."

"I shouldn't have read it?"

"Not according to diplomatic law. But between you and me, I would
have done the same thing." He patted Jacob on the shoulder. "We'll find a
way to solve this. Don't worry. Just wait right here." He turned to go back
into the room, then said over his shoulder, "Sit in Eyal's office. He'll be in
here with me while we figure this out."

— • —

In a few minutes the door to Ben-Gurion's office opened and Cohen
appeared. "Get in here," Ben-Gurion snarled. "We need to talk."

"What about?" Cohen asked as he stepped inside the office and closed
the door.

"Aharon Hartman."

"What's he done now?" Cohen asked with a roll of his eyes.

"Read this." Ben-Gurion tossed Bernadotte's letter on the desktop.
Cohen picked it up and read it quickly. "This isn't good," Cohen said when
he was through reading. "How did we get this?"

"Never mind about that. This thing has Hartman written all over it."

"You think he was the source for it?"

"That's his plan," Ben-Gurion said, stabbing the air with his finger for
emphasis. "In detail. And our courier who was assigned to Bernadotte's
detail said Hartman and Bernadotte met last night."

"He saw them?"

"He read about it in some notes Bernadotte left lying on his desk.
Hartman is one of the nonpolitical leaders that document refers to."

"Well," Cohen sighed, "I think it's clear we'll have to relieve him of
command while we investigate. And assuming this is what actually happened, we'll have to—"

"I'm not waiting to find out all the details," Ben-Gurion snapped. "I'm
done with Hartman. If we keep waiting on him, we'll lose the war, the

nation, and our heads."

"Maybe we should find a replacement first before we relieve him."

"Anyone come to mind?"

"We could send Moshe Dayan," Cohen suggested. "He's had some experience now. Proved himself very capable in defending Degania."

"Yeah," Revach chuckled. "Sent him to defend Degania and he took control of the entire Galilee."

"Good," Ben-Gurion said with a smile. "Dayan it is. I like him."

Cohen turned to leave the room. "I'll tell Hartman when—"

"No," Ben-Gurion interrupted. "I'll tell him. You contact Dayan and get him down here immediately. I want him ready to step up by tomorrow morning. I'll send for Hartman. I'm not delaying this any longer than it takes for him to get up here."

CHAPTER 52

MOSHE DAYAN WAS BACK IN DEGANIA when he received Cohen's order telling him to return to Tel Aviv. He went immediately to his room in the dormitory building and prepared to leave. Natan Shahak saw him through an open doorway and paused to ask, "Are we moving somewhere else?"

"Not *we*. Just me this time. I've been called to Tel Aviv."

"What for?"

"I'm not sure."

"Give me a minute to pack and I'll go with you."

Dayan shook his head. "No, we need you here."

"What for? The fighting's over here. And besides, I've never seen Tel Aviv."

"There's not that much to see."

"But that's where all the decisions are made."

Dayan glanced at him, remembering the eagerness he'd felt as a young soldier. "I'm leaving in ten minutes," he smiled.

Shahak bolted through the doorway and ran upstairs to his room. Ten minutes later, bag in hand, he met Dayan outside by the car. Three hours later they arrived at IDF headquarters in Tel Aviv. While Shahak waited downstairs, Dayan met with Revach upstairs for a briefing on what was about to happen.

— · —

Later that day Aharon Hartman arrived at the Jewish Agency building.

Rather than skewering him with details of what he knew, Ben-Gurion cited Hartman's unauthorized contact with Bernadotte, statements he made to Ivry Haimovitz to join him—a conversation that came to light when Cohen began his initial inquiry into the matter—then summarily relieved him of his command and dismissed him from the military.

Shortly after that, Ben-Gurion sent word to IDF headquarters for Dayan to join him. Dayan walked across the street to the Jewish Agency office and went upstairs to Ben-Gurion's office.

"I'm placing you in command of all troops in the Negev," Ben-Gurion announced as Dayan entered the room.

A frown wrinkled Dayan's brow. "Has something happened to General Hartman?"

"I've relieved him of command."

"May I ask why?"

"I'm not sure that matters," Ben-Gurion said, avoiding the question. "I want you to take control of the Negev—from Ashdod on the west coast all the way to Eilat on the Red Sea. We need Eilat for an outlet to the Indian Ocean without having to use the Suez Canal."

"All of the Negev?"

"All of it. Some in the UN want to give the Negev to the Arabs. If we can occupy it, we'll have a good argument for keeping it."

"Yes sir."

"That's your mission," Ben-Gurion said for emphasis. "Maybe you can use some of the same tactics you used so successfully in the Galilee."

"This will violate the UN's most recent cease-fire orders," Dayan pointed out. "The one they issued a few weeks ago and the second one they issued when they sent Bernadotte back."

"Let them enforce their order if they want to," Ben-Gurion scoffed. "We are not giving back the Negev."

"Very well," Dayan said and turned to leave. He paused at the door and glanced back to Ben-Gurion. "Does Hartman know I'm replacing him?"

"I didn't tell him, but I'm sure he'll find out one way or the other."

— • —

Natan Shahak was waiting when Dayan came from the meeting. "What did they want?"

"They want me to take command of the southern army."

"In the Negev?"

"Yes."

"Great. They face some of the hardest fighting left."

"The Egyptians have crack regular troops," Dayan warned. "Highly mechanized units. This won't be like what you experienced in the Galilee."

"I'm not afraid," Shahak countered. "This is the land of David. We are his people. A kingdom that has no end."

"So it is and so we are," Dayan chuckled. "Are you sure you can handle this?"

"I was born for this," Shahak grinned.

Dayan was amused by his confidence. "Then come on. We need to get you officially enlisted and assigned to me."

— · —

Later that afternoon, before Dayan could leave for the front, Haim Topol, a friend and fellow officer, invited him to a meeting at a house in Rishon LeZion.

"I need to get to Ashdod," Dayan announced.

"It's just a chance to get together," Topol said. "Zeev Gutman told me about it. You remember him?"

Dayan smiled at the mention of the name. He and Gutman had known each other since childhood. "Yeah," he said wistfully. "I remember Zeev."

"He'll be there and a lot of other people you know. I'm sure they'd love to see you. And you can still get to Ashdod before sunup."

"Okay," Dayan said finally. "I'll be there."

It was dark when Dayan arrived and he was surprised to find several IDF officers and lower-level government officials in attendance. Many of Dayan's friends were there, and as he had hoped, he and Zeev had time to get reacquainted. Before long, however, they began finding their way to their seats. When everyone was settled, Aharon Hartman came from a back room dressed in civilian clothes. Dayan was immediately ill at ease and glanced over at Topol. "Did you know he was going to be here?"

"Not when I asked you to come. It's okay. Listen to what he says."

"I'm not sure you understand the situation."

"No," Topol frowned. "I'm not sure I do." He nodded in Hartman's direction. "Why is he out of uniform?"

"That's what I'm talking about."

Just then, Hartman stepped forward to shake Dayan's hand. "Didn't expect to see you here."

Dayan stood. "I'm sure you didn't."

Then Topol jumped up from his chair. "I invited him."

"Very good," Hartman smiled.

"I can leave if you like," Dayan offered.

"No," Hartman said, apparently unaware of Dayan's new appointment. "Relax." Then a questioning look came over him. "What brings you to Tel Aviv?"

Dayan realized Hartman didn't know that he'd taken his command but he was now suspicious. "Ah, you know," Dayan replied. "Meetings."

"The war couldn't run without them," Hartman quipped.

As Hartman continued around the room shaking hands, Dayan excused himself and stepped outside. Topol followed after him. "What's wrong?"

"I need to go," Dayan said.

"Are you sure?"

"Yes."

"But—"

"I just need to, Haim," Dayan insisted. "I need to go."

"Okay. You can get back to Tel Aviv?"

"Yeah. I'll find a way."

While Topol went back inside the house, Dayan started up the street. As he approached the corner, he saw Shahak walking toward him. "What are you doing here?" he asked with surprise.

"I came to find you," Shahak said, out of breath.

"Why?"

"I talked to some of the guys in Tel Aviv. The ones who use that down-stairs room in the building where you met with Ben-Gurion."

"The couriers."

"Yeah," Shahak nodded. "They say Hartman lost his command because he was trying to get Ben-Gurion removed from office. Hartman wanted to take over."

Dayan was beside himself. "Do what?"

"They say Hartman met with that guy...the mediator."

"Folke Bernadotte."

"Yeah," Shahak continued. "Hartman met with him and they discussed it and then Bernadotte tried to send a message to New York about it. To get the UN to change its plans for Palestine. Only the message didn't get through because one of the couriers saw it and took it back to the office rather than sending it to New York."

"That explains a lot of things."

"I came to find you because someone said you'd come down here with a friend for a meeting and I wanted you to know about what happened to Hartman in case you ran into him. One of the guys said they thought that's what this meeting was about."

"It was." Dayan gestured for Shahak to follow. "Come on."

"Where are we going?"

"Back to the meeting."

"What for?"

"To listen to what he says."

Shahak started after him. "Won't he stop talking when he sees us?"

"We won't let him see us."

They hurried back to the house and crept beneath a windowsill. The evening was warm and the window was raised. Hartman's voice was clearly audible. Dayan and Shahak listened as Hartman described his plan for solving the problems of Palestine through a unified government. Then the discussion turned sinister.

"As you can see," Hartman continued, "I'm not wearing my uniform. That's because I am no longer an officer in the Israel Defense Forces." A collective gasp went up from those in the room. "David Ben-Gurion relieved me of command and dismissed me from the army."

"Why would he do such a thing?" someone asked.

"Because he has no military experience. He doesn't understand how we think and knows nothing of tactics or strategy. And worst of all, he has no a clue about the real solutions to our problems. All he cares about is gaining power and keeping power."

"What can we do to help?" someone asked.

"You could resign in protest over his meddling in military affairs," Hartman replied. "And then join me in forming a new coalition to take charge of our situation before we lose everything."

Dayan was shocked by what he heard and muttered to himself, "This is why Ben-Gurion relieved him." He glanced back at Shahak and whispered, "Come on." They hurried from the window to the front door and burst into the room. "And that is exactly why Ben-Gurion relieved you," Dayan said in a strong, authoritative voice. "Because you are a traitor."

"How dare you barge in here like this!" Hartman blurted. "Have you been listening outside?"

Dayan turned to those in the room. "The reason he's not wearing a uniform is because he's not worthy of the IDF colors. He went behind Ben-Gurion's back, defied Ben-Gurion's orders, and made a bid with Folke Bernadotte to take over. If you do as he suggests, you will be participating in a coup d'état." He turned back to Hartman. "You, sir, are under arrest." He grabbed Hartman by the arms and slammed him against the wall.

"I am a private citizen," Hartman shouted. "I can say whatever I want!"

"Not in a time of war," Dayan snarled.

Several in the room stood as if to intervene, but Zeev Gutman leapt from his chair and positioned himself between the group and Dayan. "I'd think twice about that if I were you," he said.

"There are only two of you and a roomful of us," someone chortled.

"Better count again," Shahak announced from the door. He held a rifle, which he cocked with great flare, racking a round into the chamber. "I think I count for a dozen."

The men who'd stood in protest backed away and Dayan called over his shoulder to Gutman, "Get a rope, Zeev."

Gutman glanced around quickly, then noticed the belt around Hartman's waist. "Use this," he said, stripping the belt from Hartman's pants.

While Dayan bound Hartman's hands behind his back with the belt, Idan Sakharof stepped forward. "What do you plan to do with him?"

"I'm taking him back to the Red House."

"Bring him." Sakharof gestured toward the door. "We can take my car."

Dayan held Hartman by the wrist and manhandled him toward the door. As they pushed through the group, Dayan glanced over at Shahak. "Cover us to the car."

Shahak waited while Dayan and Sakharof led Hartman from the room, then followed them outside.

— · —

Cohen was at IDF headquarters when Dayan arrived with Hartman. Dayan recounted for him what Hartman said and what he was attempting to do.

"Don't you think you're overreacting just a little?" Cohen asked.

"The man was plotting treason," Dayan snapped. "I should have shot him on the spot."

"That would raise some interesting questions."

"Like what?"

"Like a long-standing rivalry between the two of you and how you actually came to have his command."

"You know I had nothing to do with that. I didn't ask for his post. I didn't politick for his post. And from what I hear, I only got it because you suggested it."

"I didn't say any of it would be true. I'm just suggesting what people might ask. That's all."

"Well, here's the deal," Dayan declared. "You can put Hartman in jail and charge him with treason, or I'm resigning."

Topol appeared at the door. "I'll resign, too." He glanced over at Dayan. "Sorry I didn't speak up back there."

"You were at this meeting?" Cohen asked with surprise.

"Yes. And Moshe's right. It was treasonous. The man was trying to convince us to join him in overthrowing Ben-Gurion." Topol gestured over his shoulder. "Zeev Gutman was there. He'll back up every word of what Moshe said."

Reluctantly, Cohen placed Hartman in custody and confined him to the building's only jail cell. Dayan spent the remainder of the evening preparing a written report. When it was finished, he submitted it to Cohen and with an extra copy in hand started outside for the drive to Ashdod. Shahak was waiting by the car. "Nice move," Dayan said with a grin. "Where'd you get that rifle?"

"It was in the trunk of somebody's car. When you went into the house I figured there'd be trouble, so I found a weapon."

"Good thinking." Dayan patted him on the back. "I need to leave something for Revach at his office and then we'll go."

CHAPTER 53

AFTER A FEW DAYS IN TEL AVIV, Bernadotte and Hammersmith moved with their entourage to Jerusalem where they met for extended sessions with el-Husseini and an Arab League delegation. Jacob accompanied them. To his relief, Bernadotte never asked about the message he was supposed to have delivered to the French office.

Three days later, when those meetings ended, Bernadotte announced that he wanted to take a tour of Jerusalem, to see conditions in every part of the city. Hammersmith tried to dissuade him but Bernadotte insisted they had to see conditions for themselves. "Besides," he said, "I need to find suitable space to house a permanent mediator's office."

"Permanent?" Hammersmith asked. "You think you will be working here permanently?"

"Certainly for the foreseeable future."

"Do the Arabs know you are planning to replace the British mandate with the Bernadotte mandate?"

"No one knows it yet."

"Not even the Security Council?"

"Most certainly not them. Members of the Security Council have neither the vision for this sort of thing nor any respect for the depth of discord present here."

"And you think you can solve that."

"I'd like to give it a try. And I think a number of delegates on the Security Council would accept that as an alternative to a two-state approach." Bernadotte had a curious expression. "Which means this situation could require concerted attention over an extended period of time."

"Well, when you put it that way," Hammersmith finally conceded, "I guess we take the tour."

"Yes," Bernadotte nodded. "We take a tour. Doesn't need to last longer than a day. We should see what we need to see and have an eye on a permanent office by dinner tomorrow." He turned to go up to his room. "You'll see to all the arrangements?"

Hammersmith nodded. "I'll take care of it."

— • —

That evening, Levi Barak, a former Lehi member now working as a security agent in Bernadotte's delegation, contacted Halevy. They met around the kitchen table in an apartment not far from the King David Hotel to review the meetings Bernadotte held with the Arabs.

"Not much new happened," Barak said, "except now Bernadotte's talking about a permanent office."

"Permanent office?" Halevy was troubled. "He's counting on staying here?"

"Apparently. They're taking a tour of the city tomorrow."

"What for?"

"To find an office."

"That's not good. How safe is it for him to do something like that?"

"Getting an office?"

"No. Taking a tour."

"I think he'll be okay. His earlier proposal bought some time with the Arabs. They didn't like it but they could see he favored them, so they weren't too upset. But this last round of talks...I'm not sure exactly how they feel about that."

"What happened?"

"Nothing except Bernadotte kept asking them about a plan for a unified Palestine."

Halevy frowned. "A unified Palestine?"

"Yeah. I know. It's strange. You should have seen the looks on *their* faces."

"What did he say about this plan?"

"He kept asking them about whether they would agree to elections for the entire region, as if partition had not happened, and about local divisions along ethnic lines. They didn't seem to understand why he was stuck on that idea. I didn't understand it, either, but he kept coming back to it."

"I wonder why he'd ask about that," Halevy mused. "Ben-Gurion would never agree to it."

"Maybe Bernadotte thinks he can get rid of Ben-Gurion."

"But even if he did, Eyal Revach wouldn't agree to it, either. And neither would Golda."

"Golda surely wouldn't," Barak chuckled. "That is one tough woman."

Halevy leaned back in his chair. "Maybe Bernadotte thinks he can move all those people out." Halevy's eyes opened wide as if he suddenly understood. "The German." He leaned forward and tapped the tabletop with his index finger. "That's all part of it."

"Yeah," Barak nodded. "Maybe that's it. I forgot about him."

"If the German assassinates Ben-Gurion, the situation is much different. If he's gone, the others might think they need to negotiate a settlement, which is what the UN wants now—a negotiated end to the fighting."

"That might be right," Barak nodded. "But I've been wondering if something hasn't changed. I mean, the German has been here quite a while and no one of note has been killed. So, could something have happened since last month that makes the situation different?"

"Whatever it was," Halevy said, "I think the German and Hammersmith talked about it that night in the café. If things changed, that's when it happened."

"Okay." Barak propped his elbows on the table. "What could that change be? Let's think about it. Hammersmith is British—"

"But he's not just British," Halevy interjected. "He's a colonel in the British army."

"The British are in this," Barak said emphatically. "They were backing Transjordan and Egypt already. I think this unified Palestine plan is theirs."

"If they didn't come up with it, they certainly seem to support it.

They've always favored an Arab Palestine."

"Only now they're doing something to make it happen."

"Negotiation by assassination," Halevy sighed. "This is worse than we thought. This is all just one big conspiracy and Ben-Gurion doesn't even see what's coming."

"I think you're right," Barak agreed. "Bernadotte, Hammersmith, the German, and now that thing with Hartman—all of them working together in a coordinated effort to overthrow the government and give the whole place to the Arabs."

"That Hartman situation was scary," Halevy observed. "I mean, an IDF general was ready to take over. How could Gedaliah Cohen miss that?"

"Maybe he's in on it."

"Nah." Halevy shook his head. "Not Gedaliah. He just doesn't like internal conflict. The politics of it is too much for him. He likes to be in the field. This sort of thing could easily get past him."

"We should take this to Jeziernicky."

"I don't think so," Halevy said with a shake of his head. "Not this time. Let's keep him out of it."

"Why?" Barak frowned. "We need to know if we're right."

"Jeziernicky's path lies in another direction. With the men who joined IDF. They have their work. We have ours. And we don't have to be right on all these details. We know Bernadotte is trying to destroy Israel. We know he wants the Arabs to have control of the entire region. And we know Hammersmith is working to the same end, though not by the same means. That's all we need."

"Okay," Barak said with a note of hesitancy. "But what do we do about it?"

Halevy gave him a look. "You know what we have to do."

Barak took a deep breath. "All right. How do we do it?"

"I'm not sure." Halevy paused for a moment, thinking, then sat up straight as if he'd hit on a plan. "Tell me about that tour," Halevy said. "What are they doing?"

Barak took a map from his hip pocket and unfolded it on the table. "They leave from the hotel, which is right here." He pointed to a spot on the map. "That gives them two potential routes. They can go down this way." He traced with his finger along one route. "Or they can go this way," he said, tracing a route in the opposite direction.

"All right," Halevy said when he'd seen the routes. "We'll need two teams."

"Okay."

"Four men in each team," Halevy continued. "Good men. Men with experience who know how to work up close without rushing it beforehand and won't panic afterward."

"I know the men," Barak answered.

"Get them organized and plan every detail. How you'll stop the car, which ones will approach, which ones will be the shooters. And don't forget to plan how they'll get away."

"I'll take care of it."

"Don't tell me their names, and make sure the men from the teams don't know about each other."

"Right."

— · —

The next day, Bernadotte and company came from the King David Hotel and walked toward the car parked on the driveway in front of the building. Jacob held the rear door on the driver's side for Bernadotte, then walked around to get in on the opposite side. Hammersmith got there first and grabbed the rear door handle. "I'll ride back here today," he said with an arrogant tone. "You sit up front with the driver." He opened the door and got in back with Bernadotte. Jacob took a seat up front on the passenger side.

From the hotel they drove to the corner and turned left. In the middle of the next block they came to an army jeep parked in the street, blocking the way. An insignia from the Transjordanian army was emblazoned on the jeep's door. Four soldiers stood nearby with rifles slung over their shoulders. All of them wore Transjordanian army uniforms. As the car came to a stop, the soldiers stepped forward and brought their rifles from their shoulders, pointing them toward the car. They were serious and focused but appeared to be disciplined and not at all hostile or aggressive.

Hammersmith leaned forward. "Why are we stopped?"

"Just a checkpoint," the driver replied. "It's nothing."

Hammersmith settled back in the seat. "The way things are these days, this kind of stop will be the routine for a long time to come."

"I suppose so." Bernadotte peered around the driver's head and his eyes widened. "Aren't those Transjordan soldiers?"

"Yeah," Hammersmith sighed. "King Abdullah's men."

Bernadotte glanced over at him. "I thought this was a Jewish sector."

"You're right," Hammersmith replied with a note of concern. "It is."

By then the soldiers were at the car. Two of them stopped at the front bumper and stood staring through the windshield, focusing on no one in particular. Two more came alongside the car as far as the front doors, one on either side.

Hammersmith grasped the door handle and opened the rear door. "Hey, who are you?"

Without a word of warning or demand, the first soldier lowered his rifle with the muzzle only centimeters from the driver's head and squeezed the trigger. A single shot struck the driver in the forehead and exited the back of his skull. Blood, bone fragments, and brain matter sprayed the headliner of the passenger compartment.

Hammersmith's mouth dropped open and he moved his leg to climb out of the car. Bernadotte cowered behind the driver's seat, his arms over his face. But before either could say a word, both soldiers fired into the rear of the passenger compartment, striking Hammersmith and Bernadotte multiple times. Instinctively, Jacob leaned forward to get out of the way and covered his ears with his hands while the sound of gunfire exploded around him.

CHAPTER 54

WITHIN THE HOUR, news of the assassination reached Ben-Gurion at his office in Tel Aviv. He summoned Revach and Golda to his office to tell them. They met around Ben-Gurion's desk, all of them standing, while he gave them the details.

"We don't have all the facts yet," Ben-Gurion said, "but we know Bernadotte and Hammersmith are dead. They died in Jerusalem at the hands of four gunmen. It was a deliberate act. This is a big problem."

"It's the Arabs," Golda responded, unwilling to concede it could have been done by someone else. "It must be."

"But why would they?" Ben-Gurion argued. "Bernadotte was doing his best to give them what they wanted."

"Bernadotte was working for the British," Revach said flatly. "And that's what the British wanted. An all-Arab Palestine."

Golda had an inquisitive expression. "You know for a fact he was with the British?"

"Yes," Revach nodded.

"How so?"

Revach lowered his gaze. "I talked to some people."

"Who?" Ben-Gurion pressed.

"People," Revach shrugged.

"Eyal." Ben-Gurion's voice had an edge. "We don't have time for secrets now. Who did you talk to?"

"Nahum."

Ben-Gurion's eyes went cold. "Halevy?"

Revach glanced down at the floor. "Yes."

The muscles along Ben-Gurion's jaw flexed. He shoved his hands in his pockets and turned away. Golda spoke up. "What did he tell you?"

"That's where we got the tip about the assassin."

"Assassin?" Golda blurted with surprise. "This is the first I've heard about it. What assassin?"

"We thought it was better to keep it close," Revach explained.

Ben-Gurion turned toward them and pointed a finger at Revach. "*You* thought it was better. I said we should tell her."

Golda put her hands on her hips. "Did you think I couldn't be trusted?"

"I thought it was better to keep it close," Revach repeated.

Now Golda turned away. Revach moved around to face her. "Of course I trust you," he said with a solicitous tone, "but we had to limit the number of people who knew in order to contain it. If I told you then someone in your office would eventually find out about it. Not because you'd feel compelled to talk but because that's what happens. Your people know your information. My people know mine. I didn't want that to happen so I didn't tell you. But it wasn't out of disrespect. There are a lot of other people I didn't tell."

"Who?" Golda demanded.

"I didn't tell Abba. I didn't tell—"

"No," Golda snapped. "Who *did* you tell?"

"He didn't even tell me this much," Ben-Gurion interjected, letting Revach twist on his own admission.

"I told Gedaliah about it," Revach replied, "and two men from Shai. That's all."

"Shai?" Golda asked.

"So they could follow up on the information and so they could help us form a security detail."

"Security detail?" Golda was surprised again. "For who?"

"For David."

Ben-Gurion waved his hands in protest. "I didn't want it. Eyal made me take it."

Golda glared at Revach. "How long has *that* been in effect?"

Revach glanced in Ben-Gurion's direction, but Ben-Gurion once again waved his hands in a defensive gesture. "You tell her. I'm not. You swore me to secrecy."

"It still is," Revach answered. "He's still under protection."

"I haven't seen anyone," Golda said in a huff, but she was calmer than before.

"Good," Revach smiled. "That's just how it's supposed to be."

Ben-Gurion came back to the desk. "Now, if we can get to the issue at hand," he said. "We have to have a response on this. These men were here under UN order. No one is going to like it."

Golda turned to Revach. "Did Halevy do this? Was he the one who killed these two men?"

Revach glanced at the floor again. "I can't say."

"Can't say, or won't say?"

"Halevy couldn't have done this alone," Ben-Gurion suggested. "This wasn't done by a single individual. This was the work of several."

"He was the head of Lehi," Golda offered. "He had any number of men at his disposal."

"Lehi has been disbanded for a long time," Ben-Gurion said with a dismissive gesture. "Jeziernicky brought his men into the IDF with him."

Golda caught the look in Revach's eye. "What?" she asked expectantly. When Revach didn't reply she pressed for an answer. "What do you know that you aren't saying?" She stared at him a moment as the realization came over her. "Oh no." Color drained from her face. She pulled a chair to the desk and took a seat. "I don't believe it," she muttered. "They're still out there."

Ben-Gurion glanced at Revach, then to Golda with a bewildered frown. "Who's still out there?"

"Lehi," Golda groaned.

Ben-Gurion focused on Revach. "Is that true, Eyal?"

"Most of them joined up," Revach sighed.

"Most? But not all?"

"No." Revach slowly shook his head. "Not all of them."

Ben-Gurion took a seat behind the desk. "This is worse than we could have imagined. You knew about this?"

"I found out."

"How?"

Revach took a seat. "My cousin runs a café. He saw Halevy in a meeting and asked me about it. I didn't say anything, but when this business came up with Schwarz seeing Hammersmith with that guy, I found Halevy and talked to him to see if he knew who the man might be."

"Schwarz?" Golda was alert. "What guy?"

"Don't worry about it," Revach said. He was irritated by the grilling and found the drama unnecessary.

"This just keeps getting worse and worse," Golda sighed.

"How?" Revach raised his voice. "How does that make it bad for us?"

Golda sat up straight. "You are an official of the provisional government." Her voice was even and firm. "You aren't just a lackey from the Jewish Agency anymore. And you, as a government official, met with a member of a clandestine group that has been outlawed by the very government you serve. Don't you think, even though they'd been officially disbanded by parliamentary order, Halevy might have assumed after your meeting—after your request for a favor—that he and others like him were authorized to continue doing the kinds of things they'd been doing before?"

Revach lowered his voice. "We don't know for sure it was them."

"Yes, we do," Golda insisted, her voice near a shout. "Yes, we do! This operation has Lehi written all over it. Daringly brilliant. Flawlessly executed. Easy fall guy with the uniforms. It's Lehi and you know it."

Revach turned to Ben-Gurion. "You want me to contact Halevy?"

"NO!" Ben-Gurion and Golda shouted as one.

Revach had a sheepish grin. "There's no way they'll find out."

"Someone always finds out," Ben-Gurion sighed. "You know that."

"Nahum Halevy and I are the only people who know we met," Revach continued. "And he certainly—"

"No," Ben-Gurion interrupted. "You contacted Halevy directly?"

Revach slouched in his chair. "I went through someone."

"So a third person knows."

"Yeah."

"Like I said, someone always knows." Ben-Gurion stood and began to pace.

They sat in silence a moment before Revach said, "Well, one thing is for certain, this is the end of Bernadotte's plan."

"And Hartman's," Golda added.

"And the British plan, too."

"What about Jacob Schwarz?" Ben-Gurion turned back to Revach. "Was he in the car with them?"

"I don't know. I didn't think to ask."

"Call the office in Jerusalem," Golda ordered, "and see what you can find out."

"I'll call when we finish," Revach replied.

"No." Golda nudged him on the shoulder. "That man has a wife and a child. Call now. It may take a while to get through." Reluctantly, Revach stood and walked up the hall to his office.

When he was out of the room Ben-Gurion glanced at Golda. "Don't be too hard on Eyal. This was a difficult situation and he had to make a difficult decision."

"I understand," Golda acknowledged. "We need a thousand Eyal Revaches."

"But we only have one, so let's keep our emotions under control and try to understand what he was dealing with."

"I'm not nearly so angry about what he did as about not being told."

"Well, one reason he didn't tell you is because he knew he had to meet with Halevy, or someone like him, to find out the information we needed. We needed to know who that man was. But meeting with him came very close to violating the law and he didn't want to pull you into that."

"So, who was he?"

"Eyal should tell you."

"We've just seen, Eyal won't tell me much about this. Who is it?"

"A German. Former Nazi assassin. Jacob Schwarz saw him meeting with Hammersmith in a café in Jerusalem. Eyal wanted to know who it was. No one else knew. So he went to Halevy. That's how we found out."

"We know for sure you're the target?"

"They think he wouldn't be here for anyone but me."

"They're probably right. And Eyal was right to form a protection detail for you. We should have done that before. I just don't like not knowing."

"I know. But he couldn't tell you and I was too embarrassed."

A frown wrinkled Golda's brow. "Too embarrassed?"

"Our men face a bullet every day. They don't have bodyguards. Why should I be treated any differently?"

"They have each other," Golda countered. "And they know how to defend themselves."

Ben-Gurion looked away. "Perhaps so."

Golda leaned forward and rested her hands on the desktop. "Now, about this situation. You should issue a statement right away. Make a radio announcement condemning the killing. Call for a thorough investigation. This happened in a sector we control. We won't be able to avoid it. Appoint someone as medical examiner and get him up there now to preserve whatever evidence might still exist. No telling what they did with the bodies."

"Who should we appoint?"

"Ovadia Geffen. Appoint him and tell him to get busy now. Before the UN sends in a medical team and takes it away from us. If we want to be a state, we have to act like one."

Within the hour, Ben-Gurion delivered an address over Voice of Israel Radio condemning the assassinations, announcing the appointment of Dr. Ovadia Geffen as medical examiner, and promising to track down those responsible and hold them accountable. Golda prepared the text and accompanied him to the station. Revach was nowhere to be seen.

— • —

While Golda took care of the announcement, Revach called the provisional office in Jerusalem and asked for details about the shooting. Through that conversation he learned that Jacob Schwarz was unharmed but detained by an IDF unit in order to give investigators an opportunity to question him.

"Is he in your office?" Revach asked.

"No. He's over at the gym where we have the bodies."

"Get Schwarz and have him brought down here. We need him as soon as possible."

Three hours later, Jacob arrived in Tel Aviv and was taken upstairs to

Revach's office. He was still shaken from the incident but composed enough to talk. He and Revach spent an hour going over details of the event.

"Okay," Revach said when they'd talked it all the way through, "I'm going to show you some photographs. You tell me if you recognize any of them as the men who did the shooting."

"Okay," Jacob answered. "I'll try."

Revach picked up a folder from the corner of the desk and opened it, then began spreading pictures on the desktop for Jacob to see. When he laid out the fourth one, Jacob stopped him. "That's the one who came to my side of the car."

"He was a shooter?"

"He didn't actually shoot anyone," Jacob explained. "He stood at the front bumper on my side."

"But he was armed."

"Yes," Jacob nodded. "He had a rifle. There was another guy at the bumper on the other side. He had a rifle, too. Neither of them shot anyone. They just stood there."

"Okay. Look at a few more." Revach spread two more photographs on the desk and reached for a third before Jacob stopped him. "Those two," he said, pointing. "They did the shooting."

Revach collected the four photographs Jacob identified and showed them to him one more time. "These are the four men who approached the car?"

"Yes."

Revach held up the first two pictures. "These men stood near the bumper at the front of the car."

"Yes," Jacob said again.

Revach held up the other two photos. "And these two actually did the shooting."

"Yes."

Revach opened the desk drawer and put the pictures inside. "Okay," he said as he came around the corner of the desk. "We need to get you home." He took Jacob by the elbow. "Come on. I'll drive you."

CHAPTER 55

FROM AN APARTMENT deep in the Arab-controlled sector of Jerusalem, el-Husseini summoned one of his men. "There is a German visiting here. A former Nazi," Husseini instructed. "Find him and bring him to me." Later that day, the man returned with Keppler.

"I trust your stay with us has been profitable."

"Who are you?" Keppler asked. "And why did you send for me?"

"Perhaps you are not as knowledgeable as Mr. Hammersmith suggested," Husseini replied.

Keppler did his best to appear confused. "I have no idea what you are talking about."

"Mr. Hammersmith contacted me shortly before his untimely death," Husseini continued, unimpressed by Keppler's reaction. "I believe you two knew each other."

"I'm not sure," Keppler shrugged. "I don't think I know who you're talking about."

"Yes," el-Husseini replied. "I believe you do. He and I go back a long way, as I do with Lord Marbury and his son Richard." He cleared his throat and a door opened at the end of the room. Three men entered and stood nearby. "Mr. Keppler," Husseini continued, "I believe we understand each other very well. But if you persist in being obstinate, I will have you escorted from my presence and no one will ever hear from you again."

"I'm not trying to be difficult or disrespectful," Keppler responded. "I'm just not sure why you wanted to see me."

Husseini nodded to the men and waited while they left the room. "It's really quite simple," he said when they were gone. "And I will speak plainly. You were sent here to kill David Ben-Gurion and I was asked to help you do it. Now, shall we continue these word games or shall we get on with helping you complete your mission?"

"I would appreciate your assistance." Keppler gave a slight bow of his head as he spoke.

"Good," Husseini smiled. "I understand you are encountering difficulty locating your target."

"I can locate him. He's everywhere," Keppler explained. "I just haven't been able to find him in a location from which I can escape. I don't mind killing him. I'm just not interested in dying for a cause."

"Very well," Husseini nodded. "We will locate him for you."

"But it has to be the right place."

"I understand."

"And none of the places I know about will work. The office, the residence, they are all wrong."

"I believe you suspected he had a second home in Tel Aviv."

"Yes," Keppler acknowledged. "It seems that way to me and when I explained Ben-Gurion's activities to Hammersmith, he agreed."

"That will be no problem. We have someone close to the situation who can help. He will find just such a place for you."

"Good, but how will I make contact with him?"

"Not to worry," Husseini replied. "He will contact you."

— • —

The following day, Yehuda Geller left the holding room at the Jewish Agency building to deliver a message. On his way back, he turned down a street that went by the post office. As he neared the corner, he passed Keppler, who was standing in a doorway. Their eyes met and Geller acknowledged him with a nod. Keppler followed and halfway up the block they turned into an alley.

With Keppler behind him, Geller walked up the alley to the cross street, then left to the next block and into a three-story brick building.

Keppler followed him inside. A stairway stood to the right of the door. Geller started up and when Keppler hesitated, he glanced back from the second-floor landing, gesturing for Keppler to follow. They continued up to the third floor and into an apartment. When the door was closed, Geller walked over to the window. Keppler stood nearby but to one side, away from direct view.

Geller pointed. "You see the house over there with the green shutters?"

Keppler leaned around to see out and nodded. "Yes. I see it."

"That's it."

Keppler looked again. "That is Ben-Gurion's second residence?"

"Yes."

Keppler sighed. "This is no better than the other locations."

"This is the backside," Geller explained. "The entrance to the house is on the opposite side. A drive turns off the street to a small courtyard. There is only one way in and one way out." He smiled at Keppler. "It will be perfect for your purpose."

"No," Keppler shook his head. "That is the problem with all these locations. One way in and one way out. That is not good. I cannot escape from such a place."

"Ah," Geller grinned. "But this place is different."

"How so?"

"See that building on the opposite side?" Geller tapped the window-pane as he pointed. "The one that used to be red but is now a shade of pink?"

Keppler looked once more through the window. "Yes," he said, nodding slowly.

"That is an apartment building, like this one. There is an empty room on the third floor, like this one. From it you can see straight down the driveway to the building entrance. Anyone coming or going would be clearly visible from the apartment window."

Keppler glanced at him. "You are certain it is empty?"

"Yes," Geller assured. "It was rented just yesterday for that purpose. To make certain it was empty for you."

Keppler frowned. "Won't they know who rented it?"

"They might have known, but not anymore."

"No?"

"The man who rented it is no longer available. And they will never find his body." Geller had an unsettling smile. "So there is nothing for you to worry about. You can get on with your business now and finish this project." He stepped away from the window. "I must go. You can find your way out?"

"Yes."

"And you can find the other apartment building?"

"I think so."

"Good." Geller reached for the door to open it.

"Here," Keppler called to him. He drew some money from his pocket. "Take this for your trouble."

"No," Geller replied with a wave of his hand. "I cannot. It is an honor to assist you in exterminating one more of these Jewish vermin. That is payment enough for me."

"Are you not a Jew?"

"On my father's side."

"But your mother?"

"She is Arab."

"Yet you work for them."

"Yes," Geller said with an ironic smile. "I work for them so that I may work for Allah." Then he opened the door and disappeared down the hallway.

CHAPTER 56

TWO DAYS LATER, Jacob Schwarz was back in the holding room on the first floor of the Jewish Agency building. Most were surprised to see him so soon after the Bernadotte shooting. Sarah had expected him to stay at home much longer, but with the war going on he wanted to be a part of it.

A little before ten that morning, one of the women from upstairs brought him a thick envelope. "This must go to Ben-Gurion," she said. "He's at the second house, resting, but he needs it right away."

Jacob stuffed the envelope in a leather pouch, took it outside to one of the motorcycles, and roared down the street. Ten minutes later, he arrived at the driveway outside Ben-Gurion's second residence. He throttled the engine back to an idle and coasted into the courtyard, bringing the machine to a stop near the front entrance.

Two guards were present, one on the steps and another a few meters away smoking a cigarette. Jacob shoved the kickstand down with his heel, propped the motorcycle against it, and dismounted. Just then, the door to the residence opened and Ben-Gurion appeared. He came past the guard on the steps and down to the pavement, then moved out to the motorcycle.

"I assume you brought something for me," he said with his hand outstretched.

"Yes sir," Jacob replied.

As he opened the pouch to take out the envelope, a shadow caught Jacob's eye. He glanced to the left and saw the glint of sunshine off the windows on the second floor of the house. Something about the situation didn't set well with him and when he looked back at Ben-Gurion he realized why.

Standing where he was, with one guard over by the door behind him and the other all the way across the courtyard, Ben-Gurion was unprotected. He was exposed from any number of angles. Jacob turned his head to the left to check and saw, indeed, an open view straight up the driveway to where Ben-Gurion stood. He ignored Ben-Gurion's outstretched hand, stuffed the envelope back inside the pouch, and took Ben-Gurion by the shoulder. "You can't be out here like this. You're totally—"

Suddenly Jacob's left shoulder exploded as flesh ripped from his body and blood filled the air, covering Ben-Gurion in a thin red mist. An instant later he heard the report of a gunshot from behind him.

For an instant the guards, wide-eyed with fear, were frozen in place. Ben-Gurion, too, seemed unable to move as Jacob collapsed against him and slowly slid to the ground. As his knees hit the pavement, though, Jacob realized Ben-Gurion was once again completely exposed and he groaned as loudly as he could, "Get him inside."

The man nearest the door sprang into action, shielding Ben-Gurion with his body while the other guard ran toward them and shoved Ben-Gurion toward the house. As they reached the top of the steps, a second shot splintered the doorframe. One of the men threw open the door and the other drove Ben-Gurion inside as a third shot struck the wall just centimeters past Ben-Gurion's head.

— • —

When Revach arrived at Ben-Gurion's residence, Jacob was still lying on the pavement. One of the guards was bent over him with a towel trying to stanch the flow of blood from the gaping wound. Revach brought the car to a stop and jumped out. "Is he alive?" he shouted.

"Yes," the guard replied. "But not by much."

Revach stepped closer. "What happened?"

"There were two shots. Maybe three. I don't know. I know there were at least two. One hit Schwarz. The other hit the door." He pointed down the driveway. "Sounded like they came from over there."

Revach turned in that direction, then glanced back to Jacob. "Anybody hit besides him?"

"No sir."

"Ben-Gurion's okay?"

"Yes sir."

"All right, let's get him in my car." Revach stooped over to help lift Jacob from the ground. "The keys are in it," he continued. "Drive him to the hospital." They put Jacob on the back seat and closed the door. "I'm going inside."

As Revach reached the front step, the door to the house opened and a guard appeared. "Where are your snipers?" he demanded.

"They're in place," the guard replied, pointing. "Over there." He turned to the left and pointed again. "And over there. That shot came out of nowhere. I doubt they know where it came from."

Revach glanced down the driveway as his car with Jacob inside reached the street. Over the top of the car he saw the pink building and on the third floor he saw an open window. "It came from right up there," he said, pointing. "Come on. Let's check that building."

The guard at the door shouted inside and two men came out. They joined Revach as he ran down the driveway toward the pink apartment building. One of them caught up with him and handed him a pistol, which Revach held in his hand as they ran.

When they reached the building one man ran inside and up the stairs while Revach and a second man continued around back. As they came past the far corner of the building, Keppler came out the back door.

"Keppler!" Revach shouted. "Stop!"

Keppler turned to face them and drew a pistol from the waistband of his trousers. Before it cleared his belt, a shot from a sniper behind them exploded through Keppler's forehead. His head snapped back and his arms flew wide apart. Then his legs buckled and his body fell to the ground.

— • —

Hours later, Jacob became aware that he was lying in a soft, warm bed covered with clean sheets. He smelled them first and felt them long before he could lift his eyelids far enough apart to see them. As he lay there in a semiconscious state, he heard voices talking around him.

Across the room, Revach described what happened when he arrived at the house and what they thought might have happened when Jacob was shot. Another person, someone from the couriers' room, told about the first time Jacob tried to ride a motorcycle and how he crashed it into the waste bin. Jacob couldn't remember his name.

The sound of footsteps caught their attention and everyone stopped talking. Then another voice spoke. Jacob didn't recognize it, but as the voice continued he realized the man who spoke was a doctor. "He's doing as well as can be expected," the doctor said. "That was a nasty wound, as bad as any you'd see on the battlefield and expect someone to survive. We've put him back together but it will take a while for him to heal, if he can make it through the night."

"It's that bad?" he heard Ben-Gurion say.

"Yes. The next twelve hours will be critical."

Someone sobbed. From the sound of it Jacob was sure it was Sarah. She was standing close by. He wanted to reach up and touch her and tell her he was fine, but his arms wouldn't move.

A woman came and stood next to her—he could tell by the smell of perfume—the woman from upstairs who brought him the envelope. He couldn't remember her name, either, but she was standing beside Sarah and from the muffled sound of sobs he was sure they were holding each other close.

After a moment the doctor left the room and a few minutes later someone asked about Jacob's family. "They all died at Treblinka," Sarah replied. "I thought he was dead, too, for a long time."

"How did you find each other?"

"I was in one of the camps after the war, and one day someone touched me from behind. When I turned around, there he was."

"Now, that's a story someone needs to hear," a new voice said.

"Ah. Golda," Sarah said and she moved away from the bed. Jacob felt a twinge of jealousy but realized she and Golda had come to be good friends, and Golda had just arrived in the room.

"Survived the *Exodus*. Was there when Bernadotte was killed. And now this," Revach added. "That's quite an adventure."

"For someone who thought being a courier was a letdown," Golda chimed in.

Revach laughed. "Remember how enthusiastic he was to join the army?"

"That's all he talked about on the trip from Paris," Sarah explained, moving back to the edge of the bed. "When he got here he was going to join Haganah and fight for Israel. I tried to talk him out of it but he wouldn't listen to me."

The woman from upstairs asked, "How did he get the job at the office?"

"Ben-Gurion," Revach replied.

"The man had a pregnant wife." Ben-Gurion took a defensive tone. "I wasn't sending him off to the battlefield."

"Lots of men out there with pregnant wives."

"Yeah. But I don't know them, and they weren't right there in front of me asking for an assignment. Jacob was." Ben-Gurion lowered his voice. "Do you think we should send for a rabbi?"

"He's not dead yet," Golda chided. "And besides, he can probably hear you."

"I know. But I'm just saying."

"I thought you didn't like the rabbis."

"Everyone says that, but it's not true. What I don't like is the rabbinate. Rabbis can be very helpful. But the institution with the synagogues and the rules and all that—totally unnecessary."

"Hey," the courier's voice said. "I haven't seen Yehuda Geller up here. He was friends with Jacob, even better than I was. He ought to be here. Did anyone tell him?"

"Haven't seen him all day."

"Come to think of it, he wasn't there yesterday, either."

The room fell silent, and suddenly Jacob was worried. Was something wrong with Geller?

Revach spoke up. His voice had a suspicious tone. "Has he been out much before?"

"No," the courier replied. "I don't think he's missed a day since I've been here."

"Maybe you should call and check," Ben-Gurion suggested.

"Yeah," Revach replied. "I'll send someone to check on him."

Jacob heard footsteps echoing down the hall as Revach left the room, then a soft, smooth hand touched his arm. *Sarah,* he thought. *She's right here with me.*

CHAPTER 57

WHILE JACOB SCHWARZ remained in the hospital, struggling to survive, Dayan and Shahak arrived at the IDF headquarters tent at the command compound near Ashdod. They spent ten minutes meeting the staff, then went on a tour of his army's current position. When they returned, Dayan used the remainder of the day to evaluate enemy troop strength. The following morning, he called his officers to the tent.

"Based on our estimates of Egyptian strength," Dayan announced, "we can hold the Egyptian army in place with half the troops presently deployed here. The rest can break off from our present location and move toward Beersheba. Once we've secured the western half of the Negev, we can turn back to the east and attack the Egyptians from two directions."

"Finally!" someone exclaimed.

"We've been begging Hartman to do that for weeks," another shouted.

Dayan nodded to Shahak, who began passing around a list describing the units assigned for the western campaign. "Check the list. Prepare to move out in the morning."

Before sunrise the following morning, Dayan led a mechanized column of tanks and armored vehicles from Ashdod. Troops followed in trucks with artillery pieces behind. Traveling at top speed, they secured three small settlements along the way and arrived on the outskirts of Beersheba by nightfall. Dayan radioed army headquarters in Tel Aviv to report their position.

— • —

With a major military operation underway, Ben-Gurion and Revach spent much of their time at IDF headquarters in the Red House across the road from the Jewish Agency building. Ben-Gurion was present when Cohen received the update on Dayan's progress. "Finally!" he shouted. "We are on the move."

While Ben-Gurion and Cohen monitored the army, Revach walked back to his office across the street. He arrived to find an aide with a report on the search for Yehuda Geller.

"We've been through the apartment three times," he said. "There's nothing there that can help us. But as we were leaving today, a neighbor said Geller has a brother who lives in Jerusalem."

"Can we find out anything on him?"

"Already checked. His name is Saleh al-Aulaqi. He's a Muslim cleric at Nebi Akasha Mosque in the Old City."

"How did we not know this before?"

"I don't know."

"So, Geller was involved, which means the attempt on Ben-Gurion was an inside job."

"Looks that way."

In spite of the trouble he'd received over the way he handled the assassination threat, Revach knew there was only one person who could help him locate Geller. So, late that afternoon he took a jeep from army headquarters and drove out to a position near Latrun where Yitzhak Jeziernicky was stationed. The two men sat in the jeep while they talked.

"Is everything okay with Ben-Gurion?" Jeziernicky asked.

"Yes."

"Thank goodness the courier was there. How is he doing?"

"He's alive. Not much more than that, though."

"I hope he makes it."

"We do, too. He's a tough guy. He was on the *Exodus* and came back to fight."

"We have one of those guys in our unit."

"Listen, one of our couriers is missing. We need to find him."

Jeziernicky seemed worried. "Someone took him?"

"No. We think he was tied to the attempt on Ben-Gurion."

"That would be bad."

"It gets worse. His brother is Saleh al-Aulaqi."

Jeziernicky's eyes opened wide. "He's a Muslim cleric."

"Right," Revach nodded. "At Nebi Akasha Mosque."

"You want someone to find him?"

"Not the brother," Revach replied. "We need to find our missing courier. Think you can help?"

"We'd have to go back to Nahum Halevy."

"Is that a problem?"

"If you go to him once, you're just asking a favor. He would understand the nature of the request. If you go to him twice, however, he might think he has your permission to do whatever it is he does."

"I think he already thinks that," Revach said with a wry smile.

"What do you mean?"

"Bernadotte."

Jeziernicky glanced away. "I was afraid that might happen."

"I assume you know nothing about that."

"Not about Bernadotte." Jeziernicky looked him squarely in the eye. "I knew nothing at all."

"Well," Revach sighed, "we need to find Geller. Contact Halevy and tell him we need to talk."

"You want me to handle it for you?"

"No," Revach said. "If someone has to take the fall for my decision, I'd prefer it was me. I don't like hiding from myself."

— • —

That night, Revach drove to a street two blocks from the beach in Tel Aviv and parked the car at the curb. A moment later, Nahum Halevy opened the front door and got inside.

"We need to find a better way to meet," Halevy said. "If someone sees you out here, you could be in danger."

"People are in danger all over Palestine tonight," Revach replied.

"They said you wanted to talk."

"We need to find one of our couriers."

"Yehuda Geller," Halevy offered. "He's at a house in Jerusalem. Do you want him alive or dead?"

"I prefer him alive," Revach said quietly. "But if he's dead, no one will be upset."

Halevy opened the car door and stepped out. As the door banged closed, Revach put the car in gear and drove away.

CHAPTER 58

WITH HIS FORCES GATHERED at Beersheba, Moshe Dayan wasted little time in quickly tightening his grip on the city, establishing a perimeter that cut off every avenue of retreat. Then he pushed through the city and trapped the Egyptians at the southern edge of town. Rather than capture them or engage in a battle of attrition, he opened a gap in his defenses, allowing them to escape. Once they were beyond the city perimeter, he left an occupying force in Beersheba and pursued the Egyptians southward as far as Makhtesh Ramon atop Mount Negev. By then, the Egyptian army was well beyond the border.

Dayan waited there a day for the trucks carrying his infantry and the artillery pieces to catch up, then set out for Eilat, the tiny but important port at the northern end of the Red Sea, and the real goal of the operation. They arrived at Eilat expecting a fight but found the village devoid of Egyptian troops.

An itinerate fisherman explained, "When they heard how easily you took Beersheba and that you were headed in this direction, they withdrew rather than fight."

Unwilling to accept victory so easily, Dayan spent half the day searching each structure and patrolling the streets, making certain all Egyptian forces were gone and that local Arab militiamen were disarmed. Finally, shortly after noon, he radioed army headquarters in Tel Aviv to report his progress.

— · —

In addition to fighting the war, Ben-Gurion and Revach were busy forming the provisional government and preparing for the transition to permanent institutions necessary for the young nation's survival. Part of that effort involved selection of a location for buildings that would house the ministries and agencies that soon would follow. Doing that required a visit to several locations, including one at Ramat Gan, just east of Tel Aviv. They spent most of the morning there and returned to the city after lunch.

When they arrived, Ben-Gurion went to his office in the Jewish Agency building. Revach walked across the street to army headquarters in the Red House to check on the latest news from Dayan. As he entered the command center, a cheer went up from the staff that manned the room.

Cohen greeted him with a handshake and a grin. "Moshe has reached Eilat!" he said with excitement.

"You heard from him?"

"Just now. He called in to report his position."

"Any casualties?"

"None," Cohen said triumphantly. "The Egyptians were gone when they arrived."

"Wow. That's incredible."

"And our forces at Ashdod have pushed the Egyptians as far south as Gaza." Cohen had a satisfied smile. "We control the Negev."

"Well, they can keep Gaza so long as they don't advance northward."

"They are in a defensive position," Cohen explained. "I don't think they're going anywhere except home."

Just then, the door opened and Ben-Gurion arrived. Another chorus of cheers went up, this one louder than before. He waved to the room and turned to Cohen. "Did something happen?"

"Moshe reached Eilat."

Ben-Gurion's face lit up. "He took it?"

"Yes. Without resistance."

"Is he sure they aren't hiding and waiting to launch a counter strike?"

"They swept the city," Cohen explained. "House to house. Street by street. Disarmed the local Arabs. It's ours."

"Good," Ben-Gurion grinned. He looked over at Revach. "There was a message waiting from King Abdullah when I got back. He wants to talk."

"Perhaps the Egyptians will join those talks," Revach suggested.

"I think they will," Ben-Gurion agreed. "Maybe they can convince the Arab League to talk about a permanent peace."

"Our troops control the Galilee and the Negev and a portion of Jerusalem," Cohen noted expectantly. "Does that mean the war is over?"

"It's over for now," Ben-Gurion replied. "Tell our units to hold their positions while we see what happens with Abdullah."

As Cohen and Ben-Gurion continued to talk, Jeziernicky appeared in the doorway and caught Revach's attention. He gestured for him to follow and they walked outside. When they were alone, Jeziernicky said quietly, "I just heard from Halevy. They got Geller last night."

"Alive?"

"No." Jeziernicky shook his head. "There was a fight. Two of our men were wounded. Geller and his brother were killed in the process. Husseini is threatening retaliation."

Revach had an ironic smile. "And we were just celebrating the prospect of a permanent peace."

"I think we are never to have peace."

"And I think you are correct," Revach nodded. "But we will have our nation."

— · —

Across town at the hospital, Jacob Schwarz once again became aware he was lying in bed. This time, however, the sheets didn't feel so clean nor did they smell so fresh. Time had passed, he assumed. He must have been there for a while.

On the opposite side of the room hushed voices talked about him.

"There is no way of knowing how long this will last," a man said.

"Will he come out of it?" Sarah asked.

"I can't say for certain. Some do. Some do not."

"How long can he continue this way?" There was a hint of despair in Sarah's voice. Jacob did not like it.

"With a positive result," the man replied, "not very long."

"Is there no hope?"

"There is always hope," a third voice said, this one much stronger and louder than the others.

"Who are you?" the man asked.

"I am Yechiel Diskin."

Jacob felt his heart skip a beat. Diskin. The rabbi. He was the one who confronted the British and took Livney's body from the ship, appeared at the warehouse when things seemed their worst, and showed up at the hospital when Benzion was born. There was a rustling sound at Jacob's side and a hand touched his forehead.

"What are you doing?" Sarah asked in an unpleasant tone.

"You'll have to leave him alone," the man said. His voice was authoritative, but with a hint of hesitancy, as if he knew what he must say but was uncomfortable saying it.

"I wish him no harm," Diskin replied softly. His face was close. Jacob could smell his breath, stale from tobacco and coffee. He smelled of sweat, too, but over all of it there was a fruity scent. Jacob had smelled it before, somewhere, sometime. And then he remembered. Incense. And all at once an image from childhood flooded his mind.

They were in the synagogue, at home in Warsaw. His mother sat beside him while his father stood at the lectern and read from the prophets. *"Who has ever heard of such a thing?"* his father read. *"Who has ever seen such things? Can a country be born in a day or a nation be brought forth in a moment? Yet no sooner is Zion in labor than she gives birth to her children."*

Only now he didn't hear his father's voice but Diskin saying, "Jacob, today that reading from Isaiah you heard long ago has come to pass. The vision of your father and your father's father has been fulfilled. Israel has been reborn. The towns of Judah have been inhabited. The ruins have been restored."

Diskin moved his hand away and Jacob felt something warm and damp in its place. A heavy fragrance wafted through the air and he realized it was the smell of oil—olive oil. And Diskin continued. "Now, Jacob, it is time to open your eyes and come back to us. Come back to us and witness the fulfillment of what I told you before when your son was born. 'His name shall be Benzion, for he is the Son of Zion, the firstborn of the new nation.

He shall grow up to be strong and wise and will lead his people twice, once through a difficult time and once through a time of great prosperity.'" Jacob joined him as they said the words together, "And when he is old they will say of him, 'The son of Zion grew up to lead us and we have become his children.' And you shall not pass away before these words have been fulfilled." As he spoke, Jacob's eyes opened and he saw see Sarah standing over him with a doctor dressed in a white lab coat beside her.

"He was talking to himself," the doctor said.

"What were you saying, Jacob?" Sarah asked. "What was it?"

Jacob glanced around, wondering what happened to Rabbi Diskin and for a moment unsure where he was. Rather than explain it, he just smiled and said, "How long was I out?"

"Several days," she smiled and kissed him on the forehead.

Just then Golda appeared at the door and in her arms she held little Benzion. "I think he's missing you," she said to Sarah. Then she saw Jacob was awake and she came to the edge of the bed. "You're with us again?"

"Yes," Jacob replied. "I'm here."

Golda stepped closer and held the baby so he could see. "He's getting big," she said as she handed him to Sarah.

"Yes," Jacob smiled. "He is."

"And he's been missing his father," Sarah said tearfully.

Jacob lifted his good arm to make a place beside him. "Put him here for a moment." Sarah glanced at the doctor, and he responded with a shrug as if to say okay. Then carefully, she slid Benzion from her arms, laid him next to Jacob, and tucked his feet beneath the sheet. "Just for a minute," she said.

With the baby next to him, Jacob closed his eyes and whispered, "Your name is Benzion, for you are the Son of Zion, the firstborn of the new nation. You shall grow up to be strong and wise and lead your people twice, once through a difficult time and once through a time of great prosperity. And when you are old they will say of you, 'The son of Zion grew up to lead us and we have become his children.' And I shall not pass away before these words have been fulfilled." Little one, your watchword will be Jeremiah 33:3: "Call unto Me, and I will answer thee, and will tell thee great things, and hidden, which thou knowest not."

A NOTE ABOUT BORN AGAIN

This book is a work of fiction. The characters and events you encountered on these pages came from our imagination. In preparing the story, however, we drew on many of the historic events that took place during modern Israel's long march from dream to reality. Some of those events were taken out of chronological sequence, names were changed, and circumstances altered in order to fit the dramatic needs of our story. It is our hope that the result is both entertaining and informative and that in reading this book you will be inspired to discover more about the story of Israel's rise to statehood.

— . —

ACKNOWLEDGEMENTS

My deepest gratitude and sincere thanks to my writing partner, Joe Hilley, and to my executive assistant, Lanelle Shaw-Young, both of whom work diligently to turn my story ideas into great books. And to Arlen Young, Peter Glöege, and Janna Nysewander for making the finished product look and read its best. And always, to my wife, Carolyn, whose presence makes everything better.

BOOKS BY: MIKE EVANS

Israel: America's Key to Survival

Save Jerusalem

The Return

Jerusalem D.C.

Purity and Peace of Mind

Who Cries for the Hurting?

Living Fear Free

I Shall Not Want

Let My People Go

Jerusalem Betrayed

Seven Years of Shaking: A Vision

The Nuclear Bomb of Islam

Jerusalem Prophecies

Pray For Peace of Jerusalem

America's War: The Beginning of the End

The Jerusalem Scroll

The Prayer of David

The Unanswered Prayers of Jesus

God Wrestling

Why Christians Should Support Israel

The American Prophecies

Beyond Iraq: The Next Move

The Final Move beyond Iraq

Showdown with Nuclear Iran

Jimmy Carter: The Liberal Left and World Chaos

Atomic Iran

Cursed

Betrayed

The Light

Corrie's Reflections & Meditations (booklet)

GAMECHANGER SERIES:
GameChanger
Samson Option
The Four Horsemen

THE PROTOCOLS SERIES:
The Protocols
The Candidate

The Revolution

The Final Generation

Seven Days

The Locket

Living in the F.O.G.

Persia: The Final Jihad

Jerusalem

The History of Christian Zionism

Countdown

Ten Boom: Betsie, Promise of God

Commanded Blessing

Born Again

Presidents in Prophecy

TO PURCHASE, CONTACT: orders@timeworthybooks.com
P. O. BOX 30000, PHOENIX, AZ 85046